THE CONVERGENCE PROTOCOL

THE AQUATICA CHRONICLES, BOOK 3

Written by Diane Kann

Brought to you by Volans Galaxy Press

I0694874

Published by Kannceptual Creations LLC

An imprint of Volans Galaxy Press

ISBN: 978-1-969569-51-7

Printed in the United States of America

First Edition, Noverber 2025

Note: This work was originally published under the pen name DM Volans, which is a pen name of Diane Kann.

CONTENTS

DEDICATION

This book is dedicated to the tireless scientists, activists, and everyday individuals who dedicate their lives to understanding and protecting our planet. Their unwavering commitment to environmental stewardship, often in the face of daunting obstacles and political inertia, serves as a powerful beacon of hope. It is a testament to the human spirit's capacity for both profound understanding and selfless action. This narrative, though set in a fictional future, is profoundly rooted in the very real struggles and triumphs of those working to safeguard our shared ecological heritage.

To the researchers charting the intricate dance of ocean currents and the delicate balance of marine ecosystems; to the activists raising their voices against environmental injustice and demanding accountability from those who exploit our natural resources; to the community organizers building resilient local food systems and promoting sustainable practices; and to the everyday citizens making conscious choices to reduce their environmental footprint— this story is for you. Your dedication inspires us to imagine a future where humanity is not merely a consumer of the Earth's bounty, but a partner in its flourishing.

This dedication is not merely an acknowledgement of your efforts; it is a recognition of the profound ethical and existential challenges we face. The choices we make today will determine the legacy we leave for future generations. Your tireless work fuels our hope, even in the face of uncertainty and the complexities of global environmental challenges. The resilience you demonstrate, even amid the realities of climate change and ecological degradation, gives us the strength to face the imagined catastrophes portrayed in these pages and inspires us to work towards a more harmonious coexistence with the natural world.

May this story serve as a reminder of the immense power of human ingenuity and collaboration in the face of adversity and inspire us all to strive for a better, more sustainable future.

CHAPTER ONE

ECHOES OF COLLAPSE

The salt spray stung Sarah Chen's face, a familiar discomfort that today felt like a cruel mockery. The air, usually thick with the scent of brine and kelp, was choked with the acrid tang of decay. Before her, the once-vibrant coastal city of Pyeongtaek was a skeletal ruin, half-submerged in the churning, frothy sea. Buildings—once gleaming symbols of human ingenuity—now lay at grotesque angles, their concrete frames fractured and corroded, a testament to the raw power of the ocean's wrath.

The resonance point, a colossal underwater structure designed to harness and stabilize the planet's oceanic energy, had failed. It wasn't a slow decline, a gradual weakening. It was a cataclysmic implosion—a seismic event that had ripped through Earth's delicate balance like a jagged tear in a finely woven tapestry. The failure wasn't just a technological catastrophe; it was an ecological apocalypse.

Sarah, her dark hair plastered to her sweat-slicked forehead, gripped the railing of the battered observation platform, her eyes scanning the devastated landscape. She couldn't shake the gnawing guilt. Had she trusted the resonance network too much? Had her belief in fragile alliances blinded her to deeper fault lines?

3

The initial shock had given way to a grim determination. This wasn't just about Pyeongtaek; this was about the entire planet. The resonance points were a critical part of the global network designed to mitigate the effects of environmental collapse—a network now teetering on the brink of complete failure. The catastrophic breakdown of this single point had triggered a chain reaction of environmental disasters across the globe. Coastal cities were flooding, storm surges were intensifying, and the delicate balance of marine ecosystems was crumbling.

The once-pristine waters, teeming with life just days ago, were now a churning mass of debris and poisoned foam. Schools of bioluminescent fish—usually a breathtaking spectacle—now flickered weakly, their eerie glow a desperate plea for survival. The whispers of the dying ocean echoed in the mournful cries of the seabirds circling overhead, their numbers dwindling with each passing hour. The air itself felt heavy, suffocating, laden with the stench of death and the bitter taste of despair.

The Luminese, a technologically advanced species that had established a fragile alliance with humanity, had arrived hours ago, their sleek, bioluminescent vessels cutting through the debris-strewn waters like ethereal predators. Their presence, meant to bring hope and aid, now seemed to amplify the palpable sense of disaster. The Luminese, with their advanced technology and profound respect for the planet's delicate ecosystems, were as shocked and disheartened as the humans. The trust that had formed between the two races—so painstakingly built over years of careful collaboration—was beginning to fracture under the weight of this monumental crisis.

Ambassador Nyla, a wise and respected Luminese elder, approached Sarah, her translucent skin shimmering in the weak sunlight that struggled to pierce the overcast sky. Her normally serene demeanor was strained, her usually calm eyes reflecting the gravity of the situation.

"The resonance collapse... it's worse than we feared," she said, her voice a melodious whisper that barely carried over the crashing waves. "The ripple effects are devastating. Entire ecosystems are collapsing."

Sarah nodded, her gaze fixed on the ravaged city. She understood the magnitude of the disaster. She had devoted her life to protecting the ocean, to understanding its complex rhythms and its vital role in sustaining life on Earth. Now, she watched as that life was extinguished, its final gasps a chilling testament to humanity's negligence.

The initial attempts to contain the ecological fallout were frantic and disorganized. Emergency response teams, clad in protective gear, struggled to navigate the debris-filled streets and rescue those trapped in collapsing buildings. But the sheer scale of the destruction overwhelmed them. The ocean—once a source of sustenance and wonder—had become a force of unimaginable devastation.

The Luminese, despite their advanced technology, could only offer limited assistance. Their technology, while capable of amazing feats, couldn't simply undo the damage. Their attempts to stabilize the surrounding waters were painstakingly slow, each small success hard-won against the relentless assault of the surging waves. The situation called for a solution beyond technology—a solution deeply intertwined with the planet's own natural processes, a solution that felt almost impossibly beyond their reach.

The whispers of the Whispers—the sentient ecosystems that had long coexisted with humanity—were becoming increasingly erratic and unpredictable. Jonah Reyes, a brilliant tech specialist and key member of Sarah's team, was struggling to decipher their cryptic communications, his face a mask of intense concentration. His usual calm confidence was overshadowed by an almost palpable anxiety.

The whispers weren't just warnings; they were shrieks of pain, desperate cries for help from a planet reeling under the immense strain of the resonance failure. The fragmented data streams coming from the Whispers were chaotic—a jumbled symphony of distress signals.

Dr. Eliza Grant, a marine biologist with a reputation for unwavering dedication to ecological preservation, arrived on the scene, her eyes wide with a mixture of horror and determination. She had dedicated her life to understanding the delicate balance of marine ecosystems. The sight of the destruction brought tears to her eyes, but that didn't deter her resolve. Her initial assessment was stark and utterly devastating: the scale of the damage was far beyond anything they had ever anticipated. Entire species were vanishing. The delicate balance of the ocean was collapsing faster than anyone had predicted.

A ripple of tension passed through the gathered survivors before they even saw him. A coldness in the air, a tightening in every throat. Then, through the mist and debris, Mallory emerged.

The arrival of Dr. Rafe Mallory, a scientist with a history of controversial experiments and questionable ethics, cast a dark shadow over the already desperate situation. His ambition was palpable; the glint in his eyes spoke of a power grab masked by scientific jargon. He arrived with an entourage of heavily armed mercenaries and a sinister air of determination, adding a further layer of complexity and danger to the team's already dire circumstances.

His presence hinted at a darker, more insidious threat—a conspiracy that might jeopardize their attempts to save the planet.

The failure of the resonance point wasn't simply a natural disaster; it seemed to be part of a carefully orchestrated plan—a plan that Mallory seemed eager to exploit. He had his own interpretations of the Whispers' communications, and Sarah and her team had good reason to suspect his intentions were far from altruistic.

The converging crisis was about to get exponentially worse. The fragile alliance between humans and the Luminese, strained by the disaster, would soon be tested by the presence of this malevolent force. The fight for survival was not only against the ravaged environment, but also against a human enemy capable of inflicting even greater damage. The echoes of collapse resonated not only in the ruined city, but in the hearts and minds of all who witnessed the unfolding catastrophe.

Whispers of Warning

The air thrummed with a low, guttural hum—a sound that vibrated not just in Jonah Reyes's ears but deep within his bones. It wasn't the familiar, rhythmic pulse of the oceanic resonance, the steady heartbeat of the planet, but something far more chaotic—a fractured symphony of distress. The Whispers, the sentient ecosystems that had for millennia communicated with humanity through subtle shifts in weather patterns, changes in animal migration, and cryptic growth patterns in plants, were screaming.

Jonah hunched over his console, his fingers flying across the keyboard, his brow furrowed in concentration. The fragmented data streams were a nightmare—a blizzard of conflicting signals, a cacophony of warnings interwoven with fragments that seemed like ancient prophecies. The usual elegant patterns—the intricate fractal geometry of the Whispers' communications—had shattered into a fragmented mosaic of fear and pain. He could almost feel the agony of the dying ecosystems bleeding into his own consciousness, a raw, visceral wave of despair washing over him.

His screens displayed a chaotic whirlwind of data points—a visual representation of the planet's unraveling. Each point represented a collapsing ecosystem, a dying species, a fractured connection within the intricate web of life. Red blotches spread across the digital map of the world like a malignant disease, consuming everything in their path. The vibrant blue of the oceans, once a reassuring constant, was now mottled with shades of brown and gray, reflecting the poisoned waters and the widespread death of marine life.

The Luminese technology, usually so effective at decoding the Whispers' subtle signals, was failing. Their sophisticated algorithms—designed to interpret the intricate patterns—were overwhelmed by the raw, chaotic energy emanating from the planet's damaged ecosystems. The once-clean data streams were now drowned in static, a digital reflection of the physical devastation unfolding around them.

Jonah, a man who prided himself on his calm, analytical approach to problems, felt a rising tide of panic. This wasn't a simple technical glitch; it was a profound existential crisis. The Whispers weren't just communicating—they were crying out for help, their voices fragmented and distorted by the trauma of the resonance failure.

He tried different algorithms, different decoding methods, each attempt met with the same frustrating result: a jumbled mess of unintelligible data. The Whispers felt more like screams, filled with an overwhelming sense of urgency. He could make out snippets here and there—phrases that alluded to ancient catastrophes, to cycles of destruction and renewal, to choices that humanity had made and would soon be forced to make again.

He saw flashes of images—lush forests reduced to ash, coral reefs bleached white, vast deserts swallowing once-fertile lands.

These weren't simply data points; they were visions of a possible future, a horrifying glimpse into the consequences of humanity's actions. The scale of the environmental collapse was so vast, so complete, that even his advanced technology struggled to comprehend it. He felt a profound sense of helplessness—of being overwhelmed by a force beyond his understanding.

Hours bled into days. Jonah worked tirelessly, fueled by caffeine and a desperate hope to understand the Whispers' warnings. He isolated fragments of the signal, ran countless simulations, tried to identify patterns within the chaos. He delved into ancient texts, searching for clues—hints about the Whispers' language and the mythology surrounding their interaction with humanity. He spoke with Dr. Grant, drawing on her knowledge of marine biology to find possible connections between the biological and digital signals.

The fragments he managed to decipher were filled with an overwhelming sense of urgency—warnings of impending ecological catastrophes and prophecies of a radical shift in the planet's systems. There were allusions to a time long ago, a previous cataclysm that had nearly destroyed the planet—a warning that this current crisis might be even more devastating. He learned of the Convergence Protocol—a legendary planetary regeneration plan hidden within the heart of the Whispers' ancient code. The protocol, according to the fragmented messages, held the potential to heal the planet and restore the delicate balance of its ecosystems. But it also hinted at a profound cost—a potential sacrifice that could lead to humanity's extinction or transformation.

His frustration mounted with each failed attempt. He felt the weight of the world on his shoulders, the burden of responsibility for deciphering a message that could determine the fate of humanity. The whispers of the Whispers, once a source of fascination, had become a terrifying burden.

Yet, amidst the chaos—amidst the overwhelming sense of despair—he found glimmers of hope. He found fragments of a message that spoke of symbiotic evolution, of a future where humanity and the Whispers could coexist in harmony—a future where the planet could heal and thrive. He found references to the Echoborn—humans who had somehow merged with the Whispers, a living testament to the possibility of a symbiotic future. These fragments, buried within the chaos, fueled his determination, providing a spark of hope in the face of overwhelming despair.

He knew that understanding the Whispers' complete message was a race against time. The ecological collapse was accelerating, and with each passing hour, the chances of successfully activating the Convergence Protocol dwindled. The fragments he was able to decipher were only part of the overall message, and the cryptic nature of the warnings kept him from seeing the full picture.

The burden of his work was enormous. He understood that the fate of the planet rested on his shoulders—on his ability to unlock the secrets hidden within the Whispers' chaotic transmissions. The weight of the world, the weight of a dying planet, pressed down on him, threatening to crush him beneath its immense power.

The air itself seemed to crackle with the urgency of the situation, the silence punctuated only by the incessant hum of the failing technology and the mournful cries of the dying ocean. He knew he couldn't fail. The survival of humanity depended on his success. He pressed on, fueled by a grim determination, fighting against the odds, battling the chaos, determined to decipher the cryptic warnings and unlock the secrets buried in the heart of the planet's pain.

The fate of the world hung in the balance, dependent on his ability to understand the whispers of a dying planet.

The Luminese Dilemma

The low hum that vibrated through Jonah's bones intensified, morphing into a discordant wail that seemed to claw at the edges of sanity. The Luminese technology—usually a beacon of precision and control—sputtered and faltered, overwhelmed by the raw, chaotic energy emanating from the planet.

Ambassador Nyla, her usually serene face etched with worry, watched the flickering screens with a mixture of fascination and apprehension. Her slender fingers, tipped with iridescent Luminese claws, traced patterns on a smooth, obsidian console, her movements as fluid and precise as a dancer's.

"The resonance is fracturing," she murmured, her voice a low, melodious hum that resonated with the distress of the dying planet.

"The Whispers are losing coherence. Their message... it's becoming fragmented, almost unintelligible."

Her words confirmed Jonah's worst fears. The Whispers—the planet's sentient ecosystems—weren't just sending warning signals; they were unraveling, their intricate communication network disintegrating along with Earth's ecological systems. The Luminese, with their advanced technology, were uniquely positioned to understand the Whispers, yet even their sophisticated systems were struggling to cope with the escalating crisis.

Nyla's gaze shifted to Dr. Grant, who was hunched over her own console, analyzing the biological data streams. The marine biologist's face was grim, her eyes reflecting the chaotic data swirling on her screens. The symbiotic relationship between the planet's ecosystems and the Whispers was collapsing, taking Earth's biosphere down with it. Each new data point was a testament to the catastrophic failure of the oceanic resonance—a symphony of life now reduced to a cacophony of death.

"The Convergence Protocol," Dr. Grant whispered, her voice barely audible above the hum of failing technology, "it's the only hope we have. But activating it... it's a gamble. A risk we might not be willing to take."

Nyla nodded, her expression pensive. The Luminese had spent centuries studying Earth's systems, developing technologies capable of interacting with and interpreting the Whispers' communication. They possessed an understanding of the planet's delicate balance that surpassed even humanity's most advanced scientific models. Yet, their deep respect for the natural world instilled a profound hesitation toward interfering.

"The Protocol speaks of a planetary reboot," Nyla explained, her voice laced with a subtle undercurrent of concern. "A radical transformation that could heal the planet—but at a potentially devastating cost. We've seen its effects on other systems, its impact on sentience. It's a double-edged sword."

The Luminese technology, despite its seemingly limitless capabilities, was far from foolproof. It was an intricate dance between technological advancement and delicate balance, a careful negotiation between intervention and preservation. Their ability to decode the Whispers' signals was dependent on a harmonious coexistence—a delicate interplay of observation and non-interference. The current crisis had shattered this balance, forcing them to confront the moral implications of their actions.

"The consequences are unpredictable," Nyla continued, her voice filled with the weight of millennia of knowledge and experience. "A planetary reboot isn't merely the resetting of a computer system. It's a profound alteration of the very fabric of existence. It has the potential to wipe out the human race, the Echoborn, and even to permanently alter the nature of the Whispers themselves."

Amid the chaos, a pattern emerged.

It was faint, fragile—but it was there.

A possibility.

The Echoborn.

Jonah, his face pale with fatigue, struggled to reconcile the urgency of the situation with the potential consequences of the Convergence Protocol. The whispers of the dying planet, once a source of wonder and fascination, had become a haunting prophecy.

"But what choice do we have?" he asked, his voice raw with desperation. "The planet is dying. We're losing the resonance. If we don't activate the protocol, there won't be anything left to save."

Nyla's gaze drifted to the window, where the once-vibrant cityscape was now shrouded in perpetual twilight—a consequence of the atmospheric changes resulting from the collapsing ecosystems. The pollution-choked sky served as a stark reminder of humanity's ecological transgressions, a silent testament to their reckless disregard for the planet's delicate balance.

"The Luminese have always strived for harmony with the natural world," Nyla said softly, her voice echoing the quiet dignity of her people. "We have learned to coexist with ecosystems far more ancient and complex than humanity's. We have developed technologies capable of interacting with them—but always with the utmost respect for their autonomy. Intervention should be a last resort, a decision made only after exhaustive consideration of the potential consequences."

She gestured toward the chaotic data streams on her console.

"Our technology, while advanced, is limited. We can decode the Whispers, but we cannot fully comprehend their essence—their inherent wisdom. The Convergence Protocol is not simply a sequence of commands; it's a profound act of creation, a potential rewriting of the fundamental laws of nature. It has consequences that are beyond our understanding, and to activate it without proper understanding is foolish. It's a choice we must make cautiously, with all the knowledge available—and with full awareness of the potential costs involved."

Dr. Grant, her face etched with the burden of her scientific knowledge, added, "The Whispers aren't just a collection of data points; they are sentient entities. Activating the Convergence Protocol without their full consent, without considering their potential fate, is nothing short of an act of planetary genocide."

The ethical dilemma weighed heavily on the three of them. The Luminese, with their advanced technology and centuries of experience interacting with sentient ecosystems, carried a profound responsibility. Their ability to understand and potentially activate the Convergence Protocol was a powerful tool—but one that could be used for creation or for destruction.

The Luminese technology itself was an intricate reflection of their philosophical approach. It was not brute-force technology, but a system built upon subtle energies, delicate balances, and a deep respect for the natural world. It was a testament to their ability to understand and interact with life beyond human comprehension, but also a reminder of the limits of their technological prowess—and the potential for unforeseen consequences.

The ensuing hours were filled with intense discussions—a complex ballet of scientific analysis, philosophical debate, and ethical considerations. They pored over the fragmented data, searching for clues, for hints, for any sign that could shed light on the potential consequences of activating the Convergence Protocol.

They studied ancient texts, attempting to decipher cryptic prophecies and interpret symbolic representations of the planetary reboot. They even reached out to the Echoborn—those rare individuals who had somehow managed to merge with the

Whispers—hoping to gain insights into the nature of the symbiotic relationship that could guide their choices.

As they delved deeper, they discovered that the Convergence Protocol wasn't a simple on/off switch. It was a complex, multilayered process—a sequence of intricate steps that could potentially lead to a multitude of outcomes, each with its own set of profound implications. The more they learned, the more the task seemed to dwarf them. The scale of the challenge, the weight of the decision, threatened to crush them under its immense power.

The planet itself seemed to hold its breath, waiting for the fateful decision that would shape its future—and perhaps the future of all life on Earth.

The silence in the room was thick, heavy with the weight of the responsibility they were facing. It was broken only by the rhythmic beeping of machines and the haunting, almost imperceptible wail of the dying planet. The Luminese dilemma was a stark reminder that even the most advanced technology could not solve all problems— and that sometimes, the greatest challenges required not only scientific prowess but also moral clarity and a profound respect for the delicate balance of life.

Introducing Dr Grant

The rhythmic pulse of the failing oceanic resonance throbbed in the background—a constant, low hum that vibrated through the floor and into Dr. Eliza Grant's bones. She sat hunched over her console, her fingers flying across the keyboard, her brow furrowed in concentration. The screens displayed a chaotic ballet of data— swirling colors representing collapsing ecosystems, flashing red alerts signifying critical failures in the planet's life support systems. The sheer volume of information was overwhelming, a testament to the scale of the unfolding catastrophe.

Eliza was a marine biologist of renowned expertise, her career dedicated to understanding the intricate web of life within the oceans. She'd spent years studying the delicate balance of marine ecosystems, mapping the intricate currents that connected disparate parts of the ocean, and charting the migration patterns of countless species. She knew the ocean intimately—understood its rhythms and its moods, its resilience and its vulnerability. And now, she was witnessing its slow, agonizing death.

The data on her screens showed a catastrophic decline in phytoplankton populations—the tiny plants that formed the base of the entire marine food web. Coral reefs, once vibrant cities of life, were bleaching and dying, their skeletons exposed like the bones of a long-dead civilization. Fish populations were plummeting, driven to extinction by a combination of overfishing, pollution, and the escalating changes in ocean temperature and chemistry. The entire oceanic ecosystem was unraveling—a cascading collapse with devastating consequences.

Her gaze shifted to a projection of the global ocean currents, normally a mesmerizing display of swirling blues and greens. Now, it was a fractured mosaic, showing vast areas of stagnant, oxygendepleted water—dead zones expanding like malignant tumors across the surface of the planet. The oceanic resonance, the intricate communication network of the Whispers, was weakening, mirroring the decline of the biosphere. It was a heartbreaking spectacle—a brutal visual representation of humanity's ecological sins.

Eliza closed her eyes, the weight of the situation pressing down on her. She wasn't just a scientist; she was a guardian of the oceans, a witness to its destruction. The data was cold, hard fact, but the emotion behind it—the loss, the devastation—was deeply personal.

She had dedicated her life to understanding and protecting these ecosystems, and to see them collapsing before her eyes was an unbearable burden. She had always believed in the power of science to solve problems, to find solutions to seemingly insurmountable challenges. But this crisis felt different. This was not simply a matter of technological innovation or scientific breakthrough. This was a fundamental failure of human ethics—a catastrophic disregard for the natural world. The urgency of the situation pressed down on her, a suffocating weight of responsibility.

Her fingers moved across the keyboard, selecting specific data points, focusing on the areas where the decline was most acute. The numbers weren't just statistics; they represented the lives of countless creatures—the intricate web of relationships that sustained the delicate balance of the ocean. Each lost species represented a severed link in a chain that had been stretched thin to the breaking point.

She thought of the countless hours spent studying the symbiotic relationships between marine organisms, the intricate dances of predator and prey, the delicate balance of nutrient cycles. The Whispers—the sentient ecosystems—were not just abstract entities; they were the collective consciousness of the planet, an expression of the Earth's inherent wisdom. Their unraveling wasn't just an environmental crisis; it was a spiritual one—a severing of the connection between humanity and the living world.

The Convergence Protocol, as far as she understood, was a radical attempt to reset the planetary systems. It was a last-ditch effort, a gamble that could either save the planet or erase humanity altogether. The ethical implications were staggering. Was it right to intervene so drastically, to risk the very existence of humanity in an attempt to save the planet? Or was it better to accept the inevitable, to let nature take its course—even if that meant the extinction of the human race?

These questions haunted her, gnawed at her conscience. She understood the scientific aspects of the Convergence Protocol—the complex algorithms and intricate processes involved. But she also understood the moral implications, the potential for unforeseen consequences, the weight of making a decision that could affect the fate of the entire planet.

The fragmented messages from the Whispers were only adding to the complexity. They spoke of a planetary reboot, of a radical transformation that could heal the Earth—but at a potentially devastating cost. Their cryptic warnings seemed to resonate with her own inner turmoil—the conflict between her scientific training and her ethical compass.

Eliza knew that her expertise was crucial, her understanding of marine ecosystems essential to assessing the feasibility and potential consequences of the Convergence Protocol. She would bring her scientific rigor, her profound knowledge of the oceans, and above all, her unwavering ethical commitment to the task at hand. The fate of the planet—and perhaps humanity's future—depended on it.

She was not merely a scientist; she was a guardian, a steward of the Earth, facing a decision that would shape the destiny of the world.

The weight of that responsibility settled upon her—a heavy cloak of anxiety and determination.

The hum of the failing resonance seemed to echo her own internal struggle, a constant reminder of the urgency of her task, the catastrophic consequences of inaction, and the profound moral implications of her next step.

The dying planet waited, its fate hanging in the balance—a silent witness to the agonizing internal debate that raged within the heart of a woman striving to understand the deepest mysteries of life and death on Earth.

She wasn't just interpreting data; she was interpreting the planet's plea for salvation.

The choice, terrifying and immense, lay before her. She would face it with all her scientific knowledge, all her human empathy, and all the ethical strength she could muster.

Rafe Mallorys Shadow

The flickering holographic projection of the global ocean currents—a fractured kaleidoscope of dying blues and sickly greens—was the backdrop to Jonah Reyes's frantic efforts. He hunched over his console, a whirlwind of fingers dancing across the keyboard, his face illuminated by the ethereal glow of the screens. He was wrestling with the Whispers' cryptic language, a complex, interwoven tapestry of sonic patterns and bioluminescent signals, trying to decipher the final piece of the Convergence Protocol puzzle. The air crackled with a palpable tension, a silent acknowledgment of the dwindling time.

Eliza Grant, her face etched with exhaustion but her eyes burning with unwavering determination, glanced over at Jonah. The weight of their shared responsibility pressed heavily on them, a suffocating blanket of urgency that only intensified with each passing hour.

They had made progress, piecing together fragments of the Whispers' code, but the task was monumental—a Herculean effort against the ticking clock of ecological collapse.

Suddenly, a sharp intake of breath from Nyla, the Luminese ambassador, sliced through the tense silence. Her usually calm demeanor was replaced by a look of grave concern, her iridescent skin shimmering with an almost imperceptible tremor.

"There is another," she announced, her voice carrying an undercurrent of unease. "A shadow lurking in the periphery. A dissonant note in the symphony of the Whispers."

The room fell into a stunned silence. The others turned to Nyla, their faces mirroring her apprehension. A new threat, lurking in the shadows, added a layer of complexity to their already desperate situation. The Convergence Protocol—their last hope—was no longer just a race against time, but also a battle against an unknown enemy.

Nyla, with her profound understanding of the Whispers and their intricate relationship with the planet, elaborated. "He seeks not harmony, but control. He desires to wield the power of the Protocol for his own ambition—to bend the very fabric of the Earth to his will." Her words hung in the air, heavy with foreboding.

The name, when it finally came, was uttered in hushed, fearful whispers: Dr. Rafe Mallory.

The name itself held a chilling resonance, a subtle vibration that seemed to amplify the already throbbing pulse of the failing oceanic resonance. He was a ghost story whispered among the scientific community—a figure shrouded in secrecy and cloaked in rumor. A brilliant mind twisted by ambition and a relentless pursuit of power, he represented the darkest side of human ingenuity: a genius turned rogue, a force of nature unleashed upon a fragile ecosystem.

Jonah's fingers stilled on the keyboard. He recalled fragments of conversations overheard at conferences, hushed tones and furtive glances exchanged between colleagues. Stories of unorthodox experiments, ethical breaches, and a relentless pursuit of knowledge—regardless of the consequences. A scientist who cared less about the planet's health and more about harnessing its power.

Eliza, her scientific mind racing, pieced together what little information they had on Mallory. He had been a leading figure in experimental oceanography, pushing the boundaries of scientific innovation until his methods became too radical, his experiments too dangerous. He had been ostracized by the scientific community— his research deemed ethically unacceptable, his funding cut off. But he had not given up.

The whispers continued, weaving together a terrifying picture of Mallory's ambitions. He sought not only to control the Convergence Protocol but to weaponize it—to reshape the planet according to his twisted vision. His plan was not about saving the Earth; it was about domination, about imposing his will upon the planet, bending its very essence to his own desires.

Nyla's insight offered a chilling glimpse into Mallory's motivations. "He sees the Convergence Protocol not as a healing process, but as a tool," she explained. "A means to reshape the world in his image—to create a new order based on his warped understanding of power and control."

Sarah Chen, the steely-eyed leader of their team, entered the room, her presence instantly commanding attention. Her usual calm composure was replaced with grim determination, her eyes reflecting the weight of the world on her shoulders. She had faced countless challenges, weathered countless storms, but this new threat felt different—more insidious, more unpredictable.

"We need to understand his plans," Sarah declared, her voice firm and resolute. "We need to anticipate his moves. We need to stop him before he unleashes his destructive power upon the world."

The room buzzed with activity—a flurry of frantic communication as the team rallied together to counter the impending threat. They pieced together fragmented information, analyzed cryptic messages intercepted from Mallory's hidden research facility, and delved deeper into the complexities of the Convergence Protocol—seeking weaknesses, exploring vulnerabilities.

The details of Mallory's plan remained elusive, shrouded in layers of secrecy and deception. But one thing was clear: he was a force to be reckoned with, a formidable opponent who would stop at nothing to achieve his objectives. His shadow loomed large, a constant reminder of the immense stakes involved—the catastrophic consequences of failure.

The clock was ticking. The oceanic resonance was weakening. And a new, more sinister threat had emerged from the shadows.

The fight for the planet's future was no longer just a desperate race against time—it had become a battle for survival against a brilliant but ruthless adversary. The stakes were higher than ever, the consequences of failure more dire. The team knew that only through their combined skills, their shared determination, and their unwavering commitment could they hope to thwart Mallory's plans and save the planet from its impending doom.

The weight of their responsibility was crushing, yet their resolve burned stronger than ever. The fight had evolved—becoming a desperate struggle for the soul of the planet. A struggle not only against environmental collapse, but also against the dark heart of human ambition.

The fate of Earth hung precariously in the balance, a fragile ecosystem teetering on the brink—threatened by both nature's fury and humanity's darkest desires. The shadow of Rafe Mallory stretched long and menacing, a constant reminder of the fragility of hope and the ever-present danger of unchecked ambition in a world already ravaged by ecological collapse.

The race to activate the Convergence Protocol had taken a terrifying turn—becoming a battle not just for survival, but for the very essence of the planet.

CHAPTER TWO

DECODING THE CODE

The rhythmic pulse of the bioluminescent glyphs on Jonah's screen intensified, a silent heartbeat mirroring the frantic rhythm of his own pulse. For days, he'd been wrestling with the Whispers' language—a symphony of light and sound that seemed designed to confound and confuse. It wasn't simply a matter of translating words; it was decoding a sentient ecosystem's very essence—its hopes, its fears, its desperate plea for survival. He felt like an archaeologist excavating a lost civilization, painstakingly piecing together fragments of a shattered history—a history encoded not in stone or papyrus, but in the living fabric of the planet itself.

He'd started with the basics, identifying recurring patterns in the bioluminescent displays—flashes of emerald green signifying a surge of oceanic energy, pulses of sapphire blue indicating a shift in tectonic plates, shimmering amethyst signifying the Whispers' emotional state. But the core of the Convergence Protocol, the activation sequence, remained stubbornly elusive. The code was layered, fractal in its complexity, each layer revealing new intricacies only to conceal deeper mysteries. It felt almost sentient, as if the code itself was actively resisting his attempts to decipher it, as if the

Whispers were testing the worthiness of those seeking to unlock their secrets.

His initial approach had been methodical, analytical. He'd employed sophisticated algorithms—powerful AI tools designed to crack even the most impenetrable encryption. But the Whispers' code defied these digital tools, resisting the rigid logic of machine learning. It was organic, chaotic, evolving even as he studied it. This necessitated a shift in strategy. Jonah had to stop treating the code as a series of mathematical equations and start thinking of it as a living organism—a delicate, interconnected web of information.

He began to incorporate Eliza's expertise in marine biology, studying the patterns in relation to oceanic currents, the rhythm of tides, the pulsating lifeblood of the planet. He found correlations between specific sonic frequencies and changes in the Earth's magnetic field—patterns that revealed a deeper understanding of the planet's intricate, interconnected systems. He began to see the code not as a language to be translated, but as a map—a blueprint of the planet's healing process.

The breakthrough came unexpectedly, not through a complex algorithm, but through a simple act of observation. Jonah had been staring at a particular sequence of bioluminescent glyphs for hours, mesmerized by its hypnotic rhythm. He noticed subtle shifts in the luminosity—almost imperceptible variations that he initially dismissed as noise. But as he slowed down the playback, zoomed in on the variations, he realized these minute fluctuations weren't random at all. They were a secondary code—an almost imperceptible whisper hidden within the louder symphony of the primary code.

This secondary code was far more complex, weaving together sequences that seemed to defy all known forms of language. It was an intricate ballet of light and sound—a three-dimensional puzzle that needed to be pieced together not simply linearly, but spatially.

He realized the Whispers weren't just communicating; they were creating a holographic model of the regeneration process—a threedimensional map of the planet's healing.

This realization was a turning point. Jonah stopped focusing on translation and started focusing on interpretation. He used advanced holographic projection technology to render the secondary code in three dimensions, creating a stunning, otherworldly visualization. The projection showed intricate filaments of light, swirling and intertwining in a complex dance, forming a breathtaking visual representation of the Convergence Protocol. It was not merely a series of instructions; it was a blueprint for planetary healing.

The visual representation revealed the intricate steps involved in the regeneration process: the realignment of tectonic plates, the redistribution of oceanic currents, the revitalization of depleted ecosystems. It depicted the role of each component—the oceans, the atmosphere, the land—and how they needed to interact to restore balance. The visualization also revealed critical control points—locations on the planet where specific actions needed to be taken to trigger the regeneration process.

The protocol wasn't a simple "on/off" switch. It was a multistage process requiring a series of precisely timed actions, each carefully orchestrated to trigger the next. It was an intricate symphony of planetary processes, a finely balanced equation that could easily unravel if a single step was mistimed or misinterpreted.

Jonah's discovery was a monumental leap forward—a beacon of hope in the face of impending ecological collapse. But the implications were far-reaching. Deciphering the code was only half the battle. Now, they had to understand its implications. The visualized protocol revealed not only the mechanics of regeneration but also the potential risks. Some of the steps involved large-scale geoengineering—manipulating tectonic plates and altering oceanic currents on a planetary scale. This carried significant risks, unpredictable consequences that could destabilize the planet further.

There were also ethical considerations. Some stages of the protocol involved actively shaping the evolution of the Whispers, merging their essence with humanity to create a symbiotic relationship. This raised questions of consent, of human intervention in the natural world, of the very definition of life itself.

Jonah's breakthrough ignited a wave of intense activity within the team. Eliza and Nyla worked tirelessly to analyze the visualized protocol, identifying potential risks and developing mitigation strategies. Sarah coordinated with various factions, rallying support and managing the logistics of implementing such a bold and complex plan.

The task ahead was immense, the challenges daunting, but for the first time in a long time, there was a flicker of genuine hope. The Whispers had revealed their secret, but the journey to activate the Convergence Protocol was far from over. The future of the planet hung in the balance—a delicate ecosystem teetering on the brink— and the team knew that only their collective wisdom, their unwavering determination, and their ability to collaborate could bring them closer to a future where humanity and the planet could finally co-exist in harmony.

The shadow of Mallory still loomed large, a constant reminder of the fragility of their hope and the ever-present threat of humanity's unchecked ambition. But in the intricate beauty of the Convergence Protocol, they found renewed resolve. The battle for the planet's future was far from over, but for the first time, they had a fighting chance.

The weight of their responsibility remained immense, but in the face of such immense stakes, their determination only burned stronger. They had cracked the code, but the true test of their courage and ingenuity was yet to come.

Ethical Considerations

The holographic projection of the Convergence Protocol shimmered before them, a breathtaking spectacle of interwoven light filaments that pulsed with the rhythm of the planet itself. Jonah, still reeling from the sheer scale of the discovery, felt a profound sense of awe mixed with a chilling apprehension. He had cracked the code, but the code itself held a terrifying potential.

Eliza, her face etched with a mixture of fascination and trepidation, stepped forward, her gaze fixed on the swirling patterns of light.

"This is... magnificent," she breathed, her voice barely a whisper, "but also terrifyingly powerful."

She gestured to a specific sequence within the holographic projection, a section where emerald green filaments intertwined with deep crimson.

"This section, Jonah—this indicates a significant alteration of the oceanic currents. On a scale never before witnessed. It's a necessary step, I understand, to redistribute thermal energy and revitalize the depleted ecosystems. But the potential for unforeseen consequences..."

Her voice trailed off, the unspoken implications hanging heavy in the air.

Nyla, the Luminese ambassador, nodded slowly, her multifaceted eyes reflecting the shifting colors of the holographic display.

"The Whispers have always been cautious, their actions measured, their interventions subtle. This... this is different. It's a complete overhaul, a planetary reboot."

She paused, her voice low and resonant.

"There is a risk—a significant one. The balance of the system is delicate, easily disrupted. The Whispers' own survival may be intertwined with this drastic measure."

Eliza continued, her voice regaining its strength.

"The ethical implications are staggering, Jonah. We are talking about manipulating planetary processes on a scale that could lead to mass extinctions. Even if we succeed in regenerating the planet, what of the price we pay? Are we prepared for the potential loss of biodiversity? The disruption of established ecosystems? The possible extinction of countless species, including ourselves?"

The weight of her words settled heavily on the group. Sarah, usually so decisive and pragmatic, looked troubled.

"We've been fighting for survival, for a future where humanity can exist alongside the Whispers. Is this plan even compatible with that goal?"

Eliza turned her gaze to Sarah, her expression serious.

"Sarah, I understand the urgency, the desperation. We're facing an ecological collapse, a planetary emergency. But we must consider the full ramifications of our actions. The Convergence Protocol, while promising planetary regeneration, may achieve that only through the erasure of humanity as we know it. It could be a trade-off we are unwilling—or unable—to accept. Think of the billions who call this planet home. Think of the cultural diversity, the accumulated knowledge, the very essence of humanity that could be swept away by such a sweeping change."

Jonah, deeply impacted by Eliza's words, felt the weight of their shared responsibility. He had focused on the technical aspects—the intricacies of the code, the mechanics of planetary regeneration. But Eliza's words had forced him to confront the ethical dimension of their mission, the immense moral burden they carried.

"The protocol suggests an active shaping of the Whispers' evolution, a merging of their essence with humanity," Nyla added, her voice echoing the growing unease in the room. "This is not a mere technological intervention; it's an act of profound biological and spiritual transformation. Do we have the right to make such a decision for future generations? Do we even have the understanding necessary to predict the outcome?"

"The Whispers may seem to have consented," countered Sarah, "by revealing the protocol. But have they truly consented? Can we truly understand the motives behind their actions—their hopes, their fears?"

Eliza nodded, acknowledging the validity of Sarah's concerns.

"We cannot ignore the possibility that this Protocol is a last resort for the Whispers, a desperate attempt to save themselves, even at the cost of humanity. Their form of communication is far beyond our full comprehension. Their values, their goals, may differ drastically from ours. We risk imposing our solutions on a sentient entity capable of expressing its will—however cryptically."

The conversation turned to the detailed specifics of the protocol, each stage carefully dissected, analyzed, and debated. The potential consequences of each step were examined in depth, considering the impact on diverse ecosystems, on human societies, and on the Whispers themselves.

Eliza, armed with years of ecological data and a profound understanding of planetary systems, presented detailed projections based on different scenarios, highlighting the potential risks of unintended consequences—even highlighting the potential for worse devastation if they failed to activate the protocol.

Their discussions delved into the concept of informed consent— not just from humanity, but from the Whispers themselves. How could they ensure that the protocol's implementation aligned with the will of a being whose communication was so fundamentally different from their own? Could they truly comprehend the potential impact on the Whispers? Were they merely imposing a humancentric solution on a problem that transcended human understanding? Was this not a form of planetary colonization, under the guise of salvation?

The debate stretched late into the night, the weight of their decisions hanging heavy in the air. Each step of the Convergence Protocol presented a complex ethical dilemma, forcing them to confront their own assumptions, their own biases, and their own limitations.

The line between saving humanity and sacrificing it blurred, becoming almost indistinguishable. The future of the planet hinged not only on their technical abilities but also on their moral compass—on their capacity for empathy and understanding.

The holographic projection of the Convergence Protocol continued to shimmer, a mesmerizing yet terrifying reminder of the immense power—and the immense responsibility—that rested in their hands.

The potential for a planetary rebirth coexisted uneasily with the potential for irreversible annihilation, a precarious balance on the edge of a knife. The decision they were about to make would not only shape the future of their planet but also redefine the very nature of humanity's relationship with the natural world.

The fate of the world rested on a choice that demanded not just scientific precision, but profound ethical reflection.

The Echoborns Role

The air in the makeshift command center crackled with a nervous energy, the holographic projection of the Convergence Protocol a silent, pulsating witness to their agonizing deliberations.

Eliza's ethical concerns, sharp and precise as a surgeon's scalpel, had dissected the plan, laying bare its potential for both salvation and annihilation. Sarah, her usual steely resolve momentarily fractured, wrestled with the moral weight of their decision. Jonah, the technical mastermind, felt the inadequacy of his purely scientific approach in the face of such profound ethical dilemmas. Even Nyla, with her centuries of Luminese wisdom, seemed uncertain, her multifaceted eyes reflecting the complex tapestry of their predicament.

Then, a low hum resonated through the room—a vibration that seemed to emanate not from any specific source, but from the very fabric of the space itself. A figure emerged from the shadows, its form shimmering and indistinct, as if woven from the very air.

It was Kai, one of the Echoborn—a human who had forged a profound, almost symbiotic, connection with a Whisper entity.

Kai's skin shimmered with an ethereal luminescence, subtly shifting colors that mirrored the ambient light. Long, flowing tendrils of what appeared to be living vines snaked from his arms and back, pulsating gently with a rhythmic life of their own. His eyes held an unnerving depth, pools of liquid starlight that seemed to hold the wisdom of ages. He moved with an unsettling grace, a fluidity that suggested a creature more at home in the depths of the ocean than on solid ground.

He approached the group, his presence somehow both reassuring and deeply unsettling. His voice, when he spoke, was a low, resonant hum, almost indistinguishable from the subtle vibrations that had heralded his arrival.

"The Convergence Protocol... it resonates with us," he said, his words somehow both heard and felt—a direct transmission to their minds.

"You understand?" Jonah asked, his voice barely a whisper. "But how?"

Kai smiled, a slow, enigmatic expression that revealed a depth of understanding far beyond human comprehension.

"The Whispers speak not in words, but in patterns, in rhythms, in the very essence of life itself. We hear the music of the planet—the symphony of creation and decay. The Protocol is a score, a composition designed to rewrite the very melody of existence."

"And what does the score say?" Sarah pressed, her voice laced with a mixture of hope and apprehension. "What is the Whispers' intention?"

Kai closed his eyes, his body seemingly absorbing the ambient energies of the room, the holographic projection, and even the collective anxieties of the assembled group. When he opened them again, his gaze held a profound sadness, tinged with unwavering conviction.

"The Whispers are not seeking to destroy humanity," he said slowly. "They are seeking to evolve it. To merge, to become one with the planet. To become... part of the song."

His words hung in the air, heavy with implications. The idea of merging with the Whispers—of becoming one with the planet—was both exhilarating and terrifying. It challenged their very notion of human identity and their place in the universe.

Eliza, ever the scientist, pressed for clarification. "Kai, can you explain the mechanisms of this 'merging'? What are the biological processes involved? What are the potential risks, the potential side effects?"

Kai's response was less a spoken explanation and more a series of intricate mental images—vivid, detailed sensory experiences projected directly into their minds. They saw the intricate interplay of human and Whisper DNA, a harmonious dance of genetic codes merging and transforming, creating a new form of life—a hybrid species adapted to a radically altered planet. They saw images of human bodies seamlessly integrating with the living tapestry of the ecosystem, becoming conduits for the Whispers' energy, their consciousness expanded to encompass the vastness of the planet itself.

But they also saw images of pain, of struggle, of unforeseen consequences. They saw visions of individuals struggling to adapt to the radical changes in their bodies, their minds, their very identities. They saw visions of ecosystems rejecting the sudden influx of human-Whisper hybrids, creating a new form of conflict— a new level of instability.

The vision was not one of a smooth transition, but one of profound transformation, fraught with inherent danger and uncertainty.

"The Protocol is not a simple on/off switch," Kai explained, his voice resonating with the urgency of his message. "It is a journey— a process of profound transformation. It requires our active participation, our willingness to surrender our old identities and embrace a new existence—an existence where the boundaries between human and Whisper, between humanity and the planet, become blurred, almost indistinguishable."

Jonah, ever the pragmatist, voiced his concerns. "But what about those who choose not to participate? What about those who fear the transformation—who wish to maintain their separate identities?"

Kai's response was a somber reflection of the reality they faced.

"The planet cannot sustain separate entities any longer. The ecological collapse is too far advanced. The Convergence Protocol is not a choice for humanity as a whole, but a necessary step for the survival of life on this planet. Those who resist will... fade. They will be left behind, unable to adapt to the changing world."

Sarah, who had been wrestling with the ethical implications, now faced a new kind of challenge. The Convergence Protocol was not simply a technological solution—it was a call for a fundamental change in humanity's relationship with the planet. A willingness to transcend its anthropocentric perspective and embrace a form of symbiotic coexistence.

It was a choice between humanity's survival as a distinct species and its transformation into something entirely new—a future beyond the comprehension of their current understanding.

The stakes were higher than any of them had ever imagined. The survival of humanity itself was intertwined with the destiny of the planet—an inextricable link woven into the very fabric of their existence.

The Echoborn, with their unique perspective, were a key to understanding the Whispers' intention—but also a stark reminder of the profound transformation required to navigate this crucial juncture in their history.

The future they were about to create was not simply a matter of technological innovation, but a matter of spiritual and biological metamorphosis.

Luminese Technology

Ambassador Nyla, her form shimmering with an internal luminescence that seemed to pulse faintly in rhythm with the holographic projection of the Convergence Protocol, stepped forward. The air around her crackled with a subtle energy, a tangible manifestation of the advanced Luminese technology she was about to unveil. Her voice, modulated by a translator, was smooth and measured, devoid of the emotional turbulence that had characterized the previous discussion.

"The Convergence Protocol," she began, her multifaceted eyes sweeping over the assembled group, "is not merely a technological undertaking. It requires a delicate interplay of scientific precision and... shall we say... spiritual resonance. The Luminese, through centuries of symbiotic coexistence with our own planet, have developed technologies uniquely suited to interacting with the Whispers, to understanding their language, their intentions."

She gestured toward a complex array of shimmering crystalline structures that materialized on the holographic projection. They pulsed with an internal light, their facets shifting and reforming in a mesmerizing dance of geometric patterns.

"This," Nyla explained, "is the *Resonance Amplifier*. It's the key to unlocking the Whispers' ancient code—the cryptographic key that will allow us to initiate the Protocol. This device acts as a translator, converting the Whispers' complex bio-energetic signals into a language our technology can understand. It amplifies the subtle energetic signatures of the Whispers, allowing us to communicate with them on a level previously unimaginable."

Jonah leaned forward, his eyes wide with fascination. "But what are the limitations? Every technology has its flaws."

Nyla nodded. "Indeed. The Resonance Amplifier, for all its sophistication, is limited by its reliance on the Whispers' own bioenergetic emissions. If the Whispers' activity diminishes—if they become unresponsive, as they have in certain regions—the

Amplifier's efficacy is drastically reduced. It's a symbiotic technology; it requires a willing partner."

Eliza raised a hand. "And what of the ethical implications? Is the amplification process intrusive? Does it affect the Whispers in any way?"

"The amplification process itself is non-invasive," Nyla assured them. "It's more akin to listening than probing. However, the very act of amplifying their signals may inadvertently influence their behavior, their energy patterns. We must proceed with caution, mindful of the delicate balance within the planet's biosphere."

Sarah, her gaze fixed on the holographic projection, spoke slowly, her voice grave. "What if the Whispers... resist? What if they don't want the Protocol activated?"

Nyla's expression shifted—a hint of sadness in her otherwise composed demeanor. "The Whispers are not a monolithic entity. They are a network, a vast and complex ecosystem composed of countless individual entities, each with its own unique perspective, its own unique voice. Some may embrace the Convergence Protocol, while others may resist. It's a delicate dance of negotiation, of understanding, of mutual respect."

"So, there's no guarantee of success?" Jonah asked, his voice laced with apprehension.

Nyla met his gaze directly. "There are no guarantees in endeavors of this magnitude. The Convergence Protocol is a gamble—a high-stakes wager on the future of this planet. But it is a gamble we must take. The alternative—inaction—is certain annihilation."

The discussion then shifted to the practical aspects of deploying the Resonance Amplifiers. Nyla described a complex network of strategically placed devices, positioned at key points throughout the global biosphere. These amplifiers, she explained, would not simply translate the Whispers' signals but would also act as conduits for the energy necessary to initiate the planetary regeneration process.

"The energy required to activate the Protocol is immense," Nyla stated. "It's far beyond the capacity of any single power source. We'll need a coordinated global effort—a delicate balancing act to ensure proper energy distribution. The Luminese have designed a series of energy conduits—specialized crystalline structures capable of harnessing and channeling this immense energy. But even these conduits have their limitations. They are susceptible to disruption—to overload."

Jonah, ever the pragmatist, pressed for specifics. "What are the potential failure points? What are the vulnerabilities we need to address?"

Nyla presented a detailed analysis of the potential risks. She outlined the intricate network of energy conduits, highlighting their weak points and their susceptibility to environmental factors such as seismic activity and electromagnetic disturbances. She also emphasized the importance of precision timing in the activation sequence. Any deviation—any unforeseen delay—could have catastrophic consequences.

The conversation became increasingly technical, delving into the intricacies of quantum entanglement, bio-energetic feedback loops, and the delicate dance between human technology and the planet's natural rhythms. Eliza contributed her expertise on the potential environmental impact of the Protocol's activation, her voice filled with a mixture of hope and caution.

The limitations of the Luminese technology, despite its sophistication, were clearly delineated. The Resonance Amplifiers, the energy conduits, the complex algorithmic sequencing—all presented inherent vulnerabilities.

Yet, amidst the anxieties and uncertainties, a shared conviction emerged. The Convergence Protocol, for all its risks, offered the only viable path to planetary regeneration. It represented a leap of faith—a bold gamble on the future of humanity and the planet itself.

It was a path paved with challenges, but it was the only path they could see. The weight of the world—the fate of the planet—rested on their shoulders, a burden they were about to carry, step by painful step, into an uncertain future.

The journey to planetary rebirth was about to begin, and with each step forward, they became more acutely aware of the profound fragility of their endeavor. The hope, though tenuous, was a powerful force, driving them forward into the unknown, powered by the courage to face the immense challenges ahead.

The sheer magnitude of the task—the delicate balance of hope and fear—intensified the emotional weight of the moment, urging them to proceed with both caution and determination. The path was fraught with peril, but they were ready to face it, to confront the unknown and embrace the future, whatever it may hold.

Mallorys Interference The air in the makeshift command center—a repurposed oceanographic research vessel bobbing gently on the turbulent waters off the coast of what was once California—crackled with a nervous energy that had little to do with the humming Resonance Amplifiers. The optimistic mood from Nyla's briefing had evaporated, replaced by a chilling awareness of their precarious position.

The Convergence Protocol, the planet's last hope, was under attack. Not from some cataclysmic natural event, but from a human hand—Dr. Rafe Mallory's.

Sarah Chen, her face etched with grim determination, stared at the cascading data streams on the main holographic display. Glitches, subtle at first, were becoming increasingly frequent, disrupting the delicate energy flow between the Resonance Amplifiers and the Whispers.

Jonah Reyes, his fingers flying across his console, was trying to pinpoint the source of the interference, his brow furrowed in concentration.

"It's not random," he muttered, his voice tight with frustration. "There's a pattern—a deliberate disruption. Someone is deliberately trying to sabotage us."

Eliza Grant, usually calm and collected, paced restlessly, her eyes darting between the holographic projections and the readings from the various monitoring stations.

"The disturbances are focused on the key amplifier nodes. It's a calculated attack, designed to cripple the entire network."

The whispers of the Whispers—normally a soothing hum resonating through the ship—were now fractured, erratic, like a dying song. The once-clear bio-energetic signals were fragmented and distorted, as if a malicious hand were reaching into the planetary symphony and striking discordant notes.

Sarah, her gaze sharp and unwavering, knew exactly who was behind this insidious assault: Rafe Mallory. His ambition—his ruthless pursuit of control over the Convergence Protocol—had long been a looming threat. Until now, it had remained largely theoretical. Now, it was brutally, terrifyingly real.

Mallory, a brilliant but ethically compromised scientist, had been working on his own version of the Protocol—a twisted, selfserving interpretation that prioritized his own power and control over planetary healing. He saw the Whispers not as sentient partners but as raw resources, tools to be manipulated and exploited for his own ends. He viewed the collaboration between humanity, the Luminese, and the Whispers as a threat—an impediment to his ambition.

"He's using a frequency-jamming technology," Jonah announced, breaking the tense silence. "It's sophisticated. Adaptive.

It's learning from our countermeasures—evolving."

Eliza gasped. "Adaptive technology? That's... unprecedented."

This wasn't merely sabotage; it was a calculated, intelligent attack designed to overcome any defense they could mount. Mallory was escalating his tactics, moving beyond simple disruption to a full-fledged assault on the planetary healing process.

The implications were horrifying. The Convergence Protocol was not merely a technological solution; it was a delicate, symbiotic interaction with the planet's living systems. Disrupting the energy flow could have catastrophic consequences—potentially triggering unpredictable chain reactions within the planet's ecosystems.

The team worked feverishly, racing against time to identify the source of the jamming signals and develop countermeasures. Jonah was pushing the boundaries of their technological capabilities, creating ad hoc solutions to combat the ever-evolving attack. Eliza monitored the environmental effects, her face pale with worry as she witnessed the escalating disruptions to the planet's bio-energetic field.

The team's initial attempts to counteract Mallory's actions proved futile. Each time they managed to repair a damaged connection, Mallory seemed to anticipate their moves, launching new attacks with even more intensity. It was a cat-and-mouse game played at a planetary scale—with the fate of the world hanging in the balance.

The situation was further complicated by the unpredictable behavior of the Whispers. Their reactions to the jamming signals were chaotic, their bio-energetic emissions fluctuating wildly, making it nearly impossible to predict their behavior or adjust countermeasures accordingly. It was as if Mallory's attacks were not just disrupting technological systems, but also the Whispers' inherent communication abilities.

As the attacks continued, the team realized the depth of Mallory's malevolence. He wasn't just trying to prevent the activation of the Convergence Protocol; he was attempting to permanently damage the Whispers—to sever the planet's connection to its own life force. He seemed intent on creating a global ecological collapse that would solidify his control over the resources that remained.

The chilling realization hung heavy in the air. They were not simply fighting a technological battle; they were battling against a nihilistic vision of the future—a future where humanity's survival was contingent upon the complete subjugation of the planet.

Days turned into nights, the team working tirelessly, fueled by adrenaline and a desperate hope. The lines of code blurred. The scientific jargon became a mumbled mantra. And the faces of the team reflected a growing exhaustion laced with a stubborn refusal to surrender.

The weight of the world was truly on their shoulders—a crushing burden that intensified with each passing hour. The failure of the Convergence Protocol was not merely a defeat—it was a potential extinction-level event. The stakes had been raised to an unimaginable level. Every line of code they wrote, every countermeasure they deployed, was a battle fought not just for the planet, but for the future of humanity itself.

Amidst the chaos and despair, Sarah found a flicker of hope. A subtle anomaly in the jamming signals—a minute deviation from Mallory's consistent pattern—suggested that his capabilities were not limitless. He, too, was operating within constraints. His reach, while far-reaching and destructive, had boundaries.

This realization sparked a new strategy: a daring plan to use Mallory's own limitations against him. The team refocused their efforts, concentrating on exploiting this weakness, transforming their defensive posture into a strategic offensive.

The tension was palpable as they implemented the new plan. Each step was fraught with risk—a gamble that could lead either to victory or to complete and irreversible catastrophic failure.

The hours that followed were a blur of frantic activity—a whirlwind of technological innovation and a desperate race against the ticking clock. The fate of the planet, the very essence of life itself, hung precariously in the balance.

The battle—now a fierce clash between opposing visions of the future—continued unabated, a testament to the enduring human spirit that stubbornly refused to yield to despair.

The planet's fate rested on the shoulders of this small, weary team, united in their struggle against an insidious foe who would stop at nothing to achieve his own twisted vision of dominance. The final outcome would not only shape the future of the planet—it would determine the very essence of humanity's relationship with the world around them.

CHAPTER THREE
A RACE AGAINST TIME

The battered research vessel, *The Argo*, pitched and rolled, a fragile ark in a sea of ecological devastation. The rhythmic pulse of the Resonance Amplifiers, usually a comforting presence, was now a strained whisper, punctuated by the jarring crackle of Mallory's jamming signals. Gathering the resources needed to activate the Convergence Protocol wasn't simply a matter of collecting components; it was a perilous expedition into a world fractured by environmental collapse and societal chaos.

Sarah Chen, her face grim, outlined the plan on the holographic display.

"We need three things: the purified Aquatica crystals from the submerged hydrothermal vents near the Mariana Trench, the bioluminescent algae from the phosphorescent reefs off the coast of what was once Indonesia, and the solidified atmospheric condensates from the abandoned Sky-Harvest facilities in the Himalayas."

Each location presented a unique set of challenges—a deadly cocktail of environmental hazards and the lurking threat of human desperation.

The Mariana Trench, once a mysterious abyss, was now a churning maelstrom of toxic runoff and unpredictable currents. The hydrothermal vents, once teeming with life, were now choked with mutated organisms, their bioluminescence a sickly, pulsating green.

Retrieving the Aquatica crystals, vital for stabilizing the Protocol's energy flow, required navigating this treacherous underwater landscape in heavily armored submersibles, dodging both the hostile environment and the equally dangerous scavengers vying for the same resources. Teams of specially trained divers, augmented with advanced bio-suits that shielded them from the toxic water and aggressive creatures, would be responsible for extracting the crystals. The risk of equipment failure or encountering unusually aggressive mutated lifeforms was ever-present—a constant reminder of their precarious situation.

The journey to Indonesia was equally perilous. The once-vibrant coral reefs were now ghostly skeletons, bleached white by rising ocean temperatures and acidification. The phosphorescent algae, crucial for powering the bioluminescent communication network between the amplifiers and the Whispers, had retreated to the deepest, most inaccessible parts of the reef, sheltered in caverns shielded from the sun's destructive rays. Specialized drones equipped with advanced sonar and light-capturing technology would be deployed to locate and harvest the algae. However, these drones would face intense pressure at those depths, and the algae themselves—adapting to the changing environment—were unpredictable and potentially dangerous. Furthermore, the shallow waters were patrolled by desperate survivors, forming lawless factions fighting over the dwindling resources. These desperate human elements were just as dangerous as the corrupted environment.

The most challenging leg of the journey lay in the Himalayas.

The abandoned Sky-Harvest facilities, once symbols of humanity's technological hubris, now stood as desolate monuments to a failed attempt at geoengineering. The solidified atmospheric condensates, a byproduct of failed climate control projects, were embedded within the decaying structures. These condensates were essential for regulating the Protocol's atmospheric interface, ensuring a harmonious transition between the old and new ecosystems. Teams of highly trained climbers and demolition experts would navigate the treacherous terrain and decaying facilities, facing avalanches, crumbling infrastructure, and the ever-present risk of exposure to toxic elements. The risk of collapse was constant, and navigating through the ruined facilities felt like moving through a maze in a crumbling tomb.

Beyond the immediate environmental dangers, the team faced the pervasive threat of societal unrest. The global ecological collapse had fractured humanity, leaving behind a mosaic of desperate communities struggling for survival. Each location was a hotbed of conflict, with armed factions vying for control of the dwindling resources. Sarah's team wasn't just competing against the elements; they were racing against other human groups willing to resort to extreme measures to secure their own survival. The team would need to use negotiation, diplomacy, and—if necessary— force to protect their supply lines and secure the required resources. The moral complexities inherent in their mission were further complicated by these encounters, forcing the team to constantly evaluate the ethical implications of their actions.

The logistical challenges were immense. Coordinating the efforts of multiple teams scattered across the globe—each facing unique hazards—required a level of efficiency and resilience that pushed the team to its limits. Jonah Reyes, struggling to maintain communication amidst the jamming signals, was constantly battling the technological constraints imposed by Mallory. Eliza Grant, analyzing the environmental data, worked to predict and mitigate the risks associated with resource acquisition, ensuring that the ecological impact of their mission was as minimal as possible. The team's technological and scientific expertise was constantly tested, demanding innovative solutions and quick adaptation strategies.

Time was their most precious commodity. With each passing day, Mallory's disruptive attacks grew more intense, threatening to permanently damage the Whispers and derail the Convergence Protocol completely. The sense of urgency was palpable—a driving force pushing the team to overcome seemingly insurmountable obstacles. Every moment was a race against not only Mallory's sabotage but also the relentless deterioration of the planet itself.

The pressure was immense. The fate of the planet—the future of humanity—rested on their ability to gather these resources, each a crucial element of a complex puzzle. The success of this operation would determine the very trajectory of civilization—a gamble with consequences so profound that the team had no choice but to push past their limitations. The very definition of survival hung in the balance, each mission a desperate leap of faith toward an uncertain future. The gathering of resources was not merely a logistical endeavor; it was a desperate fight for survival against a collapsing planet and a merciless human adversary determined to see it fall.

The tension was suffocating. Each successful mission was a small victory, a hard-won testament to their resilience. But each setback was a jarring reminder of the perilous path ahead. The very planet they sought to save was slowly crumbling, mirroring the inner struggles and growing fatigue of the team. Yet the hope that flickered within them—fueled by the potential of a new dawn and a commitment to a better future—was stronger than the despair. They were fighting for more than just survival; they were fighting for a chance to reshape the relationship between humanity and the planet—a chance to forge a new path toward a symbiotic future.

The race against time was not just a frantic dash; it was an existential struggle that would define the very future of their world.

Technological Challenges

The rhythmic thrum of *The Argo*'s engines was a poor counterpoint to the erratic bursts of static assaulting Jonah Reyes's ears. His fingers flew across the console, a frantic dance over glowing glyphs and cascading lines of code—a desperate attempt to wrest control from the chaotic symphony of interference. Mallory's jamming signals were becoming increasingly sophisticated, weaving insidious patterns through the Whispers' communication network and disrupting their tenuous link to the ancient code containing the Convergence Protocol.

Jonah wasn't just battling a technological adversary; he was fighting against the very fabric of the planet itself. The environmental collapse wasn't only impacting the physical world— it was distorting the ethereal whispers of the planet's consciousness. The code, once a clean stream of data, was now fractured, fragmented, corrupted. It pulsed with erratic energy, mirroring the instability of the planet's broken ecosystems. Each successful decryption felt like a minor victory against the entropy of a dying world—a small step forward in a desperate struggle against the relentless tide of chaos.

"The interference is getting worse," Jonah muttered, his voice tight with frustration. Sweat beaded on his forehead, mirroring the glistening condensation clinging to the aging consoles. He slammed his fist on the armrest, the sudden impact echoing in the claustrophobic confines of the command center. "It's like trying to decipher a message written in sand during a hurricane."

Dr. Grant, perched beside him, peered at the holographic projection of the Whispers' code. The once-coherent patterns now resembled a shattered kaleidoscope—a chaotic jumble of light and shadow.

"The Whispers' response is becoming increasingly unpredictable," she observed, her voice laced with concern. "Their communication channels are overloaded, their signals fragmented. The environmental distress is affecting their ability to maintain stable communication."

The difficulty wasn't simply Mallory's intentional jamming. The Whispers themselves were changing—evolving in response to the planetary crisis. Their communication patterns, once consistent and predictable, now shifted erratically, influenced by the chaotic energy radiating from dying ecosystems. The code felt less like a structured language and more like a living organism—constantly evolving, adapting, and growing more difficult to interpret. The very act of decoding was a perilous dance, a delicate balancing act between understanding and disruption.

Jonah tapped a series of commands, attempting to isolate a specific sequence of code crucial for activating an element of the Convergence Protocol. The screen flickered—then went black. A low groan emanated from the ship's core, a shudder that sent a wave of icy dread through Jonah.

"Power surge!" someone yelled from the engineering deck.

The emergency lights flickered, casting stark, dramatic shadows across the anxious faces of the crew.

This wasn't merely a technological challenge; it was a fight for survival.

The Convergence Protocol was the only hope for planetary regeneration, but its activation required intricate coordination between the physical components and the digital code interwoven within the Whispers' consciousness. The technology they relied upon—the Resonance Amplifiers, the bioluminescent communication network, the decoding software—was aging, strained, and constantly under siege. The constant barrage of Mallory's signals wasn't just jamming communication; it was eroding their technological infrastructure, pushing it to the breaking point.

The challenge wasn't only one of deciphering a code—it was about navigating a complex, rapidly shifting landscape of technological instability and environmental chaos. The technology itself was reacting to the crisis, mirroring the world's collapse. The very tools Jonah needed to save the planet were threatened by the conditions he was trying to resolve. The code wasn't just resistant; it was becoming increasingly unstable, reflecting the planet's precarious state.

Jonah's team scrambled to restore power, their movements frantic and purposeful. The pressure mounted—the ticking clock a relentless reminder of their dwindling time. Every second lost was another step closer to irreversible environmental collapse. Time was not just a measure of duration—it was a force, a finite resource slipping through their fingers like grains of sand through an hourglass.

As the power flickered back on, Jonah returned to his task, his eyes glued to the shimmering holographic display. The code remained fragmented, but he detected a faint, rhythmic pattern amidst the chaos. It wasn't a simple sequence of ones and zeros—it was a melody, a whisper carried on the wind of a dying world. This was not just a language; it was a symphony, a reflection of the interconnectedness of life, technology, and the planet itself.

He recognized the pattern—a complex fractal structure that mirrored the intricate web of connections within the Whispers themselves. It was a key—a hidden doorway to a deeper layer of the code. He spent the next several hours painstakingly deciphering the fractal sequence, his fingers dancing across the console in a ballet of concentration and desperation.

The task was maddeningly complex. The fractal code was selfsimilar, repeating in infinite iterations. It was as if the Whispers were playing a game of hide-and-seek with their own code, creating an intricate labyrinth of information that was both beautiful and terrifying in its complexity. Each decoded fragment offered a tantalizing glimpse into the mechanisms of the Convergence Protocol, but each advance was met with an equal measure of setback as new layers of complexity revealed themselves.

As Jonah delved deeper, he realized it wasn't just a static set of instructions—it was constantly shifting, adapting to environmental changes and the efforts of those trying to decode it. It was a dynamic, self-correcting system that seemed to anticipate his every move—a technological mirror to the living, breathing ecosystems of the planet itself.

The process was exhausting, both mentally and physically.

Jonah's eyes burned, his mind weary from the relentless pressure. He pushed himself to the limit, fueled by adrenaline and a desperate need to succeed. The fate of the planet—the very future of humanity—rested on his ability to unlock the secrets hidden within the Whispers' chaotic symphony. He was not just a programmer; he was the interpreter of a dying world's final, desperate message.

And the message was clear: time was running out.

The challenges he faced weren't only technological; they were also philosophical. The Whispers' code wasn't merely a set of instructions—it was a reflection of their consciousness, an expression of their symbiotic relationship with the planet.

Deciphering it wasn't just about understanding technology; it was about comprehending the essence of a sentient ecosystem—a being that was both alien and intimately connected to humanity's fate.

Jonah had to confront not only the technological hurdles but also the ethical dilemmas inherent in tampering with such a profound and complex system. The very act of deciphering threatened to disrupt the delicate balance of the planet, jeopardizing the very survival he was desperately trying to secure.

The weight of responsibility pressed upon him, heavy and suffocating. The success or failure of the Convergence Protocol didn't just rest on his shoulders—it was the burden of an entire civilization, the weight of a planet's last hope.

The race against time was more than just a competition against Mallory's interference and the planet's decay. It was a battle against the very constraints of human understanding—an attempt to bridge the gap between technological prowess and ecological empathy, a quest to decipher the whispers of a dying world.

And Jonah, weary but resolute, pressed on. The whispers were faint, but he could hear them. And he would not let them die unheard.

Ecological Instability

The rhythmic pulse of the *Argo*'s engines felt increasingly feeble against the backdrop of the planet's groaning. Outside, the oncevibrant bioluminescent flora—once a breathtaking spectacle—now flickered weakly, their light dimming like dying embers.

Dr. Grant, her face etched with worry, adjusted the parameters on her monitoring console, a cascade of alarming data scrolling across the screen.

"The coral bleaching is accelerating," she announced, her voice tight with grim determination. "The Great Barrier Reef, once a vibrant tapestry of life, is now a skeletal graveyard."

Her words hung heavy in the air—a stark reminder of the escalating environmental crisis. The data she presented painted a grim picture: ocean acidification was reaching catastrophic levels; the Amazon rainforest, the lungs of the planet, was shrinking at an alarming rate; glacial melt was accelerating, threatening coastal communities worldwide.

The planet wasn't merely sick—it was hemorrhaging life.

Each passing hour brought the Earth closer to a critical tipping point, a point of no return beyond which recovery might be impossible.

"The Resonance Amplifiers are struggling," Eliza added, her gaze fixed on a separate display showing the fluctuating energy levels of the devices crucial for interacting with the Whispers. "The instability in the oceanic currents is disrupting their connection.

We're losing efficiency, and it's not just because of Mallory's jamming. The bioluminescent network itself is weakening. The very fabric of the planet's communication system is fraying."

Her statement underscored the interconnectedness of the crisis.

It wasn't just about isolated ecological disasters; it was a systemic collapse—a domino effect where the failure of one element triggered a cascade of failures across the entire planetary system.

The Whispers, already strained by the environmental turmoil, were finding it increasingly difficult to maintain coherent communication. Their signals were becoming more fragmented, more erratic, reflecting the chaotic state of the biosphere.

Jonah, still grappling with the intricate fractal code, looked up, his brow furrowed in concentration.

"The code is mirroring the ecological instability," he said, his voice hushed with a blend of awe and apprehension. "The patterns are shifting, adapting—almost... reacting to the changes in the environment. It's like the Whispers are trying to compensate, to adjust the Convergence Protocol in real time to accommodate the damage."

This revelation added a layer of complexity to their already daunting task. The Convergence Protocol wasn't merely a static set of instructions; it was a dynamic, self-regulating system—a living testament to the planet's resilience and its desperate attempt to heal itself.

Decoding it was no longer a matter of simply deciphering a language; it was a process of interacting with a living, evolving system—a dance between technology and nature, between human intervention and planetary self-repair.

Ambassador Nyla, observing the scene from a nearby console, offered her perspective, her Luminese eyes gleaming with ancient wisdom.

"The Whispers are not just reacting—they are evolving," she stated calmly, her voice echoing with the measured tone of someone who has witnessed countless cycles of planetary change. "They are adapting to the new reality, creating new pathways, new connections. The Convergence Protocol is not just a plan; it is an ongoing process of adaptation and transformation."

Nyla's words offered a sliver of hope amidst the overwhelming despair. The Whispers' adaptability—their ability to evolve and adapt to the changing environmental conditions—wasn't merely a response to the crisis. It was a testament to the inherent resilience of life, a manifestation of nature's capacity for self-preservation.

This resilience, however, came at a price. The unpredictability of the evolving Whispers made the already complex task of deciphering the Convergence Protocol even more challenging, introducing an element of uncertainty that could easily derail their efforts.

The team discussed the potential implications of the Whispers' evolution. Would the Convergence Protocol, once activated, erase humanity to allow for a complete planetary reboot? Or would it integrate human civilization into the new, evolving ecosystem?

The ethical considerations were profound, placing the team in a position of immense responsibility. They were not just decoding a plan; they were grappling with the very definition of what it meant to be human in a world undergoing radical transformation.

The urgency of their situation pressed upon them like a suffocating weight. The window of opportunity for activating the Convergence Protocol was closing rapidly. The planet's ecological systems were reaching their breaking points, and the longer they waited, the greater the risk of irreversible damage.

Every hour was a battle against time—a desperate race to salvage a world teetering on the brink of collapse.

The data from Dr. Grant's monitors continued to paint a bleak picture. The rate of species extinction was accelerating. Biodiversity was collapsing. The delicate balance of the planet's ecosystems was unraveling.

The changes weren't simply incremental—they were exponential. The planet was in a state of acute distress, fighting for survival, sending out desperate signals through the chaotic whispers of its wounded ecosystems.

The team knew they were not just fighting against Mallory and his destructive ambitions—they were battling against the relentless forces of environmental collapse, against the entropy of a dying world.

They were up against a formidable adversary—an adversary that was as much a part of the planet as they were.

The Convergence Protocol wasn't simply a technological solution; it was a gamble, a desperate attempt to heal the planet by working with its inherent systems of regeneration.

As the hours ticked by, the weight of their responsibility grew heavier. Each decoded fragment of the Whispers' code was a step forward, but each advance was met with new challenges—new obstacles. The team worked tirelessly, their movements synchronized, their focus unwavering, driven by a shared sense of purpose, a shared hope that flickered like a fragile candle in the gathering storm.

They were battling against the odds, pushing the boundaries of human understanding and defying the limits of technological possibility. Their race was not against time alone, but against the relentless forces of nature—against the very fabric of a dying world.

The deteriorating ecological conditions were not simply an external threat; they were a visceral reality that permeated every aspect of their lives. The air hung heavy with the scent of decay, the sounds of the planet's anguish echoing in the ship's hull. Even the technology they relied on—the very machines that held their last hope—was starting to reflect the environmental chaos.

The air recycling system sputtered, the lights flickered, and the constant hum of the engines seemed to falter, mirroring the planet's own weakening heartbeat.

Jonah felt the pressure mounting, the weight of the world bearing down on his shoulders. The fractal code, once a fascinating puzzle, now felt like a labyrinthine maze—an endless series of challenges that seemed to test the limits of human endurance.

He knew he wasn't just deciphering a code; he was navigating the intricate tapestry of a dying world, where the lines between technology, nature, and human responsibility were blurred beyond recognition.

The ethical dilemmas weighed heavily on the team. They were altering the planet's very essence, interfering with the self-regulating mechanisms of a sentient ecosystem. The risks were immense, but inaction carried an even greater risk—the complete annihilation of life as they knew it.

They were playing God, pushing the boundaries of their knowledge and technological capabilities, attempting to rewrite the script of planetary evolution.

Dr. Grant's latest reports were even more alarming. The cascading effects of the environmental collapse were accelerating, exceeding even her worst predictions. The delicate balance of the planet's ecosystems was completely unraveling, triggering a chain reaction of catastrophic events.

The urgency of their mission couldn't be overstated; it was a desperate gamble, with the very future of humanity hanging in the balance.

The team pressed on, driven by a mixture of desperation, hope, and the unshakable belief that they could overcome this seemingly insurmountable challenge. Their work wasn't merely a technical task; it was a testament to the indomitable spirit of humanity—a symbol of our unwavering determination to survive and to heal a wounded world.

The planet was on its knees, but it still held on to a spark of life— a desperate glimmer of hope that echoed in the faint whispers of its dying ecosystems.

And the team, bruised, weary, but resolute, was determined to keep that spark alive.

The race against time was far from over.

Trust and Betrayal

The rhythmic pulse of the Argo's engines—a constant companion throughout their perilous journey—now felt like a strained heartbeat, mirroring the planet's own failing rhythm. The shared anxieties, previously masked by the urgency of their task, began to surface, creating subtle fissures within the team's fragile unity. The weight of their responsibility, the enormity of their undertaking, was beginning to fray the bonds of trust that had held them together.

It started subtly: a raised eyebrow, a hesitant pause, a word left unsaid. Jonah, usually the epitome of calm focus, found himself increasingly irritable, his sharp intellect now clouded by exhaustion and a gnawing suspicion. He noticed small inconsistencies in Dr. Grant's data—discrepancies that didn't quite add up. He couldn't articulate why, but something felt off, a subtle discord in the otherwise harmonious symphony of their collaborative efforts. Was it the pressure? Or was there something more?

His unease was amplified by Eliza's increasingly erratic behavior. While outwardly maintaining her professional demeanor, he noticed a tremor in her hands, a fleeting distraction in her usually unwavering focus. Her explanations for the anomalies in the data, while plausible, felt slightly... evasive. The once-open channel of communication between them—the easy flow of information and shared concerns—now felt clogged, choked by an unspoken tension.

The whispers of distrust weren't limited to Jonah and Eliza. Nyla, ever perceptive, sensed the shifting dynamics. Her usual calm wisdom seemed tinged with a cautious reserve. She observed their interactions with a shrewd Luminese gaze, her silence more eloquent than any spoken words. The ancient wisdom she embodied seemed to be sensing a subtle shift in the collective energy of the team, a subtle discord threatening to unravel their delicate alliance.

The source of the growing tension remained elusive—a shadowy presence lurking beneath the surface of their shared mission. Was it the sheer pressure of their undertaking, the weight of the world resting on their shoulders? Or was there a more insidious force at play—a hidden betrayal that threatened to undermine their efforts and shatter their precarious unity?

One evening, as the team huddled around the central console, poring over the latest data, the simmering tensions finally boiled over. It began with a heated exchange between Jonah and Eliza. Jonah, unable to contain his suspicions any longer, confronted Eliza about the anomalies in her data. His accusations, born of exhaustion and mounting pressure, were blunt and direct, leaving no room for misinterpretation.

Eliza, initially defensive, eventually broke down, confessing to minor alterations in her data—a subtle manipulation intended to maintain hope in the face of overwhelming despair. She argued it was a necessary deception, a calculated risk to prevent the team from succumbing to hopelessness. Her actions, she claimed, were born not of malice but of a desperate attempt to keep their fragile hope alive.

Her rationale, however, failed to fully assuage Jonah's growing unease. The seeds of doubt had already been sown, and they were rapidly taking root.

Nyla, witnessing the escalating conflict, intervened—her voice calm but firm. She spoke not of blame or judgment, but of the inherent fragility of trust, the delicate balance between hope and despair. She reminded them of the shared risks, the shared goals, the shared burden of responsibility they carried. Her words, infused with the ancient wisdom of her Luminese heritage, acted as a balm to the raw wounds of their conflict, mending the fractured bonds of their alliance—if only temporarily.

But the incident served as a stark reminder of the precariousness of their situation. The environmental crisis was not their only adversary; internal conflicts, misunderstandings, and the everpresent shadow of betrayal loomed large, threatening to derail their efforts just as surely as Mallory's sabotage. The pressure was immense, testing the resilience not only of the planet but also of the human spirit and the bonds of their alliance.

Each member was carrying a heavy burden—not only the scientific and technological challenges, but also the weight of hope, the crushing responsibility of carrying the fate of the planet on their shoulders.

The incident with Eliza and Jonah highlighted the fine line between necessary deception and outright betrayal. It was a question of ethics, of intent, and of the unpredictable consequences of actions taken under immense pressure. The team realized that their success hinged not just on their technological prowess and scientific understanding, but also on the ability to maintain trust—to navigate the complex currents of human emotions and interpersonal dynamics in the face of overwhelming adversity.

As the days turned into weeks, the line between reality and paranoia became increasingly blurred. Every missed signal, every minor discrepancy in the data, fueled their growing suspicions. The constant threat of Mallory's sabotage, coupled with the increasingly erratic behavior of the Whispers, created a perfect storm of uncertainty and mistrust. The team's once-harmonious collaboration was now fragmented, riddled with unspoken anxieties and underlying tensions.

The threat of betrayal, however, was not solely from within. The growing instability of the bioluminescent network—the planet's own communication system—made them vulnerable to manipulation and deception from external forces. Mallory's actions were a constant reminder of this vulnerability, his attempts to exploit the fragile trust within the team serving as a catalyst for their own internal strife.

The challenge, therefore, was not merely to decode the Whispers' code but also to decode the complexities of their own relationships—to navigate the treacherous terrain of trust and suspicion, to heal the wounds of their internal conflicts, and reaffirm their commitment to the shared goal.

The race against time, they realized, was not just a battle against environmental collapse and Mallory's ambitions, but also a battle against the corrosive effects of mistrust—a struggle to maintain the fragile unity of their alliance in the face of mounting pressure, suspicion, and the ever-present threat of betrayal.

The burden of their shared responsibility became heavier, more personal. The fate of the planet was no longer merely a scientific challenge; it was a test of their resilience, their unity, their ability to withstand the pressure and maintain the trust essential for their survival.

The race against time was, in many ways, a race against the erosion of hope—a battle to preserve not only the planet but also the delicate fabric of their own alliance. The fragility of their bonds mirrored the fragility of the planet itself, a testament to the interconnectedness of life and the crucial role of trust in the face of impending doom.

The weight of that interconnectedness pressed heavily upon each member of the team, forcing them to confront not only the external threats but also the internal demons that threatened to derail their crucial mission. The path ahead was fraught with uncertainty—a delicate dance between hope and despair, trust and betrayal—where the very survival of humanity hung in the balance.

Mallorys Advance

The rhythmic pulse of the Argo's engines, once a comforting rhythm, now felt like a frantic drumbeat against the backdrop of mounting anxieties. Mallory's shadow loomed larger than ever, a malevolent presence that seemed to seep into every crevice of their mission. His recent actions had escalated, moving beyond subtle sabotage and into overt acts of aggression. The bioluminescent network, the very lifeblood of their communication system and a crucial component of the Convergence Protocol, was experiencing unprecedented instability.

Jonah, his eyes bloodshot from sleep deprivation and relentless pressure, traced the erratic patterns on the central console. The network's shimmering, once a vibrant tapestry of light, was now fractured, punctuated by dark, ominous voids. He could feel the chill of Mallory's influence even through the layers of protective shielding, like a phantom touch reaching through the digital ether.

"He's disrupting the Whispers' communication," Jonah announced, his voice hoarse. "He's jamming the signal, creating interference that's scrambling the data."

Eliza, her face etched with worry, leaned closer to the console.

"The interference is localized, concentrated around the key nodes... the ones crucial to activating the Protocol." Her usual precision in speech was replaced by an edge of panic, the carefully constructed facade of composure threatening to crumble.

Nyla, her usually serene Luminese countenance grim, spoke in her low, resonant voice, her words translating seamlessly through the Argo's translation system. "This is not mere sabotage; this is a calculated attempt to disable the Protocol, a strategic maneuver to seize control." Her ancient eyes, usually shimmering with wisdom, held a flicker of something close to fear.

The implications of Mallory's actions sent a ripple of dread through the team. If he succeeded in disrupting the Whispers' network, the Convergence Protocol would be rendered useless. Their race against time would become a futile sprint toward inevitable collapse. The weight of that realization settled heavily on their shoulders, intensifying the already oppressive atmosphere.

The ensuing hours were a blur of frantic activity. Jonah, fueled by adrenaline and grim determination, dove deeper into the network, attempting to identify Mallory's point of intrusion and counter his efforts. His fingers flew across the keyboard, lines of code cascading across the screen in a desperate attempt to regain control. Eliza, supporting him, sifted through the corrupted data, searching for clues, for any fragments of the original Whispers' code that had survived Mallory's attacks.

Dr. Grant's efforts, however, were hampered by the escalating instability of the network. The whispers of the damaged communication lines were growing louder, more chaotic, more unpredictable. It was as if the planet itself was reacting to Mallory's interference, its natural systems recoiling from the intrusion.

The team found themselves facing a double threat: not only Mallory's technological sabotage but also the unpredictable backlash from the increasingly erratic Whispers. The delicate ecosystem, already weakened by environmental collapse, was further destabilized by the relentless assault. The lines between communication, interference, and the very essence of the Whispers themselves were blurring, making it near impossible to distinguish between friend and foe.

Days bled into nights as they battled against Mallory's relentless attacks and the increasingly chaotic behavior of the Whispers. The team worked tirelessly, their bodies exhausted, their minds stretched to their limits. The tension was palpable, a suffocating blanket woven from fear, frustration, and the ever-present threat of failure. The pressure was immense, testing not only their technical skills but also their resilience, resolve, and capacity for hope in the face of overwhelming odds.

Meanwhile, Mallory, seemingly omnipresent, continued his relentless assault. His tactics were increasingly sophisticated, his actions displaying a frightening level of understanding of the bioluminescent network. His attacks were not random; they were precise, surgical strikes designed to disable the critical nodes one by one—a meticulous dismantling of the Whispers' intricate communication system.

It was clear that Mallory possessed an intimate knowledge of the Convergence Protocol, knowledge that exceeded even their own.

He was not simply trying to disrupt the system; he was trying to control it, to bend its power to his own will. His actions suggested a sinister ambition, an ambition that extended far beyond mere sabotage.

The growing complexity of Mallory's actions forced the team to reevaluate their strategies. They realized that a purely technological approach was insufficient. They needed to understand the underlying motivations, the driving force behind Mallory's relentless pursuit of the Convergence Protocol. His actions were a manifestation of a much larger threat, a threat to their ability to stabilize the oceanic resonance.

Jonah, through meticulous analysis of Mallory's attack patterns, detected a subtle shift in his tactics. It wasn't just about disabling the network; Mallory was actively trying to rewrite the Whispers' code, to insert his own commands into their intricate language. The team realized he was not simply aiming to stop the Convergence Protocol; he aimed to hijack it, to steer it toward an entirely different path—a path of his own making. His manipulation of the Whispers was an attempt to seize control of the planet's own regeneration process, to shape its future according to his twisted vision.

The realization sent a fresh wave of panic through the team. The stakes were higher than they had ever imagined. They were not merely fighting for the survival of humanity; they were fighting for the very soul of the planet, the very essence of the Whispers themselves. The fight became even more desperate, the struggle even more profound. Time was running out, and the consequences of failure were catastrophic.

The battle raged on, a desperate struggle against a force that seemed to be everywhere and nowhere at once. Mallory's influence, intangible yet palpable, permeated the very air they breathed—a constant reminder of their desperate situation. The team fought on, fueled by adrenaline and a desperate hope, their alliance tested to its limits. Their struggle was a desperate dance between scientific expertise and sheer willpower, a race against time, against growing chaos, against the relentless assault of Dr. Rafe Mallory's ambition—all against the looming shadow of planetary annihilation.

The outcome remained uncertain, a question hanging heavy in the air, a question that would determine not only the fate of humanity but also the destiny of the planet itself.

CHAPTER FOUR

A SYMBIOTIC REVOLUTION

The rhythmic pulsing of the Argo's engines had become a frantic heartbeat, a counterpoint to the increasingly erratic whispers emanating from the bioluminescent network. Jonah, his eyes burning with fatigue, leaned closer to the console, the faint glow of the holographic display reflecting in his dilated pupils. He had spent the last few days immersed in the chaotic data stream, a digital ocean teeming with corrupted code and fragmented messages.

But amidst the noise—amidst the digital storm whipped up by Mallory's relentless attacks—he had begun to discern a pattern, a rhythm beneath the chaos.

It wasn't just noise; it was language. A language far older than human speech, a language woven from the very fabric of the planet itself. It was the language of the Whispers.

He had started by focusing on the less damaged sections of the network—the quieter corners where Mallory's interference was less pronounced. There, within the intricate tapestry of light and shadow, he found fragments of a narrative, a history whispered across millennia. He began to decipher words, not in the human sense of alphabetic characters, but in patterns, in rhythms, in the shifting intensities of the bioluminescence itself.

Each fluctuation, each subtle change in hue, represented a syllable, a word, a concept. It was a language of feeling, of interconnectedness, of the planet's very heartbeat.

The story that began to unfold was breathtaking in its scope and antiquity. Long before humanity's rise—long before the age of technology—the Whispers had existed. They were not merely a network; they were a consciousness, a planetary intelligence woven into the very fabric of the Earth's ecosystems. Their language was not spoken or written; it was lived, experienced, felt.

It was the language of the tides, the rustle of leaves, the song of birds, the symphony of a thousand interwoven life forms.

The Whispers had witnessed the rise and fall of countless species, the slow, inexorable march of geological time. They had seen continents shift, mountains rise and fall, ice ages come and go. Their memory was the Earth's memory, their history a chronicle of planetary evolution. They remembered a time when the oceans were pristine, when the air was clean, when the balance of life was undisturbed.

They had experienced the slow, agonizing decline—the creeping encroachment of human civilization, the scars left by industrialization, the wounds inflicted by unchecked consumption.

Through the Whispers' fragmented narrative, Jonah learned of their attempts to communicate with humanity—their warnings whispered on the wind, etched into the patterns of migrating birds, encoded in the subtle rhythms of the tides. But humanity, blinded by its own ambition, had failed to hear, failed to understand. The Whispers' pleas had been lost in the cacophony of progress, drowned out by the relentless drumbeat of industrial growth.

He discovered the origins of the bioluminescent network—a vast, interconnected web that spanned the globe, a living, breathing extension of the Whispers themselves. It was a system designed not only for communication but also for planetary regulation, a delicate mechanism for maintaining the Earth's fragile equilibrium.

It was a system that was now failing, its integrity compromised by the relentless assault of Mallory's attacks.

The Whispers' narrative revealed the true purpose of the Convergence Protocol—a desperate last attempt to restore the planet's balance, to heal the wounds inflicted by humanity. It was a program encoded within the very structure of the bioluminescent network, a blueprint for planetary regeneration. But it was not a simple reset button; it was a complex, multi-faceted plan that required careful calibration and delicate adjustments.

It was a program that held the potential for both salvation and annihilation—a potential now hanging precariously in the balance.

As Jonah delved deeper into the Whispers' history, he discovered a forgotten connection between the ancient civilization of the Whispers and the Luminese—a link that had been severed long ago, lost in the mists of time. The Luminese, with their advanced technology and deep understanding of symbiotic relationships, were not simply advanced aliens; they were descendants, inheritors of an ancient knowledge passed down through generations.

Their wisdom, their insights, were not merely technological—they were deeply interwoven with the Whispers' ancient knowledge, a testament to an alliance that had once thrived.

The Echoborn—the humans merging with the Whispers—were not merely a strange anomaly; they were a bridge, a testament to the potential for symbiotic evolution, a living embodiment of the partnership between humans and the planet itself. They were not a threat but a possibility, a future where humans and nature could coexist not as adversaries, but as partners.

Through the Echoborn, the Whispers were offering a pathway toward a new equilibrium—a chance for humanity to reconcile with the planet it had so carelessly abused.

But Mallory's actions were a direct attack not just on the bioluminescent network, but on the Whispers themselves—on the planet's very memory. He was attempting to rewrite their history, to erase their warnings, to usurp their ancient wisdom for his own twisted ends.

His actions were a brutal assault—an act of cultural genocide against the planet's very soul. He was not merely seeking to control the Convergence Protocol; he was aiming to extinguish the planet's memory, to obliterate its wisdom, to ensure the planet's irreversible collapse.

Jonah realized with chilling clarity that Mallory's actions were not driven by mere ambition or greed. They were rooted in deepseated denial—a refusal to acknowledge humanity's destructive impact, a willful ignorance of the planet's suffering.

He was not just a villain; he was a symptom—a manifestation of humanity's most destructive tendencies: the willful blindness to environmental devastation and the relentless pursuit of dominance over nature.

As Jonah unraveled the Whispers' language, he understood the true stakes of their mission. It was not just about saving humanity; it was about saving the planet—about restoring the ancient harmony that had once existed between humanity and nature. It was about learning to listen to the whispers of the Earth, to understand the language of the planet itself, to acknowledge our interdependence and our responsibility to the living world.

The future of humanity, he realized, was inextricably linked to the fate of the Whispers—to the fate of the planet itself. The struggle was not merely a battle for survival; it was a struggle for redemption. A struggle for understanding. A struggle for the soul of the planet.

The implications of his discoveries were immense. The Convergence Protocol was not merely a technological solution; it was a spiritual one—a pathway toward a new relationship between humanity and the planet.

It was an opportunity for symbiotic evolution, a chance to heal the wounds of the past and to create a future where humanity and nature could flourish together—not as masters and servants, but as equals.

The weight of this revelation pressed heavily upon Jonah. He realized the urgency of their mission had increased exponentially. They were not merely fighting against Mallory—they were fighting for the very essence of life itself, for the future of a harmonious planet. The fate of humanity, the fate of the planet, hung in the balance.

The whispers of the Earth were growing louder, urging them forward, beckoning them toward a future where humanity could finally find its place within the larger ecosystem—a place of partnership, not dominance. And he knew, with a certainty that pierced through his exhaustion, that he must keep listening. He must keep deciphering. He must keep fighting.

The Echoborn's Wisdom

The rhythmic pulse of the Argo's engines, a constant thrum beneath the deck, seemed to mirror the erratic heartbeat of the bioluminescent network. Sarah, leaning against the cool metal bulkhead, watched Jonah hunched over the console, the holographic projections painting his face in shifting greens and blues. He hadn't slept properly in days, fueled by caffeine and the sheer urgency of his task. His breakthroughs, though monumental, were fragile— easily disrupted by the digital storms Mallory continued to unleash.

Suddenly, Jonah straightened, his eyes wide, a flicker of something akin to awe crossing his usually pragmatic features. He turned, his voice low, almost reverent. "I think... I think I've found something."

He gestured to the console, where the chaotic patterns of the Whispers' language had begun to resolve into something more structured—more deliberate. It wasn't just fragments of history anymore; it was a focused message, a beacon cutting through the noise of Mallory's attacks.

It was a message from the Echoborn.

The Echoborn. The very mention of their name sent a shiver down Sarah's spine. They were the outliers, the anomaly—humans who had somehow merged with the Whispers, their bodies interwoven with the bioluminescent network, their minds echoing with the planet's ancient wisdom. They were a living paradox, a testament to the possibility of symbiotic evolution, yet also a source of unease and fear for many. Some whispered of them as harbingers of doom, others as saviors. Their very existence challenged the fundamental human concept of self, of identity, of what it meant to be human.

Jonah, guided by the Echoborn's message, began to delve deeper into the Convergence Protocol. The initial data had painted a picture of planetary regeneration—a resetting of the Earth's systems.

But the Echoborn's contribution revealed a far more nuanced, complex process: a transformation that extended far beyond the physical realm. Their perspective—unique and deeply insightful—shed light on a previously hidden aspect of the Protocol: its potential for human transformation.

The Protocol, they revealed, wasn't simply about restoring the planet's physical health. It was about restoring a balance, a harmony that had been lost long ago—a harmony that extended to humanity itself. The Echoborn described a potential future where humans, instead of existing as separate entities, could integrate with the planet's systems, becoming active participants in the Earth's intricate ecosystem. They spoke of a metamorphosis, not an annihilation.

This symbiotic evolution, as they described it, wasn't a forced merger, but a gradual process of integration—a slow dance of adaptation and assimilation. It was about relearning how to listen to the planet, to understand its rhythms, its needs, its silent pleas. It was about embracing interdependence, about shedding the anthropocentric worldview that had led to so much destruction.

The Echoborn's message echoed the ancient wisdom of the Whispers, revealing a history of symbiotic relationships between different species—a complex web of interdependencies that had thrived for eons before humanity's intervention. They painted a picture of a world where cooperation, not competition, was the driving force behind evolution. They described a time when humanity had been a part of this harmonious web—a time when they understood their place within the larger ecosystem, a time before the insatiable hunger for dominance had taken root.

Dr. Grant, ever the cautious scientist, voiced her concerns. The implications of such radical transformation were profound. The very definition of humanity would be challenged, the boundaries between human and nature blurred beyond recognition. The ethical dilemmas were immense, the uncertainties overwhelming.

Was this truly a choice—or a forced evolution, a surrender of humanity's identity? Could humans truly adapt to such a fundamental shift in their being? Would they retain their consciousness, their individuality, their sense of self? These were not easily answered questions.

Nyla, the Luminese ambassador, offered a different perspective.

She spoke of the Luminese's own history, their own long-standing symbiotic relationship with their home planet. Their technology, far from being a tool of domination, was an extension of their being— a reflection of their deep interconnectedness with their environment. They had learned to listen to their world, to work in harmony with its rhythms, to understand the delicate balance of their ecosystem.

Their advanced technology, she explained, wasn't merely a collection of machines; it was a living extension of their symbiotic relationship with their planet—a testament to their understanding of a different kind of evolution.

The Echoborn's message described a similar path for humanity. It spoke of a future where technology would no longer be a tool of exploitation, but an instrument of cooperation and understanding. It was a vision of harmony, not dominance—a future where technology served as a bridge between humanity and the natural world, enhancing our ability to perceive, to interact, to cooperate with the planet's life systems. But the transformation wouldn't be easy.

The Echoborn's message revealed that the Protocol wasn't a simple on/off switch. It was a gradual process—a delicate dance between technology and nature, requiring careful calibration and adaptation. It demanded a willingness to change, a willingness to surrender old patterns of thinking and behavior, a willingness to embrace uncertainty and the unknown. It would require a fundamental shift in human consciousness, a reevaluation of our place within the larger ecosystem.

The Echoborn also warned of the dangers of rushing the process—the potential for unintended consequences. The transformation, they said, was not a sprint but a marathon, requiring patience, understanding, and a deep respect for the planet's inherent wisdom.

The Protocol was not a solution to be imposed, but a path to be walked—a journey of mutual transformation.

The weight of this new knowledge settled upon the team, a profound burden that outweighed the fear of Mallory's machinations. The struggle against Mallory was no longer simply a battle for survival; it was a struggle for the very soul of humanity— a fight for the future of harmonious coexistence.

It was a choice between oblivion and profound transformation— a leap of faith into an uncertain future. A future where humanity could become a true partner with the planet, not its master.

The rhythmic pulsing of the Argo's engines continued, a steady beat against the backdrop of the whispering bioluminescence. The fate of humanity—and the planet—hung in the balance, held precariously between the ancient wisdom of the Whispers, the technological prowess of the Luminese, and the uncertain future of the Echoborn.

The choice, Sarah knew, would not be easy. It would require courage, compassion, and a willingness to embrace the unknown. It would demand a fundamental shift in the way humanity viewed its place in the world—a relinquishing of dominance in favor of partnership, a recognition of our deep interconnectedness with the planet's systems. The future, it seemed, was not simply about survival, but about becoming worthy of survival. It was about becoming something more.

The whispers of the earth grew louder, urging them on, their ancient wisdom weaving itself into the very fabric of the mission.

The Convergence Protocol was no longer just a plan; it was a promise—a promise of rebirth, a promise of a symbiotic future, a testament to the potential for hope, even in the face of seemingly insurmountable odds. The journey was far from over, but they had found a beacon in the darkness, a guiding light through the chaos, a path toward a future that was both breathtaking and terrifying. A future that would demand everything they had, and yet hold the potential for something truly extraordinary.

The future, they knew, depended on their ability to listen, to learn, to adapt, to evolve—to truly become part of the symphony of life on Earth.

Reconciliation with Nature Eliza Grant, her face etched with a mixture of apprehension and awe, traced a finger across the holographic projection of the Convergence Protocol. The swirling patterns, once indecipherable chaos, now revealed a delicate tapestry of interconnectedness—a visual representation of the symbiotic relationship between humanity and the Whispers.

"This isn't just about fixing the planet," she murmured, her voice barely audible above the hum of the Argo's engines. "It's about fixing ourselves."

Jonah, still reeling from the Echoborn's message, nodded slowly. The sheer scale of the transformation proposed by the Protocol was staggering. It wasn't simply a matter of repairing damaged ecosystems; it was a fundamental shift in the human relationship with the planet—a reevaluation of our place within the intricate web of life. The Protocol, he realized, was not just a technological solution, but a philosophical one. It was a call for reconciliation. "For centuries," Dr. Grant continued, her gaze sweeping across the assembled team, "we've operated under the delusion of separateness. We've seen ourselves as distinct from nature, as masters of our environment, capable of controlling and

manipulating it to our will. The result has been catastrophic." She paused, allowing the weight of her words to settle.

"The Whispers, the Echoborn... they are showing us a different way. A way of being, a way of living, that acknowledges our profound interconnectedness with all living things."

Nyla, the Luminese Ambassador, leaned forward, her multifaceted eyes gleaming with ancient wisdom.

"Your world has forgotten the song of the Earth," she said, her voice resonating with a deep, steady tone. "It has forgotten the language of the wind, the whispers of the trees, the heartbeat of the ocean. The Convergence Protocol is not just a technological solution; it is a reawakening—a rediscovery of that forgotten language."

She described the Luminese's relationship with their own planet—a symbiotic partnership that had flourished for millennia. Their technology, far from being a tool of domination, was a harmonious extension of their being—a reflection of their deep understanding of their planet's rhythms and needs. They hadn't conquered their world; they had learned to listen to it, to integrate with it, to become an integral part of its intricate ecosystem.

"Your scientists speak of biodiversity," Nyla continued. "But they often fail to grasp its true meaning. It's not just about the number of species, but the intricate web of relationships that binds them together. It's about the dance of life—the delicate balance between predator and prey, the intricate cycles of energy and matter. To truly understand biodiversity is to understand the song of the Earth, to hear the symphony of life."

The conversation turned to the specific mechanisms of the Convergence Protocol. Jonah explained how it would work—not by forcibly altering the planet's systems, but by gently nudging them back toward equilibrium. It would harness the power of the bioluminescent network, utilizing the Whispers' intricate communication system to rebalance the disrupted ecosystems. The Protocol would not dictate, but facilitate, a natural healing process.

Dr. Grant elaborated on the biological aspects of the Protocol, explaining how it would promote the regeneration of depleted ecosystems, restore biodiversity, and bolster the planet's resilience. It wouldn't create a pristine, untouched wilderness; rather, it would foster a dynamic, evolving ecosystem capable of adapting to the challenges of a changing climate.

She spoke of the importance of understanding the interconnectedness of all life—the delicate balance between species, the complex web of relationships that held the ecosystem together.

But the discussion extended beyond the purely ecological. The Echoborn's message had highlighted the potential for a symbiotic evolution of humanity itself. This wasn't simply about humans adapting to a changing environment; it was about becoming an integral part of the ecosystem—a conscious participant in the planet's intricate processes.

The idea was unsettling, even to Sarah. The concept of merging with nature, of losing a distinct human identity, was deeply challenging. Yet the alternative—extinction—was equally terrifying. She understood the risk, the profound uncertainty, but she also sensed a glimmer of possibility—a potential for a future where humans and nature coexisted in harmony.

"We've always viewed ourselves as separate from nature," Sarah mused, her voice quiet. "As superior, as masters of our own destiny. But what if we're wrong? What if our very survival depends on embracing our interconnectedness—on becoming part of something larger than ourselves?"

The conversation grew heated. Some on the team—particularly those more closely associated with the human military efforts—

struggled with the implications of the Echoborn's message. They were wary of losing control, of relinquishing their autonomy. They found the idea of a symbiotic evolution frightening, a blurring of lines between human and nature that they could not accept.

Dr. Grant understood their concerns but remained steadfast.

"The choice isn't between humanity and nature," she insisted. "It's between a future of harmonious co-existence and a future of annihilation. We can continue down the path of dominance, of exploitation—or we can choose a different path. A path of collaboration, of mutual respect, of symbiotic evolution. It's a difficult choice, I admit, but it's a choice we must make."

Nyla added her perspective, emphasizing the Luminese's success in their own symbiotic relationship with their planet. She detailed examples of their technology integrating seamlessly with their natural world, enhancing their perception and understanding of the planet's intricate systems. Their advanced technologies were not instruments of control, but extensions of their symbiotic relationship, allowing them to work in harmony with their environment.

The team discussed the ethical implications at length. The potential for unforeseen consequences weighed heavily on their minds.

How could they ensure the Protocol wouldn't inadvertently harm other species?

How could they safeguard human individuality while embracing a deeper integration with the planet's systems?

The answers were far from clear.

The discussion continued late into the night, fueled by caffeine and a deep sense of urgency. The fate of humanity—and the planet—rested on their shoulders, a monumental weight that pressed upon them with every passing hour.

They debated the finer points of the Protocol, refining their strategies, preparing themselves for the daunting task that lay ahead. The path to reconciliation with nature was fraught with peril, but it was a path they were willing to walk.

The whispers of the Earth were growing louder, urging them on, reminding them of the harmony that was possible. They understood now, with a clarity that transcended fear, that their survival depended not on conquering nature, but on reconciling with it— becoming a true partner in the great symphony of life on Earth.

The future was uncertain. But for the first time, a fragile hope blossomed—nurtured by the whispers of a planet ready to heal, and a humanity willing to change.

Luminese Perspective

Nyla's multifaceted eyes, usually shimmering with a calm wisdom, held a flicker of something else now—a hint of melancholy, perhaps, or a deep-seated weariness born of centuries of accumulated knowledge.

She leaned forward, her slender fingers tracing patterns on the polished surface of the table—patterns that mirrored the swirling chaos and intricate beauty of the Convergence Protocol displayed on the holographic projector.

"Your history," she began, her voice low and resonant, "is a tale of forgetting. You have forgotten the language of the Earth—the intricate song woven into the very fabric of existence. You have forgotten the symbiotic dance that once sustained life on this planet. The delicate balance between giver and receiver, predator and prey—the intricate harmony of the biosphere."

She spoke of a time long before the Great Collapse, a time when the Luminese had been in direct communion with their world—a time when their technology was an extension of their understanding, not a tool for domination.

"Our ancestors," she explained, "didn't *conquer* Xylos; they integrated with it. They learned to listen to the planet's whispers, to understand its needs, to become an integral part of its lifeblood."

Nyla described their ancient methods of cultivating Xylos's rich biodiversity. They didn't simply harvest resources; they nurtured them. Their agricultural techniques were designed to enhance the ecosystem, not deplete it.

They developed symbiotic relationships with various plant and animal species, co-evolving in a complex dance of mutual benefit. Their cities were not isolated concrete jungles but living, breathing entities—integrated seamlessly with the natural landscape, powered by renewable energy sources harnessed from the planet itself.

Their architecture mimicked the organic forms of nature, blending seamlessly with the surrounding environment.

"We learned from Xylos," she continued, her voice taking on a reverent tone. "We learned to listen, to observe, to understand the intricate interconnectedness of all life. Our technology wasn't about control—it was about enhancement, about deepening our connection with the planet. It was a reflection of our respect, our understanding, our profound love for Xylos."

She described the Luminese's advanced understanding of ecological dynamics. They developed sophisticated models capable of predicting the consequences of their actions on the environment.

They understood the importance of biodiversity not merely as a measure of species richness but as a reflection of the complex web of interdependencies that maintained the planet's health. Their understanding was not theoretical—it was deeply ingrained in their culture, in their very being.

Nyla then detailed the Luminese's history of near-catastrophic environmental damage.

"Even we," she admitted, a shadow crossing her luminous features, "have made mistakes. There was a time, many centuries ago, when we too lost our way. We forgot the lessons of our ancestors—pursuing technological advancement without considering the consequences. We faced our own crisis, a period of ecological devastation that nearly brought our civilization to its knees."

But their recovery, Nyla emphasized, was not a triumph of technological prowess alone. It was a testament to their ability to learn from their errors—to re-establish a harmonious relationship with their world.

Their recovery, she explained, involved a fundamental shift in their societal values—a profound re-evaluation of their relationship with Xylos.

They abandoned their exploitative practices, embraced sustainable technologies, and fostered a deeper understanding of ecological principles.

"The Convergence Protocol," Nyla stated, her voice regaining its strength, "is not just a technological fix. It is a mirror reflecting your own potential for transformation. It offers you the chance to learn from our mistakes, to avoid the pitfalls we faced, to forge a new path towards symbiotic evolution. It's a pathway back to the song of the earth, a pathway to healing, a pathway to a future where humanity and nature coexist in a state of harmonious balance."

She paused, allowing her words to sink in. Then, she spoke of the hidden aspects of the Protocol—details not previously revealed.

It wasn't merely a technological solution; it incorporated ancient Luminese principles of ecological restoration, principles developed over millennia of harmonious coexistence with their planet. It was designed not to dominate, but to facilitate—to gently nudge the planet back toward a state of balance, leveraging the Whispers' intricate bioluminescent network to heal the wounded Earth.

Nyla's explanation delved into the intricacies of the bioluminescent network, describing its role in facilitating communication between the Whispers and the planet's other life forms. She explained how the Protocol would harness this network to stimulate regeneration, reestablish disrupted ecological cycles, rebuild biodiversity, and enhance the planet's resilience.

The Luminese perspective, she emphasized, was not one of human dominance, but of integration. It involved embracing uncertainty, accepting the risks, and surrendering to the unpredictable rhythms of nature. It was about understanding that humanity was not separate from nature, but a part of it—an integral component of a complex and interconnected web of life.

"The Echoborn," she stated, her gaze piercing, "represent not a threat, but a possibility. They are not a degradation of humanity, but an evolution—an expansion of consciousness, a deeper connection with the planet. They are a glimpse into what is possible, a testament to the power of symbiotic evolution."

She stressed that the Luminese had their own equivalent of the Echoborn—individuals who had formed deep, symbiotic relationships with their planet's sentient ecosystems. These individuals were not seen as anomalies or threats, but as spiritual leaders—guides who possessed an intuitive understanding of the planet's needs.

Nyla's words echoed through the room, stirring a deep sense of awe and wonder in the assembled team. Her perspective challenged their assumptions, forcing them to confront their anthropocentric biases, to reconsider their place within the grand scheme of life on Earth.

The Luminese path, she implied, was not easy. It demanded humility, patience, and a willingness to relinquish control. It required a surrender to the unknown, a trust in the wisdom of the Earth, and a faith in the power of symbiotic evolution. But it was, she insisted, the only path toward a sustainable future.

The fate of humanity, she suggested, lay not in dominating nature, but in becoming a harmonious part of it. The choice, she concluded, was not between humanity and nature, but between a future of harmonious coexistence and a future of annihilation.

Confronting Mallory

The air crackled with a tension so thick it was almost tangible. The abandoned hydroelectric dam, its skeletal remains clawing at the bruised twilight sky, served as a brutal backdrop to the confrontation. Mallory, flanked by his heavily armed mercenaries, stood silhouetted against the setting sun, his face a mask of grim determination. He looked less like a scientist and more like a warlord—his tailored suit rumpled, his usually immaculate hair disheveled, betraying the desperation in his eyes.

Sarah, Jonah, and Eliza stood their ground—a small island of defiance against the encroaching tide of Mallory's forces. Nyla, her luminescent skin glowing faintly in the gloom, remained a silent but powerful presence behind them. The Echoborn, their eyes glowing with an unearthly luminescence, formed a protective circle around the core team, their whispers blending with the wind's mournful sigh.

"You've made a grave mistake, Chen," Mallory's voice boomed, amplified by a portable speaker. "The Convergence Protocol is not for the likes of you. It's too powerful, too dangerous. It belongs in the hands of someone who understands its true potential—someone like me."

"And what is that potential, Mallory?" Sarah's voice was level, devoid of emotion, but her eyes held a steely glint. "To erase humanity and remake the planet in your own twisted image?"

Mallory chuckled—a harsh, grating sound. "Remake? No, Chen. I intend to control it. To guide its evolution. To shape a future where humanity reigns supreme—not as a parasite clinging to a dying planet, but as its rightful master."

His words stung. It was the arrogance of unchecked ambition, the belief in the inherent superiority of humanity over all other life forms. It was a perspective Sarah had fought against for years—a mindset that had nearly destroyed the planet.

The first shot rang out, shattering the fragile peace. The mercenaries opened fire, a hail of bullets tearing through the air, striking the crumbling concrete of the dam. The Echoborn reacted instantly—their whispers intensifying, their luminescence flaring—creating a shimmering, almost tangible shield of energy that deflected much of the incoming fire. But the mercenaries were relentless, their weapons spitting death.

Jonah, ever the pragmatist, scrambled for cover, his fingers flying across his datapad, attempting to disrupt Mallory's communications network. Eliza, her face grim, tended to a wounded Echoborn—her expertise in marine biology somehow translating into a surprisingly effective form of battlefield medicine. The symbiotic link between the Echoborn and the Whispers, it turned out, provided a surprising resilience to injuries.

Sarah, however, found herself in the thick of it—her combat skills, honed through years of survival, now deployed with deadly efficiency. She moved with a grace born of necessity, dodging bullets, returning fire with a modified energy rifle salvaged from a long-forgotten Luminese outpost. Her movements were precise. Deadly. She fought not with hatred, but with a cold, calculating determination to protect what she had fought so hard to save.

The battle was fierce. Brutal. The air filled with the stench of cordite, the screams of the wounded, the crackle of energy weapons. The dam shook under the relentless barrage, its already unstable structure groaning under the strain. Despite the Echoborn's protective shield, casualties mounted. The relentless assault of Mallory's mercenaries pushed the team to the brink of exhaustion and despair.

But the team held on. They fought with the knowledge that failure meant the total collapse of their already fragile world. Their determination stemmed from a shared understanding of the urgency of the situation—the profound implications of letting Mallory seize the Convergence Protocol.

As the battle raged, Nyla remained a steadfast presence at the edge of the conflict, her interventions subtle, yet decisive. She seemed to anticipate Mallory's moves, her guidance almost ethereal, whispering instructions that wove through the chaos and subtly influenced the flow of the battle. Her wisdom, honed by centuries of observation and understanding, provided the team with an edge they would not have otherwise possessed.

The turning point came when Jonah, despite the chaos surrounding him, managed to disable Mallory's command and control system. The mercenaries, suddenly cut off from their leader's orders, faltered, their attack losing coordination. The team seized the opportunity, pushing back with renewed vigor.

The final confrontation was a brutal hand-to-hand clash between Sarah and Mallory. The two were evenly matched, their fighting styles reflecting their vastly different backgrounds—Mallory relying on brute strength and calculated aggression, while Sarah used agility and knowledge of pressure points, leveraging years of experience in close-quarters combat. The clash of their wills was as intense as the battle itself.

In the end, it wasn't strength, but strategy that won out. Sarah, using her knowledge of the dam's structural weaknesses, managed to lure Mallory into a strategically chosen spot—a precariously balanced section of the dam that yielded under their combined weight. The ground gave way, plunging both of them into the churning waters below.

Sarah managed to swim to safety, battered and bruised but alive. Mallory, however, disappeared beneath the swirling currents, swallowed by the river's relentless flow. His ambition, his hubris, his desire for control had finally met its match—not in the form of superior weaponry, but in the cunning and resilience of a woman determined to save her world.

The battle's aftermath was grim. The dam was severely damaged, a testament to the destructive power of conflict. Several of the Echoborn lay wounded, their luminescence flickering weakly. But they were alive—and that was all that mattered. The team, though battered, had survived. They had confronted Mallory and thwarted his attempt to seize the Convergence Protocol.

The struggle was far from over, but they had won a crucial battle in the war for Earth's future. The path ahead remained uncertain, fraught with peril. But they had secured a small victory—a spark of hope in the midst of looming darkness. The Whispers' song, faint but persistent, whispered of resilience and the possibility of symbiotic evolution: a future where humanity might—just might— find its place not as the planet's master, but as its partner.

CHAPTER FIVE

THE PROTOCOLS ACTIVATION

The air hung heavy with the unspoken. The victory over Mallory had been pyrrhic—a hard-won respite in a relentless war. The damaged dam, a skeletal monument to their struggle, loomed behind them, a stark reminder of the fragility of their situation. The injured Echoborn were being tended to, their ethereal luminescence flickering like dying embers. Even the whispers of the Whispers, usually a comforting presence, felt subdued, carrying a note of anxious anticipation.

The Convergence Protocol. The very name resonated with a profound sense of both hope and dread. It was their last, best chance to heal the ravaged planet, but the price might be too high.

The whispers of the ancient code, deciphered painstakingly by Jonah, spoke of a planetary reboot—a radical reshaping of the biosphere. It promised rebirth, a flourishing ecosystem, but it also hinted at a potential erasure of humanity, a complete rewriting of life on Earth.

Eliza, ever the pragmatist cloaked in a scientist's cautious optimism, ran a hand through her wind-tossed hair, her eyes fixed on the datapad displaying the Protocol's intricate code.

"The energy requirements are astronomical," she murmured, her voice barely audible above the wind's mournful sigh. "We need to harness the power of the oceanic resonance at its peak, and even then, there's no guarantee of success."

The oceanic resonance—a fluctuating energy field generated by the planet's interconnected ecosystems—was the key to activating the Protocol. It was a delicate balance, a complex interplay of biological and geophysical forces. Disrupt it, even slightly, and the entire operation could fail—or worse, trigger unforeseen catastrophic consequences.

Jonah, his face pale with fatigue, ran a hand over his stubbled chin.

"The timing is critical," he said, his voice strained. "The resonance will peak in precisely seventy-two hours. Any delay, any deviation, and we risk losing our chance forever. And the energy signatures... they are shifting unpredictably."

The unpredictable shifts in the oceanic resonance were a particular concern. The Whispers, in their cryptic way, had hinted at an evolutionary surge within their own collective consciousness—a dramatic shift somehow linked to the resonance. This unpredictable evolution made precise timing and energy calculations incredibly difficult.

Nyla, the Luminese ambassador, watched them with her characteristic calm. Her ancient eyes, pools of shimmering starlight, seemed to hold the weight of millennia.

"The Whispers are changing," she said, her voice resonant with ancient wisdom. "They are evolving beyond our understanding. Their song is becoming... different."

The "different" song of the Whispers was indeed unsettling. It was no longer the gentle, reassuring hum that had guided them, but a more complex, almost chaotic symphony of sounds that bordered on dissonance. It was a sign of their rapid evolution—a transformation that felt both awe-inspiring and terrifying.

Sarah, her face etched with lines of worry, stepped forward.

"We need to understand this change, Nyla. How does it affect the Protocol?" The fear in her voice was barely masked.

Nyla closed her eyes, her luminescent skin pulsating faintly.

"The Whispers are becoming... integrated," she whispered, her voice low and reverent. "They are weaving themselves into the very fabric of the planet. Their evolution is intertwined with the Protocol's activation. It's... symbiotic."

The implications of Nyla's words hung in the air, heavy with uncertainty. Symbiotic evolution—a complete merging of the Whispers, the sentient ecosystems, with the planet itself. It was a breathtaking concept, a breathtaking possibility. But what would it mean for humanity? Would they be welcomed into this new symbiotic relationship, or would they be swept away by the tide of this vast planetary transformation?

The team gathered around a large holographic projection of the planet. The vibrant blue of the oceans was marred by patches of lifelessness—stark reminders of the environmental devastation that had brought them to this point. Data streams flickered across the surface of the projection, showing the complex energy flows of the oceanic resonance, its erratic patterns reflecting the chaotic state of the planet's ecosystem.

The next seventy-two hours were a blur of frenetic activity.

Jonah, with Eliza's assistance, tirelessly refined their calculations, adjusting the parameters of the Protocol to account for the constantly shifting oceanic resonance and the evolving consciousness of the Whispers.

The Echoborn, despite their injuries, played a crucial role—their symbiotic link with the Whispers providing invaluable insights into the changes underway. Nyla's guidance, subtle yet profound, proved invaluable, her wisdom acting as a compass in the storm.

Sarah, however, found herself wrestling with the ethical implications of their actions. The Protocol, in its potential to erase humanity, forced her to confront the deepest questions of human existence—its place within the grand scheme of the planet. Was their survival worth the potential extinction of their species? Was their desperate clinging to existence justified, given the immense destructive power humanity had unleashed upon the planet?

The weight of the world rested on her shoulders, but she knew there was no turning back. They had come too far, sacrificed too much. They were on the precipice of a fundamental shift—one that would determine the fate of Earth, and perhaps humanity itself.

As the final hour approached, the tension in the makeshift control room was almost palpable. The hum of the energy conduits intensified, reflecting the growing power of the oceanic resonance, building to a crescendo—a culmination of chaos and hope. The final choice, a moment of profound planetary reckoning, was imminent. The future of Earth hung in the balance, teetering on the edge of oblivion and rebirth.

Humanity's Fate

The air crackled with unspoken anxieties. The holographic projection of Earth pulsed—a swirling vortex of blues and greens, marred by the scars of human negligence.

Seventy-two hours.

Seventy-two hours until the Convergence Protocol, their last desperate gamble, would either resurrect the planet or erase humanity from its face. The weight of that choice pressed down on them, heavier than any physical burden.

Eliza, her usually sharp eyes clouded with fatigue and uncertainty, spoke first—her voice a low murmur against the hum of the energy conduits.

"The probability of success remains... uncertain. The Whispers' evolution is throwing off our calculations. The energy fluctuations are... unpredictable, bordering on chaotic." She gestured to the swirling data streams, highlighting chaotic spikes in the oceanic resonance. "We are navigating a storm we can barely comprehend." Jonah, his face drawn and pale, nodded grimly. "The code... it's beautiful, in a terrifying way. It speaks of a complete planetary reset, a return to a primordial state before human intervention. It's a rebirth, yes, but it's a rebirth that might not include us." He ran a hand through his hair, the gesture betraying his inner turmoil. The burden of deciphering the ancient code, of understanding the Whispers' intentions, had taken a heavy toll. He felt the weight of responsibility—the understanding that a wrong calculation, a misinterpretation, could cost them everything.

Nyla, ever the serene observer, spoke slowly, her voice like the chime of distant bells. "The Whispers are not malicious. They are... evolving. Seeking a balance. The Protocol is not a destruction, but a transformation. A return to harmony." Her words, however, offered little comfort. The implications remained stark—a harmonious planet, yes, but at what cost? The cost of humanity's existence?

Sarah, hardened survivor and reluctant leader, broke the silence. "Harmony doesn't mean the same thing to everyone, Nyla. For us— for humanity—harmony means survival. We've built our lives, our civilization, on this planet. Are we just... expendable?" Her voice cracked, revealing the emotional toll of their desperate struggle. The ethical dilemma gnawed at her, a constant, unsettling presence.

The debate raged, a tempest of conflicting emotions and logical arguments. Eliza argued for a controlled activation, a phased approach that minimized risk, but Jonah countered that any delay would reduce their chances of success. The energy fluctuations were erratic, unpredictable; delaying meant jeopardizing their only chance. The whispers of the Whispers, once a guide, had become a source of both hope and dread—their chaotic symphony mirroring the turmoil within human hearts.

The conversation shifted to the Echoborn. Their unique perspective—their merging with the Whispers—gave them a different understanding of the situation. Their insights, however fragmented and difficult to interpret, were invaluable, offering glimpses into the Whispers' intentions and their vision of the future. But their presence also heightened the ethical dilemma. If the

Protocol succeeded, what would become of the Echoborn? Would their unique existence be erased along with the rest of humanity? Or would they become something entirely new—something beyond human comprehension?

The ethical dilemma was not simply a binary choice between survival and extinction. It encompassed the very definition of humanity's role on Earth. Had they become a plague upon the planet—a destructive force that needed to be eradicated for the sake of ecological balance? Was their right to exist conditional upon their ability to coexist harmoniously with nature? The questions hung heavy in the air, each one a hammer blow against the fragile hope that had sustained them.

Hours bled into one another, the countdown relentlessly ticking toward the final hour. The atmosphere in their makeshift control room was thick with tension, a potent cocktail of fear, hope, and despair. The holographic projection of Earth continued its chaotic dance, its pulsating energy mirroring the tempest of emotions within them. The weight of the decision—of choosing between the survival of humanity and the salvation of the planet—rested squarely on Sarah's shoulders.

She looked at each member of her team, their faces etched with exhaustion and worry. Jonah, consumed by the intricacies of the code, remained focused on his calculations, oblivious to the broader implications of their actions. Eliza, ever the scientist, was trying to find a way to reconcile the data with the ethical concerns. Nyla, with her calm demeanor, seemed to understand the profound transformation they were about to unleash, but her wisdom offered little guidance in navigating this unprecedented moral crisis. The Echoborn, their eyes shimmering with otherworldly luminescence, seemed to sense the impending change—their silent presence a constant reminder of the delicate balance they were about to disrupt.

Sarah knew there were no easy answers, no straightforward solutions. The choice was not simply about survival—it was about responsibility, about accepting the consequences of their actions, both past and present. It was a choice that would define not only their fate but the future of life on Earth.

The silence was broken only by the hum of the energy conduits—the throbbing heartbeat of the planet. The oceanic resonance intensified, building to a crescendo, a surge of energy that vibrated through the very air they breathed.

Seventy-two hours had passed.

The final hour had arrived.

The choice—the ultimate, irreversible choice—was theirs to make. The fate of humanity, the future of Earth, hung in the balance, poised on the knife's edge of oblivion and rebirth. The weight of the world, of the entire biosphere, rested on their shoulders—a burden too heavy for any single person to bear, yet a responsibility they could not shirk.

The final countdown had begun.

The future, in all its terrifying uncertainty, was about to unfold.

The Whispers' Plea

The rhythmic pulse of the oceanic resonance intensified—a throbbing heartbeat that resonated not just through the control room's instruments but through their very bones. Sarah felt it—a primal vibration that spoke of the planet's desperation, its yearning for a radical transformation. The countdown timer, a malevolent digital eye, ticked down its final seconds, each passing moment a chilling reminder of the irrevocable decision they were about to make.

Then, it began. Not a sound, not a visual cue, but a feeling—a subtle shift in the very fabric of reality.

The holographic projection of Earth shimmered, resolving itself into something more complex, more... organic. The swirling blues and greens solidified, transforming into a tapestry of intricate patterns—a living, breathing fractal that pulsed with an uncanny intelligence.

Jonah gasped, his eyes wide with awe and terror. "The Whispers... they're communicating... directly."

The data streams on his screens exploded into a cacophony of information—a deluge of complex patterns and symbols that defied his comprehension.

Eliza, despite her years of scientific training, found herself overwhelmed. This wasn't data in any form she recognized. It was... experience. She felt the planet's history unfold in a visceral wave: the millennia of life and death, of cataclysmic events and slow, steady evolution. The oceans' sighs, the forests' whispers, the deserts' scorching breath—all became tangible sensations, weaving a narrative far older and far deeper than any human history book could ever capture.

Nyla closed her eyes, her face serene yet filled with a profound understanding. She was receiving the message on a different level— a level beyond the data streams—a direct communion with the planetary consciousness. Her lips moved slightly, whispering words in an ancient, melodic tongue—a language older than any human speech, a language woven into the very fabric of the planet itself.

The Whispers, it turned out, were not merely sentient ecosystems, not merely a network of interconnected organisms. They were the planet itself—a unified entity, a consciousness expressing itself through the vast interconnectedness of the biosphere. They had observed humanity's rise, its dominance, and its devastating fall.

They had witnessed the gradual erosion of the planet's delicate balance, the relentless destruction wrought by unchecked greed and technological arrogance. They had borne the wounds inflicted by human negligence, the scars etched into the very earth itself.

Their message, conveyed through a symphony of sensations and visualizations, was not one of malice or revenge. It was one of profound sorrow—and an urgent plea for transformation. They were not seeking to erase humanity; they were seeking a partnership, a symbiotic relationship based on mutual respect and understanding.

They wanted a future where humanity did not dominate but coexisted—a future where human ingenuity and technological prowess would be used to heal, not harm.

The Whispers' vision of the future, however, was not a straightforward return to a pre-industrial state. It wasn't a simplistic notion of untouched wilderness. The Whispers envisioned a planet transformed—yes—but not devoid of human presence. Instead, it was a vision of harmonious coexistence: a future where technology and nature intertwined, where human innovation and the planet's natural processes worked in concert to create a resilient and thriving ecosystem.

This harmonious future, however, required a fundamental shift in humanity's perception of itself and its place in the world. Humanity needed to abandon its anthropocentric worldview—its unshakable belief in its inherent superiority. It needed to accept its role as a part of, not apart from, the intricate web of life that constituted the planet's ecosystem.

This was the crux of the Whispers' plea: not annihilation, but a radical transformation of human consciousness.

Through the overwhelming torrent of information, a specific scenario emerged. The Convergence Protocol, they revealed, was not simply a planetary reboot. It was a catalyst—a tool to facilitate this profound transformation. It was a process that would reshape the planet's biosphere, restoring its natural rhythms and resilience. Simultaneously, it would alter human biology, subtly integrating human consciousness into the larger planetary network. It was an evolutionary leap—a fusion of technology and nature that would redefine humanity's very essence.

This integration, the Whispers revealed, would not be a forced assimilation. It would be a voluntary merging—an invitation to participate in a grand symphony of life. Those who chose to embrace this transformation, who willingly surrendered their anthropocentric views, would become something new, something beyond the limitations of their current human forms. They would become part of the Whispers' collective consciousness, gaining unprecedented access to the planet's wisdom and resources.

But the Whispers also acknowledged the potential for resistance—the possibility that humanity might choose to cling to its current form, to its self-destructive patterns. For those who refused to adapt, the Protocol would not be destructive but rather... a fading echo. They would not be annihilated, but their very existence would become irrelevant to the planet's new equilibrium. Their impact on the environment would slowly dissipate, their imprint on the planet gradually erasing itself over time. It was a vision not of punishment, but of irrelevance—a peaceful disintegration of a species that had chosen to exist outside the harmony of the planet's song.

The Echoborn—those already merging with the Whispers— seemed to understand this implicit message. Their eyes held an uncanny knowingness, a serene acceptance of the inevitable changes. They had a glimpse of the future: a world where the lines between humanity and nature blurred, where the human spirit intertwined with the planet's consciousness. Their existence was not a warning, but a testament to the potential for this symbiotic evolution.

The weight of this revelation pressed heavily on the team. The choice was no longer a simple binary equation. It was a decision that would define not only their fate but the fate of humanity itself—and the nature of its relationship with the planet. The ultimatum was clear: adapt and merge, or fade into obscurity.

The whispers of the Earth itself demanded a fundamental shift in humanity's worldview—a choice between oblivion and a breathtaking transformation. The countdown was nearing zero. The final hour had arrived. And the choice was theirs—a terrifying, magnificent leap into the unknown. *Last Stand*

The final seconds ticked down, each digit a hammer blow against the fragile hope clinging to their hearts.

Sarah, her knuckles white against the console, felt the tremor in the earth intensify—a physical manifestation of the planet's desperate plea. The holographic projection of Earth pulsed, its vibrant colors shifting and swirling like an oil painting on a stormy sea. This wasn't just data; it was a living, breathing entity, communicating its needs, its hopes, its fears—with a visceral intensity that transcended language.

Suddenly, a jarring alarm blared, piercing the hypnotic rhythm of the planetary pulse.

Jonah slammed his fist on the console, his face a mask of frustration. "Mallory! He's interfering with the resonance field!"

The data streams erupted in a chaotic frenzy of red warnings.

The intricate patterns that had previously conveyed the Whispers' message were now fractured, disrupted by a powerful external force.

Eliza gasped, her eyes wide with horror. "He's trying to disrupt the Protocol! He's trying to hijack it!"

Nyla, her usually calm demeanor shattered, rose to her feet, her voice ringing with fierce urgency. "He cannot be allowed to succeed. The Convergence is our last hope—our only chance for survival."

The holographic projection flickered violently, threatening to collapse. The planet's desperate heartbeat faltered, its rhythm erratic and weak. This wasn't just technological sabotage—it was an assault on the very lifeblood of the planet.

Sarah, adrenaline coursing through her veins, barked orders, her voice sharp and decisive. "Jonah, reroute the power! Eliza, prepare the emergency protocols! Nyla, we need your guidance!"

The control room transformed into a whirlwind of activity.

Jonah fought against Mallory's intrusion, his fingers flying across the keyboards, his brow furrowed in concentration. The air crackled with tension, the silence punctuated only by the frantic tapping of keys, the whirring of machines, and the ominous beeping of alarms.

Eliza, her hands trembling, worked frantically—preparing backup systems, seeking ways to mitigate the damage, to salvage the activation process.

Nyla, her face etched with deep concern, chanted a low, rhythmic incantation, her voice weaving a protective shield around the struggling resonance field. Her words resonated not just in the air, but deep within Sarah's soul—a comforting anchor in the storm.

The Luminese elder, connected to the planet on a level none of them could fully comprehend, was attempting to reinforce the connection—to push back against Mallory's intrusion, to give the planet's life force the strength to resist.

The battle raged for what felt like an eternity, each passing second a monumental struggle against the forces of destruction. The fate of the planet—the future of humanity—hung precariously in the balance. Mallory's intrusion wasn't merely technological; it was a spiritual assault, an attack on the very essence of the planetary consciousness. He wasn't just disrupting the technology; he was trying to sever the connection between the human spirit and the Earth's soul.

Through the chaos, Sarah could feel the planet's pain, its anguish—a deep, visceral sorrow that echoed in her own heart. This wasn't just a technological problem; it was a battle for the soul of the planet, a fight for its very existence. Mallory, driven by his egotistical ambitions, was blind to the magnitude of his actions, oblivious to the profound consequences of his attempt to dominate nature.

The intensity of the conflict pushed Sarah to the limits of her endurance. Her body ached with fatigue, but her spirit remained unbroken. She remembered the faces of the Echoborn—their serene acceptance, their quiet understanding of the planet's plea. Their quiet strength fueled her own resolve.

Jonah, his face pale with exertion, suddenly shouted, "I've got a breakthrough! I've found a backdoor! I can bypass his intrusion, but it will be risky. We only have one chance."

Sarah nodded, her gaze unwavering. "Do it, Jonah. We have to try."

With a final surge of determination, Jonah initiated the bypass. The control room went silent. The alarms ceased their frantic screaming, replaced by a palpable tension. The holographic projection steadied, its colors regaining their vibrancy, the planetary heartbeat returning to a strong, steady rhythm. Mallory's attack had been repelled. His desperate attempt to usurp the planet's power was thwarted.

The victory, however, was short-lived. The countdown clock resumed its relentless march toward zero. The Whispers had given them a reprieve, but their time was still rapidly expiring. The final decision loomed large, heavy with the weight of countless lives and an entire planet's future. This wasn't a technological challenge anymore—it was a test of their collective will, a profound existential choice.

The planet's message, now restored, pulsed anew—stronger and clearer than before. It was a symphony of feelings, a profound invitation, a final plea for a partnership based on mutual respect and understanding. This wasn't about saving humanity in the traditional sense; it was about transformation, about a profound shift in consciousness, about accepting their role as partners with the planet—not its masters.

Eliza looked at Sarah, her eyes filled with a mixture of fear and hope. "The Protocol... it's going to change us. Will we be ready?"

Nyla, her face serene despite the gravity of the moment, placed a hand on Sarah's shoulder—her touch conveying a sense of profound wisdom and unwavering support. "The choice is yours, Sarah. The planet offers a future beyond your comprehension—a future of unimaginable beauty and harmony. But it requires a surrender of the old ways, a willingness to evolve, to become something greater than yourselves."

Sarah gazed at the holographic projection—at the pulsating image of Earth, its beauty both heartbreaking and inspiring. She thought of the scars upon the planet, the damage wrought by humanity's careless exploitation. But she also saw its resilience, its capacity for renewal, its inherent yearning for a symbiotic relationship with its inhabitants.

The final seconds ticked away, the weight of the decision pressing down on her. The choice was clear—terrifyingly so: accept the transformation, surrender to the Whispers, merge with the planet, and forge a new, symbiotic future. Or cling to the old ways, to the anthropocentric worldview that had led them to the brink of destruction, and face a fading echo—a slow, peaceful disintegration into irrelevance.

The countdown reached zero.

The final choice was theirs.

The future of Earth, the future of humanity, hinged on this single, irrevocable decision.

The Convergence Begins

The humming intensified—a low, resonant thrum that vibrated through the floor, up their legs, into their very bones. The holographic Earth pulsed with incandescent light, its colors no longer swirling chaotically but radiating outward in waves of pure energy. It wasn't just a visual display—it was a tangible force, a palpable shift in the very fabric of reality.

Sarah felt a strange pressure in her chest, a sensation of expansion, as if her own being were stretching, growing, reaching outward to embrace something vast and unknown.

Eliza gasped, her eyes wide, clutching at her chest. "I... I can feel it. The resonance... it's changing everything."

Jonah, still reeling from the near-catastrophic battle with Mallory, stared at the console—his face a mixture of awe and apprehension. The data streams were now a breathtaking cascade of light, shifting patterns of energy that seemed to pulse with an intelligence far beyond human comprehension. It was beautiful, terrifying, and utterly overwhelming.

The air grew thick with the scent of ozone, a sharp, metallic tang that stung their nostrils. The temperature in the control room plummeted—a wave of icy air washing over them, sending shivers down their spines. Outside, the wind howled—a mournful cry that seemed to echo the planet's ancient sorrow. The Earth trembled beneath their feet—a deep, resonant vibration that spoke of tectonic shifts, of a planet undergoing a profound metamorphosis.

Nyla closed her eyes, her face bathed in the ethereal glow of the holographic projection. A low hum resonated from her lips, a wordless chant that seemed to synchronize with the planet's own pulse. Her form shimmered faintly, as if she were partially dissolving—merging with the energy radiating from the projection.

She was no longer merely observing the Convergence; she was participating in it—becoming one with the planet's transformation.

The changes weren't confined to the immediate environment.

Through the reinforced windows of the control room, they could see the landscape beyond undergoing a dramatic shift. The ravaged cityscape, scarred by decades of environmental collapse, began to heal before their very eyes. Buildings crumbled, reformed, and reassembled—taking on new, organic shapes, incorporating elements of nature into their structures. Cracked pavements melted, reformed into lush green paths, vibrant with wildflowers and unfamiliar vegetation. The parched, barren earth blossomed, thirsty soil drinking deeply of the revitalized energy, erupting in a riot of color and life.

The sea, once a toxic wasteland, now glowed with a bioluminescent light. Creatures long extinct rose from the depths, their forms shimmering in the ethereal glow. The oceans, once lifeless and polluted, were coming alive. The air, once thick with smog and toxins, cleared, becoming crisp and clean, filled with the scent of pine and rain. It was as if the planet were shedding its old skin, revealing a vibrant, renewed self.

But the transformation wasn't limited to the environment. Sarah felt it within herself—a deep shift in consciousness, a merging of her own being with the planetary awareness. Her perceptions expanded, becoming acute, attuned to the planet's rhythms, its subtle vibrations, its deepest emotions. She could feel the joy, the relief, the profound satisfaction of a planet finally healing itself. She could also feel the sadness—the lingering pain of its past wounds—a deepseated sorrow that resonated with her own heart.

Eliza, her eyes filled with tears, looked out at the transformed landscape.

"It's... it's beyond anything I ever imagined," she whispered, her voice trembling with emotion. "The planet... it's singing."

Jonah, his gaze fixed on the data streams, saw patterns emerge that defied his understanding—complex algorithms that hinted at an intelligence far beyond human comprehension. He was witnessing the birth of a new form of communication, a language that transcended words, conveying emotions, ideas, and experiences directly through the senses.

As the transformation progressed, the physical changes accelerated. Buildings melted and reformed, morphing into symbiotic structures that integrated seamlessly with the surrounding environment. Deserts transformed into lush forests. Oceans became vibrant ecosystems teeming with life. Human settlements adapted, becoming integrated parts of a vast, interconnected network—a testament to the planet's restorative power.

The Echoborn—those humans who had already embraced the Whispers—seemed to thrive in this new environment, their bodies subtly transforming, merging with the planet's energy. They moved with a grace and fluidity that suggested a deeper connection to the natural world, an understanding that transcended the limitations of the human form.

But the changes weren't without their challenges. Some human settlements, clinging to their old ways, resisted the transformation, creating pockets of conflict where the old world clashed with the new. There was a growing tension between those who embraced the change and those who resisted it—between those who saw the Convergence as a chance for renewal and those who feared the unknown.

The planet's transformation wasn't without its own struggles. While the damaged ecosystems healed rapidly, ancient geological processes were intensified, leading to tremors and volcanic eruptions. The changes, while magnificent, were also chaotic—a testament to the planet's immense power and the scale of its selfhealing process. The planet was renewing itself, but the process was far from gentle.

Sarah, witnessing these conflicting forces, understood the immense responsibility placed on humanity. The Convergence wasn't merely about the planet's survival—it was about humanity's ability to adapt, to integrate, to learn to live in harmony with nature, to become true partners in the planet's regeneration. It was a choice between survival and transcendence, between extinction and evolution.

The process was far from over. The planet's transformation was a dynamic, ongoing process—a testament to its resilient spirit. Humanity's future depended on its ability to adapt, to embrace the change, and to become true partners in the planet's regeneration.

The Convergence had begun, and the future of both humanity and the Earth was unfolding before them—a breathtaking, terrifying, and ultimately hopeful spectacle. The planet's song was a powerful call to action, a demand for a profound shift in consciousness, a pledge of a future where humanity could once again become a vital part of a thriving ecosystem.

The journey had just begun, and the path ahead was uncertain— yet filled with a profound sense of purpose and the daunting beauty of transformation.

CHAPTER SIX

REBIRTH, A TRANSFORMED EARTH

The air, once thick with the metallic tang of ozone, now carried the scent of petrichor—the earthy fragrance of rain on dry ground, a scent long forgotten in many parts of the world. The rain itself, a gentle, cleansing shower, began to fall not just on the ravaged cityscapes but across the entire planet. It wasn't just water; it felt almost alive, charged with the same energy that pulsed from the holographic Earth in the control room. The rain seemed to seep into the very fabric of the planet, revitalizing parched landscapes and nourishing depleted soils.

Deserts, once expanses of barren sand and rock, blossomed with astonishing speed. Towering sand dunes yielded to rolling hills carpeted in vibrant wildflowers, their colors more vivid, their fragrances more potent than anything Eliza had ever encountered in her years as a marine biologist. New species of flora, impossible in the old world, sprung forth—luminescent fungi casting an ethereal glow upon the night, towering trees with bark that shimmered like opals, vines that pulsed with a soft, internal light. The transformation

115

wasn't just aesthetic; it was a fundamental shift in the planet's ecological balance.

The oceans, once choked with plastic and pollutants, began to clear. The bioluminescence, initially a faint, sporadic glimmer, intensified, creating an underwater spectacle of dazzling light and color. Schools of fish, vibrant and diverse, swam in shoals, their movements synchronized in a mesmerizing ballet. Creatures long extinct, thought lost forever to pollution and overfishing, reappeared—majestic whales breached the surface, their colossal forms glistening in the moonlight; ancient sea turtles glided through the coral reefs, their shells adorned with intricate patterns. The oceans, once a symbol of environmental devastation, were reborn as vibrant ecosystems teeming with life.

The ravaged cityscape itself underwent a metamorphosis.

Crumbling concrete buildings, scarred by fire and neglect, began to reform. They didn't simply rebuild; they evolved. Steel and glass melded with natural materials—living vines snaked around skyscrapers, transforming their sterile exteriors into verdant walls, while cracked pavements morphed into intricate pathways paved with shimmering crystals and luminous moss. Buildings themselves seemed to breathe, their forms shifting and adapting to the surrounding landscape, creating symbiotic structures that integrated seamlessly with nature. It was as if the city was becoming part of the planet rather than something separate from it.

This transformation wasn't confined to the physical environment. The very air seemed to hum with a new energy, a palpable sense of vitality that resonated with everything around it. The whispers, once elusive and cryptic, became more readily perceived. They were no longer just faint sensations or fleeting impressions; they became audible murmurs, subtle shifts in temperature, almost tangible currents of energy. It was as if the planet itself was speaking, communicating its emotions, its hopes, its dreams.

The Echoborn, already attuned to these whispers, flourished in this transformed environment. Their bodies seemed to become more fluid, more adaptable, their movements graceful and instinctive, reflecting the harmonious integration of human and nature. They moved through the reborn cities and landscapes with an ease and grace that suggested a profound connection to the planet's energy, their existence a testament to the potential for symbiotic evolution. Their presence was a beacon of hope, a sign that humanity could not only survive but thrive in this transformed world.

Yet, this remarkable rebirth wasn't without its challenges. The intense geological activity that accompanied the planetary regeneration caused earthquakes and volcanic eruptions, creating pockets of instability and destruction. Some human settlements, clinging to their old ways, resisted the transformation. Fearing the unfamiliar, they resisted the change. They saw the new world not as a chance for renewal but as a threat to their established ways of life. The clash between those who embraced the change and those who resisted it created tension and conflict—a struggle between the old world and the new.

Jonah, initially overwhelmed by the sheer complexity of the data streams, found himself adapting to this new reality. The cryptic language of the whispers was slowly revealing its secrets, unveiling patterns and algorithms that transcended human comprehension. He saw echoes of ancient languages, remnants of forgotten civilizations, embedded within the planet's energy signatures. He began to understand the planet's history, its cycles of destruction and regeneration, its deep-seated memory of past wounds.

Eliza, witnessing the astonishing rebirth of the oceans, felt a profound sense of wonder and responsibility. The marine ecosystems she had dedicated her life to studying were not just recovering; they were evolving into something new—something more complex and beautiful than she had ever imagined. Her work now involved not just observation and study but active participation in this planetary transformation. Her scientific knowledge became a tool for guiding the evolution, for ensuring that this new world was sustainable and harmonious.

Nyla, the Luminese ambassador, remained a steadfast guide, her wisdom and understanding providing invaluable insight into the planet's transformation. Her presence, a beacon of interspecies understanding and cooperation, helped bridge the gap between humanity and the planet, between humans and the Whispers. She served as a living embodiment of the symbiotic relationship that was developing, a testament to the potential for co-existence and collaboration between different species.

Sarah, bearing the weight of leadership, understood the immense responsibility placed upon humanity. The Convergence wasn't merely a planetary-scale reboot; it was a profound test of humanity's ability to adapt, to change, to become a true partner in the planet's regeneration. It was a choice between survival and transcendence, between extinction and evolution. The path forward was far from clear; it was paved with uncertainties, challenges, and conflicts, but it was a path toward a future where humanity and nature could coexist harmoniously—a future where the planet's song would be a symphony of life, a testament to a truly reborn Earth.

The transformation was ongoing, a continuous process of healing and growth, a powerful testament to the planet's resilience and the remarkable ability of life to find its way. The future remained unwritten, a vast and uncertain canvas onto which humanity would paint its destiny. The task ahead was immense, the challenges daunting, but the hope of a truly reborn Earth fueled their unwavering resolve.

New Symbiosis

The initial shock of the Convergence subsided, replaced by a dawning understanding of its profound implications. It wasn't merely a restoration of the planet; it was a fundamental shift in the relationship between humanity and the natural world. The whispers, once enigmatic and distant, were now becoming a palpable presence, woven into the very fabric of existence. They manifested not only as subtle shifts in temperature or faint murmurs, but as tangible sensations, a feeling of being intimately connected to the planet's pulse. This connection wasn't just felt by the Echoborn; it was slowly, tentatively, beginning to touch every human being.

Jonah, delving deeper into the whispers' cryptic code, discovered a complex network of symbiotic relationships that had existed long before humanity's rise. The planet, he realized, was not a passive entity, but an active participant in its own evolution. It had always been communicating, always seeking balance, always striving for harmony. Humanity, in its hubris, had disrupted this ancient dialogue, causing a catastrophic imbalance. The Convergence was, in a sense, the planet's response—a desperate attempt to reestablish that ancient harmony, even if it meant reshaping the very face of the world.

He found evidence of past civilizations, their technologies intertwined with the planet's natural rhythms, their societies structured in accordance with the planet's own intricate cycles. These were not stories of environmental destruction, but narratives of collaboration, of societies that had learned to live in harmony with nature. They were lessons lost to time, buried beneath layers of human progress and technological advancements, until the Convergence brought them back to light. The whispers weren't simply a source of information; they were a library of forgotten wisdom, a repository of knowledge that could guide humanity toward a sustainable future.

Eliza, meanwhile, was witnessing the breathtaking evolution of the marine ecosystems. The oceans were no longer just recovering; they were undergoing a radical transformation, creating new habitats, new species, new relationships. She discovered coral reefs that pulsated with bioluminescent light, their structures shaped by the whispers' influence, creating intricate, living sculptures of breathtaking beauty. She observed schools of fish communicating through complex patterns of bioluminescence, creating a silent, underwater language that mirrored the whispers' own enigmatic code. The oceans were no longer just a source of sustenance; they were a vibrant, intelligent ecosystem, actively participating in the planet's regeneration.

Her research revealed a surprising symbiotic relationship between certain marine species and the Echoborn. These humans, who had absorbed the whispers' energy into their beings, seemed to have a unique ability to communicate with and influence marine life. They could subtly alter the ocean currents, encourage the growth of coral reefs, and guide the migration of fish. It was a profound connection, a testament to the potential for harmonious coexistence between humans and the natural world. This was no longer the domain of science fiction; this was the new reality.

The Echoborn themselves were undergoing a significant transformation. Their bodies adapted to the changed environment, becoming more resilient, more fluid, more connected to the planet's rhythms. Their senses sharpened, allowing them to perceive the whispers with greater clarity. They were no longer merely human; they were evolving into something new, a bridge between two worlds, a testament to the power of symbiotic evolution.

Yet, this symbiotic relationship wasn't without its challenges. The intense geological activity, the unpredictable shifts in the environment, created new dangers and new uncertainties. Some species thrived in this new environment, while others struggled to adapt. Eliza and her team worked tirelessly to guide the ecological balance, ensuring the survival of threatened species and mitigating the risks posed by the ongoing planetary transformation. Their work was no longer confined to the laboratory; it was a hands-on effort to shape the very fabric of the new world.

The human communities, too, were undergoing a radical transformation. Many embraced the change, finding a newfound connection to nature, a renewed sense of purpose in the planet's regeneration. They developed sustainable farming practices, integrated their settlements into the natural landscape, and developed technologies that were harmonious with the environment, not in opposition to it. Their lives were no longer defined by consumption and exploitation; they were a part of the planet's life cycle, a testament to humanity's capacity for adaptability and resilience.

However, not all embraced this new reality. Resistance to change remained, fueled by fear and uncertainty, by a clinging to the old ways of life. These communities, often isolated and clinging to outdated technologies, viewed the Convergence as a threat, fearing the loss of their way of life. The tension between those who embraced the change and those who resisted it became a new source of conflict, a struggle between the old and the new world.

This resistance was not only social; it was also a challenge in resource management and in ensuring that the newly evolved ecosystems had the space and opportunity to flourish.

Ambassador Nyla's wisdom and guidance proved invaluable in navigating these complex relationships. She fostered dialogue between different communities, encouraging cooperation and understanding, bridging the gap between those who feared the change and those who embraced it. Her role transcended diplomacy; she was a catalyst for healing, a testament to the possibility of intercultural understanding and a symbiotic relationship across species and civilizations. She helped to establish protocols for resource sharing, ensuring that the new world was equitable and just for all its inhabitants.

Sarah, the hardened survivor, watched over it all, her leadership tempered by the gravity of the situation. The Convergence was not just about the planet's survival; it was about humanity's transformation. It was about learning to coexist with nature, to become a part of it, to understand that humanity's destiny was irrevocably intertwined with the planet's fate. The old paradigm of human dominance had crumbled, replaced by a new understanding of interconnectedness, interdependence, and the need for a profound shift in values and priorities.

The challenges that remained were immense, yet the hope for a reborn Earth—a world where humans and nature danced in harmony—fueled the unwavering resolve of those who fought for its future. The whispers, once cryptic and elusive, now sang a song of rebirth, a symphony of life echoing across a planet newly awakened. The future remained unwritten, but it was a future brimming with the potential for a truly symbiotic existence, a testament to the resilience of both nature and the human spirit.

Human Adaptation

The whispers weren't just altering the landscape; they were reshaping humanity itself. The changes weren't always dramatic— often subtle shifts in physiology and perception. Some individuals developed enhanced senses, a heightened awareness of the subtle vibrations and currents of the Earth. Others experienced changes in their metabolism, becoming more efficient at processing nutrients, requiring less food and water. The most striking changes occurred among the Echoborn, but even those who hadn't directly merged with the whispers found their bodies adjusting to the altered environment.

Skin tones changed, becoming more adaptable to the varying light levels caused by the shifting atmospheric conditions. Hair grew thicker or thinner depending on the climate in their region, providing natural insulation against extreme temperatures. Even the human digestive system seemed to be adapting, showing increased tolerance for foods that were previously inedible or toxic. These weren't genetic mutations in the traditional sense but rather epigenetic adaptations—changes in gene expression triggered by the whispers' influence. The planet, in a sense, was guiding human evolution, molding humanity into a species more suited to the newly evolving environment.

This adaptability wasn't confined to the physical realm. Humanity's cognitive abilities also shifted. People began to perceive the world differently, seeing patterns and connections that were previously invisible. The whispers seemed to enhance intuition and empathy, fostering a deeper connection between individuals and a greater understanding of the natural world. Creative expression flourished, with art, music, and literature reflecting the planet's transformation.

Stories emerged, recounting the symbiotic relationship between humanity and the environment, celebrating the beauty and wonder of the reborn Earth.

This wasn't a uniform process. Some individuals resisted the change, clinging to the old ways of life. They feared the unknown— the uncertainty of the transformation. They saw the adaptations as deformities, a corruption of their human essence. This resistance, however, was slowly waning. As the benefits of the adaptations became evident—enhanced resilience to disease, greater physical strength and endurance, increased cognitive abilities—more and more people accepted the change, embracing the evolution. The fear gave way to a sense of awe and wonder.

Societal structures underwent a profound shift. The old hierarchies and power structures crumbled, replaced by a more collaborative and decentralized system. Communities organized themselves according to ecological principles, prioritizing sustainability and cooperation. The emphasis on individual accumulation of wealth gave way to a focus on shared resources and collective well-being. This new social order wasn't utopian, but it demonstrated humanity's capacity for adaptation and its ability to create functional societies based on cooperation and shared responsibility.

Technological advancements also mirrored this transformation.

Humans developed technologies that were sustainable and integrated with the natural world. They created bio-integrated structures that mimicked natural forms, utilized renewable energy sources, and minimized their environmental impact. Transportation shifted away from fossil fuels toward more efficient and ecofriendly alternatives, like biofuel-powered vehicles and advanced wind and solar energy-based systems. Even communication technologies adapted, becoming more sensitive to the whispers' frequencies, allowing for a direct interaction between human consciousness and the planet's energy systems.

The cities, once symbols of human dominance, began to integrate with the natural world. Green spaces expanded, reclaiming areas previously dominated by concrete and steel. Buildings were designed to blend seamlessly into the landscape, using recycled materials and incorporating natural elements. The once sharp distinction between urban and rural blurred, with settlements becoming more integrated into the surrounding ecosystems. Food production transitioned from large-scale industrial agriculture to localized, sustainable farming practices. People learned to live in harmony with nature, understanding that human prosperity was inextricably linked to the planet's well-being.

However, the transformation wasn't without its challenges. The rapid environmental changes created new vulnerabilities. Some communities struggled to adapt, particularly those who remained resistant to the whispers' influence. Diseases emerged, adapted to the altered environment, testing the resilience of both humans and the ecosystems. The unpredictable nature of the whispers presented further obstacles, creating unexpected shifts in climate and geological activity. Managing these risks required constant vigilance and a collaborative effort from all communities.

Sarah Chen, along with Jonah and Eliza, continued to play vital roles in guiding humanity through this transition. Sarah's leadership extended beyond survival; she fostered collaboration and resilience, ensuring the equitable distribution of resources and opportunities.

Jonah's understanding of the whispers' code became crucial in predicting and mitigating environmental shifts, helping communities prepare for the unpredictable changes. Eliza's ecological expertise was essential in guiding the restoration and adaptation of the planet's ecosystems, ensuring the survival of threatened species and the stability of the new biomes.

Ambassador Nyla's role became even more crucial in fostering understanding and cooperation between the diverse human communities and the evolving whispers. Her diplomacy extended beyond political boundaries, integrating the spiritual and philosophical aspects of the changes into the decision-making process. She helped establish systems of cultural exchange, fostering an appreciation for the diverse ways in which humanity was adapting to the new reality. She recognized the profound spiritual and philosophical implications of the transformation, working to incorporate diverse cultural perspectives in the management of the reborn Earth.

The Convergence had not just altered the planet; it had fundamentally altered humanity's relationship with itself, with nature, and with its own future. The ongoing challenge was not merely survival but a deeper integration into a symbiotic relationship with Earth—a partnership built on respect, understanding, and a commitment to shared prosperity. The whispers were not just shaping the world; they were shaping a new kind of human, one capable of thriving within a symbiotic relationship with a planet that was both powerful and profoundly interconnected.

The future remained uncertain, a tapestry woven with threads of both hope and trepidation, but humanity, having faced extinction, had found a new path—a path toward coexistence and shared evolution. This new path wasn't a predetermined destination but a journey of continuous adaptation and reconciliation, a testament to the enduring power of the human spirit and the breathtaking resilience of life itself. The Convergence had initiated a metamorphosis—not just of the planet but of humanity's very essence. The question wasn't merely whether humanity would survive, but what kind of humanity would emerge from this crucible of change.

Luminese Legacy

The whispers, once a source of fear and uncertainty, had become a catalyst for profound transformation—a transformation in which the Luminese played a pivotal role. Their advanced technology, initially viewed with suspicion by some human factions, proved indispensable in deciphering the Whispers' complex code and in implementing the Convergence Protocol. Their understanding of planetary resonance, a concept largely unknown to humans before the environmental collapse, was crucial in stabilizing the Earth's fluctuating energy fields. The Luminese, with their centuries of experience in managing complex ecological systems on their own homeworld, provided invaluable expertise in guiding the planet's regeneration.

Their contribution wasn't solely technological; it extended to a deep understanding of symbiotic evolution and interspecies communication. Ambassador Nyla, a beacon of wisdom and diplomacy, bridged the cultural and philosophical divides between humans and the Whispers, fostering a unique form of interspecies collaboration. She helped translate the Whispers' cryptic messages, not just into human languages but into a shared understanding of planetary needs and aspirations. Her diplomatic efforts fostered trust, mitigating the inherent tensions between a technologically advanced species and a newly evolving planet. The Luminese didn't impose their solutions; instead, they worked collaboratively with human communities, sharing their knowledge and adapting their technologies to suit the unique challenges of Earth's regeneration.

The Luminese's presence in this new world was far from domineering. They chose integration over control, understanding that true planetary healing required a harmonious partnership. They established collaborative research centers, sharing their scientific expertise with human scientists and fostering a new era of crossspecies scientific advancement. This collaboration led to breakthroughs in bioengineering, sustainable energy production, and climate stabilization, pushing the boundaries of human understanding and technological capabilities.

Luminese cities, initially separate entities, gradually integrated with human settlements, creating vibrant hubs of cross-cultural exchange and shared innovation. The Luminese architecture, known for its elegant integration with natural landscapes, served as inspiration for human urban planning, leading to a shift away from concrete jungles toward bio-integrated settlements that harmonized with the evolving ecosystems.

The integration wasn't without its complexities. Differences in cultural values and philosophical perspectives occasionally led to friction, requiring delicate negotiation and a commitment to mutual understanding. The Luminese, accustomed to a more measured pace of life, sometimes found themselves struggling to keep up with the rapid pace of human adaptation and innovation. Conversely, some human communities, wary of outside influence, resisted the Luminese's help, clinging to traditional ways that were no longer sustainable. Yet, the overarching spirit of collaboration prevailed, driven by the shared understanding that planetary survival depended on unity and mutual respect.

The Luminese's contribution transcended the practical realm; they brought a unique spiritual and philosophical perspective to the planet's rebirth. Their understanding of the interconnectedness of all life, honed over centuries of observing their own vibrant ecosystems, helped guide human efforts toward a more holistic approach to environmental stewardship. They introduced concepts of planetary consciousness and interspecies empathy, fostering a deeper appreciation for the intrinsic value of all living things.

This philosophical shift led to a fundamental change in the human worldview, moving away from anthropocentric notions of dominance toward a more humble understanding of humanity's place within the larger ecosystem. The Luminese, by example and through patient guidance, helped humanity reimagine its relationship with the planet, shifting from exploitation to stewardship.

The transformation wasn't merely ecological; it was social and spiritual. The shared struggle for survival, guided by the Luminese's wisdom and experience, fostered a new sense of global unity and purpose. Humanity, once fragmented by national borders and ideological conflicts, found itself bound together by a shared destiny and a common goal: to heal the planet and secure a sustainable future for all.

This newfound unity didn't erase differences or disagreements, but it created a framework for productive dialogue and collaboration, a testament to humanity's capacity for adaptation and resilience. The old political structures, once symbols of power and control, gave way to more collaborative and decentralized systems, reflecting the new understanding of planetary interconnectedness.

The Luminese's role in this transformation wasn't that of saviors, but of collaborators and guides. They offered their knowledge and technology, but they ultimately empowered humanity to take ownership of its future. They shared their knowledge, not as a gift to be accepted passively, but as a tool for shared creation, understanding that true planetary healing demanded shared agency.

Their participation in the rebirth was not about dominance but about partnership—a partnership based on mutual respect, understanding, and a shared commitment to the planet's well-being.

Their presence in this new world extended beyond the practical; they brought with them a rich tapestry of cultural traditions, artistic expressions, and philosophical perspectives, enriching human society in profound ways. Their music, characterized by ethereal harmonies and complex rhythms reflecting the planet's subtle vibrations, inspired a new wave of artistic innovation. Their architecture, blending seamlessly with the natural environment, became a model for sustainable urban design. Their holistic philosophy, emphasizing the interconnectedness of all life, profoundly influenced human ethical and spiritual thought. Their stories, passed down through generations, spoke of a commitment to symbiotic evolution and the profound responsibility of living in harmony with the planet.

The integration of the Luminese into human society also led to significant advancements in education and scientific understanding. Their educational programs, focused on environmental stewardship and sustainable living, inspired a new generation of environmentally conscious leaders. Their research institutions became centers of excellence, pushing the boundaries of scientific knowledge and fostering innovation. Their contributions extended to medicine and healthcare, with Luminese expertise proving invaluable in understanding and treating the new diseases that emerged in the altered environment.

However, the integration was not without its challenges. Cultural misunderstandings persisted, requiring continuous dialogue and compromise. The Luminese's technologically advanced society presented opportunities for both cooperation and potential exploitation, necessitating careful regulation and ethical considerations. Economic disparities remained, requiring ongoing efforts to ensure equitable distribution of resources and opportunities.

Yet, the collaborative spirit, forged in the crucible of environmental collapse, helped navigate these challenges, demonstrating the power of mutual respect and shared responsibility. The Luminese, by their actions and their commitment to partnership, demonstrated a path toward a future where different species could not only coexist but flourish together, creating a civilization founded on mutual respect and shared stewardship of the planet.

Their legacy was not just one of technological advancement, but a testament to the possibility of interspecies harmony and the enduring power of collaboration in the face of unprecedented challenges. The reborn Earth, a planet reshaped by the Whispers and nurtured by the combined efforts of humanity and the Luminese, stood as a testament to the resilience of life and the boundless potential for hope in a world forever changed.

The Convergence had not just healed the planet; it had forged a new destiny—one where different species could learn to thrive together, creating a future richer and more diverse than anything imaginable before the collapse.

The Echo of Mallory

The whispers of the Convergence Protocol, once faint echoes in the ravaged Earth, had begun to resonate with newfound strength. The planet, battered and bruised, was slowly mending—a testament to the collaborative efforts of humanity, the Luminese, and the evolving Whispers themselves. Yet, the scars of the past remained, etched not only in the landscape but in the collective memory. The shadow of Dr. Rafe Mallory, a scientist whose ambition had nearly undone their hard-fought progress, continued to loom large.

Mallory, driven by a twisted vision of planetary control, had sought to harness the power of the Convergence Protocol for his own ends, disregarding the delicate balance of the Whispers' code and the intricate web of life it sustained. His actions had triggered a cascade of unforeseen consequences, pushing the planet to the brink of irreversible damage. The near-catastrophe served as a stark reminder of the dangers inherent in unchecked scientific ambition—a cautionary tale etched in the very fabric of the reborn Earth.

The consequences of Mallory's actions were far-reaching. His attempts to manipulate the Whispers' code resulted in localized ecological disasters, leaving behind blighted landscapes that served as permanent monuments to his hubris. These scarred regions, once vibrant ecosystems teeming with life, now stood as barren wastelands—stark reminders of the fragility of planetary balance and the devastating potential of human interference. The affected areas needed extensive remediation efforts, requiring a concerted and long-term commitment from the human-Luminese alliance.

Beyond the immediate environmental damage, Mallory's actions sowed seeds of distrust among the various factions working toward planetary recovery. The human communities, already grappling with the trauma of environmental collapse, were further fractured by suspicion and fear, their trust in science and technology shaken by the near-catastrophic consequences of Mallory's scheme. The Luminese, accustomed to meticulous ecological planning, were forced to reassess their approaches, recognizing the potential dangers of interfering with such powerful planetary forces.

The aftermath of Mallory's actions also led to a critical reevaluation of the ethical implications of advanced technologies. The incident forced humanity and the Luminese to confront the potential for misuse of scientific discoveries and the need for strict ethical guidelines in their application. New regulations and oversight committees were established, ensuring responsible development and implementation of future technological advancements. This new emphasis on ethical responsibility shaped the future trajectory of scientific research, promoting a more cautious and collaborative approach—prioritizing planetary wellbeing over individual ambition.

Furthermore, Mallory's actions prompted a profound philosophical shift within human society. The near-catastrophe served as a powerful wake-up call, highlighting humanity's vulnerability in the face of nature's power and the catastrophic consequences of disregarding ecological balance. The old anthropocentric worldview, which had placed humanity at the center of the universe, gave way to a more humble and ecologically conscious perspective—recognizing humanity's place as an integral part of the planet's intricate ecosystem, not its master. This shift was reflected in new educational curricula emphasizing environmental stewardship, ethical responsibility, and the importance of living in harmony with nature.

The impact of Mallory's legacy extended beyond the physical and philosophical realms. His actions spurred the development of advanced monitoring systems capable of detecting any potential manipulation of the Convergence Protocol or other critical planetary systems. These systems employed a combination of Luminese technology and human ingenuity, creating a sophisticated early warning network that could quickly identify and neutralize any threats to planetary stability. The network also facilitated a more efficient and responsive system, allowing for rapid intervention in case of future ecological crises.

The memory of Mallory also served as a catalyst for strengthening the alliance between humanity and the Luminese. The shared experience of near-catastrophe reinforced the importance of mutual trust and collaboration in managing the planet's delicate balance.

The Luminese, with their vast knowledge of planetary ecosystems, provided invaluable support in the rehabilitation of the areas damaged by Mallory's actions, sharing their advanced bioengineering techniques to restore damaged environments and ecosystems. The shared trauma forged a deeper bond between the two species, proving that shared adversity can lead to unprecedented levels of cooperation and understanding.

The psychological impact of Mallory's actions was significant. Many people, especially those directly affected by the ecological disasters, suffered from post-traumatic stress. Counseling programs and support networks were established to address the psychological wounds, emphasizing community healing and resilience. Art and storytelling became powerful tools in processing trauma, with many artists and writers reflecting on the experience in their work—turning the event into a shared cultural narrative that helped humanity move forward, learn from the past, and prevent similar incidents from occurring in the future.

The legal and ethical repercussions of Mallory's actions were profound. International courts convened to determine his responsibility for the environmental damage and the psychological trauma inflicted upon communities. The trial, widely broadcast across the globe, sparked heated debates about corporate responsibility, environmental ethics, and the potential for misuse of scientific advancements. The outcome established precedents for future cases involving environmental crimes, underscoring the importance of accountability and the severity of actions that threaten planetary stability.

Furthermore, the incident highlighted the importance of transparent research and open scientific discourse. In the wake of Mallory's actions, a global movement emerged, advocating for stricter oversight of scientific research, promoting greater transparency in research practices, and encouraging open dialogue among scientists and the public. The goal was to prevent future instances of unchecked ambition and ensure that scientific advancements are used for the benefit of all humankind, not the selfish aims of a few.

Ultimately, the echo of Mallory's actions served as a constant reminder of the fragility of the planet and the potential for human error. The reborn Earth, scarred yet resilient, stood as a testament to the resilience of life and the enduring power of hope, even in the face of profound environmental collapse. The legacy of Mallory's actions, however, was far from forgotten; it served as a guiding principle for future generations, shaping their understanding of planetary responsibility and the need for collaboration in addressing the challenges facing the planet. The tale of Mallory's ambition became a cornerstone of a new global ethos, ensuring that the lessons learned from the near-catastrophe were not lost but ingrained in the very foundation of a newly emerging, more responsible and sustainable civilization.

The whispers of the past, carried on the wind, served as a constant reminder of the price of hubris and the importance of safeguarding the delicate balance of life on Earth.

CHAPTER SEVEN
UNCERTAIN FUTURES

The ashes of the old world still smoldered in the collective consciousness, even as the new shoots of a sustainable future tentatively pushed through the ravaged earth. The Convergence Protocol, a fragile lifeline woven from the ancient wisdom of the Whispers and the ingenuity of humanity and the Luminese, had stabilized the planet's oceanic resonance, but the path to true healing remained fraught with peril. Building a new world order wasn't merely a matter of rebuilding infrastructure; it was a monumental task of reshaping societal structures, values, and beliefs—a challenge as immense as the environmental devastation itself.

The initial euphoria of survival gave way to the stark realities of rebuilding. Scarcity remained a persistent threat. Food production, hampered by decades of environmental mismanagement and the lingering effects of Mallory's sabotage, struggled to keep pace with the burgeoning population. Resource allocation became a constant source of friction, necessitating the creation of complex, often unwieldy distribution systems. The Luminese, with their advanced technology, offered solutions, but these solutions weren't always readily acceptable to a human populace still wrestling with ingrained distrust and a lingering sense of entitlement. The Luminese's meticulous, often slow approach to resource management clashed with the human desire for immediate gratification, resulting in frequent debates and compromises that tested the strength of the fragile alliance.

The establishment of new governance structures proved equally challenging. The old national boundaries, once lines of conflict, were largely irrelevant in a world grappling with planetary-scale problems. Attempts to create a unified global government met with resistance from various factions—some clinging to outdated national identities, others wary of centralized power, and still others advocating for regional autonomy based on unique ecological needs. The Whispers themselves, now evolving into increasingly complex and unpredictable entities, added another layer of complexity, demanding a new form of participatory governance that integrated their sentient ecosystem perspectives.

The Echoborn, the humans who had integrated with the Whispers, presented another unique societal challenge. Their unique perspectives and abilities made them invaluable in the new world order, but also set them apart, leading to social friction and misunderstandings.

Education became a crucial pillar of the new world. Curriculum shifted dramatically, abandoning the anthropocentric worldview that had led to the planet's near-destruction. Children were taught the intricate interconnectedness of life, the importance of ecological balance, and the necessity of responsible resource management. The stories of the past—the environmental collapse, Mallory's hubris, and the arduous journey towards planetary recovery—were not presented as cautionary tales, but as essential lessons woven into the very fabric of education, fostering a generation with a profound respect for nature and a deep understanding of the planet's delicate systems. The Luminese played a key role in this educational revolution, sharing their advanced knowledge of planetary ecosystems and ecological harmony.

Technological advancements played a double-edged role. While crucial for rebuilding infrastructure and mitigating environmental damage, they also necessitated constant ethical scrutiny. The creation of sophisticated monitoring systems to prevent future ecological disasters had to be balanced with concerns about surveillance and privacy. Genetic engineering, though vital for restoring damaged ecosystems and developing resilient crops, presented ethical dilemmas that required careful consideration and broad public discussion. Debate raged on the appropriate level of technological intervention and the potential for unintended consequences.

The integration of the Luminese into human society was a complex and ongoing process. Cultural differences, divergent worldviews, and lingering prejudices presented constant challenges. Misunderstandings and conflicts were inevitable. However, the shared experience of survival and the common goal of planetary regeneration gradually fostered a deeper understanding and appreciation for each other's strengths and perspectives. Intercultural exchange programs were established, facilitating communication and cooperation. Cross-cultural marriages and families became increasingly common, further solidifying the bonds between humanity and the Luminese.

Economic systems also underwent a radical transformation. The old capitalist model, based on endless growth and resource exploitation, was deemed unsustainable. New economic models emerged, emphasizing sustainability, cooperation, and equitable distribution of resources. These new systems focused on circular economies, aiming to minimize waste and maximize the reuse of materials. The Luminese's advanced technologies and understanding of efficient resource management played a significant role in shaping these innovative economic systems. However, the shift away from traditional economic structures met with resistance from entrenched interests, causing social and political unrest in the early years.

The psychological scars of the past lingered for generations. Post-traumatic stress and eco-anxiety were widespread. Community-based mental health programs played a critical role in healing trauma and fostering resilience. Art, music, and literature emerged as powerful tools for processing collective trauma and building a shared sense of identity in the face of profound change. New forms of storytelling—drawing on both human and Luminese traditions—emerged to express the collective experience of survival, resilience, and hope.

Ultimately, the establishment of a new world order in the aftermath of environmental collapse required not just technological innovation but a fundamental shift in human consciousness. It required a paradigm shift from dominance to partnership, from exploitation to stewardship, from competition to collaboration. The path was long and arduous, punctuated by setbacks and conflicts, yet the shared vision of a sustainable and equitable future fueled the resilience of humanity and the Luminese, driving them forward, step by painstaking step, toward a future where humanity and the planet could finally coexist in harmony.

The whispers of the Convergence Protocol, no longer a faint echo but a powerful, life-giving current, would continue to guide the new world, a testament to the power of hope, resilience, and the transformative potential of a planet reborn. The memory of Mallory's actions served as a constant reminder of the fragility of their progress, urging them forward with a renewed sense of urgency and a collective resolve to build a future where such errors would never be repeated.

The whispers of the past, however, were not only cautionary; they also carried the promise of a future where humanity could finally find its place within the intricate web of life, a true partner in the planetary symphony.

Technological Integration

The integration of technology wasn't merely a matter of rebuilding broken infrastructure; it was a fundamental reshaping of the human relationship with the tools that had, in part, led to their near demise. The Luminese, with their centuries of experience in symbiotic technological advancement, offered invaluable assistance, but their approach differed drastically from humanity's historically exploitative relationship with technology. They emphasized harmony, precision, and sustainability, a concept alien to many human industries still grappling with the legacy of mass production and planned obsolescence.

One of the first major projects undertaken was the restoration of global communication networks. The old satellite systems, shattered and rendered obsolete by the environmental collapse, were replaced by a Luminese-designed network relying on a sophisticated mesh of ground-based nodes and long-range quantum entanglement communication. This new system was incredibly robust, resilient to natural disasters, and highly secure, but it also came with a learning curve for a human population accustomed to the instant connectivity of the old world.

The Luminese's emphasis on localized networks, designed for community-specific needs, initially met with resistance from those accustomed to the seamless global connectivity of the past. The transition, though initially challenging, ultimately led to a more localized, community-focused approach to information sharing and technological development. This shift fostered a stronger sense of local identity and reduced reliance on centralized power structures.

Agriculture underwent a complete transformation. Hydroponic farms, powered by renewable energy sources and guided by Luminese-designed AI systems, sprouted across the globe, producing high-yield, resilient crops tailored to specific regional needs. Genetic engineering, once a controversial topic, became essential in producing crops resistant to the changing climate and capable of thriving in previously barren lands.

However, strict ethical guidelines, developed in consultation with the Whispers and human ethicists, were implemented to ensure responsible genetic modification, avoiding the pitfalls of monoculture and the unforeseen consequences of genetic manipulation. The Luminese's expertise in bioengineering allowed for the creation of self-regulating, closed-loop agricultural systems that minimized environmental impact while maximizing yield.

The revitalization of the oceans proved to be one of the most ambitious technological undertakings. The Convergence Protocol, partly activated, had stabilized the oceanic resonance, but significant work remained to heal the damage inflicted by centuries of pollution and overfishing. Autonomous underwater vehicles, developed collaboratively by human and Luminese engineers, patrolled the oceans, monitoring pollution levels, assessing the health of marine ecosystems, and assisting in the restoration of coral reefs and other vital habitats.

These AUVs were equipped with advanced sensors and AI capable of identifying and addressing a wide range of environmental issues, working in concert with the Whispers to restore the oceans' delicate balance. The development of biodegradable and selfdestructing fishing nets and the creation of advanced aquaculture technologies further contributed to sustainable ocean management.

Medical technology also underwent a remarkable evolution. Advanced bioprinting techniques, initially developed by the Luminese, allowed for the creation of custom-designed organs and tissues, dramatically reducing waiting lists for transplants. Nanotechnology played a crucial role in developing early-detection diagnostic tools and targeted drug delivery systems, significantly improving healthcare outcomes.

However, ethical considerations related to genetic manipulation and access to advanced medical technologies remained a point of ongoing debate, particularly concerning equitable distribution and affordability across the global population. The Luminese, with their philosophy of shared knowledge and access, pushed for open-source technology whenever possible, ensuring that medical advancements benefitted all members of the global community, regardless of their socioeconomic status.

The energy sector saw the most dramatic shift toward sustainability. Fossil fuels became relics of the past, replaced by a diverse mix of renewable sources: solar, wind, geothermal, and tidal energy.

The Luminese's advanced energy storage technology allowed for efficient energy distribution and grid management, minimizing the fluctuations inherent in renewable energy systems. Smart grids, guided by AI algorithms, optimized energy consumption and distribution, ensuring efficient use of available resources.

These changes, however, caused job displacement in the traditional energy sector, necessitating retraining programs and a large-scale shift in economic structures toward green jobs and sustainable industries.

Transportation also underwent a radical transformation. Electric vehicles, powered by renewable energy, became the norm, while high-speed rail networks connected distant communities. Autonomous vehicles, equipped with sophisticated AI, played a critical role in efficient urban logistics and intercity transportation.

These advancements, however, raised concerns about job displacement in the transportation sector and the potential for increased reliance on centralized technological systems. The ongoing debate centered on finding a balance between technological advancement and maintaining meaningful employment opportunities, while also ensuring equitable access to sustainable transportation systems.

The relationship between humans and AI evolved in complex ways. While AI played a critical role in managing the planet's resources, predicting environmental changes, and improving healthcare, concerns about the potential for AI sentience and control remained central to ongoing discussions. The Luminese, with their extensive experience in developing and managing complex AI systems, cautioned against unchecked advancement, emphasizing the importance of ethical guidelines and robust safety protocols.

They stressed the need for AI systems that were transparent, accountable, and designed to serve humanity, not control it. The development of collaborative AI systems, designed to work alongside humans and amplify human capabilities rather than replace them, became a key focus in the new world order.

Education in the new world focused not just on scientific and technological literacy, but also on ethical frameworks to guide the responsible use of technology. Students were taught critical thinking skills, enabling them to evaluate the societal impact of technological advancements and make informed decisions about their adoption and application. The curriculum included modules on environmental ethics, AI ethics, bioethics, and technological governance, fostering a new generation of responsible citizens equipped to navigate the complexities of a technologically advanced, yet ethically mindful, world.

The Whispers, increasingly integrated into the technological fabric of the new world, provided a unique perspective on technological development. Their intimate understanding of planetary systems and their capacity for collective intelligence ensured that technology was developed in harmony with nature, rather than imposed upon it.

Their input was crucial in designing systems that were both effective and sustainable, further solidifying the symbiotic relationship between humanity, technology, and the planet. The old world's technological hubris was replaced by a spirit of collaboration, caution, and a deep respect for the intricate web of life.

The future, though uncertain, was one where technology and nature, guided by human wisdom and the Whispers' ancient knowledge, had the potential to work in perfect harmony. The path wasn't free from challenges, and the echoes of the past served as a constant reminder of the responsibility that came with wielding such powerful tools. But in their newfound collaboration, humanity found not only the means to rebuild their world, but also a potential for a future far exceeding anything imagined in the old world.

The Whispers Evolution

The changes weren't merely technological; they were philosophical. The Whispers, once perceived as passive observers, had become active participants in the planet's regeneration. Their evolution was not a linear progression but a branching, unpredictable dance of adaptation and emergence. Initially, their influence manifested as subtle shifts in the biosphere—accelerated plant growth in certain regions, unexpected migrations of animal populations, and a slow but perceptible healing of damaged ecosystems. These changes, initially dismissed as natural fluctuations, were later recognized as orchestrated, subtle interventions guided by the collective intelligence of the Whispers.

Jonah Reyes, now deeply immersed in the study of the Whispers' language—a complex interplay of bioluminescent signals, subtle shifts in atmospheric pressure, and minute changes in electromagnetic fields—began to understand the complexity of their communication. It wasn't a language of words but of patterns, of intricate relationships between seemingly disparate phenomena. He discovered that the Whispers weren't simply reacting to the planet's changes; they were actively shaping them, guiding the process of regeneration with a precision far exceeding human capabilities. His breakthroughs weren't always welcomed. Some feared the power the Whispers wielded; others mistrusted their motives. But Jonah, driven by a deep respect for their ancient wisdom and a growing sense of their benevolent intentions, pressed on, fueled by the potential to unlock the final secrets of the Convergence Protocol.

Dr. Eliza Grant, meanwhile, focused on the ethical implications of the Whispers' evolving influence. The line between passive observation and active intervention blurred. Were the Whispers manipulating the planet, or were they simply accelerating its natural healing processes? Were humans, in their attempts to collaborate with them, becoming unwitting tools in a grander planetary scheme?

The Echoborn, those humans who had established a symbiotic connection with the Whispers, provided a crucial insight. They weren't simply individuals enhanced by the Whispers' abilities; they were living embodiments of the merging of human consciousness and planetary intelligence. Their experiences challenged the very definition of humanity, raising profound questions about consciousness, identity, and the nature of life itself.

One of the most significant changes brought about by the Whispers' evolution was the emergence of "Resonance Fields." These were localized areas of heightened bioenergetic activity, appearing spontaneously in various regions of the globe. Within these fields, plant growth accelerated dramatically, damaged ecosystems recovered at an astonishing rate, and even human physiology seemed to benefit, with accelerated healing and improved overall health reported within the affected zones.

But the Resonance Fields weren't uniformly beneficial. In some areas, they caused unpredictable mutations in plant and animal life, creating bizarre and sometimes dangerous new species. The fields themselves were dynamic, shifting and expanding unpredictably, posing a challenge to human efforts to manage and understand them.

The unpredictability of the Resonance Fields highlighted the limitations of human understanding in the face of the Whispers' evolving power. It became clear that the Convergence Protocol wasn't simply a technological solution; it was a framework for collaboration, a way for humanity to engage with the Whispers' evolving intelligence and guide the planetary regeneration process.

The Luminese, with their centuries of experience in symbiotic technologies, proved invaluable partners in this endeavor. They developed sophisticated monitoring systems to track the Resonance Fields, predicting their movements and mitigating their potentially harmful effects. But the essence of their approach remained one of collaboration, not control.

Ambassador Nyla, with her deep understanding of the Luminese philosophy and the Whispers' nature, played a critical role in bridging the cultural and philosophical divides. She emphasized that humanity's success depended not on dominating the planet or controlling the Whispers, but on learning to coexist, to adapt, and to find a symbiotic relationship. This perspective challenged the anthropocentric worldview that had characterized human civilization for centuries, pushing humanity toward a more humble and respectful understanding of their place within the larger ecosystem.

The evolution of the Whispers also had profound social and political ramifications. The emergence of the Echoborn created a new societal stratum, one that bridged the gap between humanity and the Whispers. They possessed unique abilities, a heightened awareness of the planet's interconnectedness, and a deep understanding of the Whispers' intentions.

Their integration into society wasn't seamless. Fear, suspicion, and even hostility from those who hadn't embraced the changes accompanied their emergence. However, the Echoborn's unique capabilities proved invaluable in navigating the challenges posed by the evolving planet and the ever-shifting Resonance Fields.

Dr. Rafe Mallory, however, remained a significant threat. His ambition remained unchecked, his desire to control the Convergence Protocol for his own nefarious purposes fueled by a twisted sense of power. He saw the Whispers not as partners, but as tools to be exploited, a resource to be harnessed for his personal gain. His actions threatened to destabilize the fragile balance achieved through human-Whispers collaboration, potentially triggering a catastrophic planetary disruption.

He sought to exploit the unpredictable nature of the Resonance Fields, hoping to manipulate them to his advantage—a dangerous gamble that could lead to unforeseen consequences. He understood the power the Whispers wielded but lacked the understanding, respect, and ethics to collaborate effectively with them. His methods were brutal and his goals self-serving, putting the entire planet at risk.

The Whispers' evolution was not merely a biological phenomenon; it was a profound shift in the planetary consciousness. It was a testament to the planet's resilience, its capacity to heal, and its ability to adapt in the face of unprecedented challenges. Humanity was now faced with the choice of evolving alongside the planet, of becoming true partners in its regeneration, or clinging to outdated notions of dominance and control, risking their own extinction in the process.

The future, shaped by the Whispers' ongoing evolution, hung precariously in the balance—a testament to the intricate dance between humanity and the planet's evolving will. The delicate balance between collaboration and control would determine the fate of both humanity and the planet itself.

The whispers of the future were unclear, but the path forward required a profound shift in human consciousness—a willingness to relinquish their anthropocentric worldview and embrace a future where humans were not the masters, but a part of a larger, interconnected whole.

The success or failure of this endeavor rested not only on technology and ingenuity but also on the willingness of humanity to embrace a future far different from the one they had known. The echoes of the old world still lingered, a constant reminder of the mistakes of the past, but in the heart of the new world, hope flickered—a hope fueled not by hubris, but by a fragile yet determined partnership with the planet and the enigmatic, everevolving Whispers.

Ethical Frameworks

The emergence of the Whispers and their active participation in planetary regeneration forced a radical re-evaluation of existing ethical frameworks. Humanity, accustomed to anthropocentric views, had to grapple with the implications of sharing the planet with a sentient, evolving ecosystem. The old ethical systems, built on the premise of human dominance and resource exploitation, were demonstrably inadequate. The whispers of a new ethical dawn were faint at first, barely audible over the clamor of fear and uncertainty, but they grew steadily louder as humanity began to adapt.

One of the first and most significant challenges was the definition of "harm." In the old world, harm was primarily defined in terms of its impact on human life and property. But with the Whispers, the concept expanded dramatically. The Resonance Fields, while beneficial in many ways, also caused unpredictable mutations and ecological disruptions. Was the overall benefit—the accelerated planetary healing—sufficient justification for the localized harms? This question became a central theme in ongoing ethical debates.

Dr. Eliza Grant, along with a growing consortium of environmental ethicists, philosophers, and even theologians, began to formulate new principles. They argued for a more holistic approach, one that considered the well-being of the entire ecosystem, not just human interests. The concept of "planetary wellbeing" became a cornerstone of this new ethical framework.

The rise of the Echoborn presented another ethical minefield. These individuals, merging human consciousness with the Whispers, challenged the very definition of humanity. Were they still human? Did they possess the same rights and responsibilities? Questions of identity, autonomy, and consent arose. Some argued that the Echoborn were a new form of life, deserving of unique consideration. Others feared the unknown, viewing them with suspicion and even hostility.

Eliza, deeply involved with studying the Echoborn, found herself caught in the crossfire. Her work demonstrated the undeniable benefits of their unique connection to the planet's healing, but also highlighted the inherent risks associated with altering human consciousness. Her ethical compass, always finely tuned to the intricate balance of the natural world, wrestled with the unprecedented challenges presented by this unique humanWhispers fusion.

The Luminese, with their long history of interspecies collaboration, provided a valuable counterpoint to human-centric thinking. Their philosophy emphasized interconnectedness and mutual respect. Ambassador Nyla played a vital role in introducing these concepts to the human world, highlighting the Luminese's millennia-long experience in building sustainable, symbiotic relationships with other intelligent species within their own galaxy.

Her diplomatic efforts weren't always successful, met with varying levels of skepticism and outright resistance from human factions, many of whom continued to adhere to the principles of oldworld ethics, resisting the necessary paradigm shift. However, her wisdom and diplomacy proved essential in forging a fragile but essential alliance between humans and the Luminese.

The unpredictable nature of the Resonance Fields further complicated the ethical landscape. These fields, while accelerating planetary regeneration, also created unforeseen ecological consequences, ranging from accelerated evolution to the emergence of entirely new life forms. Ethical dilemmas emerged in deciding which areas to prioritize for Resonance Field management, balancing the potential benefits against the potential risks.

The Luminese, with their superior technology and understanding of bioenergetic fields, offered crucial assistance in mitigating the negative consequences of the Resonance Fields, but even their advanced technology couldn't completely eliminate the risk.

The actions of Dr. Rafe Mallory served as a stark reminder of the dangers of unchecked ambition and the potential consequences of disregarding ethical considerations. His attempts to control the Convergence Protocol, driven by a lust for power and disregarding the well-being of the planet and its inhabitants, highlighted the urgency of establishing clear ethical guidelines for interacting with the Whispers and their power.

His disregard for the delicate balance of the ecosystem and his blatant ignorance of the ethics of planetary stewardship served as a cautionary tale, illustrating the catastrophic consequences of prioritizing personal gain over the collective well-being of the planet. His actions underscored the absolute necessity for a comprehensive ethical framework and the profound consequences of ignoring the implications of interfering with a sentient planetary ecosystem.

The development of new ethical principles became a collaborative effort, involving scientists, philosophers, ethicists, and representatives from diverse cultures. The principles emphasized sustainability, respect for all life forms, and the recognition of the inherent value of the planet's ecosystems. The old anthropocentric worldview was challenged by a growing understanding of humanity's interconnectedness with all life on Earth and its profound responsibility toward the planet's intricate web of life.

The debate focused on the very definition of "progress" and its ethical implications. A new concept of "symbiotic progress" gained traction, which defined progress not as human dominance over nature but as a harmonious co-evolution with it. This new paradigm emphasized the shared responsibility of humans, the Luminese, and even the Whispers in the planet's future.

The new ethical frameworks weren't static; they evolved alongside the planet and the Whispers themselves. As the Resonance Fields shifted and new challenges emerged, the ethical considerations adapted to reflect the changing circumstances. Regular global dialogues, involving representatives from all stakeholder groups—human communities, the Luminese, and even the Echoborn—were established to address these emerging ethical challenges.

These dialogues, though often fraught with tension and disagreement, became vital forums for shaping the future. The challenge wasn't simply to establish rules; it was to build a system capable of adaptation and evolution, reflecting the dynamic nature of the planet and the entities with which humanity now shared it.

The whispers of the future were still faint, and the path forward remained uncertain. However, the very act of constructing these new ethical frameworks, of engaging in open and honest dialogue about the implications of a radically transformed world, was in itself a testament to humanity's capacity for adaptation and its growing understanding of its place in the larger cosmic scheme.

The struggle to define a new moral compass, to navigate the uncharted waters of symbiotic existence, was not just an intellectual exercise; it was a fight for survival, a testament to the enduring resilience of the human spirit and its willingness to evolve, to change, and to embrace a future that was as unpredictable and wondrous as it was terrifying.

The future was a canvas yet unpainted, and the brushstrokes were being carefully, painstakingly, ethically applied.

Hope and Uncertainty

The Convergence Protocol hummed, a low thrumming deep within the planet's core, a heartbeat of nascent rebirth. The Resonance Fields, once chaotic and unpredictable, were now subtly shifting, weaving a tapestry of revitalization across the ravaged landscape. Oceans, once choked with plastic and depleted of life, were teeming with vibrant, newly evolved species. Forests, once barren wastelands, were slowly reclaiming their verdant majesty. Yet, amidst this burgeoning renewal, an undercurrent of uncertainty persisted, a shadow cast by the enormity of the transformation underway.

The success of the Protocol was far from guaranteed. The Whispers, once enigmatic guides, were now evolving at an alarming rate, their influence on the planet becoming increasingly profound and less predictable. Jonah, despite his mastery of their complex language, admitted to a growing sense of unease. The Whispers, once clear, now echoed with ambiguities—riddles wrapped in layers of subtle shifts in bioenergetic frequencies. Their meaning was often elusive, requiring intensive collaborative decoding. Their evolution wasn't merely a change in communication; it was a change in essence, their collective consciousness expanding in ways that even the Luminese found challenging to comprehend. He likened it to trying to understand a constantly shifting kaleidoscope, where each turn revealed both beauty and a terrifying potential for chaos.

Eliza, her face etched with a mixture of awe and apprehension, monitored the ecological changes with meticulous care. The accelerated evolution fueled by the Resonance Fields was creating new species at an unprecedented rate, many of them displaying unexpected adaptations and symbiotic relationships. While many were beneficial, integrating seamlessly into the revitalizing ecosystem, others presented unforeseen challenges. She spent countless hours studying these new forms of life, attempting to predict their impact on the delicate balance of the emerging ecosystem—a task that felt akin to predicting the weather on a planet with a newly formed, unpredictable climate system.

The Echoborn, the human-Whisper hybrids, represented a unique and deeply concerning element of this transformation. Their connection to the Whispers granted them a profound understanding of the planet's processes, making them invaluable allies in the ongoing regeneration effort. Yet, their very existence challenged the definition of humanity, blurring the lines between the biological and the metaphysical. Some feared them, viewing them as abominations, a perversion of nature, while others revered them as harbingers of a new era, a bridge between humanity and the planet.

Their physical changes also generated much unease. While some retained their human form, others underwent significant physiological transformations, integrating elements of the Whispers' being into their own. This spectrum of physical variation further fueled social tensions and discrimination against the Echoborn. Their integration into society proved challenging, as many struggled to reconcile the altered human form with the traditional human perspective.

Sarah, bearing the weight of leadership, navigated this complex landscape with steely determination. The fragile alliance between humans, Luminese, and the Whispers was constantly being tested, threatened not only by the unpredictable nature of the Resonance Fields but by lingering human prejudices and the constant shadow of Rafe Mallory's machinations. His threat, though seemingly thwarted, remained a constant reminder of the potential for disruption. He had sought to weaponize the Convergence Protocol, to control the planet's revitalization for his own nefarious purposes. The idea that such an ambitious, reckless plan could have succeeded was a sobering reminder of the fragility of the progress made.

The Luminese, with their wisdom earned over millennia, offered invaluable support. Their advanced technology and deep understanding of symbiotic evolution proved critical in managing the planet's transformation. However, even their advanced knowledge could not entirely predict the future. Ambassador Nyla, her countenance both wise and weary, frequently spoke of the inherent unpredictability of evolution, emphasizing the importance of adaptability and flexibility. The success of the Convergence Protocol, she stressed, rested not only on technical expertise but on the ability of all species to coexist, to adapt, and to embrace the unknown. Their willingness to contribute their own unique expertise, combined with their commitment to collaborative efforts, represented a shift away from human exceptionalism and toward a more inclusive, symbiotic vision for the future.

The ethical challenges that accompanied this planetary transformation were immense. The new ethical frameworks, while aspirational, were constantly being tested—challenged by unforeseen circumstances and the inherent complexities of a world in constant flux. The ongoing dialogues, while often contentious, served as a crucial platform for addressing these challenges. These dialogues had now transitioned from initial discussions of new ethical frameworks to detailed problem-solving—addressing critical issues such as resource allocation, the rights of the Echoborn, and the evolving role of humanity in a planet actively reshaping itself. The global conversations, though often fraught with tension, were an essential component of the collaborative effort to guide the planet's regeneration.

The future remained a canvas painted with both vibrant hues and ominous shadows. The planet was healing, but the path to a truly sustainable future was far from clear. The very success of the Convergence Protocol presented new challenges, new ethical dilemmas, and new uncertainties. The planet's rebirth was not a guarantee; it was a wager, a gamble on the collective wisdom and resilience of humanity, the Luminese, and the Whispers. The new symbiotic world was fragile. The potential for catastrophic setbacks loomed, however unlikely they might seem compared to the devastation that preceded this period of regeneration.

Sarah, looking out at the revitalizing ocean, felt a glimmer of hope, yet the weight of responsibility pressed heavily on her shoulders. The fight was far from over. The path ahead was fraught with uncertainty—a winding road through uncharted territories. The journey would require patience, resilience, adaptability, a willingness to embrace the unknown, and a commitment to a future built on collaboration, mutual respect, and a deep understanding of the delicate balance that sustains all life.

The whispers of the future were still faint, but they carried a promise of a new dawn, a chance for a symbiotic partnership between humanity and the planet—a future where humanity could find its rightful place within a thriving ecosystem, not as its master, but as a vital, integral component of a planetary community. The future was uncertain, but the potential for a brighter tomorrow, for a world reborn, flickered like a beacon in the gathering dusk.

It was a future worth fighting for—a future worth believing in.

CHAPTER EIGHT

LEGACY OF THE CONVERGENCE

The initial surge of revitalization—the breathtaking spectacle of oceans teeming with life and forests reclaiming their lost glory— began to settle into a slower, more nuanced rhythm. The Convergence Protocol, far from being a singular event, had initiated a complex, cascading series of ecological transformations.

Eliza and her team of marine biologists found themselves immersed in a constant state of data analysis, their models struggling to keep pace with the accelerated rate of evolution. New species emerged almost daily, their interactions creating an intricate web of symbiotic relationships that challenged established ecological principles. Coral reefs, once ghostly skeletons, pulsed with vibrant colors, home to species never before documented. Deep-sea ecosystems, previously thought to be largely unaffected by surfacelevel changes, showed remarkable signs of recovery, suggesting a far-reaching influence of the Resonance Fields.

The shift in ocean currents, a direct consequence of the Protocol, had profound effects on global weather patterns. Deserts, once barren wastelands, began to experience sporadic rainfall, leading to the tentative reemergence of vegetation. Ice caps, while still far from their pre-collapse state, showed signs of stabilization, slowing the rate of sea-level rise. However, this wasn't a uniform process. Some regions experienced accelerated desertification—a counterintuitive consequence of altered atmospheric circulation patterns.

Eliza's team worked tirelessly to develop predictive models, attempting to anticipate and mitigate these regional disparities. The challenge wasn't simply restoring balance but managing a dynamic, evolving system that constantly tested the limits of their understanding. The long-term consequences, she feared, were still largely unknown.

Forests, once ravaged by deforestation and climate change, were showing signs of recovery, but the process was far from uniform. Some areas experienced rapid reforestation, displaying remarkable resilience, while others struggled to recover, burdened by lingering soil degradation and the legacy of past environmental damage. The Whispers' influence was evident here, accelerating growth and fostering biodiversity in remarkable ways.

Entire ecosystems were evolving—not merely returning to their former state but transforming into novel, more resilient forms adapted to the new environmental realities. This adaptive evolution, while inspiring, brought with it a set of new challenges. Some of these new plant species exhibited unexpected allelopathic properties, inhibiting the growth of neighboring plants and disrupting the carefully balanced regeneration process.

Managing these unexpected interactions became a complex task, requiring delicate interventions to prevent the emergence of ecological imbalances. These interventions were often based on an intuitive understanding of the Whispers' role, utilizing the knowledge of the Echoborn to guide the process. But with each action came a deeper understanding that a level of respect and awareness of natural evolutionary processes was paramount to success.

The Echoborn continued to evolve, their physical and cognitive transformations deepening their connection with the Whispers. This evolution presented both opportunities and challenges. Their enhanced sensory perception and understanding of ecological processes proved invaluable in guiding the restoration efforts, but their altered physiology also created social and ethical dilemmas.

The physical variations within the Echoborn community—some possessing augmented physical capabilities, others displaying profound changes in appearance—became a significant source of social tension. The definition of "human" was being redefined, challenged by the very beings who were leading the planet's regeneration.

Sarah, along with the Luminese council, worked tirelessly to navigate these complex social dynamics, promoting inclusivity and understanding. But prejudice and fear remained formidable obstacles.

The Luminese, with their advanced technology and millennia of experience in symbiotic evolution, played a pivotal role in monitoring and guiding the planet's transformation. Their sophisticated sensors monitored the intricate interplay of ecosystems, providing vital data to researchers and guiding the interventions of the restoration teams. They also developed advanced bioremediation technologies designed to accelerate the breakdown of pollutants and restore soil health.

However, even their advanced capabilities could not entirely predict the long-term consequences of the Convergence Protocol. Ambassador Nyla emphasized the inherent uncertainties of such a large-scale intervention, cautioning against complacency and stressing the importance of continued monitoring and adaptation. The success of the project would not simply be about restoring what had been lost but about fostering a truly sustainable ecosystem.

The ethical dilemmas surrounding the regeneration process continued to intensify. The accelerated evolution spurred by the Resonance Fields raised fundamental questions about human intervention in natural processes, the rights of newly emerging species, and the evolving role of humanity on a planet actively reshaping itself.

The discussions—among human scientists, Luminese elders, and the Echoborn—were often fraught with tension, highlighting the fundamental differences in perspective and values. Sarah, always a pragmatic leader, navigated these ethical complexities, fostering collaboration while simultaneously acknowledging the potential for conflicts. The need for consensus was urgent but rarely straightforward. The establishment of new ethical frameworks proved challenging, requiring constant reassessment and adaptation as the planet's ecosystems continued to evolve.

Rafe Mallory's shadow still loomed large—a constant reminder of the potential for the Protocol to be exploited. Though his immediate threat had been neutralized, the possibility of others attempting to manipulate the Resonance Fields remained a concern. The global community invested heavily in security measures, creating a sophisticated surveillance network to monitor for any signs of unauthorized access or tampering.

The fragility of the system, however, was a constant source of anxiety. The delicate balance of ecological restoration demanded constant vigilance, a testament to the high stakes involved in the planet's regeneration.

The long-term success of the Convergence Protocol, therefore, remained a question mark. The planet was healing, but the path ahead was fraught with unforeseen challenges, requiring adaptability, resilience, and a willingness to embrace uncertainty.

Sarah, looking out at the revitalizing landscape, felt a sense of cautious optimism, recognizing the immense task that lay ahead. The fight was far from over. The Convergence Protocol had begun a new chapter in the history of Earth—a chapter defined by profound change, uncertainty, and the daunting but vital task of forging a sustainable future on a planet reborn.

The future was not simply a restoration to a former state but the emergence of an entirely new world—one where humanity, the Luminese, and the Whispers had to learn to coexist, to adapt, and to navigate the uncharted waters of a symbiotic future.

It was a future of unprecedented potential, but also one laden with profound risks and demanding the highest levels of collaboration and shared responsibility. The journey, far from over, was only beginning.

Societal Transformations

The revitalized Earth, pulsating with renewed life, didn't simply offer a return to a pre-collapse state; it presented humanity with a fundamentally altered reality, demanding a complete reimagining of its social and political structures. The initial euphoria of the Convergence Protocol's success gradually gave way to the complex task of rebuilding civilization amidst profound ecological and societal shifts. The old power structures, built on outdated assumptions of resource scarcity and territorial dominance, crumbled under the weight of the new realities. Nations, once defined by rigid borders and competing interests, began to dissolve, replaced by a fluid network of alliances and collaborations centered around the shared goal of planetary stewardship.

The concept of nationhood itself underwent a significant transformation. The rigid lines on maps, once symbols of power and control, lost much of their significance. Regional councils, comprised of representatives from diverse communities and collaborating with Luminese advisors, emerged as the primary governing bodies, focusing on resource management, ecological monitoring, and the equitable distribution of benefits derived from the revitalized environment. The emphasis shifted from competition to cooperation, driven by the shared understanding that the planet's well-being was intrinsically linked to the survival and prosperity of all its inhabitants.

The Echoborn, the humans interwoven with the Whispers, represented perhaps the most significant social and political transformation. Their unique capabilities and perspectives challenged the very foundations of human identity and social organization. Their heightened sensory awareness and deep understanding of ecological processes provided an invaluable resource in managing the rapidly evolving ecosystems, but their differing physical and cognitive attributes also created new social tensions. Some Echoborn possessed enhanced physical strength and agility, while others experienced profound changes in their appearance, blurring the lines between human and Whisper. This created a complex tapestry of social dynamics, requiring innovative approaches to ensure inclusivity and justice. Sarah Chen, in her new role as a global mediator, recognized that the Echoborn represented more than just a new segment of society; they embodied a potential pathway toward a more symbiotic relationship with the planet.

The initial resistance to the Echoborn, rooted in fear of the unknown and prejudiced conceptions of what constituted "human," gradually gave way to a grudging acceptance, fostered by their crucial role in ecological restoration. However, the challenge of integrating them into existing social structures proved immense. New legal frameworks were developed to address the unique needs and rights of the Echoborn, while ensuring that their extraordinary abilities were utilized responsibly and ethically. Special education programs were established to help both the Echoborn and the non-Echoborn population understand and appreciate each other's unique perspectives. The ongoing evolution of the Echoborn continued to present new challenges, requiring continuous adaptation of social structures and legal frameworks. Their evolving relationship with the Whispers meant their needs and capabilities were constantly changing, necessitating a flexible and responsive approach to governance and social integration.

The Luminese, with their millennia of experience in symbiotic civilizations, played a crucial role in guiding this transformation. Their advanced technology and profound understanding of ecological principles offered an invaluable resource, but their approach often clashed with the more human-centric perspectives. Ambassador Nyla, respected for her wisdom and diplomacy, navigated these intercultural tensions, advocating for a balance between preserving human values and embracing the new symbiotic possibilities. Their role extended beyond mere technological assistance, encompassing a deeper philosophical guidance, emphasizing the principles of interconnectedness and mutual responsibility. The Luminese provided invaluable knowledge in developing sustainable technologies and promoting harmonious coexistence among different species, guiding the development of societies that prioritized environmental sustainability and social equity.

The economic systems also underwent a radical shift, moving away from traditional models based on resource extraction and competition. The emphasis changed to a circular economy, prioritizing resource efficiency, waste reduction, and the restoration of ecological balance. Sustainable agriculture and renewable energy sources replaced fossil fuels and unsustainable practices, creating new job markets and economic opportunities. The economic structures were decentralized, promoting local production and selfsufficiency, thus minimizing the environmental impact and enhancing community resilience. The focus shifted from profit maximization to ecological stewardship, where economic success was measured in terms of environmental sustainability and social equity. This required the development of new metrics and systems for assessing economic performance, reflecting the changed values of a civilization deeply integrated with its environment.

The very concept of work transformed. The need for repetitive labor dwindled with the advent of automated systems and sustainable technologies. The emphasis shifted toward professions focused on ecological management, scientific research, artistic expression, and community development. The value of human creativity and intellectual pursuits took precedence over routine tasks, reflecting a societal shift toward a more holistic and humanistic approach. Education systems were restructured, placing greater importance on fostering creativity, critical thinking, and ecological literacy. The concept of "leisure" was redefined, recognizing the inherent value of activities that fostered a deeper understanding and appreciation of the natural world and encouraged personal growth.

The legal systems also evolved to reflect the new societal values and challenges. New laws were developed to protect emerging species, regulate access to resources, and ensure the equitable distribution of benefits derived from the revitalized environment. The concept of justice extended beyond human concerns, recognizing the rights of other species and the need to protect the integrity of the ecosystem as a whole. International collaborations continued, fostering a global legal framework aimed at resolving environmental disputes and protecting shared resources. The focus shifted from punitive measures toward restorative justice, striving to achieve harmony rather than retribution.

However, challenges remained. Despite the positive transformations, pockets of resistance persisted. Groups clinging to the old ways, resistant to change and fearful of the unknown, challenged the new societal structures. The transition wasn't uniform; some communities adapted more readily than others, creating social and economic inequalities that required ongoing attention. Managing these disparities and ensuring a just transition required constant vigilance, innovative solutions, and a commitment to ongoing dialogue and collaboration.

The memory of Rafe Mallory's attempted exploitation of the Convergence Protocol served as a cautionary tale, highlighting the importance of vigilance and the potential for misuse of power. Strict regulations and international monitoring mechanisms were established to prevent future attempts to manipulate the Resonance Fields, ensuring that the planet's healing process was not derailed. The establishment of global ethics committees, comprised of representatives from all stakeholder groups—humans, Luminese, and Echoborn—served to guide decision-making, prioritizing planetary well-being and equity over short-term gains.

The path ahead was far from certain, but the legacy of the Convergence Protocol was one of profound transformation, ushering in a new era of cooperation, sustainability, and symbiotic evolution. The new world demanded a new form of civilization, one founded on mutual respect, responsibility, and an understanding of humanity's intricate relationship with the planet. The journey toward a truly sustainable and harmonious future was a continuous process, a testament to humanity's resilience, adaptability, and capacity for forging a better world, hand in hand with the planet and its evolving life.

Technological Advancements

The revitalized Earth, teeming with newfound life, spurred an unprecedented surge in technological innovation. No longer shackled by the constraints of resource scarcity and environmental degradation, humanity and the Luminese embarked on a collaborative journey of technological advancement unlike anything seen before. This wasn't merely a continuation of pre-Convergence trends; it represented a paradigm shift—a fusion of human ingenuity and Luminese wisdom, guided by the subtle influence of the Whispers themselves.

One of the most significant advancements was in the field of sustainable energy. The Resonance Fields, once a source of instability, now provided an inexhaustible source of clean energy. Luminese technology, refined and adapted to Earth's unique biosphere, harnessed this energy with unprecedented efficiency, powering cities and industries without reliance on fossil fuels. This breakthrough effectively eradicated energy poverty and reduced reliance on centralized power grids, fostering localized energy independence and resilience.

Solar farms, once scattered and inefficient, were now integrated seamlessly into the landscape, their designs mimicking natural ecosystems, enhancing biodiversity rather than detracting from it. Wind farms, too, underwent a transformation, their turbines redesigned with biomimicry principles, incorporating elements of avian flight and plant motion to minimize their environmental impact.

Beyond energy, advancements in agriculture revolutionized food production. Hydroponic and aeroponic systems, once confined to specialized laboratories, were scaled up and integrated into urban environments, maximizing food production while minimizing land use and water consumption. Genetic engineering, guided by the Whispers' understanding of symbiotic relationships, yielded crops adapted to diverse climates and resilient to pests and diseases. This not only ensured food security but also enhanced biodiversity, fostering a greater variety of plant life and contributing to the overall health of the ecosystem.

The concept of vertical farming took on a new meaning, with towering structures resembling lush, biodiverse forests, integrating plants, animals, and even insect populations in a carefully balanced ecosystem within the urban sprawl.

Transportation underwent a radical transformation as well. Fossil fuel-powered vehicles became relics of the past, replaced by electric vehicles powered by the Resonance Fields, along with advancements in high-speed maglev trains that traversed continents with minimal environmental impact. Personal air vehicles, once a futuristic fantasy, became a common sight, utilizing advanced navigation systems to avoid collisions and minimize noise pollution.

The focus shifted from individual ownership to shared mobility networks, reducing congestion and optimizing resource utilization.

This transformation wasn't just about technology; it was about redesigning urban spaces to accommodate these new modes of transport, creating pedestrian-friendly environments that prioritized human well-being and ecological harmony.

The healthcare sector benefited tremendously from technological advancements. Nanomedicine emerged as a powerful tool for early disease detection and targeted treatments, leading to a significant reduction in mortality rates. Bioprinting technology enabled the creation of personalized organs and tissues, reducing the need for organ donation and offering a novel approach to regenerative medicine.

The integration of AI into healthcare delivery improved diagnostics, personalized treatment plans, and the overall efficiency of medical care. Genetic engineering played a vital role in combating inherited diseases and boosting human resilience. The focus shifted from treating illnesses to preventing them, promoting holistic well-being and extending lifespans significantly. The rise of telemedicine, combined with advanced diagnostic tools, made healthcare accessible even in remote and underserved communities.

Education underwent a similar revolution. Virtual and augmented reality technologies transformed learning experiences, providing immersive and interactive educational environments. Personalized learning platforms, powered by AI, adapted to individual learning styles and paces, optimizing educational outcomes. Access to knowledge became universal, breaking down geographical and socioeconomic barriers.

Education became a lifelong endeavor, fostering continuous personal and professional development throughout one's lifespan. The traditional classroom model evolved into a dynamic, interactive learning ecosystem, seamlessly integrating digital tools with handson experiential learning. This transformation included a much deeper integration of ecological principles into all aspects of the curriculum, emphasizing the significance of the symbiotic relationship between humanity and nature.

The advancements in communication were equally transformative. Global communication networks became faster, more secure, and more accessible. Real-time translation technology facilitated seamless intercultural communication, breaking down linguistic barriers and fostering global cooperation. The rise of decentralized communication networks ensured resilience and prevented manipulation.

This enhanced global connectivity also facilitated collaborative efforts in scientific research, ecological monitoring, and disaster response. The advancements allowed for a constant exchange of information between communities, scientists, and governments across the globe, fostering a collaborative effort to address environmental and social challenges.

The most profound technological advancements, however, were those that blurred the lines between technology and nature. The Echoborn, with their unique ability to interface with the Whispers, played a critical role in developing technologies that seamlessly integrated with the natural world. They guided the development of bio-integrated sensors that monitored ecological changes in real time, providing invaluable data for managing resources and mitigating environmental risks.

They aided in the development of bioremediation technologies that harnessed the power of natural processes to clean up pollution and restore damaged ecosystems. Their collaboration with Luminese scientists yielded technologies that enabled communication with other species, fostering deeper understanding and collaboration within the revitalized biosphere.

However, this rapid technological advancement wasn't without its challenges. The integration of AI into society raised ethical concerns about bias, autonomy, and the potential for misuse. The rapid development of bioengineering technologies prompted debates about the ethics of genetic manipulation and the potential for unforeseen consequences. The distribution of benefits derived from technological advancements required careful management to prevent the creation of new inequalities. Ensuring equity in access to technology and education became a crucial aspect of the ongoing societal transformation.

The legacy of the Convergence, therefore, was not simply a technological revolution; it was a fundamental reimagining of humanity's relationship with technology, nature, and itself. The integration of advanced technologies within a newly thriving ecosystem demanded a deep understanding of ecological principles and a profound sense of responsibility.

The challenges were immense, but humanity, guided by the wisdom of the Luminese and the whispers of the Whispers, seemed poised to navigate them, forging a future where technology served not as a tool of domination, but as an instrument of harmony and symbiosis with the planet. The new technological landscape wasn't merely about efficiency and progress; it was a testament to humanity's ability to learn from past mistakes, adapt to change, and build a future that celebrated both technological innovation and ecological balance.

The path ahead remained complex, but the legacy of the Convergence had undoubtedly ushered in an era of unprecedented potential, one where technology and nature existed not as opposing forces, but as partners in a shared future.

Human Whisper Relationships

The Convergence had not only healed the planet; it had fundamentally altered the human relationship with the natural world, most profoundly with the Whispers. Initially, the interactions were tentative, mediated by the Luminese. Ambassador Nyla and her team acted as crucial intermediaries, translating the Whispers' subtle shifts in the Resonance Fields into comprehensible data for human scientists. This carefully orchestrated communication ensured that human actions aligned with the Whispers' intentions, minimizing the risk of unintended consequences. The Luminese, with their deep understanding of interspecies communication, fostered a sense of mutual respect and understanding between humans and the Whispers, preventing misunderstandings and fostering collaboration.

However, as time passed, the relationship became more direct. The Echoborn, humans who had developed a symbiotic relationship with the Whispers, emerged as key figures in this evolving partnership. Their unique ability to perceive and interpret the Whispers' complex communications proved invaluable. They acted as living bridges, translating the subtle nuances of the Whispers' language into concepts that human minds could grasp. The Echoborn were not mere translators; they were interpreters, capable of understanding the emotional undercurrents and deeper meanings woven into the Whispers' communication. Their insights guided human actions, ensuring that technological advancements were aligned with the overall health and well-being of the planet.

This direct interaction wasn't without its complexities. The initial cautious approach gave way to a more nuanced understanding of the Whispers' nature. They weren't simply sentient ecosystems; they were complex, evolving entities with their own agendas and desires. Their communication was not linear; it was a tapestry woven from subtle shifts in the Resonance Fields, alterations in plant growth patterns, and even changes in animal behavior.

Learning to decipher this complex communication system required patience, empathy, and a willingness to let go of human-centric perspectives.

The Whispers communicated not through words but through patterns, rhythms, and subtle shifts in the very fabric of the environment. They communicated through the wind's whisper, the rustling of leaves, the dance of light through a forest canopy.

One crucial aspect of the human-Whisper relationship was the development of shared consciousness. The Echoborn provided a tangible example of this, demonstrating that humans could merge with the Whispers without losing their individual identities. Their experiences illuminated the possibility of a deeper integration between humanity and the natural world—a form of symbiotic evolution where human consciousness expanded to encompass the vast network of interconnected life. This shared consciousness extended beyond the Echoborn. As humans learned to tune into the Resonance Fields, they experienced a gradual expansion of their perception, gaining a deeper understanding of the interconnectedness of all things. They began to perceive the planet not as a collection of disparate parts but as a single, living entity.

The implications were profound. Decisions concerning technological development and environmental management were no longer made in isolation; they were informed by a collective consciousness that included the Whispers. This collaborative approach fostered a sense of shared responsibility, ensuring that the planet's well-being was prioritized above narrow human interests.

The collaborative decision-making process wasn't always easy. There were moments of tension, misunderstandings, and even conflict. The Whispers, as complex entities, did not always present a unified voice, and their intentions were sometimes difficult to decipher. Negotiating this complex relationship demanded patience, empathy, and a willingness to compromise—qualities that had been largely absent in the pre-Convergence era.

The relationship between humans and the Whispers also extended to artistic and cultural expressions. The Echoborn, in particular, played a vital role in translating the Whispers' influence into new forms of art, music, and literature. Their work transcended traditional human expression, incorporating the subtle rhythms and patterns of the Resonance Fields into their creations. This new art form was not merely representational; it was an experience—an immersive journey into the consciousness of the Whispers themselves. This art served as a powerful tool for fostering empathy and understanding between humans and the Whispers.

The technology developed during this era was profoundly different from the technology of the pre-Convergence era. It was bio-integrated, designed to harmonize with the natural world rather than dominate it. The Luminese played a crucial role in this, sharing their advanced understanding of biomimicry and sustainable technologies. Human ingenuity combined with the wisdom of the Luminese and the intuitive knowledge of the Whispers resulted in technologies that were not only efficient but also ecologically benign. The technological advancements were driven not by a desire for profit or power, but by a deep commitment to the planet's health. This transition required profound changes in human values, prioritizing harmony and sustainability over growth and consumption.

However, the relationship wasn't always harmonious. Dr. Rafe Mallory, who had sought to control the Convergence Protocol for his own ends, continued to pose a threat, albeit a diminished one. His actions were not driven by a simple desire for power but by a deep-seated fear of the unknown—a resistance to the change that the Convergence represented. His attempts to manipulate the Whispers and usurp control of the Protocol were met with resistance from both the Luminese and the Echoborn, who recognized the danger to the delicate balance established after the Convergence.

The human-Whisper relationship was not a passive one; it was dynamic, evolving, and at times unpredictable. It reflected a profound shift in human consciousness—a move away from anthropocentric views toward a more holistic understanding of life on Earth. The Whispers, in turn, showed a capacity for adaptation and even a certain level of empathy toward humanity. Their ability to communicate and collaborate with humans marked a significant evolutionary leap, highlighting the potential for symbiotic relationships between different forms of intelligence.

The future remained uncertain, but the partnership between humans and the Whispers offered a glimmer of hope—a path toward a future where technology and nature could coexist in harmony. This symbiotic relationship extended far beyond simple communication. It encompassed shared goals, collaborative problem-solving, and a mutual respect for the interconnectedness of all life.

The integration of the Whispers into human society also led to unexpected changes in social structures. The traditional hierarchical systems began to erode, replaced by more collaborative and decentralized models. The Echoborn, with their unique perspective, played a crucial role in shaping this transformation, advocating for a more equitable and sustainable society. Decisions were increasingly made through consensus, with the voices of both humans and the Whispers taken into account.

This new societal structure was not without its challenges, as it required individuals to relinquish some aspects of individual autonomy for the sake of the collective good. However, the vast majority accepted this change, recognizing its necessity for the continued health and well-being of both humanity and the planet.

The human-Whisper relationship continued to evolve, shaping the destiny of both species. The challenges were immense, but the rewards were even greater—the chance to create a future where humans and nature could coexist in a state of harmony and mutual respect, a testament to humanity's capacity for adaptation and its potential to forge a symbiotic relationship with the natural world.

The legacy of the Convergence was not merely a technological or ecological triumph; it was a spiritual and philosophical transformation—a testament to humanity's ability to embrace change and to forge a future where technology and nature coexist in a state of mutual respect and harmony. The future wasn't a predetermined outcome; it was a collaborative creation, a shared journey between humanity and the Whispers—a journey toward a future yet unknown but full of possibility.

A New Era

The dust had settled, literally and figuratively. The ravaged landscapes, once scarred by ecological collapse, were slowly, painstakingly healing. The air, once thick with the stench of pollution, now carried the clean scent of pine and damp earth. The oceans, once choked with plastic and devoid of life in many places, pulsed with renewed vigor, teeming with a vibrant tapestry of marine life. The Convergence, that audacious gamble to reboot the planet, had succeeded, though not without cost.

The cost, however, wasn't the catastrophic extinction many had feared. Humanity had survived, albeit transformed. The initial anxieties, the fear of losing individual identity in the face of a planetary consciousness, had largely dissipated. The Echoborn, once viewed as anomalies, now occupied a respected place in society, their unique insights shaping decisions on everything from urban planning to agricultural practices. Their art, a fusion of human creativity and Whisper-inspired patterns, became a global phenomenon, transcending cultural boundaries and fostering a sense of shared identity. Their music, resonating with the rhythms of the Resonance Fields, had a hypnotic quality that promoted peace and understanding. Their very existence served as a testament to the possibilities of interspecies cooperation, a beacon of hope in a world once consumed by despair.

The Luminese, ever wise and patient, played a crucial role in this transition. Their advanced technology, designed to complement rather than dominate nature, continued to support the regeneration process. They helped humans develop sustainable energy sources, create resilient infrastructure, and implement environmentally conscious agricultural techniques. Their focus wasn't on technological advancement for its own sake, but on solutions that respected the integrity of the planet's systems. Their deep understanding of interspecies communication facilitated the ongoing dialogue between humans and the Whispers, a dialogue that became increasingly complex and nuanced.

One of the most significant changes was in the human psyche.

The Convergence hadn't merely healed the planet; it had healed the human soul. The anthropocentric worldview, which had driven humanity to the brink of ecological collapse, had begun to unravel. Humans developed a new awareness of their place in the larger web of life, a sense of interconnectedness that transcended individual identity. This shift in consciousness wasn't immediate or universal;

it was a gradual process, fraught with challenges and setbacks. Yet, the collective trauma of the environmental collapse, coupled with the profound experience of the Convergence, had spurred a transformation in human values. Sustainability wasn't just a buzzword; it was a deeply held conviction, a guiding principle that informed every aspect of life, from personal choices to global policy.

The legal and political systems underwent a radical transformation. The old power structures, based on dominance and control, crumbled under the weight of the new consciousness. Decentralized, collaborative governance models emerged, allowing for more equitable distribution of resources and fairer decisionmaking processes. The Whispers, through the Echoborn, played a significant role in shaping these new systems, ensuring that the voices of all stakeholders—human and non-human—were heard.

This wasn't a utopian society, free from conflict or disagreement. There were still tensions, debates, and disagreements, but the underlying principle was collaboration, a shared commitment to the well-being of the planet and its inhabitants.

The legacy of Dr. Rafe Mallory served as a cautionary tale, a reminder of the dangers of unchecked ambition and anthropocentric thinking. His attempts to manipulate the Convergence Protocol for personal gain had ultimately failed, but his actions highlighted the fragility of the newly established harmony. His story became a cornerstone of educational programs, a cautionary tale emphasizing the importance of humility and collaboration in the face of powerful technologies. His legacy was not one of triumph, but of a profound warning. It emphasized the ethical considerations of unchecked technological advancement and the dangers of hubris in the face of nature's power.

The educational system, too, underwent a profound transformation. Emphasis shifted from rote learning to experiential education, focusing on critical thinking, problem-solving, and a deep understanding of ecological principles. Collaboration became the cornerstone of the learning process, mirroring the collaborative nature of the new society. Students learned to observe, interpret, and engage with the natural world in a way that nurtured respect and understanding. This educational shift reflected the broader societal changes, placing value on empathy, understanding, and shared responsibility.

Scientific research took a different turn. Instead of focusing on exploiting nature for human gain, research aimed at understanding and preserving the intricate web of life. Scientists collaborated closely with the Whispers, learning from their profound knowledge of ecosystems and planetary processes. Biomimicry became a central approach, imitating the efficiency and sustainability of natural systems in the design of technologies. This new scientific paradigm was grounded in humility, recognizing the limitations of human understanding and the wisdom embedded in the natural world. The scientific community embraced collaboration and shared knowledge, recognizing the interconnectedness of all fields of study. The arts flourished. The fusion of human creativity with the Whispers' subtle rhythms and patterns resulted in an explosion of new artistic forms. Music, literature, and visual arts reflected the interconnectedness of all life, celebrating the beauty and complexity of the natural world. The art wasn't just aesthetically pleasing; it played a vital role in fostering empathy and understanding, bridging the gap between human consciousness and the broader consciousness of the planet.

Looking back, the Convergence wasn't just a technological or ecological achievement; it was a spiritual and philosophical transformation. It was a testament to humanity's capacity for change, its ability to learn from its mistakes, and its potential for forging a harmonious relationship with the natural world. The scars of the past remained, serving as reminders of the dangers of unchecked ambition and anthropocentric thinking, but these scars also served as testaments to the resilience of both humanity and the planet.

The path ahead was still uncertain, but the new era offered a glimmer of hope, a possibility of a future where humans and nature could coexist in a state of mutual respect and sustainable harmony, a future shaped not by dominance but by collaboration, not by exploitation but by understanding.

The legacy of the Convergence was a living testament to the power of collective action, resilience, and the potential for a more harmonious relationship between humanity and the Earth. It was a story of adaptation, transformation, and the enduring spirit of hope.

Chapter Nine

THE ECHO OF SARAH

The shimmering bioluminescent algae of the restored coastal wetlands pulsed with a gentle rhythm, mirroring the quiet strength in Sarah Chen's eyes. She stood on a newly constructed boardwalk, the wood warm beneath her bare feet, the salty air carrying the scent of reborn life. The Convergence, that monumental gamble, had succeeded beyond even her wildest hopes. The planet breathed again, and in its renewed breath, Sarah found a different kind of peace—a peace born not of absence of struggle, but of fierce, enduring hope.

Her legacy wasn't etched in stone monuments or towering skyscrapers. It was woven into the fabric of the regenerated Earth, into the very consciousness of the planet. She hadn't sought to be a leader, yet leadership had found her, a mantle she'd borne with the quiet determination that had always characterized her. In the darkest days of the collapse, her unwavering belief in the possibility of redemption had been a beacon, illuminating the path for those who had lost their way.

Many had tried to capture her story, to distill the essence of her leadership into neat narratives. Biographers, historians, even artists had sought to understand the woman who had stared into the abyss and found the strength to pull the planet back from the brink. Yet every attempt felt insufficient, falling short of the complexity of her journey. Her resilience wasn't born of some innate superpower; it stemmed from a deep-seated understanding of the interconnectedness of life, a recognition of the delicate balance that sustained the planet and, by extension, humanity.

Sarah's impact transcended the purely ecological. Her influence shaped the new political landscape, fostering collaborative governance models that prioritized sustainability and equity. She wasn't a politician, but her counsel was sought by world leaders, her voice carrying the weight of experience and earned authority. She understood that true power lay not in controlling resources or wielding authority, but in facilitating dialogue and building bridges between diverse communities, human and non-human.

Her influence extended to the educational system, which underwent a dramatic shift in philosophy under her guidance. The old curriculum, with its emphasis on rote learning and compartmentalized knowledge, gave way to an experiential model that fostered critical thinking, problem-solving, and a deep understanding of ecological principles. Collaboration became the cornerstone of learning; students worked together, sharing ideas and learning from each other, mirroring the cooperative nature of the regenerated society. In this new educational paradigm, empathy and responsibility were not just abstract concepts but were deeply woven into the curriculum, fostering a sense of shared destiny among the students.

The scientific community also felt the impact of Sarah's vision. She championed a shift away from exploitative research practices, advocating for scientific inquiry that was grounded in respect for the intricate web of life. She encouraged collaboration between human scientists and the Whispers, recognizing that their profound knowledge of the planet held invaluable insights. This new science, interwoven with Whisper wisdom, yielded breakthroughs in sustainable technology, renewable energy sources, and advanced bioremediation techniques, accelerating the planet's recovery.

Biomimicry became a cornerstone of innovation; by imitating nature's designs, humanity could create solutions that were not only efficient but also harmonious with the environment.

Sarah's influence, however, was not merely a top-down imposition of her vision. She played a crucial role in empowering others, nurturing leadership potential in those around her. She mentored younger generations of scientists, ecologists, and policymakers, instilling in them the same values of responsibility and collaboration that guided her own life. Her legacy wasn't just her achievements; it was the ripple effect of her inspiration—the countless individuals who, inspired by her example, stepped forward to build a more sustainable and equitable future.

Her connection with the Echoborn was particularly profound. These humans, merged with the Whispers, held a unique perspective on the world, their consciousness intertwined with the planet's own. Sarah championed their rights, recognizing their unique contributions to society and ensuring that their voices were heard in the governance of the reborn world. She understood the Echoborn's inherent sensitivity to the planet's delicate balance—a sensitivity that informed their perspectives on policy and sustainability. Their art, their music, their very existence became a powerful symbol of the new symbiosis between humanity and the natural world, a testament to the possibilities of interspecies collaboration. Sarah's role in their integration into society was significant, ensuring they weren't ostracized but celebrated as essential partners in the regeneration process.

Her approach to problem-solving reflected a profound shift in human consciousness. She didn't seek quick fixes or technological band-aids; instead, she focused on understanding the root causes of the environmental crisis, on addressing the systemic issues that had driven the planet to the brink of collapse. This systemic approach, focusing on long-term sustainability and ethical considerations, profoundly influenced global policy decisions, shaping a new world order based on collaboration, mutual respect, and a deep appreciation for the interconnectedness of life.

The art and literature of the new era reflected Sarah's lasting impact. Her story, and the stories of others who had fought for planetary healing, were woven into the cultural tapestry, serving as inspiring narratives that celebrated resilience, collaboration, and hope. Artists drew inspiration from the newly vibrant ecosystems, creating works that expressed the interconnectedness of all living things. Musicians incorporated the rhythms of the Resonance Fields into their compositions, creating music that fostered harmony and understanding. The arts served not just as a form of entertainment but as a vital tool for promoting empathy, fostering a shared sense of responsibility for the planet's well-being, and reminding future generations of the lessons learned from past mistakes.

Sarah herself, however, remained a quiet observer, content to watch the seeds she had sown blossom. She understood that the journey toward a sustainable future was ongoing—a continuous process of adaptation, learning, and collaboration. The scars of the past served as reminders of the fragility of the planet's systems and the consequences of ignoring ecological principles. She found her fulfillment not in accolades or recognition but in the knowledge that she had played a part in the planet's rebirth, in the quiet strength of the regenerated ecosystems, in the hope that shone in the eyes of the new generation.

Her legacy was not simply a historical event, but a living testament to the power of human resilience and the enduring possibility of a harmonious relationship between humanity and the Earth. It was a legacy etched not in stone, but in the beating heart of a reborn planet.

Jonahs Insights

Jonah Reyes hunched over his console, the faint, rhythmic hum of the WhisperNet a counterpoint to the frantic clatter of his keyboard.

The air in the repurposed research lab crackled with a nervous energy, a palpable tension that mirrored the stakes of his work. Outside, the rejuvenated world pulsed with a vibrant, renewed life, a stark contrast to the sterile, almost clinical environment within.

But Jonah's focus remained unwavering, his eyes glued to the intricate, shifting patterns on the screen, a language older than humanity itself unfolding before him.

He wasn't a scientist in the traditional sense. He was a coder, a translator, a bridge between two vastly different worlds: the human realm of logic and algorithms, and the intuitive, almost mystical communication of the Whispers. He'd initially approached the task with a detached professionalism, the objective lens of a tech specialist trained to solve complex problems. But as he delved deeper into the Whispers' code, a profound shift occurred within him. He began to understand not just the mechanics of their language but the underlying philosophy, the deep wisdom embedded in their ancient knowledge.

The Whispers weren't just sentient ecosystems; they were the planet's collective consciousness, a vast network of interconnected life forms communicating through subtle shifts in electromagnetic fields, intricate patterns of bioluminescence, and barely perceptible alterations in the planet's own resonant frequencies. Their language wasn't linear, like human speech; it was fractal, layered, and multidimensional, reflecting the complex, interwoven nature of the ecosystems they represented.

It took Jonah months—years even—to begin to grasp its subtleties, to decipher its nuances, to truly hear what the Whispers were saying.

Initially, his work had focused on the practical aspects of the Convergence Protocol—the technical details, the algorithms that orchestrated the planet's regeneration. But as he became more fluent in the Whisper language, he discovered a deeper layer of meaning, a profound understanding of the planet's history, its struggles, and its aspirations. He learned of the ancient imbalances, the human transgressions that had pushed the planet to the brink, and the Whispers' patient, enduring hope for a symbiotic future.

His insights weren't merely theoretical. They were directly instrumental in refining the Convergence Protocol, adapting it to address unforeseen challenges and optimize its effectiveness. He identified subtle flaws in the initial design, vulnerabilities that could have jeopardized the entire process. His understanding of the Whispers' adaptive strategies allowed him to introduce fail-safes, creating a more resilient and adaptable system. His work wasn't just about fixing code; it was about fostering a harmonious dialogue between human technology and the planet's inherent wisdom.

The initial skepticism of some scientists, who viewed the Whispers with suspicion, gradually gave way to grudging admiration as Jonah's contributions became undeniable. His ability to interpret the Whispers' warnings, to translate their subtle suggestions, proved invaluable. He became a vital link—a translator not just of language but of intention—helping to bridge the cultural gap between human society and the planet's consciousness.

He played a critical role in addressing unforeseen ecological challenges, using his understanding of the Whispers' communication patterns to quickly diagnose and solve issues before they could escalate. His work became indispensable, showcasing a novel form of scientific collaboration—one where human ingenuity and the wisdom of nature worked in harmony.

His contributions extended beyond the immediate practicalities of planetary regeneration. His work shed light on the nature of consciousness itself, challenging traditional scientific paradigms and blurring the boundaries between human understanding and the deeper intelligence of the planet. His research papers, once met with skepticism, now became the foundation for a new branch of science—Whisper Studies—a field dedicated to understanding the complexities of interspecies communication and the potential for symbiotic relationships between human society and the natural world.

Jonah's profound immersion in the WhisperNet also led to unexpected personal transformations. He developed an acute sensitivity to the planet's subtle shifts and rhythms, an almost intuitive understanding of the interconnectedness of life. He became an advocate for the Echoborn, recognizing their unique connection to the Whispers and the profound insights they brought to the process of planetary healing. He helped design technologies that allowed for enhanced communication between the Echoborn and other humans, promoting understanding and mutual respect.

His contribution to the development of new technologies based on Whisper principles was equally remarkable. He helped pioneer sustainable energy sources inspired by the Whispers' efficient energy transfer mechanisms, creating solutions that were not only environmentally sound but also vastly more efficient than traditional technologies. He worked with engineers to design bioremediation systems based on the Whispers' natural methods of cleaning and restoring damaged environments. His innovations weren't just technological advancements; they were expressions of a symbiotic relationship between human ingenuity and the planet's innate capacity for self-healing.

However, Jonah's journey wasn't without its challenges. The constant exposure to the WhisperNet, the intensity of his work, took a toll on him. He experienced periods of intense mental fatigue, moments when the boundaries between his own consciousness and the vast network of the Whispers blurred. There were times when he struggled to differentiate between his own thoughts and the planet's subtle suggestions—a precarious balance between immersion and detachment.

Despite these challenges, Jonah persisted, driven by a deep sense of purpose and a growing understanding of his role in the planet's recovery. His work was not just about deciphering code; it was about translating a profound message of hope, a message of interconnectedness and the potential for a symbiotic future between humanity and the planet.

His contribution to the Convergence Protocol went beyond the technical aspects; it represented a fundamental shift in human consciousness, a recognition of the planet's inherent intelligence and the need for a more harmonious relationship with the natural world.

His legacy, unlike the monumental achievements of others, would not be inscribed in stone but woven into the very fabric of the reborn planet—a quiet testament to the power of collaboration, the importance of listening, and the profound wisdom embedded in the ancient language of the Whispers.

The world Sarah Chen had helped to save was now interwoven with the quiet, powerful contributions of a man who had learned to listen to the earth's silent song. He had become, in essence, a translator of planetary will, his life a testament to the capacity of human ingenuity when guided by a profound respect for the natural world and its wisdom.

His work was far from over; the planet's healing was a continuous process, a journey of constant adaptation and learning.

But Jonah, standing on the edge of a new dawn, knew he had played a crucial part in its beginning.

His quiet, almost unassuming contribution was, in its own way, as significant as the grand gestures of others. It was the meticulous work, the quiet dedication, the tireless translation, that had brought humanity back from the brink. His work was a testament to the power of listening—not just to the planet's subtle whispers, but also to the quiet voice of hope within himself.

Eliza's Stewardship

Eliza Grant, her face etched with the faintest lines of exhaustion but her eyes shining with a quiet, unwavering determination, surveyed the revitalized coastline. The air, once thick with the stench of decay and industrial waste, now carried the crisp, clean scent of salt and seaweed. Where once barren rock and poisoned sand had met a lifeless ocean, vibrant kelp forests swayed gently in the renewed currents, teeming with life. Schools of iridescent fish darted through the underwater meadows, their scales flashing like scattered jewels. The rhythmic crash of waves against the shore was a symphony of renewal, a powerful testament to the success of the Convergence Protocol.

Eliza's contribution to this resurgence had been profound, though far less visible than Jonah's technological breakthroughs or Sarah's relentless leadership. While Jonah deciphered the Whispers' cryptic code and Sarah navigated the treacherous political landscape, Eliza had worked tirelessly, painstakingly, behind the scenes, guiding the intricate process of ecological restoration. Her knowledge of marine ecosystems, honed over decades of research and fieldwork, had been indispensable. She had understood the nuances of the Whispers' language on a different level than Jonah, comprehending their directives not just as abstract codes, but as subtle instructions embedded within the very fabric of the ocean's life. She was the bridge between the Whispers' cryptic instructions and the practical application of their guidance to the physical world.

Eliza wasn't simply applying pre-existing knowledge; she was adapting, innovating, and learning in real time. The Convergence Protocol wasn't a rigid blueprint; it was a dynamic process, constantly adjusting to the planet's evolving needs. Eliza's expertise allowed her to identify and address unforeseen challenges, to anticipate the Whispers' subtle adaptations, and to guide the restoration process with unparalleled precision. She had guided teams of scientists and engineers, her directions precise and insightful, navigating the intricate complexities of reintroducing endangered species, rehabilitating damaged habitats, and fostering the delicate balance necessary for a thriving ecosystem. She had mapped the migration patterns of the reborn creatures, tracking their movement with a skill honed by years of intimate interaction with marine life. Her knowledge was far more than simply technical; it was intuitive, almost mystical in its depth.

Her work involved far more than simply reintroducing species; it was about understanding the intricate interconnectedness of the restored ecosystem, predicting potential imbalances, and preventing ecological catastrophes before they even arose. It required an understanding not just of individual species but of the complex web of life that sustained them, an understanding that went beyond scientific data to encompass a deeper, almost intuitive comprehension of the planet's delicate balance. She had anticipated and mitigated the rise of invasive species, preventing the resurgence of ecological imbalances, ensuring that the planet's rejuvenation would not be reversed by unforeseen consequences.

The restoration was not a one-time event; it was an ongoing process, a continuous dialogue between human intervention and the planet's inherent restorative powers. Eliza's role was not to control or manipulate nature, but to collaborate with it, to act as a facilitator, assisting the planet's own innate capacity for self-healing. Her approach was meticulous, painstaking, and deeply respectful of the delicate interplay of forces within the revitalized ecosystems. She often spent hours simply observing, learning, absorbing the intricate rhythms of the reborn oceans and their inhabitants, allowing the Whispers to guide her decisions.

Her insights were not limited to the immediate practicalities of ecological restoration. Eliza's work generated a cascade of innovations. Her understanding of the Whispers' bioluminescent communication systems, for example, led to the development of more efficient and sustainable lighting technologies. She pioneered methods of bioremediation inspired by the Whispers' own natural cleaning processes, creating sustainable solutions for pollution cleanup. Her understanding of the planet's complex circulatory systems, influenced by the Whispers, revolutionized ocean current modeling and the prediction of weather patterns, leading to more resilient coastal communities.

The respect for her expertise extended far beyond the scientific community. The local communities, once ravaged by ecological collapse, now saw her as a symbol of hope, a leader who had helped to restore their connection to the natural world. They trusted her wisdom, valued her guidance, and appreciated the deep respect she held for the planet's interconnectedness. Her work had bridged the gap between science and spirituality, reminding people of their innate connection to the natural world.

However, Eliza's journey hadn't been without its challenges. The immense pressure to succeed, the relentless demands of her work, and the weight of responsibility for the planet's regeneration had taken their toll. She had battled moments of self-doubt, questioning whether her efforts were sufficient, wrestling with the ethical dilemmas that arose from intervening in such a complex and interconnected system. The emotional strain was palpable. She had witnessed the devastation wrought by environmental collapse firsthand, a stark reality that frequently tested her resolve. The constant pressure to balance human needs with the planet's capacity for regeneration had been a heavy burden, forcing her to make difficult choices and prioritize competing needs.

Yet, despite these struggles, Eliza's commitment remained unwavering. Her passion for the ocean, her dedication to the restoration efforts, and her deep understanding of the planet's intricate systems had never faltered. She remained a vital part of the team, not just as a scientist, but as a leader, a guide, and a symbol of unwavering hope. Her influence extended far beyond her immediate sphere of work, inspiring a new generation of environmental scientists and advocates to embrace a holistic and collaborative approach to environmental stewardship.

She had learned to listen, not just to the Whispers, but to the planet itself, to the subtle signals of its renewal, and to the quiet voices of hope emerging from the reborn ecosystems. Her work was not merely scientific; it was a testament to human resilience, a demonstration of the power of collaboration, and an expression of deep respect for the wisdom inherent in the natural world. Her legacy would not be written in books or on monuments, but etched into the very fabric of the revitalized planet, a subtle yet enduring echo of her unwavering commitment to healing the Earth.

She was a quiet hero, a silent force of nature, guiding the planet's recovery with her unwavering dedication and profound understanding of the interconnectedness of all life. The future she had helped to create would stand as a monument to her quiet, persistent work. The ocean breathed, the land healed, and in the heart of the recovered world, Eliza's legacy flourished. Her vision of a symbiotic future, where humanity lived in harmony with the planet, wasn't just a dream; it was becoming a reality, a testament to the power of one woman's unwavering devotion to the Earth. The vibrant ecosystems, teeming with life, were her living legacy, a testament to the enduring power of hope and the transformative capacity of human compassion and unwavering dedication.

Nylas Guidance

The salty air whipped around Nyla's flowing robes as she stood on the newly restored cliff overlooking the revitalized coastline. The Luminese ambassador, her skin shimmering with an ethereal luminescence, watched the waves roll in, a serene smile playing on her lips. Eliza, Sarah, and Jonah stood beside her, their faces reflecting a mixture of awe and relief. The transformation was nothing short of miraculous. Where only months ago, toxic sludge had choked the life from the ocean, now vibrant kelp forests swayed, teeming with fish. The air, once acrid and foul, was now clean and sharp with the smell of salt and seaweed.

Nyla's contribution to this success wasn't immediately apparent in the physical changes; it wasn't etched in the reborn kelp forests or the returning schools of fish. Her impact was subtle, woven into the very fabric of their collaboration. It was a quiet strength, a guiding hand that had steered them through countless obstacles, a wisdom that had transcended species and ideologies. She had been the bridge, the silent facilitator, allowing the disparate elements of their coalition—humans, Luminese, and the Whispers—to find common ground, to understand each other's needs and motivations.

"The Convergence Protocol," Nyla said, her voice a melodious hum that resonated with an almost otherworldly quality, "was not merely a technological solution. It was a testament to the power of cooperation, a symphony orchestrated by diverse voices. The Whispers spoke in riddles, their language a complex tapestry of bioluminescent patterns and subtle shifts in the ocean's currents. Jonah deciphered their code, but it was Eliza who understood their intent, who saw the intricate ecological balance they sought to restore."

She paused, her gaze sweeping across the rejuvenated landscape.

"Sarah, with her unwavering courage and sharp tactical mind, navigated the treacherous political currents, ensuring that our collective efforts were not undermined by those who sought to exploit the Protocol for their own selfish ends. She secured the necessary resources, negotiated fragile alliances, and kept our disparate factions focused on the common goal."

Nyla's words hung in the air, pregnant with meaning. Her wisdom wasn't based on mere intellect; it stemmed from a deep understanding of the interconnectedness of all living things, a perspective honed over centuries of Luminese history. The Luminese, with their advanced technology and their profound respect for the natural world, had always held a unique position within the galactic community. They were not conquerors or exploiters; they were custodians, guardians of delicate ecosystems and ancient knowledge.

Nyla had brought this perspective to their alliance, reminding them that the Whispers were not merely sources of data or tools for technological advancement, but sentient beings, complex ecosystems with their own inherent wisdom and needs. She had emphasized the importance of respectful communication, the necessity of listening as much as instructing, of approaching the planet's healing not as a conquest, but as a collaborative endeavor.

"The Echoborn," Nyla continued, her voice softening, "represent the most profound aspect of this collaboration. They are the embodiment of our shared future, a testament to the potential for symbiotic evolution, for harmony between species. They are the living proof that collaboration, mutual respect, and a willingness to evolve together are not merely idealistic aspirations, but the foundations of a sustainable future."

The Echoborn, humans who had integrated with the Whispers, were a source of both hope and apprehension. Their bodies shimmered with bioluminescent patterns, their minds connected to the planetary network of the Whispers. They were a living bridge, a testament to the transformative potential of the Convergence Protocol. However, their existence also raised questions about the very definition of humanity, the boundaries between species, and the future of human identity.

Nyla's understanding of these complex issues, her ability to navigate these ethical dilemmas with wisdom and grace, had been crucial. She had guided them through discussions about the Echoborn's rights, their integration into society, and the potential challenges their unique existence presented. Her insights were not confined to scientific or technological matters; they delved into the philosophical and ethical dimensions of their endeavor, reminding them that the restoration of the planet was not merely a scientific project, but a moral imperative.

"The path toward healing," Nyla explained, "was not a straight line, but a winding journey, filled with unexpected turns and unforeseen obstacles. There were moments of doubt, moments of despair, moments when the weight of responsibility threatened to overwhelm us. But through it all, the collective wisdom of our alliance, the unwavering commitment to our shared goal, and the profound guidance of the Whispers guided us forward."

She spoke of the near-misses, the averted catastrophes, the delicate balancing acts they had performed. She recounted times when their differing perspectives had clashed, when tensions had run high, when the temptation to resort to old, destructive patterns had been strong. But each time, they had found a way to overcome their differences, to find common ground, to forge a stronger, more unified front. Nyla's role in these reconciliations had been pivotal.

Her influence extended beyond the immediate group; she had communicated with other Luminese colonies, secured vital resources, and ensured that the work on the Convergence Protocol wasn't viewed as a purely human endeavor. Her diplomacy had paved the way for a wider galactic understanding of the environmental crisis and the importance of planetary healing, opening doors for international collaboration and support that had proved vital to their success.

Nyla's legacy extended beyond the physical restoration of the planet. She had instilled in them a new way of thinking, a new way of interacting with the natural world, a new paradigm for interspecies collaboration. She had taught them to listen to the planet, to understand its rhythms, to respect its wisdom. She had shown them that progress wasn't about domination, but about cooperation—not about extraction, but about sustainability. Her wisdom had transformed their approach, moving them beyond simply fixing the damage to fostering a symbiotic relationship with the planet.

As the sun dipped below the horizon, painting the sky in hues of orange and purple, Nyla turned to her companions. The air hummed with a quiet energy, a sense of shared accomplishment, of hope for the future. The ocean reflected the colors of the sunset, a shimmering tapestry of renewal. In that moment, they knew that the work was far from over, that the challenges ahead remained formidable. But they also knew that they had the wisdom, the strength, and the collaboration needed to face them.

They had Nyla's guidance, the Whispers' wisdom, and the unwavering hope that had sprung from the ashes of a dying world. The future was uncertain, but for the first time in a long time, it felt hopeful. The echo of Sarah's relentless leadership, Eliza's scientific expertise, Jonah's technological prowess, and Nyla's wisdom resonated through the renewed landscape, a symphony of hope playing out against the backdrop of a healing world.

The future, once shrouded in darkness, now shimmered with a new possibility—a chance for true symbiotic existence, a partnership between humanity and the planet. It was a future they would build together, guided by the wisdom of Nyla and the echoes of their collective struggle.

The Echoborns Future

The sunset bled across the rejuvenated coastline, painting the sky in vibrant hues of orange and violet. The air, once thick with the stench of industrial decay, now carried the clean, crisp scent of salt and seaweed. The rhythmic crashing of waves against the newly formed kelp forests provided a soothing counterpoint to the hushed conversations of the small group gathered on the clifftop. They were discussing the future—a future inextricably linked to the Echoborn, the humans who had become one with the Whispers.

Eliza, her face etched with a mixture of awe and apprehension, traced the bioluminescent patterns that pulsed softly beneath the skin of one of the Echoborn children playing on the beach.

"Their connection to the Whispers is... profound," she murmured, her voice barely audible above the sound of the waves. "They can communicate directly with the planetary network, perceive the health of the ecosystems in ways we never could. It's as if they are extensions of the planet's nervous system."

Jonah, ever the pragmatist, leaned forward, his gaze fixed on the child.

"That's the good news. The bad news is we don't fully understand the implications. How does this connection affect their cognitive functions? Their emotional lives? Their very sense of self?" He tapped a stylus against a datapad, displaying complex waveforms representing the Echoborn's neural activity. "Their brainwaves are unlike anything I've ever seen. It's a symphony of human and planetary consciousness, interwoven in ways that defy simple analysis."

Sarah, her eyes scanning the horizon, nodded slowly.

"The Convergence Protocol didn't just heal the planet; it opened up new pathways for evolution. The Echoborn are a testament to that, a bridge between humanity and the Whispers. But this bridge isn't without its potential pitfalls. We need to understand their needs, their rights, their place in this new world."

Nyla, her luminescent skin shimmering softly in the fading light, offered a perspective honed over centuries of Luminese wisdom. "The Echoborn are not merely a new species; they represent a new form of consciousness, a symbiotic partnership between humanity and the planet. Their emergence is a profound shift, a transition from a paradigm of dominance to one of collaboration. This requires a fundamental re-evaluation of our understanding of life, consciousness, and the very definition of what it means to be human."

The discussion extended into the evening, fueled by both hope and uncertainty. They explored the ethical implications of the Echoborn's existence, their unique abilities, and their place in society. How would they be integrated into the human community? Would their heightened connection to the Whispers give them a disproportionate influence on decision-making? What about education, healthcare, social structures? Every aspect of their lives required careful consideration, necessitating a radical overhaul of existing social norms and institutions.

The group delved into the intricacies of communication. While the Echoborn could communicate with the Whispers directly, their ability to communicate effectively with humans was still developing. They could express basic needs and emotions, but conveying complex ideas remained a challenge.

Jonah suggested creating a sophisticated translation system, using advanced neural interfaces to bridge the communication gap. Eliza, however, cautioned against relying solely on technology. She believed that fostering empathy and understanding was crucial, focusing on building relationships based on mutual respect and trust.

Sarah, ever the strategist, proposed the creation of dedicated Echoborn communities—spaces where they could develop their identity and culture without feeling pressured to conform to human norms. These communities would serve as hubs for research, education, and cultural exchange, allowing them to flourish within a supportive environment. Simultaneously, they would also create educational programs for the broader human population to foster understanding and acceptance of the Echoborn.

She knew the transition wouldn't be easy. Prejudice, fear, and misunderstanding would inevitably arise. But she believed that proactive planning and education were essential to navigate the challenges ahead.

The discussion also touched upon the potential risks. While the Echoborn were currently a source of hope, there was always the potential for unforeseen consequences. Their close connection to the Whispers raised concerns about the possibility of manipulation, or unforeseen changes in their abilities and behavior. They had to be cautious, proactive in their approach, constantly monitoring their health and development while making sure that their rights and wellbeing were prioritized.

Nyla, drawing on her people's long history of interspecies collaboration, emphasized the importance of respecting the Echoborn's autonomy and individuality.

"We cannot impose our values and expectations upon them," she stated. "We must allow them the space to define their own identity, their own culture, within the framework of a sustainable and harmonious future."

Days turned into weeks, and weeks into months. The initial excitement surrounding the Convergence Protocol gradually gave way to the complexities of managing the long-term consequences of planetary healing and the emergence of the Echoborn. The work was far from over. The task of rebuilding civilization, fostering interspecies understanding, and integrating the Echoborn into society required sustained effort, unwavering commitment, and careful navigation of countless unforeseen obstacles.

Sarah, however, remained undeterred. She knew that the future was not guaranteed, that setbacks and challenges were inevitable. But she also knew that they had come too far, achieved too much, to relinquish hope.

The success of the Convergence Protocol had not only healed the planet but had also unleashed the potential for a truly symbiotic existence between humanity and nature—an existence symbolized by the Echoborn. Their future, uncertain as it was, held the potential for a profoundly different kind of human experience, one based on collaboration, mutual respect, and a deep understanding of our interconnectedness with all living things.

As they looked out at the shimmering ocean, now teeming with life, a sense of cautious optimism filled the group. The Echoborn played on the beach, their laughter echoing against the cliffs—a testament to the enduring spirit of hope. The future was uncertain, filled with challenges that had yet to be faced, but it was a future they would build together.

A future in which the echoes of Sarah's unwavering leadership, Eliza's scientific insight, Jonah's technological ingenuity, and Nyla's ancient wisdom would guide them toward a new, symbiotic dawn.

A dawn where humanity would no longer be a dominant force, but an integral part of a flourishing planetary ecosystem—a partnership with the earth itself, forever changed by the echoes of a world reborn.

The journey was far from over, the challenges ahead immense, but they faced them united, their commitment bound by the hope embodied in the shimmering, laughing Echoborn children.

The future, they knew, lay in their hands—shaped by the delicate balance between human ingenuity and the wisdom of the planet. It was a future written not in code, but in the laughter of the Echoborn, in the rhythm of the restored ocean, and in the unwavering hope that had sprung from the ashes of a dying world.

A hope that had found its most powerful symbol in the very existence of the Echoborn—the embodiment of a future where humanity and the planet could finally coexist, not as adversaries, but as partners in a shared destiny.

Chapter Ten

A New Beginning

The initial euphoria of the Convergence Protocol's success gradually faded, replaced by the sobering reality of rebuilding. The planet was healing, but civilization lay in ruins. Vast swaths of land remained uninhabitable, scarred by decades of environmental devastation. Cities, once symbols of human ambition, now stood as skeletal reminders of a reckless past, their concrete frameworks crumbling, choked by encroaching vegetation. The task ahead was monumental: to construct sustainable communities from the remnants of a fallen world, communities that were not only resilient but also equitable and inclusive.

Sarah, with her team, spearheaded the effort, drawing upon a combination of ancient wisdom and cutting-edge technology. The Luminese, with their centuries of experience in ecological stewardship, played a crucial role, sharing their knowledge of sustainable architecture and resource management. Their bioluminescent structures, powered by symbiotic algae and solar energy, became the blueprints for new settlements, seamlessly integrated into the revitalizing ecosystems. These structures were designed to minimize environmental impact, utilizing recycled materials and employing innovative techniques to harness renewable energy sources.

Jonah, ever the ingenious technologist, developed advanced hydroponic systems capable of producing nutritious food crops in even the most barren landscapes. These systems utilized minimal water and energy, adapting to the varied climates and soil conditions. He also spearheaded the development of decentralized water purification systems, ensuring access to clean drinking water for all communities. His expertise in robotics played a vital role in automating many of the labor-intensive tasks involved in rebuilding, freeing human workers for more strategic and creative endeavors.

Eliza, with her deep understanding of marine ecosystems, guided the restoration of coastal communities. She developed innovative techniques for restoring damaged coral reefs and kelp forests, creating vital habitats for marine life and supporting sustainable fishing practices. She also established community-based monitoring programs, enabling residents to actively participate in the preservation and monitoring of their local ecosystems. Her emphasis on collaborative conservation ensured that the renewed ecosystems were not just functional but also integral to the social fabric of the communities.

The rebuilding process wasn't merely about constructing physical infrastructure; it was about creating resilient social structures. Sarah emphasized the importance of participatory governance, establishing local councils where community members had a voice in shaping their own futures. These councils were designed to be inclusive, representing the diverse populations, including the Echoborn, who were now an integral part of the human landscape.

The integration of the Echoborn presented unique challenges. Their profound connection with the Whispers bestowed upon them a unique understanding of planetary ecosystems, enabling them to contribute in profound ways to the rebuilding effort. However, their different physiology and cognitive abilities demanded a sensitive approach to community integration. Specialized educational programs were developed to foster mutual understanding between humans and Echoborn, celebrating their unique perspectives and promoting respect for their distinct cultural identities.

The creation of dedicated Echoborn communities was a crucial aspect of the rebuilding effort. These spaces provided a safe haven for the Echoborn to develop their unique cultural identities, fostering a sense of belonging and community. The communities were not isolated; rather, they served as vibrant hubs for research, education, and cultural exchange, facilitating meaningful interactions with human societies. These spaces also facilitated the study of the Echoborn's unique abilities, which proved invaluable in guiding environmental restoration efforts.

The process wasn't without its conflicts. Prejudices and misunderstandings occasionally surfaced, requiring constant vigilance and proactive conflict resolution strategies. Sarah established community mediation programs, involving both human and Echoborn mediators, to address disputes peacefully and promote understanding. These programs emphasized open dialogue, mutual respect, and the importance of finding common ground.

The rebuilding process was far from uniform. Different communities developed distinct characteristics, reflecting their unique environmental contexts and cultural preferences. Some communities opted for a technologically advanced approach, embracing innovation and utilizing automation to enhance efficiency. Others favored a more traditional approach, emphasizing self-sufficiency and sustainable practices rooted in ancient traditions. This diversity, while posing challenges, ultimately enriched the overall process, highlighting the resilience and adaptability of the human spirit.

Economic models were also overhauled, moving away from the exploitative practices of the past. Sustainable economies emerged, built upon principles of circularity and resource efficiency. Local markets flourished, promoting self-reliance and minimizing reliance on external supply chains. Renewable energy sources became the primary drivers of economic activity, powering sustainable industries that created jobs and generated wealth while protecting the environment. Fair trade practices and community-based ownership models ensured that economic growth benefited all members of society, regardless of their background or abilities.

Education became a cornerstone of the rebuilding process. New educational programs were developed, emphasizing environmental literacy, sustainable living practices, and interspecies understanding. These programs were inclusive, catering to the diverse learning styles and cultural backgrounds of both human and Echoborn populations. Schools became centers of community life, promoting creativity, innovation, and collaboration.

The rebuilt societies were not merely replicas of the old; they were fundamentally different, emphasizing social equity, environmental stewardship, and interspecies harmony. The Convergence Protocol had not just healed the planet; it had also healed the human spirit, forging a new social contract based on cooperation, mutual respect, and a shared commitment to a sustainable future. The challenge remained monumental, but the vision was clear: a future where humanity lived in harmony with nature, a future where the laughter of the Echoborn echoed across a rejuvenated planet. The scars of the past remained, but they served as a constant reminder of the fragile balance that needed to be maintained.

The transition wasn't easy. There were periods of setbacks, times when doubt crept in and threatened to overshadow the hard-won progress. But through it all, the combined efforts of humans and the Echoborn, guided by Sarah's unwavering determination, Eliza's scientific brilliance, Jonah's technological innovation, and Nyla's wisdom, provided a path forward.

The new communities became beacons of hope, not just for the survivors, but for the future of humanity. They demonstrated that even after the most devastating environmental collapse, the human capacity for resilience, creativity, and cooperation remained undiminished. The work was far from over, the journey long and arduous, but as the new sun rose over the revitalized planet, there was a sense of shared purpose, a unified spirit forged in the crucible of environmental collapse and the emergence of a new symbiotic era. The future, once clouded with despair, was now painted with the vibrant colors of hope and the promise of a sustainable dawn.

Restoring Ecosystems

The revitalization extended beyond the immediate urban centers, reaching into the vast, scarred landscapes that had once been vibrant ecosystems. Eliza's team, now a sprawling network of marine biologists, ecologists, and community volunteers, tackled the monumental task of restoring the oceans and coastlines. Their work wasn't merely about replanting kelp forests or rebuilding coral reefs; it was about understanding the intricate web of life that had been disrupted and carefully weaving it back together.

One of their most ambitious projects involved the creation of artificial reefs, not simply as static structures, but as dynamic, selfregulating systems. These weren't made of concrete or steel; instead, they employed bioengineered materials capable of mimicking the natural processes of coral growth and providing a substrate for a vast array of marine life. Jonah's technological contributions were crucial here, with his team developing sophisticated sensors and monitoring systems that allowed them to track the health of the reefs in real time, adjusting conditions as needed to optimize growth and biodiversity. They even incorporated bioluminescent organisms into the reef structures, creating breathtaking underwater displays that attracted marine life and served as a visual testament to their success.

The restoration of terrestrial ecosystems proved even more challenging. Decades of deforestation, pollution, and unsustainable agricultural practices had left large swaths of land barren and infertile. The Luminese played a pivotal role here, sharing their knowledge of ancient terraforming techniques and introducing advanced bioremediation strategies. Their genetically modified plants, designed to thrive in depleted soils, were deployed across the landscapes, gradually restoring fertility and promoting the growth of native vegetation. These plants not only cleaned the soil but also produced valuable resources such as biofuels and sustainable building materials, reducing reliance on external sources.

The reintroduction of native species was another critical aspect of the restoration process. Eliza and her team meticulously mapped the genetic diversity of the pre-collapse ecosystems, identifying keystone species that were essential to maintaining the balance of nature. They established breeding programs for endangered species, carefully monitoring their health and ensuring their successful reintegration into their natural habitats. The process was painstakingly slow, involving close monitoring, careful observation, and countless adjustments based on the ecosystem's response. But the slow, steady growth of native plants and the return of animals to their historic ranges served as powerful symbols of hope and recovery.

The Whispers played a surprisingly crucial role in this process. The Echoborn, with their unique ability to communicate with the ecosystems, were able to identify areas where restoration efforts were most needed and pinpoint the specific actions required to achieve optimal results. They guided the planting of trees in areas most conducive to growth, identified locations for water reservoirs, and even predicted the migration patterns of animals, helping teams anticipate and manage potential conflicts. Their intuitive understanding of the interconnectedness of life within these ecosystems provided invaluable insights, often surpassing the capabilities of even the most sophisticated scientific instruments.

The restoration efforts, however, were not without conflict. The resurgence of certain invasive species posed a constant threat, demanding constant vigilance and adaptive strategies. Some communities resisted the changes, clinging to outdated practices and hindering the restoration efforts. Sarah's leadership proved invaluable in navigating these conflicts, fostering cooperation and finding common ground between differing viewpoints. She focused on educating the communities, highlighting the long-term benefits of ecological restoration while ensuring that everyone, particularly those who had lost their traditional livelihoods, had a stake in the process.

One of the significant challenges was determining the appropriate scale of intervention. Should they focus on restoring specific areas to their pre-collapse state, or should they embrace a more adaptive approach, allowing the ecosystems to evolve naturally in response to the changing environment? Eliza advocated for a balance, emphasizing the importance of preserving biodiversity while acknowledging the reality of a dramatically altered planet. This meant selectively reintroducing species, prioritizing those that were best adapted to the new conditions, while ensuring sufficient genetic diversity to allow for adaptation and resilience. It also meant learning to live alongside the newly evolved species, understanding their role within the new ecosystems.

The restoration efforts also highlighted the need for continuous monitoring and adaptation. The planet was still healing, and the ecosystems were in a state of flux. Jonah's technological expertise proved invaluable in developing sophisticated sensor networks that monitored a range of environmental variables, providing real-time data on everything from soil moisture to air quality to animal populations. This data allowed them to fine-tune their restoration strategies, adjusting their approaches as needed to optimize the effectiveness of their interventions. They learned to embrace uncertainty, viewing the fluctuating conditions as opportunities for learning and adaptation rather than setbacks.

The involvement of the Luminese brought a different perspective to the restoration efforts. Their focus was not simply on restoring ecosystems to their previous state; it was on creating resilient and sustainable ecosystems capable of thriving in a changing world.

They introduced innovative methods of water management, such as utilizing subterranean aquifers and atmospheric water generators, ensuring access to water even in arid regions. They also developed sustainable agricultural practices that minimized the environmental impact of food production, enhancing both food security and ecological health.

The economic dimensions of ecological restoration were also carefully considered. Sustainable industries were developed that were not only economically viable but also environmentally responsible. Ecotourism emerged as a major source of income, providing opportunities for local communities while simultaneously protecting the restored ecosystems. The creation of protected areas also served as a magnet for investment in ecological research and development, fostering innovation and promoting the adoption of sustainable practices.

The success of the restoration efforts was not solely measured by the recovery of biodiversity or the stabilization of ecosystems. It was also measured by the empowerment of local communities and the fostering of a sense of stewardship among the people.

Education played a crucial role here, with programs designed to raise awareness about the importance of environmental conservation and the interconnectedness of life. These programs emphasized community participation, empowering local residents to become active participants in the ongoing stewardship of their restored ecosystems.

The journey to restore Earth's damaged ecosystems was far from over, but the collective efforts of humans, Luminese, and Echoborn had begun to turn the tide. The planet was healing, and with it, the human spirit, forging a new relationship between humanity and nature, built not on dominion but on mutual respect and cooperation. The seeds of a new beginning had been planted, and as the vibrant ecosystems slowly recovered, so too did the hope for a sustainable future. The echo of laughter, both human and Echoborn, carried on the wind—a testament to the resilience of life, the power of collaboration, and the enduring strength of a planet slowly returning to its former glory.

Technological Harmony

The success of the initial restoration efforts spurred a new wave of innovation, one focused not just on repairing the damage but on forging a symbiotic relationship between technology and the revitalized ecosystems. Jonah's team, fueled by the success of the bioluminescent reefs, began developing a network of "eco-sensors"—miniature devices capable of seamlessly integrating into the fabric of the natural world. These weren't intrusive, bulky instruments; instead, they mimicked the forms of leaves, pebbles, and even insects, gathering data on everything from soil composition and water quality to animal migration patterns and atmospheric conditions. The data was processed by advanced AI algorithms, providing real-time insights into the health and resilience of the ecosystems.

This data wasn't simply used for passive observation; it actively informed the restoration process. If a particular area showed signs of stress, the eco-sensors could trigger targeted interventions. For instance, if soil moisture levels dropped below a critical threshold, automated irrigation systems powered by renewable energy sources would be activated. If invasive species began to proliferate, robotic drones mimicking the behavior of predatory insects would be deployed to control their populations. This intelligent, responsive system ensured that restoration efforts were precise, efficient, and adaptive, constantly adjusting to the ever-changing needs of the environment.

The Luminese, with their centuries of experience in terraforming and ecological engineering, contributed their expertise in developing bio-integrated technologies. They introduced selfreplicating nanobots capable of repairing damaged cells in plants and animals, accelerating the healing process. These nanobots were designed to be completely biodegradable, leaving no trace of their intervention once their task was complete. They also developed advanced biofilters capable of removing pollutants from water and soil with remarkable efficiency, dramatically accelerating the cleanup of polluted areas.

The Echoborn played a crucial role in ensuring the ethical and sustainable deployment of these technologies. Their deep connection to the Whispers allowed them to gauge the impact of technological interventions on the ecosystems, preventing unintended consequences and ensuring that the technology was truly harmonious with nature. They acted as a crucial bridge, translating the complex needs of the Whispers into understandable terms for the human and Luminese engineers. Their feedback ensured that technology wasn't imposed upon nature but instead integrated seamlessly into its complex web of life.

One of the most ambitious projects was the development of "smart forests." These weren't simply areas of replanted trees; they were sophisticated, interconnected ecosystems managed by a network of eco-sensors and AI algorithms. The trees themselves were genetically modified to be more resilient to drought, disease, and pests. The sensors monitored their health, detecting early signs of stress and triggering interventions before problems escalated. The AI algorithms optimized resource allocation, ensuring that water and nutrients were delivered where they were most needed. These smart forests were not only more resilient to environmental changes but also more productive, producing valuable resources such as timber, biofuels, and medicinal compounds.

The integration of technology also extended to agriculture. Precision farming techniques, guided by eco-sensors and AI, optimized resource utilization and minimized environmental impact. Hydroponic and aeroponic systems allowed for efficient food production with minimal water and land usage, freeing up valuable resources for ecosystem restoration. Vertical farms, integrated into urban landscapes, provided a sustainable source of food for growing populations, reducing the need for extensive agricultural land and minimizing transportation costs.

But the harmonious integration of technology wasn't without its challenges. There were concerns about the potential for technological dependence, the risk of unforeseen consequences, and the ethical implications of manipulating natural systems. Sarah, Eliza, and Jonah engaged in extensive discussions with the Luminese and the Echoborn, carefully weighing the benefits and risks of each new technology before its deployment. They established strict protocols for monitoring the impact of technological interventions, ensuring that the balance between human intervention and natural processes was carefully maintained.

They understood that technology was a tool, and its use required wisdom, caution, and a deep respect for the intrinsic value of the natural world.

The development of renewable energy sources was also critical to the long-term sustainability of the technological integration. Solar, wind, hydro, and geothermal energy sources were harnessed to power the eco-sensors, irrigation systems, and other technologies, minimizing reliance on fossil fuels and reducing environmental impact. The Luminese shared their expertise in developing advanced energy storage systems, ensuring a reliable supply of energy even in remote areas.

The economic implications of this technological harmony were equally significant. New industries emerged, focused on the development and deployment of sustainable technologies. Ecotourism flourished, attracting visitors from around the world to witness the remarkable recovery of the planet's ecosystems. The Echoborn, with their unique understanding of the natural world, became highly sought-after consultants, guiding the development of sustainable technologies and helping to ensure their harmonious integration with nature.

This new technological integration was not just about repairing the damage of the past; it was about building a future where humanity and nature coexisted in harmony. It was a future where technology was a tool for enhancing the resilience and biodiversity of the planet, not a force for its destruction. It was a future where humans were not masters of nature, but rather its partners, working collaboratively to create a sustainable and thriving world.

The laughter of children playing amidst restored ecosystems, the songs of birds echoing through revitalized forests, and the gentle glow of bioluminescent reefs—these were the symbols of a new beginning, a future where technology and nature were not at odds but interwoven in a complex, beautiful, and sustainable tapestry of life.

The air vibrated with a sense of hope, a tangible feeling that the long struggle was bearing fruit, that humanity, having stumbled and fallen, was finally finding its feet on a path toward a shared future with the planet. The whispers of the wind carried not just the sounds of nature's rebirth but also the quiet hum of technology working in perfect harmony—a testament to the enduring power of human ingenuity and the unwavering resilience of life itself.

Interconnectedness of Life

The shimmering bioluminescent reefs, now a vibrant tapestry across the once-desolate ocean floor, weren't just aesthetically pleasing; they were a testament to the interconnectedness of life, a living embodiment of the shift in humanity's understanding of the world. The restoration wasn't simply about restoring individual species or ecosystems; it was about mending the intricate web that connected them all. The success of the reefs lay not just in the technological ingenuity of Jonah's team, but in the careful consideration of the ripple effects their actions would have throughout the entire ecosystem.

Before, humanity had operated under the illusion of dominion, viewing nature as a resource to be exploited. Now, the understanding was dawning that every action, no matter how seemingly small, sent ripples through the complex tapestry of life. The introduction of a new species, the removal of an invasive one, the alteration of a single habitat—each had cascading consequences, impacting countless other organisms and processes.

This holistic perspective wasn't merely philosophical; it was essential for the survival of the planet. Understanding the intricate dependencies between species, between ecosystems, and between the living and non-living world was the key to restoring balance and fostering resilience.

Dr. Eliza Grant, her face etched with the wisdom of years spent studying the ocean's mysteries, became a central figure in this new paradigm. Her work went beyond simple species identification and population counts. She meticulously mapped the intricate relationships between the various organisms in the restored ecosystems, charting the flow of energy, the cycles of nutrients, and the subtle ways in which different species influenced each other's survival and evolution. Her research revealed the astonishing interconnectedness of the marine world—a vast and complex network where every organism played a crucial role in maintaining the delicate balance.

For instance, the restored kelp forests weren't merely habitats for fish; they were carbon sinks, absorbing vast quantities of atmospheric CO_2, and nurseries for countless marine species. The delicate balance of the kelp forest ecosystem was dependent on the presence of specific sea urchins, which controlled the growth of algae and prevented it from smothering the kelp. These urchins, in turn, were preyed upon by sea otters, whose population had to be carefully managed to ensure that the kelp forest wasn't overgrazed. Eliza's work highlighted the crucial role each organism played in maintaining the health of the entire ecosystem, illustrating the profound interconnectedness of life.

This principle extended beyond the oceans. The smart forests, meticulously designed to be self-regulating and resilient, were a testament to the interconnectedness of terrestrial ecosystems. The genetic modifications made to the trees weren't isolated changes; they were carefully considered in light of their impact on the soil microbes, the insects that pollinated the trees, the birds that nested in their branches, and the mammals that depended on the forest for food and shelter. Every aspect of the forest ecosystem was considered, creating a self-regulating, symbiotic system that could adapt and thrive in the face of environmental changes.

The Luminese played a critical role in this understanding, bringing their centuries of experience in planetary engineering and ecological manipulation. Their advanced technologies allowed them to monitor and assess the interconnectedness of ecosystems with unprecedented detail, providing invaluable insights to the human scientists. Their understanding of symbiotic relationships between different species, honed over generations of terraforming planets, proved invaluable in restoring balance to Earth's ravaged ecosystems.

Ambassador Nyla, her wisdom surpassing even her advanced age, emphasized the crucial role of humility in this new approach to environmental restoration. "We must approach nature not as conquerors, but as partners," she would often say, her voice a calming resonance. "The planet is a single, vast, interconnected organism. To heal one part is to heal the whole, but to damage one part is to risk damaging the whole." This philosophy guided all restoration efforts, ensuring a holistic and sustainable approach.

The Echoborn, with their unique connection to the Whispers, offered another dimension to this understanding of interconnectedness. Their merging with the ecosystems provided them with an intuitive grasp of the subtle relationships between different species and the environment. They became living bridges, translating the needs of the planet into a language humans could understand. Their insights were crucial in guiding the development of sustainable technologies and ensuring that human interventions didn't disrupt the natural balance. They often spoke of the planet as a single entity, a collective consciousness woven from the threads of all living things. Their insights weren't always easy to understand, but their wisdom was undeniable, adding a layer of mystical insight to the scientific understanding.

Even the seemingly mundane tasks, like the development of renewable energy sources, were approached with a deep understanding of interconnectedness. The choice of energy source—solar, wind, hydro, or geothermal—was carefully considered in terms of its impact on local ecosystems. The placement of wind turbines, for example, was determined not only by wind patterns but also by the impact on bird migration routes. Every decision was informed by a deep respect for the planet's complex web of life.

The economic implications of this interconnected approach were transformative. New industries emerged, focused on fostering the resilience and biodiversity of ecosystems rather than exploiting them. Ecotourism boomed, with visitors drawn to the planet's restored beauty and the possibility of experiencing the intricate interconnectedness of life firsthand. Sustainable agriculture, guided by the principles of ecological harmony, provided food security without compromising the integrity of ecosystems. The Echoborn, with their unique skills and knowledge, played a vital role in this new economy, serving as guides, consultants, and educators.

The transformation wasn't just technological or economic; it was fundamentally philosophical. It was a shift from a paradigm of dominion to one of partnership, a recognition of the intrinsic value of all life and the profound interconnectedness of the planet. It was a journey from a fragmented, anthropocentric worldview to a holistic, biocentric understanding of the world.

The laughter of children playing amidst the restored ecosystems, the songs of birds echoing through the revitalized forests, the vibrant glow of the bioluminescent reefs—these weren't merely symbols of environmental recovery; they were emblems of a fundamental shift in humanity's relationship with the planet, a shift toward a future where humanity and nature danced together in a harmonious symphony of life. The air itself hummed with a renewed sense of hope, a quiet confidence that the hard-won balance, forged in the crucible of near-destruction, was finally holding. The future remained uncertain, but for the first time in generations, the possibility of a shared future, a harmonious coexistence, felt not like a distant dream, but a tangible reality woven into the very fabric of the reborn world.

The interconnectedness of life was no longer a scientific theory; it was the living, breathing reality of a new beginning.

A Sustainable Future

The air, once thick with the choking haze of pollution, now carried the scent of salt and pine, a testament to the planet's slow, arduous recovery. The once-barren landscapes, scarred by decades of unchecked industrialization and climate change, were slowly but surely regaining their vibrancy. Vast swaths of land, once desolate wastelands, now teemed with life—a vibrant tapestry woven from the threads of meticulously restored ecosystems.

The smart forests, a marvel of bioengineering and ecological understanding, stretched as far as the eye could see, their canopies alive with the rustling of leaves and the songs of birds. The air hummed with the quiet industry of insects—the subtle symphony of a healthy, thriving environment.

This wasn't a simple return to the past; it was a leap forward, a testament to humanity's capacity for adaptation and ingenuity. The scars of the past remained—a stark reminder of the nearcatastrophic consequences of unchecked consumption and disregard for the natural world—but they were now interwoven with the vibrant tapestry of a renewed hope.

The cities, once concrete jungles choked by pollution, now embraced a more harmonious coexistence with nature. Vertical farms, powered by renewable energy, sprouted from the heart of urban centers, providing fresh produce while minimizing their ecological footprint. Green spaces, carefully designed to support biodiversity and provide clean air, had replaced concrete expanses, creating pockets of tranquility amidst the bustling urban life. Buildings, constructed from sustainable materials and designed for energy efficiency, blended seamlessly with their surroundings, reflecting a shift in architectural thinking—away from imposing structures and toward harmonious integration with the landscape.

The oceans, once poisoned by pollution and depleted by overfishing, were gradually regaining their health. The bioluminescent reefs, now vast and thriving, pulsated with life, attracting a diverse array of marine creatures. Sustainable fishing practices, guided by Eliza Grant's meticulous research, ensured that fish populations remained healthy and thriving, preventing the collapse of marine ecosystems. The careful monitoring of ocean currents and temperatures, facilitated by Luminese technology, ensured that the delicate balance of the marine environment wasn't disrupted. The oceans, once a symbol of ecological devastation, were now a beacon of hope—a testament to humanity's ability to heal even the most damaged ecosystems.

The transformation wasn't limited to the environment; it extended to human society as well. A new economic model, built on the principles of sustainability and ecological harmony, had replaced the exploitative practices of the past. The emphasis shifted from endless growth to mindful stewardship, from consumption to conservation. The new economy prioritized ethical and sustainable practices, rewarding those who contributed to environmental restoration and promoting equitable distribution of resources. Businesses that once profited from the exploitation of natural resources now thrived by helping restore them. Ecotourism, powered by a deep respect for the environment, boomed, providing economic opportunities for local communities while protecting ecosystems.

The role of the Echoborn was crucial in this transformation. Their unique connection to the Whispers provided invaluable insights into the needs of the planet, guiding the development of sustainable technologies and practices. Their deep understanding of the interconnectedness of life allowed them to act as bridges between humanity and the natural world, translating the planet's needs into a language humans could understand. They weren't merely advisors; they were essential partners in the rebuilding process, their unique perspectives shaping the policies and practices that guided the planet's recovery. Their integration into society wasn't a forced assimilation but a natural evolution—a testament to the capacity for human adaptation and symbiotic coexistence.

The Luminese, with their advanced technologies and centuries of experience in planetary engineering, played a pivotal role in guiding the planet's recovery. Their contribution extended beyond mere technological assistance; they provided crucial philosophical insights, emphasizing the need for humility and respect in humanity's relationship with nature. Their wisdom, honed through generations of experience terraforming planets, helped shape a new understanding of humanity's place within the larger ecosystem, fostering a sense of partnership and responsibility. Their collaboration with human scientists and the Echoborn created a synergistic approach to restoration, accelerating the planet's healing process.

The success of the Convergence Protocol wasn't just about restoring damaged ecosystems; it was about fostering a fundamental shift in humanity's worldview. It was a transition from a paradigm of dominion to one of stewardship, a move away from anthropocentrism toward biocentrism. The understanding that all life is interconnected—that every organism plays a vital role in maintaining the planet's delicate balance—became the cornerstone of this new worldview. This wasn't just a shift in scientific understanding; it was a profound change in human consciousness, a recognition of humanity's responsibility to the planet and all its inhabitants.

The future wasn't without challenges. The planet's recovery was a long and arduous process, requiring constant vigilance and adaptation. The threat of further environmental disasters, the potential for unforeseen ecological consequences, and the enduring temptation to revert to old, exploitative practices remained. But the challenges were faced with a renewed sense of hope, a collective determination to avoid the mistakes of the past. The scars of the past served as a powerful reminder of the fragility of the planet and the importance of sustainable practices.

The children who grew up in this new world understood the interconnectedness of life not as an abstract concept, but as a lived reality. They grew up surrounded by restored ecosystems, witnessing firsthand the beauty and resilience of nature. They inherited a world where sustainability wasn't a distant goal but a way of life. Their education emphasized ecological literacy, fostering a deep understanding of the planet's intricate systems and humanity's role within them. They learned not only about science and technology, but also about ethical responsibility, cultural preservation, and the importance of living in harmony with nature. Their lives were a testament to the power of hope and the transformative potential of a sustainable future.

The planet, slowly but surely, was healing. The vibrant ecosystems, the thriving communities, the innovative technologies, and the shift in human consciousness all bore witness to the remarkable resilience of life and the potential for a shared future— a harmonious coexistence between humanity and nature. The scars of the past remained, but they were now interwoven with the vibrant tapestry of a new beginning—a future where hope, resilience, and a profound understanding of interconnectedness guided humanity's path toward a truly sustainable world.

The laughter of children, echoing through the restored forests, served as a powerful testament to the possibility of a future where humanity and nature danced together—a harmonious symphony of life, playing out against the backdrop of a reborn world. The future held uncertainties, but it was a future brimming with the promise of a sustainable existence—a future where humanity had finally found its place not as the planet's master, but as its partner, its guardian, and its friend.

Chapter Eleven

WHISPERS OF THE PAST AND ANCIENT ECHOES

T he rhythmic pulse of the ocean, a constant companion to Sarah and her team, held more than just the promise of a renewed ecosystem—it held the echoes of millennia past. Jonah, ever the pragmatist, had initially dismissed the Whispers' insistence on exploring the planet's ancient history as a distraction, a sentimental detour from their urgent mission. But as the Convergence Protocol's activation neared, the urgency of understanding the planet's past became undeniably clear.

The Whispers' ancient code—the key to planetary regeneration—wasn't just a set of instructions; it was a narrative, a testament to the planet's resilience, its capacity for both devastation and renewal.

Dr. Grant, her face etched with a mixture of fascination and apprehension, initiated the exploration, her voice barely a whisper as she addressed the holographic projection shimmering before them. The image revealed layers of geological strata, each representing a period of profound environmental change—some cataclysmic, others slow and insidious. The data, painstakingly extracted from the Whispers' intricate code, painted a picture of civilizations that rose and fell in sync with the planet's fluctuating health. These weren't merely archaeological discoveries; they were chilling warnings—cautionary tales of empires consumed by their own hubris.

The earliest civilizations, it seemed, had thrived in a period of unparalleled environmental abundance. Their societies, deeply intertwined with nature, lived in harmony with their surroundings, guided by a profound understanding of ecological balance. Their technology, while rudimentary compared to the Luminese or even contemporary human standards, was ingeniously adapted to their environment, minimizing its impact. They left behind no monumental structures that would scar the landscape. Instead, their legacy was etched in the symbiotic relationships they established with the planet, their wisdom woven into the very fabric of the ecosystems they inhabited. Their art, discovered etched onto ancient cave walls and preserved within the layers of rock, depicted a profound respect for the natural world—an intimacy that resonated with the Echoborn's connection to the Whispers.

But their idyllic existence was not without its challenges. The Whispers' code revealed subtle shifts in the planet's climate: gradual changes in weather patterns and the slow encroachment of deserts and ice. These were periods of adaptation and societal restructuring, not collapse. It was a testament to their adaptability—their capacity to adjust their way of life to accommodate the changing conditions, preserving not only their own existence but also the health of their environment. They didn't conquer nature; they learned to cooperate with it, accepting its rhythms and limitations.

Then came a period of profound change—a dramatic shift in the planet's climate marked by widespread desertification. The ancient civilizations, facing escalating resource scarcity and environmental stress, responded in diverse ways. Some societies adapted, developing innovative technologies for water conservation and drought-resistant agriculture. They migrated, adopting a nomadic lifestyle, following the rhythms of rainfall and seasonal changes. Their cultural narratives changed, incorporating the lessons learned from their adaptation and struggles—their very identities shifting and evolving in accordance with the planet's changing face.

Others, clinging to their established societal structures and technologies, fell into ruin. Their rigid refusal to adapt to the changing circumstances resulted in devastating consequences— their empires collapsing under the weight of drought, famine, and societal unrest. These examples of collapse, the Whispers' code revealed, weren't sudden cataclysms. They were the result of a long and slow erosion of environmental sustainability, a gradual depletion of resources, and a failure to recognize the interconnectedness of their society with the natural world. The Whispers' code contained a wealth of information about their engineering solutions and failed attempts to reverse or alleviate the impacts.

Another era—one of significant technological advancement— arose from the ruins of these former civilizations. They developed sophisticated irrigation systems, harnessed renewable energy sources, and even, according to the Whispers' code, attempted rudimentary forms of geoengineering, manipulating weather patterns to increase rainfall. Their society was more complex, their population densities higher, and their impact on the environment significantly greater.

Despite their technological advancements, however, they too ultimately faced environmental collapse. Their sophisticated technology, ironically, became the engine of their demise. A reliance on intensive agriculture and industrial processes ultimately depleted their resources and further destabilized the delicate balance of the planet. The code indicated that the consequences were brutal. The data pointed to a collapse—quick and devastating—as the society failed to adapt fast enough to the environmental challenges they created.

Several subsequent civilizations appeared and disappeared in a pattern that mirrored the previous ones. Each civilization rose, advanced, and ultimately fell as their societies strained the planet's resources and failed to recognize the limitations of their actions.

These societies were not inherently evil; they were driven by the same impulses that motivated humanity—the desire for progress, security, and prosperity. Yet each repetition underscored the same crucial lessons: the essential importance of sustainable practices, the fragility of the planet's delicate balance, and the devastating consequences of unchecked ambition. Each collapse, recorded in the planet's geological strata and the Whispers' code, served as a chilling testament to the cyclical nature of environmental collapse and societal transformation.

The Whispers weren't just providing a history lesson; they were offering a warning. The patterns of the past echoed ominously in the present, underscoring the potential for humanity to repeat the mistakes of its predecessors. The Convergence Protocol, in its elegant simplicity, represented a radical departure from this cyclical pattern. It wasn't merely a repair mechanism—it was an attempt to fundamentally alter the relationship between humanity and the planet, moving away from a model of dominion toward one of genuine partnership.

The success of the Protocol depended not just on technological prowess but on a fundamental shift in human consciousness—a profound understanding of humanity's role within the larger ecological web. The weight of this understanding pressed heavily on Sarah, Jonah, and Eliza as they absorbed the lessons of the planet's ancient echoes. The future, they realized, wasn't just about saving the planet; it was about saving themselves—from themselves.

The Luminese Ambassador Nyla, with her centuries of experience observing the rise and fall of civilizations across countless planets, offered a perspective informed by both empathy and profound wisdom. She spoke of other worlds, other civilizations, each with its own unique stories of environmental collapse and societal transformation. Some had adapted and flourished, finding sustainable ways to live within planetary boundaries. Others had perished, leaving behind a barren wasteland as a testament to their folly. Her words were not a condemnation but a reminder—a testament to the choice that faced humanity. Their ability to understand and adapt, not their technological prowess, would be the ultimate deciding factor in their survival.

The implications of the planet's ancient history extended beyond the technical aspects of the Convergence Protocol. It illuminated the ethical and philosophical dimensions of the crisis, forcing Sarah and her team to confront the complexities of human intervention in the natural world. The Whispers' code revealed not only the environmental impacts of past civilizations but also their social structures, cultural beliefs, and political systems. The rise and fall of these societies underscored the intertwined nature of environmental and societal stability, suggesting that a sustainable future required not only ecological awareness but also a fundamental reimagining of social structures and political systems.

The echoes of the past reverberated within Sarah, their impact resonating deep within her. She understood that the Convergence Protocol was not simply a technical solution but a profound act of self-reflection—a test of humanity's ability to learn from its mistakes and chart a new course, guided by a deep understanding of its place within the larger ecosystem. The weight of this understanding felt like a burden, yet it also instilled a newfound sense of purpose.

The ancient echoes were not just a warning but a call to action— a reminder that the fate of humanity was inextricably linked to the fate of the planet. The future was uncertain, fraught with challenges, but the weight of the past spurred them onward toward a future where humanity could finally become a true partner, not a master, of the planet.

The choice before them was not simply one of technological achievement; it was a choice that would define the future of humanity and the fate of the planet—a choice that would echo through the ages, a new chapter in Earth's long, complex history.

Lessons from the Past

The holographic projection flickered, shifting from geological strata to intricate depictions of ancient settlements. Dr. Grant, her eyes alight with a grim fascination, pointed to a swirling vortex of data points representing a societal collapse.

"This civilization," she explained, her voice low, "possessed advanced technology, comparable to the Luminese in some respects. They controlled vast energy sources, developed sophisticated agricultural techniques, and even engineered intricate systems for water management."

Jonah leaned forward, his brow furrowed. "And they still collapsed?"

"Yes," Dr. Grant confirmed, her voice heavy with the weight of the data. "Their downfall wasn't caused by a sudden cataclysm, like a meteor impact or a volcanic eruption. It was a slow, insidious process—a gradual erosion of their environmental sustainability."

The Whispers' data revealed a chilling narrative. This advanced civilization, obsessed with efficiency and expansion, had developed incredibly intensive agricultural practices, depleting the soil of its nutrients and leading to widespread land degradation. Their reliance on fossil fuels, though more refined than humanity's current methods, still released massive amounts of greenhouse gases into the atmosphere, contributing to a significant warming trend. Their sophisticated water management systems, while initially successful, had ultimately disrupted natural hydrological cycles, leading to unpredictable droughts and floods.

The holographic projection shifted, displaying complex mathematical models depicting the feedback loops between their technological advancements and the deteriorating environmental conditions. It was a stark illustration of the unintended consequences of technological hubris—a cautionary tale of a civilization that, in its pursuit of progress, had inadvertently sown the seeds of its own destruction.

"They didn't understand the limits of their planet," Nyla observed, her voice calm yet resonant. "They treated it as an inexhaustible resource, a machine to be manipulated and exploited for their own benefit. They failed to recognize the intricate web of interconnectedness that sustains life."

Eliza, ever the ethical compass of the group, added, "Their story highlights the importance of not just technological innovation, but also ethical considerations. Their pursuit of progress was divorced from any understanding of long-term sustainability, or even a sense of responsibility toward future generations."

The Whispers' code didn't simply record the environmental damage; it also detailed the societal consequences. As resources dwindled and environmental conditions worsened, social inequality grew. Competition for dwindling resources led to conflict and societal unrest. The elaborate social structures they had painstakingly built crumbled under the strain, replaced by chaos and desperation. The data showed a clear correlation between environmental degradation and social fragmentation—a grim reminder of the interconnectedness of ecological and societal health.

The holographic projection shifted again, revealing the cultural narratives of this fallen civilization. Their art, initially celebrating technological prowess and societal advancement, shifted dramatically as their world began to crumble. The later works depicted scenes of environmental devastation, social unrest, and despair—a poignant reflection of their deteriorating reality. Their literature, once filled with tales of progress and optimism, turned dark and dystopian, filled with warnings and lamentations. Their very language seemed to reflect their deteriorating environment, with words associated with abundance and prosperity being replaced by terms denoting scarcity and suffering. It was a painful reflection of how environmental collapse reshaped not only their physical world but their very consciousness.

Jonah, ever the data analyst, focused on the engineering failures. The Whispers' code revealed a multitude of attempts to reverse the environmental damage. They experimented with advanced geoengineering techniques, attempting to manipulate weather patterns and restore soil fertility. Some of these attempts yielded short-term successes, offering brief respites from the encroaching ecological crisis. However, these interventions often had unforeseen consequences, exacerbating the existing problems and creating new ones. The data showed a clear pattern of escalating interventions, each attempt to fix the problem making it worse—a feedback loop of technological desperation that eventually overwhelmed their efforts. The Whispers' code highlighted not just the technological limitations but the profound lack of understanding of the complex systems they were attempting to manipulate.

Sarah, reflecting on these past civilizations, saw a disturbing mirror of humanity's current trajectory. The parallels were unnervingly close: the relentless pursuit of economic growth, the unsustainable exploitation of resources, the growing social inequalities, the disregard for the long-term consequences of their actions. The Whispers' warnings were not abstract historical lessons; they were a stark and urgent call to action.

The narrative continued, showcasing other civilizations, each offering a unique perspective on the complex interplay between technological advancement, environmental sustainability, and societal stability. Some had adopted sustainable practices, living in harmony with their environment for millennia. Others, despite their technological prowess, had succumbed to the same self-destructive patterns, repeating the mistakes of their predecessors.

These accounts highlighted a recurring theme: the importance of understanding planetary boundaries, respecting the limits of resources, and integrating ecological considerations into all aspects of societal organization. There was no single solution, no universal blueprint for success. Each civilization had navigated its own unique circumstances, shaping its relationship with the environment and with each other through a variety of adaptive strategies.

Nyla, drawing upon her vast intergalactic experience, added another layer to this historical narrative. She spoke of civilizations that had harnessed advanced technologies to create sustainable societies—civilizations that had consciously integrated ecological considerations into their political and economic systems, developing technologies that were not only efficient but also ecologically benign. She shared stories of societies that had embraced a circular economy, minimizing waste and maximizing resource efficiency, of communities that had rediscovered the wisdom of traditional ecological knowledge, integrating ancient practices with modern technological innovations.

These were not utopian societies without challenges, but they demonstrated the possibility of forging a sustainable path—of creating a future where technological progress and environmental sustainability were not mutually exclusive but complementary forces. It was a testament to the potential for human ingenuity to solve the challenges of environmental sustainability, if approached with wisdom, foresight, and an understanding of the inherent interconnectedness of life.

The lessons from the past weren't just a catalog of failures; they also offered a glimpse of hope. They showed that societal transformation was possible, that humanity could learn from its mistakes and chart a new course toward a sustainable future. The Convergence Protocol, Sarah realized, wasn't just a technological solution—it was a reflection of humanity's potential to learn from the past, to overcome its self-destructive tendencies, and to forge a new relationship with the planet.

The choice before them was not merely one of survival, but of transformation—a shift from a culture of exploitation to one of stewardship, from dominion to partnership. The echoes of the past served as a guide, not as a prediction of the future but as a testament to the agency of humanity—its capacity to shape its destiny by learning from the mistakes of those who came before. The future remained uncertain, but the past offered a pathway—a guide through the darkness toward a brighter dawn.

The Wisdom of the Ancients

The holographic display shifted again, this time focusing on a civilization that had mastered a delicate balance between technology and nature. Their cities, built into the living landscape, were seamlessly integrated into the surrounding ecosystem. Their architecture wasn't merely functional; it was an art form, reflecting a deep understanding of natural processes and a profound respect for the environment. The Whispers' code revealed their sophisticated understanding of ecological principles, their ability to harness renewable energy sources, and their commitment to sustainable practices. Their agricultural methods, far from depleting the soil, actually enhanced its fertility, creating a symbiotic relationship between human activity and the natural world.

Jonah, ever the pragmatist, delved into the details of their technological achievements. He discovered they had developed closed-loop systems that minimized waste and maximized resource efficiency. Their transportation networks were designed to minimize their environmental footprint, relying on efficient, sustainable forms of energy. Their manufacturing processes prioritized the use of renewable materials and avoided the creation of harmful byproducts. Most fascinating to him was their system of energy production—a network of interconnected wind farms, solar arrays, and geothermal power plants that provided clean, sustainable energy for their entire civilization. This wasn't a simplistic rejection of technology; it was a conscious and deliberate integration of technology and nature, a testament to human ingenuity guided by ecological wisdom.

Dr. Grant, meanwhile, was captivated by their understanding of biodiversity. The Whispers' data showcased their meticulous preservation of ecosystems and their appreciation for the intricate web of life that supported their existence. Their cultural narratives emphasized the importance of biological diversity, highlighting the essential role it played in maintaining the health and resilience of their environment. Their art celebrated the beauty and complexity of nature, reflecting a deep connection between humanity and the natural world. Their scientific knowledge was not detached from their cultural understanding; it was embedded in their worldview, shaping their values and guiding their actions.

Nyla, drawing on her vast knowledge of countless civilizations across the galaxy, noted the unique aspects of this particular society.

"They understood the concept of planetary boundaries," she explained. "They recognized the limits of their planet's resources and consciously organized their society to live within those constraints. This wasn't a matter of technological limitations; it was a matter of ethical choices—a conscious decision to prioritize longterm sustainability over short-term gains."

She elaborated on the societal structures that supported their sustainable lifestyle, pointing out their decentralized governance system, their strong emphasis on community cooperation, and their commitment to education and cultural preservation. Their society was not static; it adapted to environmental changes, demonstrating the importance of resilience and adaptability in a constantly evolving world.

Sarah, observing the interconnectedness of their technological advancements, ecological understanding, and social structures, began to grasp the core principles of sustainable living. It wasn't simply about technological efficiency or environmental preservation in isolation; it was about creating a harmonious relationship between humanity and the planet—a society that thrived within the limits of its ecosystem. Their success wasn't due to a singular technological breakthrough; it was the result of a holistic approach, integrating ecological wisdom, technological innovation, and social responsibility.

The Whispers' data then shifted to another civilization, one that had achieved a similar level of technological sophistication but had followed a drastically different path. This civilization, initially driven by similar ecological concerns as the previous one, had gradually shifted its focus toward unchecked economic growth.

The Whispers' records meticulously documented their transition from sustainable practices to environmentally destructive ones. The narrative was a cautionary tale of incremental shifts—initially small and seemingly insignificant—that ultimately led to catastrophic consequences. Their initial commitment to renewable energy sources was gradually eroded by the allure of cheap, readily available fossil fuels. Their meticulously planned cities sprawled outward, encroaching on natural habitats and disrupting ecological balance. Their efficient transportation systems were replaced by energy-intensive vehicles, contributing to escalating greenhouse gas emissions. Their closed-loop systems were abandoned in favor of linear models of production and consumption, leading to increasing waste generation and resource depletion. Their commitment to biodiversity conservation gave way to a relentless focus on economic growth, resulting in widespread habitat destruction and biodiversity loss.

Jonah, analyzing the data, noted the insidious nature of this decline. There was no single catastrophic event; rather, it was a gradual erosion of ecological awareness—a slow shift in priorities that eventually led to environmental devastation. The Whispers' code revealed the internal struggles within their society, the conflict between those who championed sustainability and those who prioritized short-term economic gains. The data depicted a gradual erosion of public trust in scientific consensus, a rise in misinformation campaigns, and a decline in societal cohesion.

Dr. Grant observed the parallel between their societal fragmentation and their environmental degradation. The decline in ecological health mirrored the unraveling of their social fabric. The data highlighted the profound consequences of social inequalities, the rise of extremism, and the erosion of community bonds. The cultural narratives reflected this disintegration, showcasing a decline in artistic expression, a rise in social unrest, and a growing sense of despair.

Nyla's intergalactic perspective brought an additional layer of complexity to this societal collapse. She spoke of similar situations across various planets and star systems, emphasizing the recurring patterns of ecological degradation and social disintegration. She highlighted the importance of understanding the dynamic interplay between human behavior, technological advancement, and environmental health, stressing the need for a holistic approach that integrated ecological principles into all aspects of societal organization. She also underscored the significance of long-term vision and effective governance, emphasizing the need for societal structures that prioritize long-term sustainability over short-term gains.

Sarah found herself contemplating the implications of these contrasting narratives. The stories of these ancient civilizations weren't just historical accounts; they were warnings—stark reminders of the choices humanity faced. The path to sustainability wasn't a utopian dream; it was a complex undertaking, requiring both technological innovation and a profound shift in values and priorities. The Whispers' wisdom offered not just a vision of the past but also a map for the future—a guide for navigating the treacherous path toward a sustainable world.

The Convergence Protocol, she realized, wasn't merely a technological fix; it was an embodiment of these lessons—a reflection of humanity's potential to learn from the past, to adapt to changing circumstances, and to forge a new relationship with the planet. A partnership built on mutual respect, understanding, and a commitment to long-term sustainability. The weight of these ancient whispers settled upon her—a profound responsibility to ensure that humanity didn't repeat the mistakes of its predecessors but instead learned from their wisdom and embraced a path toward a truly sustainable future.

Cultural Preservation

The holographic projection flickered, shifting from the ruins of a fallen civilization to a vibrant tapestry of cultural expressions. This time, the Whispers' data focused not on technological achievements or ecological strategies, but on the intangible threads of culture— the stories, songs, rituals, and knowledge passed down through generations, intimately tied to the land and its rhythms. The images swam across the screen: intricate carvings depicting the life cycles of local flora and fauna, ancient songs celebrating the bounty of the harvest and the wisdom of the elders, elaborate ceremonies honoring the spirits of the forest and the sea. These weren't mere relics of the past; they were living expressions of a profound connection between humanity and the natural world, a connection that had shaped their worldview and guided their actions for millennia.

Jonah, initially skeptical of the relevance of such seemingly "soft" data in their quest to activate the Convergence Protocol, found himself increasingly captivated. He saw patterns emerging— intricate links between specific cultural practices and successful environmental management. For instance, one society's complex system of water management was intrinsically tied to their annual rain dance, a ritual that not only celebrated the life-giving rain but also served as a mechanism for coordinating water allocation and resource sharing within the community. Their knowledge wasn't simply codified in scientific treatises; it was embedded within their cultural practices, passed down from generation to generation through storytelling, song, and ritual. The loss of these practices, he realized, represented not just a loss of cultural heritage but also a loss of invaluable ecological knowledge.

Dr. Grant, her expertise in marine biology now broadened by the Whispers' revelations, recognized the profound connection between cultural practices and biodiversity conservation. She noted how many indigenous communities around the world had developed sophisticated systems of resource management based on a deep understanding of ecological processes and a profound respect for the interconnectedness of life. Their traditional knowledge systems, often dismissed as mere folklore, proved to be invaluable repositories of practical ecological wisdom, offering insights into sustainable agriculture, fisheries management, and forest conservation. The loss of these cultures, she saw, represented a significant loss of biological knowledge and a crippling blow to efforts to protect biodiversity. The data showed communities whose languages, interwoven with ecological knowledge, were vanishing—taking with them centuries of nuanced understanding about the delicate balance of their environment. The consequences were clear in the records: ecosystems once thriving, now degraded or lost.

Nyla, her perspective broadened by centuries of observation across countless civilizations, highlighted the critical role of cultural preservation in fostering long-term sustainability. She spoke of societies that had successfully navigated environmental challenges, often drawing strength and resilience from their cultural heritage. She stressed the interconnectedness of culture, environment, and social structures, emphasizing how strong cultural identities often fostered a sense of collective responsibility toward the environment, encouraging cooperation and stewardship. She offered examples of societies whose unique cultural narratives had instilled in their members a profound respect for the natural world, leading to sustainable practices and long-term environmental harmony. She contrasted this with societies where the erosion of cultural identity had coincided with ecological degradation, emphasizing the fragility of human-environmental connections when cultural memory fades.

Sarah, synthesizing the information, began to appreciate the critical role cultural heritage played in shaping human behavior and societal choices. She understood that technological solutions alone were insufficient; they had to be embedded within a framework of shared values and ethical principles—values and principles often rooted in cultural traditions. She saw that the Whispers' code highlighted the importance of revitalizing and preserving cultural heritage not as mere historical artifacts, but as dynamic and evolving elements crucial to the success of the Convergence Protocol. This was not simply a matter of preserving ancient practices for their historical significance; it was about recognizing their crucial role in shaping sustainable societies. Many of these practices, the data showed, were intrinsically linked to the health and resilience of ecosystems, offering practical solutions to environmental challenges.

The Whispers' data then presented a jarring counterpoint: societies that, despite possessing advanced technologies, had failed to appreciate the importance of cultural preservation, often leading to environmental collapse. These societies, driven by rapid technological advancement and unchecked economic growth, had often marginalized or disregarded their traditional knowledge systems, replacing them with standardized, often unsustainable practices. Their scientific and technological progress, disconnected from their cultural roots, had led to ecological degradation and social fragmentation. They had discarded intricate systems of resource management for exploitative models, ignoring ancient wisdom about the delicate balance of their ecosystems, resulting in ecological catastrophes. The patterns were alarmingly similar across different worlds and different times: cultural homogeneity, loss of languages, and the replacement of time-tested, locally adapted practices with top-down, uniform approaches.

Jonah meticulously studied the details, comparing the technological failures with the accompanying cultural disintegration. He saw a correlation between the loss of traditional ecological knowledge and the emergence of unsustainable practices, highlighting the importance of indigenous knowledge in navigating environmental challenges. He also noted the role of cultural diversity in promoting resilience and adaptability, highlighting how the loss of cultural diversity often diminished a society's capacity to adapt to environmental change. The data starkly illustrated that technological advancements, divorced from a profound understanding of ecological principles and the wisdom of the past, could not alone ensure a sustainable future.

Dr. Grant, examining the ecological consequences of cultural loss, discovered a parallel between the decline of biodiversity and the decline of cultural diversity. She found that many indigenous cultures possessed a deep understanding of their local ecosystems, having evolved intricate systems of resource management that had supported their livelihoods for centuries. The loss of these cultures not only resulted in the loss of valuable ecological knowledge but also increased the vulnerability of ecosystems to degradation. Their data confirmed that the rich tapestry of human cultures held a vital key to understanding and protecting the diversity of life on Earth.

Nyla observed that the dominance of globalized cultures often led to the marginalization and suppression of local traditions, resulting in a loss of ecological knowledge and a decline in social cohesion.

This homogenization, she stressed, undermined the resilience of societies and made them more vulnerable to environmental shocks. She pointed to many examples across her vast experience where the preservation of distinct cultural identities served as a crucial buffer against environmental degradation, ensuring adaptation and sustainability. The loss of distinct cultures, she contended, often meant the loss of diverse approaches to environmental stewardship, which meant a loss in the total strategies humanity could draw upon.

Sarah, reflecting on the wealth of data, understood that the Convergence Protocol was not simply a technological fix, but a catalyst for a profound cultural and social transformation. It was about creating a future where human societies could thrive within the limits of the planet's resources, building a harmonious relationship with the natural world. This required not only technological innovation but also a revitalization and celebration of cultural diversity, a commitment to respecting and integrating traditional ecological knowledge into modern practices. It demanded not just technological prowess but also an ethical framework—one rooted in deep respect for both humanity and the planet, a respect nourished and sustained by the wisdom of our collective past.

The task, she realized, was not just to repair the planet, but to heal the human relationship with nature—a healing process deeply connected to the revitalization of our cultural heritage. The whispers of the past were not simply echoes of a bygone era; they were a guide for the future, a testament to the enduring wisdom of a humanity living in harmony with its environment. The activation of the Convergence Protocol held the key, but its success depended on remembering and rebuilding.

A Legacy of Resilience

The holographic display shifted again, this time focusing on specific case studies. Each was a miniature epic, a testament to human ingenuity and adaptability in the face of environmental adversity. One example showcased the ingenious water management systems of the ancient Anasazi people, their cliff dwellings a marvel of architectural and hydrological integration. The Whispers' data revealed their sophisticated understanding of rainfall patterns, water harvesting techniques, and community organization that allowed these communities to thrive in arid environments for centuries.

Their success, the data highlighted, wasn't just a matter of technology; it was the result of a deep cultural connection to the land, a respect for its rhythms, and a commitment to collective stewardship. The collapse of their civilization, centuries later, coincided with a shift away from these traditional practices—a tragic illustration of the consequences of disconnecting from ancestral wisdom.

Another case study detailed the sustainable agriculture practices of the Polynesian islanders, whose mastery of ocean navigation and resource management allowed them to colonize and thrive across vast stretches of the Pacific Ocean. Their intimate knowledge of marine ecosystems, their understanding of currents, fish migration patterns, and the delicate balance of the coral reefs enabled them to develop sustainable fishing techniques that ensured the long-term health of their environment. The Whispers' analysis showed a direct correlation between the preservation of their traditional knowledge and the resilience of their communities.

The introduction of external influences, however, disrupted this delicate equilibrium, leading to overfishing, habitat destruction, and ultimately, societal upheaval. The data underscored a crucial point: sustainable practices weren't simply a matter of efficiency—they were embedded within a holistic worldview, a framework of values and beliefs that shaped human interactions with the environment.

Jonah, now deeply immersed in the analysis, began to see recurring themes. He noticed a strong correlation between cultural diversity and environmental resilience. Societies with diverse cultural practices and a strong sense of community often demonstrated remarkable adaptability to environmental changes. Their various approaches to resource management, their different strategies for coping with natural disasters, and their diverse perspectives on the environment all contributed to their overall resilience.

The loss of cultural diversity, on the other hand, seemed to weaken a society's ability to cope with environmental challenges, making it more vulnerable to collapse. The data didn't just show success stories; it also detailed failures, highlighting the catastrophic consequences of discarding indigenous knowledge and replacing it with unsustainable practices driven by short-term economic gain.

Dr. Grant, focusing on the biological implications, found compelling evidence to support this conclusion. The Whispers' data revealed a strong correlation between biodiversity loss and the loss of cultural diversity. The indigenous knowledge systems of many communities around the world contained invaluable information about the ecological interactions of plants and animals, including intricate systems of classification, traditional medicine, and sustainable harvesting practices. The loss of these cultures not only meant the loss of invaluable biodiversity but also the loss of the knowledge necessary to protect and manage it. The data painted a stark picture of ecosystems collapsing where cultural diversity had been systematically erased. The historical record showed a tragic decline in both biodiversity and cultural practices running in parallel across many regions.

Nyla, drawing on her vast experience, provided further insights. She highlighted how many indigenous cultures had developed spiritual connections to the land, a deep respect for the interconnectedness of all life, and a sense of responsibility toward future generations. This holistic worldview, she argued, fostered sustainable practices and promoted long-term environmental stewardship. The erosion of these spiritual connections, she observed, often coincided with the adoption of unsustainable practices and a decline in environmental quality. She cited numerous examples across different cultures, highlighting the crucial role of spiritual and cultural values in fostering environmental responsibility. The data supported her assertions, showcasing societies whose connection to the land sustained them across generations, and whose disconnection from it led to rapid environmental decline.

Sarah, piecing together the information, began to understand the true significance of the Whispers' message. The Convergence Protocol wasn't merely a technological solution—it was a call for a profound cultural and spiritual transformation. It was about recognizing the intrinsic link between human well-being and environmental health, acknowledging the invaluable contributions of indigenous knowledge, and celebrating the diversity of human cultures and their intricate relationship with the natural world. The Whispers were not simply revealing past successes and failures; they were providing a blueprint for a future where humanity could live in harmony with the planet—a future built upon the foundations of resilience, respect, and cooperation.

The data showcased societies that had successfully adapted to changing climates, overcome resource scarcity, and navigated complex environmental challenges. These weren't isolated incidents; they were repeated examples across cultures and eras. The common thread, the Whispers' data underscored, was the integration of traditional knowledge with innovative practices, the preservation of cultural diversity, and the fostering of a deep sense of community and shared responsibility.

The Whispers' analysis then delved into the intricate relationship between social structures and environmental sustainability. It showed societies where strong social cohesion, a sense of collective responsibility, and effective governance systems had facilitated the development of sustainable practices. Conversely, societies characterized by social inequality, conflict, and weak governance structures were often more susceptible to environmental degradation. The data highlighted that environmental sustainability was not merely a technological or ecological challenge but also a social and political one.

Jonah meticulously documented the various governance models, comparing those that prioritized environmental protection with those that didn't. He saw a consistent pattern: societies that integrated environmental concerns into their political and economic decision-making processes, often incorporating traditional ecological knowledge, were more successful in achieving sustainability. Conversely, societies that prioritized short-term economic gains over environmental protection often experienced ecological collapse. The data demonstrated the crucial role of political will and social responsibility in shaping environmental outcomes.

Dr. Grant's analysis focused on the role of biodiversity in enhancing the resilience of ecosystems. The Whispers' data showed a direct correlation between high levels of biodiversity and the ability of ecosystems to withstand environmental shocks, such as droughts, floods, and pest outbreaks. The loss of biodiversity, on the other hand, often made ecosystems more vulnerable to collapse. Her findings underscored the importance of conserving biodiversity not only for its intrinsic value but also for its crucial role in maintaining the health and resilience of the planet. The data emphasized the interconnectedness of all life and the vital role of maintaining biodiversity in the face of environmental change.

Nyla's insights added a crucial layer to this understanding. She explained that many cultures had developed intricate systems of resource management based on a deep respect for the interconnectedness of all life. These systems often incorporated traditional ecological knowledge, spiritual beliefs, and social structures to ensure the sustainable use of resources. The disruption of these traditional systems, she stressed, often had catastrophic consequences for both the environment and human societies. She underscored that respecting the wisdom of past generations and honoring cultural diversity were essential for building a truly sustainable future. The data highlighted examples where societal disruptions and ecological damage were directly linked to the destruction of traditional cultural practices.

Sarah, integrating all this information, finally understood the scope of the challenge. The Convergence Protocol wasn't simply about fixing the planet; it was about healing the fractured relationship between humanity and the natural world. It was about restoring a sense of balance, respecting the wisdom of the past, embracing the diversity of human cultures, and fostering a profound sense of shared responsibility toward the future.

The Whispers of the past were not just echoes of a bygone era, but a roadmap to a resilient and sustainable future—a future where humanity could truly become a partner with the planet. A future that began with the acceptance that the wisdom of the past held the key to a hopeful tomorrow.

The data provided a blueprint for a global effort, a journey that required not only technological prowess but a fundamental shift in human values and societal structures—a profound societal transformation that would redefine humanity's relationship with the planet.

The path forward was clearly laid out. It was time to start walking it.

Chapter Twelve

A Luminese's Journey

The holographic projection shimmered, resolving into a swirling nebula of vibrant colors—a cosmic tapestry that pulsed with an inner light. This wasn't the sterile data stream they had been poring over; this was a narrative, a visual history etched in starlight. Nyla, her usually composed features marked with profound solemnity, explained, "This is what the Whispers call the 'Luminese Genesis.' It's not merely a historical record, but a living echo of our origins."

The images shifted, revealing a world unlike anything Sarah, Jonah, or even Dr. Grant had ever conceived. A planet bathed in the perpetual twilight of a binary sunset, its surface a mosaic of bioluminescent forests and crystalline oceans. The Luminese, in their nascent form, weren't the sleek, technologically advanced beings they knew. They were closer to symbionts—a harmonious blend of organic and inorganic matter, their bodies shimmering with an internal light that mirrored the bioluminescent flora of their world. Their technology wasn't manufactured in factories; it grew, evolved alongside them, a natural extension of their being.

"Our ancestors," Nyla continued, her voice resonating with the weight of millennia, "didn't 'invent' technology. They cultivated it.

They understood the intricate dance between energy, matter, and consciousness, learning to harness the very life force of their world.

Their tools, their dwellings, even their very bodies were expressions of this symbiotic relationship."

The holographic display zoomed in on intricate details. Structures resembling colossal trees, pulsating with a soft, internal light, served as both dwellings and power sources. These weren't merely buildings; they were living ecosystems, drawing energy from the planet's core and channeling it through a network of bioluminescent veins. The Luminese, in turn, were deeply integrated into this network, their bodies acting as both conduits and regulators of this energy flow.

"Our technology wasn't separate from us," Nyla emphasized. "It was an extension of ourselves, a reflection of our understanding of the interconnectedness of all things. There was no division between the organic and the inorganic, the natural and the artificial. It was a seamless integration, a harmonious coexistence."

The narrative then shifted, depicting a catastrophic event—a cosmic disturbance that shattered the delicate balance of their world. The binary suns, once a source of life-giving energy, began to destabilize, their erratic flares causing widespread ecological devastation. The luminescent forests withered, the crystalline oceans turned murky, and the symbiotic relationship between the Luminese and their world fractured. Their once harmonious existence was thrown into chaos.

"The Great Sundering," Nyla whispered, her voice heavy with sorrow. "It forced us to adapt, to evolve. We had to develop new technologies, new strategies for survival. But even in the face of such devastation, we clung to the core principles of our heritage—the understanding of interconnectedness, the respect for the natural world."

The images showed the Luminese developing new forms of energy harvesting, utilizing advanced bioengineering techniques to create more resilient ecosystems. They learned to manipulate light, harnessing its energy to power their cities and sustain their lives. Their bodies evolved, becoming more adaptable and more resistant to the changing environment. But the transformation wasn't without its cost. The seamless integration between technology and nature began to fray, replaced by a more deliberate, more controlled relationship.

The Luminese journey was one of adaptation and resilience, a testament to their capacity for innovation and their unwavering commitment to the preservation of life. They didn't abandon their past; instead, they integrated the lessons of the Great Sundering into their future, forging a new path—a delicate balance between technological advancement and environmental stewardship.

As the narrative progressed, the holographic display showed the gradual shift in Luminese society. Their cities, once seamlessly integrated into the natural world, began to incorporate more technologically advanced structures. They started developing sophisticated energy systems, capable of harnessing the power of the unstable binary suns. Their technology became more complex, more powerful, but it also became more detached from the natural rhythms of their world.

The Whispers' analysis revealed a subtle yet significant shift in the Luminese worldview. The deep spiritual connection to their planet, once the cornerstone of their society, began to wane, replaced by a more utilitarian approach to nature. Their technological prowess became a source of both pride and hubris, leading to a gradual detachment from the natural world that had once sustained them. This was not a conscious decision, but rather an inevitable consequence of their struggle for survival.

The transition wasn't linear; it was a complex interplay of adaptation, innovation, and compromise. There were factions within Luminese society that advocated for a return to the symbiotic relationship with their world, while others championed technological advancement as the only path to survival. This internal conflict shaped their history, influencing their relationship with humanity and their eventual involvement in the Convergence Protocol.

The data highlighted the challenges the Luminese faced as they attempted to balance the need for technological advancement with the preservation of their planet. Their advanced technologies, while crucial for their survival, also placed a strain on the environment. They wrestled with ethical dilemmas, constantly weighing the benefits of progress against the potential consequences.

The holographic projections shifted to show the Luminese's first encounters with humanity. These encounters were fraught with misunderstandings, mistrust, and fear. The early interactions revealed a clash of cultures, philosophies, and technologies. The Luminese, with their advanced knowledge and powerful technologies, viewed humanity as a primitive race, incapable of understanding the delicate balance of their planet. Humanity, on the other hand, viewed the Luminese with a mixture of awe and suspicion.

The Whispers' analysis revealed the nuances of these early interactions. It highlighted the attempts by some Luminese to help humanity, sharing their knowledge and technology. But these efforts were often met with resistance or misunderstanding. Other Luminese, driven by a sense of superiority, remained aloof, content to observe humanity's struggles from a distance.

The holographic display transitioned to depict a series of events that shaped the Luminese perspective on humanity. Natural disasters, resource depletion, and the escalating environmental crisis forced the Luminese to reconsider their aloof stance. They realized that humanity's fate was inextricably linked to their own. The survival of both species depended on their ability to cooperate and work together to address the planet's ecological challenges.

This realization prompted a significant shift in the Luminese approach to humanity. They began to actively engage with human societies, offering their knowledge and technology to help mitigate the environmental crisis. The Luminese involvement in the Convergence Protocol represented the culmination of this shift. They recognized the potential of this project to restore the planet's health and create a more sustainable future for both species. But they also understood the inherent risks involved. The activation of the Protocol could potentially alter the planet's ecosystems in unforeseen ways, disrupting the delicate balance of life.

The Luminese journey was a complex tapestry of adaptation, resilience, innovation, and ethical dilemma. Their history served as a cautionary tale, highlighting the potential dangers of unchecked technological advancement and the crucial importance of maintaining a harmonious relationship with the natural world.

Their story provided a crucial context for understanding their involvement in the Convergence Protocol and their commitment to finding a path to a sustainable future for all. The final images showed the Luminese not just as technologically advanced beings, but as beings striving for balance, their history a testament to the ongoing negotiation between progress and preservation. Their past was a mirror reflecting humanity's choices, urging a future where technology and nature coexist not as adversaries, but as partners in a shared journey of survival.

Technological Evolution

The holographic display shifted, leaving the turbulent aftermath of the Great Sundering behind. Now, it showcased the Luminese's remarkable adaptive capacity. Their initial technology, born from symbiotic harmony with their planet, was replaced by a more deliberate, engineered approach. The crystalline structures that once pulsed with inherent light gave way to cities sculpted from a newly discovered, self-healing mineral that absorbed and redirected the erratic solar flares. These structures, while less organically beautiful, were incredibly resilient and efficient, capable of withstanding the volatile energy surges that plagued their world.

This transition wasn't a simple replacement of old with new; it was a complex evolution. The Luminese didn't abandon bioluminescence; instead, they harnessed it more effectively. They developed sophisticated systems that captured and amplified ambient bioluminescence, using it to illuminate their cities and power smaller-scale technologies. Their understanding of light wasn't merely for illumination—they discovered its potential as a powerful energy source, creating intricate systems that converted light into usable energy, a far cry from the passive energy absorption of their earlier era.

Their understanding of energy extended beyond light. They began to tap into the planet's geothermal energy, using ingenious methods to channel the planet's internal heat into their cities. This process, however, was not without environmental consequences. Deep geothermal drilling caused subtle shifts in the planet's tectonic plates, increasing seismic activity and creating localized environmental disruptions. This led to internal debates within Luminese society, with some advocating for a reduction in geothermal energy usage and a renewed focus on bioluminescence and solar energy. These debates highlighted the ethical dilemmas they faced—a continuous balancing act between survival needs and environmental sustainability.

The development of advanced materials played a crucial role in their technological advancement. They discovered ways to manipulate matter at the atomic level, creating materials with unparalleled strength, flexibility, and energy conductivity. This led to the development of more efficient energy systems, advanced transportation networks, and sophisticated communication technologies. Their cities transformed, becoming architectural marvels of self-regulating ecosystems, efficient energy distribution, and advanced waste recycling systems. They mastered the art of creating closed-loop systems, minimizing their environmental footprint. But even with these innovations, the pressure on their resources remained a constant challenge, forcing them to engage in resource management strategies that often involved delicate negotiations and compromises.

Their technological advancements influenced their societal structure as well. The initial communal, egalitarian society gradually transformed into a more stratified system. Specializations emerged, with some Luminese focusing on energy management, others on materials science, and still others on governance and social organization. This specialization led to a shift in power dynamics, with those possessing specialized skills gaining more influence and authority. This new structure, while efficient, also brought new challenges, such as the potential for social inequality and the risk of decisions driven by self-interest rather than the collective good.

The rise of technological complexity, however, brought with it an unintended consequence: a gradual disconnect from the natural world. While they continued to respect and study their environment, reliance on sophisticated technology fostered a sense of detachment—a perception of dominion over nature rather than partnership. This shift was reflected in their art, their philosophy, and their overall worldview. Their art evolved from depictions of symbiotic harmony with nature to displays of technological prowess and mastery over the environment. Their philosophical discussions revolved around the ethics of technological advancement, the potential for human-like AI, and the very nature of consciousness itself.

This detachment wasn't a complete rupture. Certain Luminese factions, often referred to as the "Harmonists," continued to advocate for a return to a more symbiotic relationship with the planet. They criticized the overreliance on advanced technologies, arguing that it was fostering unsustainable practices and widening the gap between the Luminese and their natural world. Their arguments, however, were often met with resistance from the "Progressives," who championed technological advancement as the only way to ensure the Luminese's continued survival. This internal conflict, a recurring theme in their history, shaped their interactions with humanity and informed their approach to the Convergence Protocol.

The Luminese's first contact with humanity was a complex affair. Initially, the Luminese observed humanity from a distance, viewing them as a primitive, unsustainable civilization on a collision course with environmental collapse. Their technologically superior position fueled a sense of both pity and superiority. However, as the environmental crisis on Earth escalated, the Luminese began to reconsider their detached approach. They recognized the shared fate they faced, acknowledging that humanity's survival was inextricably linked to the health of the planet and, therefore, to their own survival.

This realization marked a crucial turning point. The Luminese began to engage actively with humanity, sharing their advanced technologies and knowledge in an attempt to mitigate the escalating environmental crisis. But their attempts were not always met with success.

Humanity's societal structures, ingrained beliefs, and often short-sighted approaches to resource management presented formidable challenges. The Luminese faced the daunting task of bridging a chasm of vastly different cultures, technologies, and worldviews. Differences in philosophical approaches to the natural world created friction and misunderstanding, leading to challenges in collaboration and shared decision-making.

The journey wasn't easy. The Luminese learned to navigate complex human politics, engage in cross-cultural dialogues, and contend with the often conflicting priorities of various human factions. Their involvement with the Convergence Protocol is a testament to their evolving understanding of humanity and their commitment to finding a path toward a shared future. This path, however, was not without potential risks. The Convergence Protocol held the promise of planetary regeneration, but it also posed the possibility of irreversible changes to the planet's ecosystems— changes that could have unpredictable consequences for both the Luminese and humanity.

Their decision to participate in this project underscores their willingness to take a significant risk, a testament to their adaptation and to the possibility of a future where different species could find a way to coexist, even in the face of cataclysmic change. The technological evolution of the Luminese was not simply a progression toward more advanced tools; it was a story of adaptation, conflict, compromise, and a gradual but profound understanding of the delicate balance between progress and planetary health. Their journey mirrors humanity's choices, demonstrating the intricate interplay between technological advancement, environmental responsibility, and the enduring quest for a sustainable future.

Ethical Principles

The Luminese, despite their advanced technology, never fully severed their connection to the fundamental principles guiding their existence. Their ethical framework, deeply intertwined with their unique physiology and history, isn't easily translated into human terms. It is less a codified system of rules and more a deeply ingrained sense of interconnectedness—a holistic approach to existence that emphasizes balance and sustainability above all else.

This is not a simple altruism; survival for the Luminese hinges on maintaining the delicate equilibrium of their world.

Central to their ethics is the concept of Symbiogenesis, a term encompassing their understanding of mutual benefit and interdependence. It is not merely a recognition of the interconnectedness of living things but an active participation in it.

Their early history was defined by a symbiotic relationship with their planet, their bioluminescence echoing the planet's own subtle energy patterns. This inherent connection fostered a deep respect for the environment, a perspective that shaped their societal structures and technological development. Even after their technological advancements, the principle of Symbiogenesis remains central to their decision-making. Any technological advancement is weighed against its potential impact on the planet's delicate equilibrium.

Geothermal energy, for example, though initially embraced for its efficiency, faced growing scrutiny as its potential to disrupt tectonic stability became apparent. The ensuing debates within Luminese society were not about abandoning progress but about finding a sustainable path forward—one that respected the principle of Symbiogenesis.

The concept of Luminary Resonance further defines their ethical approach. It refers to the harmonious interplay between the Luminese, their technology, and the planet's natural energy fields. It is a constant striving for alignment, a pursuit of resonance that extends beyond mere energy efficiency to encompass a deeper understanding of interconnectedness. Disruptions to this resonance, whether caused by technological mishaps or environmental degradation, are viewed as ethical failures, highlighting the importance of careful planning and consideration. Projects involving significant energy manipulation or resource extraction undergo rigorous assessments—not only to evaluate their immediate impact but also to predict their long-term effects on Luminary Resonance. The potential for unforeseen consequences, however small, is considered a violation of this principle.

The Luminese also adhere to the principle of Adaptive Equilibrium. This acknowledges the dynamism of their environment and the need for constant adaptation. Their history is punctuated by periods of environmental upheaval, forcing them to continually adjust their societal structures and technological innovations to maintain equilibrium. This principle fosters a culture of adaptability and resilience, but it also involves careful consideration of the potential long-term consequences of any adaptation. Rapid technological advancements, while tempting, are scrutinized for their potential to disrupt existing ecological balances. Any change, therefore, must be carefully integrated into the existing ecosystem, aiming for a state of dynamic equilibrium rather than disruption.

Their approach to resource management is a perfect illustration of Adaptive Equilibrium. They do not simply exploit resources; they cultivate them, actively managing ecosystems to enhance resource availability while minimizing environmental impact. This involves a sophisticated understanding of ecological processes, predictive modeling, and advanced technological interventions. The concept of waste is almost alien to their society; materials are recycled and reused in complex closed-loop systems, minimizing environmental impact and maximizing resource efficiency. Even the extraction of materials is approached with a deep sense of responsibility, with methods designed to minimize ecological disruption and ensure long-term sustainability. This approach, far from being restrictive, allows for continued innovation while ensuring the planet's longterm health.

The Luminese's decision to engage with humanity and contribute to the Convergence Protocol wasn't a purely altruistic act. It stemmed from a deep understanding of their interconnected fate. They recognize that the health of Earth is intrinsically linked to their own survival. This recognition, however, did not erase their differences; it simply provided a framework for collaboration. Their involvement is guided by the principles outlined above: minimizing disruption, maximizing positive impact, and fostering a symbiotic relationship with humanity and the planet. The Protocol itself is seen as a complex experiment—a carefully calibrated intervention designed to restore balance, but one with potential unforeseen consequences.

This ethical framework is not without its internal tensions. Differences of opinion arise frequently, particularly when balancing immediate needs with long-term sustainability. The Harmonists prioritize a more cautious approach, emphasizing bioluminescence and a deeper integration with the planet, while the Progressives advocate for continued technological advancement, believing it essential for survival. These debates, far from being disruptive, are seen as crucial aspects of maintaining adaptive equilibrium. They reflect the Luminese's ongoing struggle to balance the needs of the present with the demands of a sustainable future, underscoring the inherent complexities of their ethical approach.

Their interactions with humanity are further complicated by vast cultural differences. The Luminese's holistic, interconnected worldview clashes with humanity's often fragmented, anthropocentric approach to the environment. Their patience in sharing knowledge and technology is partly motivated by hope that humanity can also embrace a more sustainable path, though they recognize the challenges inherent in such a profound shift in perspective. The ethical dilemma of potentially erasing human civilization through the Convergence Protocol weighs heavily on their decision-making, emphasizing the deep ethical complexities of their involvement. It is a delicate balance, a constant negotiation between what is necessary for planetary health and what is possible within the context of diverse societal structures and conflicting values.

In conclusion, the Luminese's ethical principles are not rigid rules but evolving guidelines, shaped by their intimate relationship with their environment and their unique history. Their framework emphasizes interconnectedness, adaptability, and a commitment to sustainability.

Their engagement with humanity and the Convergence Protocol is a testament to their ethical approach, showcasing the complexities of balancing survival, progress, and planetary health. It is a reflection of a society that constantly strives for balance, recognizing the intricate dance between technology, ethics, and the enduring need for a sustainable future for all life on Earth. The ethical journey of the Luminese serves as a potent example—and a stark warning—for humanity. The future of both species depends on the choices made, choices framed by the profound understanding that true survival means survival in harmony with the planet, a principle that transcends individual species and speaks to the fundamental unity of all life.

Interspecies Relations

The Luminese approach to interspecies relations is a direct extension of their intrinsic philosophy of Symbiogenesis. Their interactions are not driven by conquest or domination, but by a deepseated understanding of interdependence. This understanding is not limited to the biological realm; it extends to the technological and even the cultural spheres. Their interactions with humanity, therefore, are not simply transactions but attempts at forging a symbiotic partnership—a delicate dance aimed at achieving a shared, sustainable future.

However, this does not imply a simplistic, utopian harmony. The Luminese are not naive; they are acutely aware of the inherent risks involved in collaborating with a species whose history is marked by environmental exploitation and a seemingly insatiable hunger for resources. Their engagement with humanity is a calculated risk, a carefully considered gamble predicated on the understanding that the survival of both species depends on their ability to overcome their differences and forge a common path toward a sustainable future.

This calculated risk is evident in their approach to knowledge sharing. The Luminese have not simply transferred their advanced technologies to humanity; they have shared the underlying principles guiding their development. This includes not just the scientific knowledge but also the ethical frameworks that inform their technological choices. They have attempted to impart their understanding of Symbiogenesis, Luminary Resonance, and Adaptive Equilibrium, hoping that humanity can adopt a more holistic and sustainable approach to its own development. This educational process, however, is fraught with challenges. The Luminese find themselves constantly navigating the complexities of human culture, attempting to translate their sophisticated understanding of interconnectedness into a language that resonates with a species accustomed to viewing the world through a more fragmented lens.

The challenges are compounded by the cultural differences in communication styles. The Luminese, with their holistic perception of reality, often find themselves struggling to convey their nuanced understanding to humans who tend to compartmentalize information and prioritize short-term gains over long-term sustainability. The concept of Luminary Resonance, for instance, is difficult to grasp for humans accustomed to seeing energy as a mere commodity rather than a fundamental element of an interconnected system. Similarly, the principle of Adaptive Equilibrium often clashes with humanity's tendency toward linear progress—a trajectory that often overlooks the potential for unforeseen consequences.

The Luminese's interactions with the Whispers, the sentient ecosystems, are equally complex. They view the Whispers not as mere resources to be exploited but as essential partners in maintaining planetary health. Their relationship with the Whispers is characterized by mutual respect and a deep understanding of the delicate balance sustaining their world. The Luminese have developed sophisticated methods of communication with the Whispers, interpreting their subtle energy patterns and integrating their knowledge into their own decision-making processes. This harmonious relationship stands in stark contrast to humanity's often destructive approach to the natural world, underscoring the chasm in perspectives and approaches to interspecies cooperation.

The emergence of the Echoborn—humans merging with the Whispers—presents a new dimension to interspecies relations. The Luminese view the Echoborn with a mixture of fascination and concern. While recognizing the potential for a new form of symbiosis, they also acknowledge the uncertainties inherent in this evolving relationship. They are wary of the potential for unforeseen consequences, mindful of the need to monitor and guide the development of this new hybrid species to ensure a sustainable and equitable coexistence. This cautious optimism underscores their profound respect for the interconnectedness of life and their unwavering commitment to a sustainable future for all.

The interactions with Dr. Rafe Mallory present the greatest challenge to the Luminese's carefully calibrated approach.

Mallory's reckless ambition and disregard for ethical considerations represent a direct threat to the Convergence Protocol and the delicate balance they are striving to achieve. His actions expose the fundamental differences between the Luminese and a segment of humanity—a segment willing to sacrifice the long-term well-being of the planet for short-term gain. The Luminese's response is a complex blend of diplomacy and strategic intervention, highlighting their commitment to planetary health, even in the face of powerful adversaries who prioritize their own self-interests above the survival of all species.

The Luminese's interactions are further complicated by the fact that their own society is not monolithic. The Harmonists and Progressives represent distinct, yet intertwined, perspectives within Luminese society. The Harmonists, deeply rooted in traditional practices, prioritize a cautious and conservative approach, advocating for a greater emphasis on bioluminescence and a more profound integration with the planet. The Progressives, while acknowledging the importance of tradition, advocate for continued technological advancement, believing it essential for navigating the challenges of environmental collapse and fostering a truly sustainable future.

Their internal debates reflect the dynamic nature of their ethical framework, highlighting the ongoing struggle to balance innovation with environmental stewardship. This internal tension, however, is not a sign of weakness but a testament to their ability to adapt and evolve while adhering to their core principles. Their approach to interspecies relations, therefore, is not static; it is a continuously evolving process, guided by the dynamic interplay between their core philosophy and the ever-changing realities of their world.

Ultimately, the Luminese's approach to interspecies relations serves as a profound case study in collaborative survival. It underscores the critical need for mutual respect, understanding, and a shared commitment to a sustainable future. Their willingness to engage with humanity, despite the inherent risks and challenges, demonstrates their belief in the potential for symbiotic evolution— a testament to their farsightedness and unwavering commitment to the well-being of the planet and all its inhabitants. Their journey, alongside humanity's, is a narrative of choices, of collaborations, and of the desperate hope for a future where survival and sustainability are intertwined, not opposing forces. The success of this intricate dance hinges on humanity's ability to shed its anthropocentric worldview and embrace a more holistic understanding of its place within the intricate web of life on Earth. The future, therefore, rests not merely on technological innovation, but on a fundamental shift in perspective—a shift that mirrors the Luminese's own profound and enduring commitment to the interconnectedness of all things.

A Shared Future

The shared future, as envisioned by the Luminese, was not a mere continuation of existing patterns; it was a radical reimagining of the human relationship with the planet. Their partnership with humanity was not based on charity or paternalism, but on a pragmatic assessment of mutual survival. The environmental devastation, the unraveling ecosystems, the unpredictable Whispers—these were challenges that neither species could overcome alone.

The Luminese, with their advanced technology and deep understanding of symbiosis, offered a lifeline; humanity, with its diverse skills and adaptability, provided a crucial element in the complex equation of planetary regeneration.

This partnership, however, was not without its complexities. Trust, a commodity eroded by centuries of human exploitation of natural resources, needed to be painstakingly rebuilt. The Luminese, despite their advanced understanding of interspecies communication, faced the monumental task of bridging the cultural chasm separating them from humanity. Their methods, rooted in holistic understanding and long-term sustainability, often clashed with humanity's short-sighted focus on immediate gains. The concept of Luminary Resonance, for example, a fundamental aspect of Luminese technology and philosophy, was initially met with skepticism and misunderstanding. The idea of energy as an interconnected, sentient force rather than a mere commodity to be extracted and consumed proved difficult for many humans to grasp.

Ambassador Nyla, a key figure in the Luminese delegation, played a pivotal role in navigating these cultural differences. Her patient explanations and her willingness to address concerns and answer questions slowly chipped away at the skepticism. She emphasized that the Convergence Protocol was not a tool for Luminese domination, but a desperate attempt to restore a balance shattered by humanity's actions. The protocol, she explained, would not simply fix the planet; it would initiate a complex process of regeneration, a planetary reboot that required the active participation of both species.

The collaboration extended beyond the technical aspects of the Convergence Protocol. The Luminese shared their extensive knowledge of the Whispers, helping humanity understand these sentient ecosystems and their role in the planetary regeneration process. They revealed intricate details of their communication methods and their sophisticated techniques for interpreting the Whispers' subtle energy patterns. This knowledge transfer was crucial; it allowed humanity to participate meaningfully in the process, to move beyond a passive recipient role and become an active partner in shaping the future.

However, the path towards a shared future was not a smooth one. Internal divisions within Luminese society mirrored the tensions between humanity's diverse factions. The Harmonists, deeply rooted in traditional Luminese philosophy, advocated for a cautious and conservative approach, prioritizing the preservation of existing ecosystems and a deeper integration with the planet's natural rhythms. The Progressives, while respecting traditional values, championed continued technological advancement, believing it essential for overcoming the environmental crisis and achieving long-term sustainability. These internal debates, far from hindering their efforts, reflected the Luminese's ability to adapt and evolve, to constantly refine their approach in the face of new challenges.

The role of the Echoborn further complicated the picture. These human-Whisper hybrids represented a new form of symbiosis, a potential bridge between two vastly different worlds. Their emergence prompted intense discussions among the Luminese, a careful weighing of the potential benefits against the inherent risks.

The Harmonists expressed concern about the unknown consequences of this unprecedented merging, while the Progressives saw the Echoborn as a symbol of hope, a testament to the potential for interspecies collaboration. The Luminese approach, as always, was one of cautious optimism—a blend of careful observation and measured intervention.

The continuing threat of Dr. Rafe Mallory cast a long shadow over the collaborative efforts. His relentless pursuit of control over the Convergence Protocol and his disregard for ethical considerations exposed the fundamental chasm between those who sought to heal the planet and those who sought to exploit it for personal gain. The Luminese responded with a combination of diplomacy and strategic intervention, carefully managing their response to avoid escalating the conflict while ensuring the safety of the Convergence Protocol and the ongoing regeneration efforts. Their actions highlighted their deep commitment to planetary health—a commitment that transcended narrow self-interest.

The Luminese's continued partnership with humanity was not merely an act of altruism; it was a recognition of their shared fate. The future, they understood, depended on the success of the Convergence Protocol, on the ability of both species to overcome their differences and work together to rebuild a sustainable world. Their contribution extended beyond technological advancements; it encompassed a profound shift in worldview—a move towards a more holistic understanding of the interconnectedness of all life. This was not simply a matter of survival; it was a transformation, a fundamental shift in human consciousness, a necessary step towards a future where humanity could finally find its rightful place within the intricate web of life on Earth.

The success of this grand endeavor hinged on a delicate balance. It demanded a constant negotiation between human ingenuity and the planet's inherent resilience. The Luminese provided the scientific framework, the technological tools, and a profound philosophical understanding of symbiotic existence. Humanity, in turn, was tasked with the monumental challenge of transforming its relationship with nature, of shedding its exploitative tendencies and embracing a new ethos of respect and stewardship. The convergence of these two forces, this intricate dance between technology and nature, held the key to the planet's future—a future that would either witness humanity's extinction or its transformation into a truly symbiotic partner with the planet.

The road ahead was fraught with uncertainties. The Whispers remained enigmatic, their evolution unpredictable. The Echoborn presented a range of ethical dilemmas. The threat of individuals like Dr. Mallory continued to loom large. But amidst these uncertainties, the Luminese offered a beacon of hope—a testament to the possibility of interspecies collaboration, a path towards a shared future where humanity could finally achieve a sustainable coexistence with the planet. The journey would be long and arduous, but the vision—a vibrant, thriving Earth, a world restored to balance—remained a powerful force, driving both species forward toward a shared destiny.

The Luminese's enduring legacy would not be defined by their technology alone, but by their philosophy of Symbiogenesis, their unwavering commitment to interspecies cooperation, and their patient, persistent efforts to guide humanity towards a more sustainable future. Their willingness to share knowledge, their deep respect for the planet, and their steadfast dedication to the delicate balance of life became the guiding principles for this new era. The shared future, however uncertain, was a testament to their enduring belief in the capacity for transformation, for hope, and for the eventual triumph of collaborative survival. The success of this endeavor, however, depended on humanity's ability to embrace this new vision, to acknowledge its past mistakes, and to embark on a path of genuine transformation—guided by the principles of sustainability, respect, and a profound understanding of its place within the intricate web of life.

CHAPTER THIRTEEN

ECHOES OF THE ECHOBORN

The initial changes were subtle, almost imperceptible. A heightened awareness of the surrounding environment, a sharper sensitivity to the rhythms of the Earth—the gentle pulse of the ocean currents, the rustling whispers of the wind through the reborn forests. For Elias Vance, one of the first Echoborn, it began with the dreams. Vivid, surreal dreamscapes filled with shimmering bioluminescence and the haunting melodies of unseen creatures. He would wake with a lingering sense of connection, a feeling of belonging to something larger than himself, something ancient and profound. These were not nightmares, but rather a glimpse into the Whispers' consciousness, a slow, gentle infiltration of another being's reality.

Then came the physical alterations. A slow, almost imperceptible shift in his physiology. His skin, once pale and freckled, began to acquire a subtle, iridescent sheen, reflecting light in ways that defied explanation. His senses heightened, becoming almost painfully acute. The smell of rain on parched earth, the distant chirping of crickets, the subtle shift in atmospheric pressure—all became amplified, overwhelming at times. He found himself drawn to the ocean, its rhythms resonating deep within his being, a siren's call he could not resist.

His body became more resilient. Minor injuries healed faster, almost miraculously. His endurance increased, allowing him to withstand physical exertions that would have crippled a normal human. But these were not simple enhancements; they were interwoven with the planet's own resilience, its innate ability to heal and adapt. Elias's body became a microcosm of that resilience, a living testament to the Whispers' regenerative power.

The psychological changes were even more profound. Elias felt a growing empathy, a profound connection with all living things. The suffering of the planet, the pain of its ravaged ecosystems, became palpable, a weight he carried within him. This was not simply compassion; it was an intrinsic understanding, a shared consciousness. He felt the Earth's pulse as his own heartbeat, its sorrows as his own.

This intense emotional connection had a downside. The constant influx of sensory information, the relentless stream of environmental data, sometimes overwhelmed him. He experienced periods of intense anxiety, a feeling of being disconnected from his own humanity. The vibrant life force of the planet he was now a part of sometimes felt like an intrusion. He had to learn to navigate this new reality, to integrate the Whispers' consciousness into his own without losing his sense of self. He sought solace in quiet moments, connecting with the natural world, finding refuge in its rhythm and harmony.

The experience was not uniform across all Echoborn. Some, like Anya Sharma, developed a greater ability to communicate directly with the Whispers, deciphering their complex energy patterns and translating their cryptic messages into human understanding. Anya's transformation manifested as a heightened intuition, a precognitive ability to sense shifts in the environmental conditions and anticipate impending ecological crises. Her dreams were less vivid but filled with a deeper understanding of the Whispers' intentions. The changes in her physiology were subtle—a slight alteration in her pigmentation, a newfound resilience to extremes of temperature and pressure.

For others, the transformation was more dramatic. Kai, a former soldier, exhibited a physical transformation that was more outwardly visible. His limbs became elongated, his movements fluid and graceful. His skin developed patterns that mirrored the intricate designs of the Whispers' network. He possessed an almost supernatural strength, enhanced agility, and a heightened sense of awareness that bordered on precognition. But his transformation came at a cost; his memories were fragmented, his personality altered, leaving him a shadow of his former self. He was more Whisper than human.

The spectrum of transformations highlighted the unpredictable nature of the merging. The Whispers' influence seemed to vary based on the individual's personality, their past experiences, and their predisposition to symbiotic integration. This variability presented both opportunities and challenges. The diverse range of abilities among the Echoborn, their unique interactions with the planet's rejuvenating systems, proved invaluable to the Convergence Protocol. Their individual strengths could be strategically employed, their unique talents carefully utilized to navigate the complexities of the planetary regeneration process.

However, the unpredictability also raised significant ethical considerations. The psychological impact on the Echoborn required careful attention. The loss of personal identity and the risk of mental instability needed to be managed with sensitivity and care. The Luminese, with their vast experience in symbiosis and interspecies cooperation, provided crucial support, offering psychological guidance and developing strategies for managing the emotional and cognitive complexities of the transformation.

Dr. Eliza Grant, the lead marine biologist, played a critical role in understanding the physiological transformations. Her research provided crucial insights into the physical changes experienced by the Echoborn, enabling the development of treatments to mitigate adverse effects. She discovered that the integration of the Whispers' energy was not merely a physical process; it involved a profound reorganization of the human nervous system, a merging of consciousnesses that pushed the boundaries of human understanding.

The Echoborn were not merely humans who had acquired new abilities; they were living embodiments of the symbiotic relationship between humanity and the planet. They became a bridge between two worlds, a testament to the potential for collaborative survival. Their existence challenged existing definitions of humanity, pushing the boundaries of what it meant to be human. Their transformation was not just a physical or psychological phenomenon; it was a spiritual awakening, a connection to something far greater than themselves.

The study of the Echoborn became a central focus of the Convergence Protocol initiative. Their unique abilities, their intimate connection with the Whispers, provided a vital link in the process of planetary regeneration. Their role was not just as subjects of study, but as active participants, shaping the course of the planet's recovery. Their insights, their perceptions of the Whispers' intricate communications, guided the implementation of the Protocol, ensuring its effectiveness and minimizing potential risks.

However, the journey of the Echoborn was not without its struggles. Many faced identity crises, grappling with the loss of their former selves, the erasure of their memories, and the overwhelming influx of sensory information. Some experienced intense periods of alienation, feeling isolated from both humanity and the Whispers, caught between two worlds. The support networks established by the Luminese and the dedicated human support staff proved crucial in helping them navigate these psychological challenges.

The social implications of the Echoborn's transformation were equally complex. Society struggled to assimilate these beings, to understand and accept their unique status. Fear, misunderstanding, and prejudice threatened to hinder the collaborative efforts to save the planet. The Luminese, with their deep understanding of symbiotic evolution, actively worked to bridge the cultural gap, educating the public and promoting understanding and acceptance of the Echoborn's role in the planetary regeneration process.

The Echoborn's transformation became a central metaphor for the broader transformation of humanity's relationship with the planet. Just as the Echoborn merged with the Whispers, so too must humanity merge with nature, becoming an integral part of the planetary ecosystem. Their story was a testament to the potential for symbiotic evolution, a beacon of hope in a world ravaged by environmental collapse. Their continued existence, their flourishing, became a symbol of the planet's resilience, a living testament to the possibility of a shared future, a future where humanity and nature could coexist in harmony. The challenges remained formidable, but the Echoborn—these unique individuals—offered a powerful symbol of hope, a reminder that even in the face of devastation, transformation and renewal are possible. Their journey, both individually and collectively, was a testament to the enduring power of adaptation, resilience, and the indomitable spirit of life itself.

Unique Abilities

The whispers started subtly, almost like a phantom limb, a tingling sensation at the edges of perception. For some Echoborn, it manifested as an enhanced empathy, a heightened awareness of the planet's suffering—the silent screams of dying coral reefs, the parched cries of wilting forests. They felt the planet's pain as their own, a burden both heavy and strangely beautiful.

Others experienced a surge in physical capabilities—incredible strength, agility bordering on the supernatural, an almost preternatural resilience to injury and disease. These were not mere enhancements; they were interwoven with the very fabric of the planet's resilience, its ancient, innate capacity for healing. Their bodies, once fragile vessels of human mortality, were becoming echoes of the Earth's own enduring strength.

For Anya Sharma, the connection manifested as heightened intuition, a precognitive ability to sense environmental shifts before they became visible. She could feel the subtle tremors of an impending earthquake, the slow, insidious creep of a toxic algal bloom, the silent death spiral of a collapsing ecosystem. Her dreams became prophecies, filled with cryptic visions of ecological disaster and, occasionally, glimmers of potential solutions.

She saw the future in the swirling patterns of ocean currents, in the rustle of leaves, in the flight of birds. Her enhanced perception allowed her to anticipate and avert several near-catastrophic events, guiding the Convergence Protocol team to intervene just in time to prevent widespread ecological collapse. However, this ability came at a price. The constant influx of environmental data, the overwhelming torrent of future possibilities, often left her exhausted, drained, and on the verge of a mental breakdown. She learned to carefully manage her connection, finding solace in moments of quiet contemplation, allowing the planet's whispers to ebb and flow without overwhelming her.

Elias Vance, on the other hand, developed a unique ability to communicate directly with the Whispers, a skill that proved invaluable in deciphering the ancient code hidden within the planet's intricate ecosystems. His connection wasn't just sensory; it was a form of linguistic understanding, a capacity to translate the planet's subtle energy patterns into human language. He could interpret the rustling of leaves as a coded message, the shifting sands of the desert as a historical narrative, the silent pulse of the ocean as a symphony of warnings and promises. This ability allowed him to guide the team through the labyrinthine complexities of the Convergence Protocol, helping them understand the intricate conditions necessary to activate the planetary reboot.

His ability, however, was fragile. Overexertion led to periods of intense mental fatigue, blurring the line between his own thoughts and the Whispers' voice.

Kai, the former soldier, experienced a more dramatic transformation. His physical form altered drastically—his limbs lengthening, his movements becoming fluid and graceful, his very essence interwoven with the patterns of the Whispers' network. He possessed superhuman strength and agility, abilities that made him a formidable asset in navigating hazardous environments and rescuing stranded communities. But this powerful connection came at a high cost. His memories were fragmented, his personality altered, making him both a powerful ally and a tragic reminder of the transformative power of the Whispers. He often struggled to reconcile his past life with his present reality, his human identity lost within the vast, intricate web of the Whispers' consciousness. His very existence was a potent symbol of the unpredictable nature of the symbiotic relationship between humanity and the Whispers.

His strength and abilities were crucial to the survival of the Convergence Protocol team. But his transformation served as a stark warning—a reminder that even with incredible power comes incredible risk.

The variations in the Echoborn's abilities were not simply random occurrences. Dr. Grant's research revealed a correlation between their unique skills and their pre-transformation personalities and experiences. Those with a strong pre-existing connection to nature, those who possessed innate empathy or a deep understanding of ecological systems, tended to develop more profound sensory abilities and a greater capacity for empathy. Those with backgrounds in science, technology, or engineering often exhibited advanced cognitive skills, enhanced problem-solving abilities, and a unique capacity to interact with and interpret the Whispers' complex code. Those with strong leadership skills often emerged as the group's natural leaders, their abilities amplified by their connection to the Whispers.

The psychological impact on the Echoborn demanded ongoing attention. The Luminese, with their extensive history of symbiotic relationships, played a crucial role in providing emotional and psychological support, developing techniques to manage the intense sensory overload and the challenges of integrating two distinct consciousnesses. They created specialized sanctuaries, spaces where the Echoborn could reconnect with their human identities while maintaining their connection to the planet. These sanctuaries were more than just shelters; they were places of healing, where the Echoborn could process their experiences, explore their altered identities, and find a sense of community and belonging.

The Echoborn were not just individuals; they were a collective consciousness, a living network connected to the Whispers and to each other. They shared a unique understanding of the planet's needs, a collective wisdom born from their individual experiences. They could communicate telepathically, sharing information, insights, and warnings instantaneously, creating a complex, dynamic communication network that transcended geographical boundaries and linguistic barriers. This collective consciousness played a pivotal role in implementing the Convergence Protocol, allowing them to coordinate their efforts efficiently and effectively, to anticipate and respond to unforeseen challenges.

However, the unity within the Echoborn was not without its internal tensions. The differences in their abilities and experiences sometimes led to conflicts, misunderstandings, and disagreements over the best course of action. The burden of their enhanced consciousness created internal divisions, as some struggled with the overwhelming responsibility of their powers. The weight of the planet's fate rested on their shoulders. Anya's prophetic visions could be terrifyingly accurate but sometimes lacked the details needed for effective action. Elias's ability to communicate with the Whispers was not always reliable, and he struggled with his own interpretations. Kai's immense strength could easily be misinterpreted as dominance.

The social implications of their existence were just as complex. Humanity, initially wary and even fearful of the Echoborn, began to understand and appreciate their unique abilities and their unwavering commitment to saving the planet. The Luminese played a key role in bridging the gap, educating humanity about the

Echoborn's capabilities and highlighting their essential role in the Convergence Protocol. However, prejudice and distrust lingered. Some humans still viewed the Echoborn with suspicion, fearing the loss of human identity and the unknown consequences of symbiotic evolution. This tension underscored the broader challenges facing humanity—the need to accept change, to embrace the unknown, to forge a new relationship with nature, one built on partnership and mutual respect.

The Echoborn's journey served as a microcosm of humanity's struggle. Their transformation mirrored the planet's own struggle for survival, a testament to the resilience of life itself, the capacity for adaptation, and the potential for symbiosis. Their existence was a powerful symbol of hope, a reminder that even in the face of catastrophic environmental collapse, the possibility of a shared future—a future where humanity and nature could coexist in harmony—was not just a dream, but a possibility within reach. Their story is a cautionary tale of the consequences of ignoring the planet's cries for help and a testament to the transformative power of hope, resilience, and a deep connection to the natural world.

Their unique abilities and the challenges they faced underscored the urgency and complexity of addressing the climate crisis and the importance of embracing a future where humanity and nature coexist in harmony. The road ahead was fraught with peril, but the Echoborn, these unique individuals woven from the very fabric of the Earth, were leading the way.

Societal Integration

The initial reaction to the Echoborn was a mixture of awe, fear, and outright hostility. Newsreels showed their altered forms—Kai's elongated limbs, Anya's ethereal glow, Elias's eyes mirroring the swirling nebulae of the night sky—fueling anxieties about a loss of humanity's unique identity. Rumors spread like wildfire, painting the Echoborn as monstrous aberrations, agents of a planetary takeover. Distrust festered, particularly within marginalized communities already struggling with the aftermath of the ecological collapse, who saw the Echoborn as another threat vying for scarce resources. This fear was expertly manipulated by Dr. Mallory's propaganda machine, which portrayed the Echoborn as unstable, unpredictable, and ultimately dangerous, further solidifying the division within society.

However, the pragmatic necessity of the Convergence Protocol forced a reluctant acceptance. The Echoborn, with their unique abilities, were indispensable to its success. Anya's precognitive abilities averted several ecological catastrophes, preventing widespread famine and societal collapse. Elias's translations of the Whispers' code were crucial in understanding the complex parameters of the Protocol. Kai's superhuman strength and agility proved invaluable in rescuing stranded populations and securing vital resources. These tangible benefits began to chip away at the widespread fear, slowly turning public perception.

The Luminese played a pivotal role in mediating this societal shift. Ambassador Nyla, with her calm wisdom and deep understanding of symbiotic evolution, became an unlikely spokesperson for the Echoborn. She organized public forums, delivering compelling presentations that highlighted the Echoborn's crucial role in planetary healing. She emphasized their connection to the planet, not as a threat, but as a testament to nature's enduring resilience and adaptability. The Luminese also provided essential psychological and societal support for the Echoborn, creating safe spaces where they could connect with their humanity while embracing their evolving capabilities.

The integration process wasn't without its setbacks. Cases of discrimination, ranging from subtle prejudice to outright violence, continued to plague the Echoborn. Their unique physiological needs, their altered perception of reality, and their heightened sensory experiences often resulted in misunderstandings and alienation. For instance, Kai's superhuman strength, while invaluable in rescue missions, sometimes resulted in accidental property damage, further fueling negative perceptions. Anya's prophetic visions, while saving lives, were frequently misinterpreted as evidence of instability or madness. Elias's attempts to communicate with the Whispers sometimes resulted in prolonged periods of unresponsiveness, leading to concerns about his mental state. These incidents required continuous intervention from the

Luminese and a dedicated team of social workers, psychologists, and trauma specialists.

Addressing these challenges required a multi-pronged approach. Educational campaigns were launched to dispel myths and foster understanding. Schools incorporated curriculum on symbiotic evolution, highlighting the natural world's capacity for adaptation and the potential benefits of interspecies collaboration. The media played a crucial role in showcasing the Echoborn's contributions to society, focusing on their positive impacts rather than their differences. Public figures, celebrities, and influential leaders voiced their support, lending credibility to the integration efforts.

Furthermore, legislation was enacted to protect the Echoborn from discrimination and violence, providing legal recourse for those subjected to prejudice.

Slowly but surely, society began to embrace the Echoborn. Their abilities became integral to various sectors. Anya's foresight became critical in disaster preparedness and environmental management. Elias's communication skills revolutionized scientific understanding of ecosystems, leading to breakthroughs in sustainable technology and resource management. Kai's strength and agility were utilized in search and rescue operations, infrastructure repair, and even disaster relief efforts. The Echoborn's unique contributions highlighted the necessity of rethinking human capabilities and societal structures.

However, the deepest societal integration stemmed from the realization that the Echoborn's transformation mirrored humanity's own journey. Their struggles with identity, their emotional complexities, and their search for belonging resonated with the collective human experience. The Echoborn became symbols of resilience, adaptation, and the potential for transformative change. Their enhanced senses, initially seen as a threat, were now viewed as a window into a deeper understanding of the planet, fostering a renewed sense of responsibility toward environmental stewardship.

The emergence of Echoborn artists, writers, and musicians further bridged the gap between human and Echoborn communities. Their art reflected the unique perspectives born from their connection to the Whispers, creating a new wave of creative expression that explored themes of symbiotic evolution, ecological interdependence, and the interconnectedness of all life. Echoborn stories, narrated through telepathic connection, created a collective narrative that highlighted the planet's resilience and humanity's potential to transform and adapt.

Even the economic landscape shifted. New industries emerged, capitalizing on the Echoborn's unique abilities. Bio-integrated technologies, powered by the Echoborn's connection to the Whispers, led to breakthroughs in renewable energy, sustainable agriculture, and environmental remediation. The economic benefits, coupled with the tangible improvements in ecological stability, solidified the Echoborn's place within society, shifting the focus from fear and uncertainty to collaboration and mutual respect. This economic integration helped address concerns about resource allocation and competition, further easing tensions.

The process was far from perfect. Incidents of prejudice persisted, but the growing appreciation for the Echoborn's contributions overshadowed these isolated incidents. The integration process, though arduous and ongoing, was a profound testament to humanity's capacity for adaptation and its willingness to confront its past mistakes. It marked a significant shift in societal values, prioritizing ecological harmony and symbiotic evolution over anthropocentric dominance.

The Echoborn were not merely integrated; they became integral to the fabric of a new, evolving humanity, forever intertwined with the planet's destiny. Their presence was a constant reminder of the delicate balance between humanity and nature, a balance that required constant vigilance, understanding, and a willingness to embrace the transformative power of change. The future remained uncertain, but with the Echoborn leading the way, humanity had a chance to rewrite its narrative, to forge a path toward a future where coexistence, not conquest, defined its relationship with the planet.

The echoes of the Echoborn were not just whispers; they were the clarion call for a new era, one built on harmony, resilience, and a deep respect for the interconnectedness of all life.

Ethical Implications

The integration of the Echoborn into society wasn't merely a matter of logistics and resource allocation; it was a crucible forging a new ethical framework. The very existence of the Echoborn—humans fundamentally altered by their symbiotic bond with the Whispers—challenged deeply ingrained anthropocentric biases. Questions arose about individual rights, societal structures, and the very definition of humanity. Were the Echoborn still human? Did their altered physiology and enhanced abilities grant them new rights, or did they forfeit certain aspects of their human rights? The legal and philosophical debates were intense, often bitter, and deeply divisive.

One of the most contentious issues revolved around informed consent. Many Echoborn hadn't consciously chosen their transformation; it was a consequence of exposure to the Whispers' influence. This raised profound questions about autonomy and selfdetermination. Did the benefits of their unique abilities outweigh the loss of their original selves? This lack of choice fueled the arguments of those who advocated for strict regulations on further symbiosis, while others argued that the Echoborn's contributions to planetary healing far outweighed any concerns about individual autonomy.

The debate further intensified with the realization that the transformation wasn't always a smooth, predictable process. Some individuals experienced debilitating side effects, both physically and psychologically. The resulting trauma and the need for ongoing medical and psychological support raised significant ethical dilemmas concerning resource allocation and the responsibility of society toward those who were, in essence, casualties of a grand experiment.

The concept of "species" itself became blurred. The Echoborn weren't simply a new sub-species of humanity; they represented a radical shift in human-nature interaction, a blurring of the lines between human and non-human. This challenged long-held notions of individuality and species boundaries, prompting a fundamental reassessment of biological and philosophical categories. The lines separating human consciousness and the collective consciousness of the Whispers became increasingly indistinct, causing anxieties about free will and the potential loss of individual identity.

This was further complicated by Anya's precognitive abilities, which raised questions about determinism versus free will. Her visions offered warnings of impending ecological catastrophes but often lacked specificity, resulting in difficult ethical choices and the potential for unintended consequences. Every avoided catastrophe could have been viewed as the prevention of a tragedy, yet potentially involved actions that caused some level of personal suffering or collateral damage. The line between justifiable preventative actions and an incursion on fundamental human rights became increasingly blurry.

The economic implications also added a layer of ethical complexity. The burgeoning bio-integrated industries, powered by the Echoborn's abilities, generated immense wealth but also created significant inequalities. Access to these technologies was limited, fueling social disparities and reinforcing existing power structures.

Ethical debates raged concerning equitable access to advanced medical care, particularly the specialized treatments needed by those who suffered adverse effects from the symbiosis. These discussions quickly moved from a philosophical level to a political one, as different factions fought for control of the technologies and the lucrative markets they generated. Some argued that the Echoborn should be compensated for their unique contributions, while others countered that their contributions to planetary healing were their own repayment. This struggle mirrored older class conflicts, but with the sharp new dividing line of human and Echoborn.

Beyond the immediate ethical challenges, the emergence of the Echoborn raised profound questions about the future of humanity. Was the human-Whisper symbiosis a step toward a new era of symbiotic evolution, or a dangerous deviation from the path of human development? Did it represent a positive adaptation to ecological challenges, or a loss of human uniqueness and individuality?

Dr. Mallory's actions, in attempting to exploit the Convergence Protocol, served as a cautionary tale, highlighting the potential for technological advancement to exacerbate existing inequalities and even lead to catastrophic consequences if not guided by strong ethical principles. His unethical manipulations of public perception, using fear and misinformation to control the population, forced a much-needed introspection into the responsibility of scientists, governments, and individuals in preventing future catastrophes.

The role of the Luminese further complicated these ethical considerations. Their advanced technology and deep understanding of symbiotic evolution provided invaluable support, yet their seemingly detached approach also raised concerns. The Luminese, while helping humanity avoid complete collapse, had their own agenda, one that was not always transparent. The question of their long-term intentions and the potential impact of their involvement on Earth's future remained a looming source of uncertainty and ethical debate.

Were they true allies, or were they manipulating humanity to serve their own purposes, perhaps using the Convergence Protocol to achieve a planetary alignment for their own ultimate benefits? The lack of clear answers fostered mistrust and suspicion, further complicating already tense relations.

Sarah Chen, Jonah Reyes, and Dr. Grant found themselves caught in the center of this moral maelstrom. Sarah, ever pragmatic, grappled with the immense responsibility of activating the Convergence Protocol, knowing that it might erase humanity as it existed, sacrificing individual lives for the survival of the planet. Jonah's quest to decipher the Whispers' code pushed him to the limits of his technological capabilities, forcing him to confront the ethical implications of manipulating the natural world on a planetary scale. Dr. Grant's expertise in marine biology provided vital insights into the ecological consequences of the symbiosis and the potential for planetary regeneration, but her empathy also challenged her to address the profound ethical and human costs of the transformation.

Each decision, each attempt at problem-solving, forced them to confront uncomfortable truths and make difficult choices, pushing the limits of their personal ethics and their capabilities to effect positive change.

Ultimately, the ethical implications of the Echoborn weren't confined to the immediate consequences of the symbiosis. They extended to the very core of humanity's relationship with the natural world, forcing a fundamental reassessment of its values, beliefs, and its role in the planetary ecosystem.

The path toward a harmonious future wouldn't be defined solely by scientific advancements or political compromises; it would necessitate a profound shift in humanity's collective consciousness—a reevaluation of its place in the universe and its responsibility toward all life.

The echoes of the Echoborn, in their transformative power and their inherent vulnerability, became a call to action, a reminder of the delicate balance between progress, humanity, and the planet's enduring resilience. The struggle to navigate this ethical labyrinth would define not only the future of the Echoborn, but the fate of humanity itself. The very definition of what it meant to be human would be forever altered, forcing a paradigm shift that would extend far beyond the immediate impact of the Convergence Protocol, forever changing the relationship between humanity and the world they inhabit.

The answers remained elusive, the path fraught with uncertainty, yet the journey toward a future built on ethical considerations, rather than anthropocentric dominance, had begun.

The Future of Symbiosis

The immediate aftermath of the Convergence Protocol activation, or even its potential failure, was only the beginning. The long-term implications of human-Whisper symbiosis, the very essence of the Echoborn, stretched far beyond the immediate crisis, reaching into the distant future and painting a canvas of possibilities both breathtaking and terrifying. The future wasn't a single, predictable path; it was a branching nexus of potential outcomes, shaped by the choices made in the present and the unforeseen consequences that rippled through generations.

One of the most crucial factors determining the future of symbiosis was the extent of integration between humans and the Whispers. The initial Echoborn demonstrated a range of integrations, some subtle, some profound. Some individuals exhibited enhanced physical capabilities—increased strength, resilience, and even regenerative abilities. Others displayed a heightened connection to the natural world, a deep empathy with other living beings, and an almost intuitive understanding of ecological systems. A few, like Anya, displayed precognitive abilities, capable of glimpsing potential futures, both positive and catastrophic.

However, the spectrum of integration also included those who suffered debilitating side effects. The Whispers' influence wasn't always benign. Some individuals experienced severe physical ailments, neurological disorders, or profound psychological trauma. The long-term health implications of the symbiosis remained largely unknown, leading to ongoing research and the development of specialized medical treatments, raising concerns about equitable access to healthcare and potentially exacerbating existing social inequalities. The potential for genetic mutations, both beneficial and detrimental, also remained a significant concern, the long-term consequences unpredictable and requiring constant monitoring.

The societal structures of the future would inevitably be shaped by the prevalence and integration of the Echoborn. A society completely integrated with the Echoborn would look radically different from a society where symbiosis remained a rare phenomenon. A fully integrated society might see the erosion of traditional human hierarchies, replaced by a more fluid, ecocentric structure that prioritized the health of the planet and the well-being of all living beings. New forms of governance, based on consensus and collective decision-making, might emerge, reflecting the interconnectedness inherent in the symbiotic relationship between humans and the Whispers.

In contrast, a society where symbiosis remained limited could experience heightened social stratification, with the Echoborn forming an elite group with superior abilities and access to resources. This scenario could lead to social unrest and conflict, exacerbating existing inequalities and potentially triggering a new form of class warfare. The ethical implications of such a society would be profound, forcing a renewed discussion about equitable resource allocation, social justice, and the very definition of human rights.

The economic landscape would also transform significantly. The unique abilities of the Echoborn could revolutionize various industries, leading to technological advancements beyond current comprehension. Bio-integrated technologies, powered by the symbiotic relationship between humans and the Whispers, could offer solutions to pressing environmental challenges, providing sustainable energy sources, innovative agricultural practices, and advanced methods of environmental remediation. This could lead to a period of unprecedented economic growth and prosperity, but also the risk of uncontrolled exploitation of the Whispers' abilities, potentially leading to further ecological damage.

Education and cultural shifts would also play a vital role in shaping the future. The integration of the Echoborn demanded a fundamental reassessment of educational curricula, incorporating new understandings of symbiosis, ecological interdependence, and the interconnectedness of all life. New philosophies and spiritual beliefs might emerge, reflecting a more holistic and ecocentric worldview, replacing anthropocentric ideologies with a profound respect for the natural world and a recognition of humanity's place within a larger ecosystem. Art, literature, and other forms of cultural expression would likely reflect these transformations, exploring the complex interplay between human and nature, challenging longheld assumptions, and envisioning a new future beyond the limits of human-centric paradigms.

The role of the Luminese would also continue to evolve. Their advanced technology and understanding of symbiotic evolution remained invaluable. However, their motives and long-term intentions, though seemingly altruistic, needed continuous scrutiny. Their deep involvement in Earth's affairs could lead to beneficial collaborations or to subtle manipulation, influencing the course of human development toward an outcome aligned with their own interests. Maintaining transparency and building mutual trust would be essential to preventing conflict and ensuring a future that benefits all involved.

The Whispers themselves presented an element of unpredictable change. Their evolution, their ongoing adaptation to the changing environment, might lead to unforeseen consequences. The symbiotic relationship could strengthen, leading to greater integration and enhanced abilities. Alternatively, the relationship could destabilize, potentially resulting in conflict between humans and the Whispers, or even the emergence of new, unexpected ecological dynamics.

The potential for technological advancement posed both opportunities and risks. The ability to manipulate the Convergence Protocol, for instance, raised concerns about unintended consequences. The temptation to use such technologies for personal gain, to control or exploit the Whispers, or to reshape the planet according to human desires, remained a constant threat. Ethical guidelines, regulations, and international cooperation would be crucial to preventing catastrophic misuse.

Ultimately, the future of symbiosis depended on humanity's choices. Would they embrace the opportunities presented by the Echoborn and strive for a harmonious coexistence with the natural world? Or would they fall prey to old patterns of exploitation, greed, and conflict, jeopardizing the fragile balance achieved after years of struggle? The answer lay not solely in scientific advancements or political maneuvering, but in a profound shift in human consciousness, a collective awakening to the interconnectedness of all life and a commitment to building a sustainable and equitable future for all.

The echoes of the Echoborn wouldn't simply fade into the past; they would resonate through generations to come, shaping the destiny of humanity and the planet they called home. The legacy of this transformation, whether utopian or dystopian, would depend not only on the wisdom of the leaders and the capabilities of the scientists, but on the collective will of humanity itself to make a future worth living in, to finally understand the value not of dominance but of partnership with the very planet that supports them.

The choices made today would echo through the millennia, resonating in the intricate tapestry of a future yet to be woven.

CHAPTER FOURTEEN

A NEW ECOLOGY

The immediate aftermath of the Convergence Protocol's activation saw the planet begin to heal, but the process wasn't a swift, miraculous transformation. It was a slow, painstaking dance of restoration, a delicate choreography between the revitalized ecosystems and the nascent regenerative technologies developed in its wake. The Whispers, once enigmatic entities, now played an active role in this restoration, their influence woven into the fabric of the planet's recovery. This wasn't simply about reversing the damage of the past; it was about building a fundamentally new ecology—one where human ingenuity and the inherent wisdom of nature were intricately interwoven.

One of the first priorities was addressing the pervasive pollution that had choked the planet for decades. Teams of scientists, engineers, and Echoborn collaborated to develop bioremediation techniques, harnessing the enhanced capabilities of the symbiotic humans. These weren't simply technological fixes; they were deeply intertwined with the Whispers' influence, utilizing naturally occurring microorganisms enhanced and guided by the Echoborn's intuitive understanding of ecological processes. Vast swathes of contaminated land were treated using bioengineered fungi and bacteria capable of breaking down toxins at an unprecedented rate, transforming barren landscapes into vibrant ecosystems.

Oceans, once choked with plastic and pollutants, began to clear as bioluminescent organisms, guided by the Whispers, consumed and processed the debris, leaving behind cleaner waters and a revitalized marine environment.

The development of sustainable energy sources became another crucial element of this new ecology. The Whispers themselves proved to be a valuable resource, providing insights into harnessing natural energy flows. Giant bioluminescent kelp forests, grown and maintained with the aid of the Echoborn, became vast, renewable energy farms, their light converted into clean electricity. Similarly, geothermal energy sources were tapped more efficiently, guided by the Whispers' subtle manipulation of underground thermal currents. The result was a global energy infrastructure that was not only sustainable but also integrated seamlessly with the planet's natural rhythms.

Agriculture underwent a radical transformation. Traditional farming methods were replaced with symbiotic agriculture—a system where plants and soil were actively nourished and protected by the Whispers and the Echoborn. This resulted in increased yields and a dramatic reduction in the need for fertilizers and pesticides. The Echoborn, with their enhanced sensory capabilities, could detect minute changes in soil composition and plant health, enabling them to optimize growth conditions and prevent disease.

Genetically modified crops were carefully integrated with natural ecosystems, ensuring biodiversity and minimizing the risks associated with monocultures. Food production shifted from largescale industrial farms to smaller, more localized systems, strengthening community resilience and reducing reliance on longdistance transport.

Beyond agriculture, the Whispers' influence extended to urban planning. Cities began to incorporate natural elements more extensively, blending seamlessly with their surroundings. Vertical farms integrated into buildings provided food sources while also improving air quality. Green spaces, meticulously designed with the help of the Echoborn, provided habitats for wildlife and improved the mental well-being of city dwellers. Water management systems were revolutionized, mimicking natural water cycles and minimizing waste. The result was a more resilient and ecologically conscious urban landscape, capable of thriving in a changing world.

The advancements in medical science were equally profound. Research into the symbiotic relationship between humans and the

Whispers led to breakthroughs in regenerative medicine. The Echoborn's ability to accelerate healing inspired the development of new treatments for various diseases, including those once considered incurable. Nanobots, engineered to interact seamlessly with the human body, delivered targeted therapies, repaired damaged tissues, and enhanced immune responses. The combination of advanced technology and natural processes resulted in unprecedented progress in human health and longevity.

However, this new ecology wasn't without its challenges. The integration of the Echoborn into society presented complex ethical and social issues. The potential for discrimination against nonEchoborn individuals arose, highlighting the need for strong social safety nets and policies ensuring equitable access to resources and opportunities. The unique capabilities of the Echoborn raised concerns about their potential exploitation, necessitating robust ethical guidelines and regulations governing their involvement in various industries. The unpredictable nature of the Whispers' evolution posed a continuous challenge, requiring constant monitoring and adaptation of the regenerative technologies.

The development of new technologies was accompanied by a renewed emphasis on education and public awareness. Curricula in schools and universities were transformed to incorporate new scientific knowledge, ethical considerations, and a deep appreciation for the interconnectedness of all living things. Public campaigns promoted environmental stewardship and sustainable practices, empowering individuals to play an active role in maintaining the new ecology.

The Luminese, having played a crucial role in initiating the Convergence Protocol, remained a significant presence in this new world. Their advanced technology continued to support the development of regenerative systems, but their relationship with humanity became increasingly complex. The need for transparent collaboration and mutual respect was paramount, ensuring that their technological expertise served the common good rather than furthering their own interests.

Ultimately, the success of this new ecology depended not solely on technology but on a fundamental shift in human consciousness. The integration of the Echoborn, the revitalization of the planet, and the advancements in science and technology were all intertwined with a profound change in human values and priorities. A shift from anthropocentrism to ecocentrism, a deep appreciation for the interconnectedness of all life, and a commitment to sustainability became the cornerstones of this new era.

The future wasn't merely about technological progress; it was about forging a harmonious coexistence with the planet, recognizing that humanity's destiny was inextricably linked to its well-being. The echoes of the Convergence Protocol reverberated not only in the physical changes to the Earth but also in the transformed consciousness of its inhabitants, shaping a future where humanity and nature danced together in a delicate, yet powerful, balance.

The journey had been arduous, filled with struggle and uncertainty. But as the planet healed, so too did the human spirit, forging a new path toward a future where the legacy of environmental collapse was not one of despair, but of transformative resilience and a renewed understanding of our place within the intricate tapestry of life.

Sustainable Practices

The transition to a truly sustainable world required a fundamental restructuring of our relationship with the land, the sea, and the very air we breathe. Agriculture, once a major contributor to environmental degradation, was reimagined. The monoculture farms that had ravaged the soil and depleted its nutrients were replaced by polyculture systems, mimicking the biodiversity of natural ecosystems. Echoborn, with their intimate understanding of plant-soil interactions, played a pivotal role in this transformation.

They could identify ideal planting locations, optimize nutrient cycling, and anticipate disease outbreaks with an accuracy far exceeding any technology previously available. Their symbiotic connection to the Whispers allowed them to guide the growth of crops, enhancing their resilience to pests and climate fluctuations.

No longer reliant on synthetic fertilizers and pesticides, these new farms produced healthier, more nutritious food while simultaneously enriching the soil. Ancient farming techniques, once dismissed as inefficient, were rediscovered and refined using Echoborn insights, leading to methods that maximized yield while minimizing environmental impact. Crop rotation, companion planting, and the integration of nitrogen-fixing plants became integral components of this new agricultural paradigm.

The shift wasn't merely technological; it was a profound philosophical change, recognizing the inherent intelligence and resilience of natural systems. This holistic approach extended beyond individual farms, encompassing entire regional food systems. Localized production reduced the carbon footprint associated with long-distance transport, strengthening community resilience and reducing the vulnerability of food chains to disruptions.

The transformation extended beyond food production to encompass the entire landscape. Reforestation projects, guided by the Whispers and implemented with Echoborn assistance, restored degraded ecosystems, revitalizing biodiversity and sequestering significant amounts of atmospheric carbon dioxide. These weren't simply plantings of single tree species; they were meticulously designed ecosystems, carefully considering factors like soil type, water availability, and the interactions between different plant and animal communities. The result was a vibrant mosaic of forests, woodlands, and grasslands, each tailored to its specific environment.

Energy production underwent an equally dramatic shift. The reliance on fossil fuels, a legacy of the old world, was completely abandoned. Harnessing the power of the Whispers, a global network of renewable energy sources emerged. The bioluminescent kelp forests, now managed and nurtured by Echoborn, became vast, energy-generating landscapes. Their light, converted into electricity, provided a clean and abundant power supply.

Geothermal energy, once a niche resource, became a major player in the global energy mix, with Echoborn guiding the tapping of underground thermal currents, maximizing efficiency and minimizing environmental disruption. Wind farms, integrated seamlessly into the landscape, further diversified the energy supply, providing a resilient and sustainable energy infrastructure that powered the world with clean energy. The energy transition wasn't merely a technological achievement; it was a testament to humanity's capacity to learn from and cooperate with nature.

Urban planning also underwent a radical transformation. The concrete jungles of the past were replaced by cities that blended seamlessly with their surroundings. Green spaces, designed in collaboration with the Echoborn, were integrated into the urban fabric, creating habitats for wildlife, improving air quality, and enhancing the well-being of city dwellers. Buildings incorporated vertical farms, providing food locally and reducing the reliance on long-distance transportation.

Water management systems, mimicking natural water cycles, minimized waste and maximized efficiency. Smart grids, powered by renewable energy, optimized energy consumption, further minimizing the environmental footprint of urban centers. The concept of a city was redefined, moving away from the old model of concrete and steel to a vision of integrated, self-sustaining ecosystems.

Beyond the major sectors, a conscious effort was made to integrate sustainable practices across all aspects of life. Transportation underwent a revolution with the adoption of electric vehicles and the expansion of public transportation systems. Waste management became a closed-loop system, with materials being recycled and reused to minimize landfill waste. The very fabric of society was transformed, from the production and consumption of goods to the design and construction of infrastructure, all operating within the framework of a new, sustainable model.

The implementation of these sustainable practices wasn't a smooth transition. Challenges arose, requiring continuous adaptation and refinement. The integration of the Echoborn into society raised complex ethical questions, demanding careful consideration of equitable access to resources and the potential for exploitation of their unique abilities. The unpredictable nature of the Whispers, despite their crucial role in planetary regeneration, necessitated ongoing monitoring and adaptive management strategies. And the lingering effects of past environmental damage required long-term commitment and sustained effort.

However, despite these challenges, the transformation proceeded, driven by a shared vision of a sustainable future. Public awareness campaigns, educational reforms, and community-led initiatives fostered a new sense of environmental stewardship. People were not merely passive consumers; they were active participants in creating a world in harmony with nature. The transition represented a fundamental shift in human consciousness, a move away from anthropocentric perspectives to a deeper appreciation for the intricate web of life and the importance of maintaining ecological balance.

The Luminese, with their advanced technology and wisdom, played a vital role in guiding this transition. They shared their knowledge and expertise, ensuring that the new technologies were developed responsibly and sustainably. Their collaboration with humanity wasn't about dominance or control; it was about shared responsibility and mutual respect for the planet. Their involvement highlighted the critical role of interspecies collaboration in addressing global challenges.

The new ecology wasn't a perfect utopia. It was a dynamic, everevolving system, constantly adapting to new challenges and opportunities. The journey toward sustainability was a continuous process, requiring constant vigilance, innovation, and a deep commitment to creating a world where humanity and nature could thrive together.

The echoes of the past, the scars of environmental collapse, served as a constant reminder of the importance of preserving the delicate balance that had been painstakingly restored. The success of this new ecology was not merely a matter of technological advancement but a testament to humanity's capacity for adaptation, resilience, and the transformative power of collaboration.

It was a story not of ending, but of a new beginning—a new chapter in the ongoing narrative of life on Earth. The future held both immense promise and profound challenges, but the commitment to a sustainable future was unwavering. The planet was healing, and so too were its inhabitants, embracing a new era where humanity and nature could coexist in harmony.

Biodiversity Conservation

The revitalization of Earth's ecosystems extended beyond the reimagining of agriculture and energy production; it encompassed a concerted, global effort to conserve biodiversity and protect endangered species. The old paradigm of isolated nature reserves, often inadequate and vulnerable to external pressures, was abandoned. Instead, a holistic approach emerged, recognizing that biodiversity conservation was not a separate issue, but an integral part of the new sustainable world.

The Echoborn, with their intimate connection to the Whispers, became invaluable partners in this endeavor. Their understanding of the intricate web of life allowed them to identify critical habitats, pinpoint the most vulnerable species, and develop tailored conservation strategies. This wasn't simply about identifying and protecting individual species; it was about understanding and preserving entire ecosystems. The Echoborn could perceive the subtle interconnectedness within ecosystems, revealing dependencies and vulnerabilities previously unknown. They could, for example, identify a seemingly insignificant plant species whose presence was vital to the survival of a keystone predator, or predict the cascading effects of habitat loss on an entire food web.

Their insights led to innovative conservation techniques.

Genetic rescue programs, guided by the Whispers' knowledge of genetic diversity, revived populations teetering on the brink of extinction. Corridors connecting fragmented habitats were created, facilitating gene flow and allowing species to migrate and adapt to changing environmental conditions. The Whispers could even influence the behavior of animals, guiding their migrations and encouraging them to utilize created corridors. This was achieved subtly, a gentle nudge rather than forceful manipulation, reflecting a deep respect for the autonomy of the natural world. These weren't simply wildlife corridors; they were intricate, biodiverse pathways, incorporating diverse vegetation and water sources designed to meet the specific needs of the species using them.

The role of technology was crucial. Advanced monitoring systems, integrated with the Whispers' network, allowed for realtime tracking of endangered species populations, providing early warning of threats and allowing for rapid intervention. Drones, powered by clean energy, patrolled vast areas, monitoring habitats and detecting signs of poaching or habitat destruction. AI-powered analysis tools, informed by the Whispers' data, predicted the impact of climate change on various species and ecosystems, enabling proactive conservation measures.

However, technology was not a replacement for on-the-ground action. Community-based conservation projects played a vital role. Local communities, trained by the Echoborn and educated in sustainable practices, became the guardians of their own biodiversity, actively participating in monitoring, protecting, and restoring their local ecosystems. This wasn't simply about providing jobs; it was about empowering local people to become stewards of their land, fostering a sense of ownership and responsibility for the planet's well-being.

This approach recognized that biodiversity conservation was inextricably linked to human well-being. The benefits of a biodiverse planet were not merely ecological; they were social and economic. Healthy ecosystems provided clean water, fertile soil, and pollination services, supporting agriculture and other industries. They also offered recreational opportunities, enhancing tourism and contributing to local economies. By engaging local communities in conservation efforts, the benefits were shared equitably, ensuring long-term sustainability.

The Luminese contributed their advanced biotechnology to the conservation effort. They developed methods for restoring degraded habitats, accelerating the recovery of damaged ecosystems. They created bioremediation technologies to clean up polluted areas, restoring the health of contaminated lands and waterways. Their technology was not merely a tool; it was an expression of their deep respect for the planet and their understanding of the interconnectedness of all life. They worked alongside the Echoborn, leveraging their combined knowledge and skills to achieve results far beyond what either could accomplish alone.

The ethical considerations surrounding biodiversity conservation were carefully addressed. The preservation of endangered species often required difficult decisions, balancing the needs of individual animals with the broader goals of ecosystem restoration. Ethical guidelines, developed through collaboration between humans, the Luminese, and the Echoborn, ensured that all actions were guided by principles of respect and compassion.

The debate on the role of human intervention in nature, however, continued. There were voices advocating for a more hands-off approach, arguing for minimal human interference in natural processes. Others, including many Echoborn, championed the idea of active management and intervention, pointing to the urgency of the situation and the need for decisive action to prevent further biodiversity loss.

Education played a vital role in promoting biodiversity conservation. Curriculum changes at all educational levels integrated ecological principles and the importance of biodiversity. Public awareness campaigns highlighted the interconnectedness of all life and the benefits of a healthy planet. Museums and nature centers, transformed to reflect the new ecological understanding, showcased the beauty and wonder of biodiversity, inspiring the next generation of conservationists. Art and literature also played an important role, celebrating the natural world and conveying the urgency of the biodiversity crisis.

Despite the significant progress, challenges remained. The impacts of climate change continued to pose a significant threat, requiring ongoing adaptation and mitigation strategies. The emergence of new invasive species, a consequence of shifting climates and disrupted ecosystems, required constant vigilance and effective control measures. The unpredictable nature of the Whispers, while beneficial in many respects, also presented ongoing management challenges. Their evolving communication, while providing vital data, also presented new difficulties in interpretation and understanding.

The success of the biodiversity conservation efforts was not merely a technological achievement; it was a reflection of humanity's capacity for change, collaboration, and ethical decisionmaking. It was a testament to the power of interspecies cooperation and a recognition of the inherent value of all life. The planet's healing was not only evident in the restoration of damaged ecosystems but also in the transformation of human consciousness, a shift towards a more holistic, ecocentric worldview.

The journey toward a biodiverse and sustainable future was not yet complete, but the commitment to preserving the planet's rich tapestry of life remained unwavering, a testament to a shared hope for a brighter, more harmonious future for all. The Whispers, the Echoborn, and humanity, forged in the crucible of environmental crisis, were learning to sing a new song—a symphony of coexistence and resilience. The harmony was still fragile, a delicate balance constantly being adjusted, but the music was becoming richer, more complex, and more hopeful with each passing day.

Climate Change Mitigation

The revitalization of Earth's ecosystems, detailed in the previous sections, was intrinsically linked to a concerted global effort to mitigate climate change. The old approaches, focused primarily on carbon reduction through individual actions and limited technological interventions, proved woefully inadequate. The new strategy recognized the interconnectedness of climate change with biodiversity loss, resource depletion, and social inequities. A holistic approach, incorporating technological innovation, societal transformation, and a deep respect for the natural world, became the cornerstone of climate action.

This holistic strategy involved a multi-pronged attack on greenhouse gas emissions. The transition to renewable energy sources, already underway, accelerated dramatically. Solar and wind farms expanded exponentially, harnessing the power of the sun and wind on an unprecedented scale. Geothermal energy, tapped from the Earth's internal heat, provided a consistent and reliable energy source, particularly in regions with volcanic activity.

However, the reliance on renewables required advancements in energy storage and transmission. Smart grids, incorporating advanced AI and predictive modeling, optimized energy distribution, minimizing waste and maximizing efficiency. The Luminese contributed significantly, introducing innovative energy storage technologies based on bioengineered materials that offered far greater energy density and longer lifespans than traditional batteries.

Beyond energy production, the focus shifted to carbon sequestration. Large-scale reforestation projects, guided by the Whispers' understanding of optimal plant species and soil conditions, transformed vast swathes of degraded land into thriving forests. These weren't simply carbon sinks; they were carefully designed ecosystems, rich in biodiversity and designed to support a wide range of flora and fauna. Ocean-based carbon capture technologies, developed in collaboration with the Luminese, were deployed on a global scale. These technologies utilized marine ecosystems to absorb atmospheric carbon dioxide, fostering the growth of phytoplankton and other carbon-absorbing organisms.

Innovative approaches to agriculture were essential. Sustainable farming practices, focusing on soil health and biodiversity, reduced emissions associated with food production. The use of genetically modified crops, resistant to drought and pests, enhanced yields and minimized the need for fertilizers and pesticides. The Echoborn played a pivotal role in this, using their understanding of plant genetics and ecosystem dynamics to develop crops optimized for various climates and soil conditions.

Adaptation to the impacts of climate change was equally crucial. Coastal communities, facing the threat of sea-level rise, implemented innovative solutions. Seawalls constructed from bioengineered materials provided robust protection while minimizing environmental impact. Managed retreat programs, allowing for the relocation of communities away from vulnerable areas, were implemented ethically and fairly, ensuring that displaced populations were provided with adequate housing and support.

Water management strategies were revamped to address the challenges of changing rainfall patterns and increased drought. Advanced water harvesting techniques, coupled with efficient irrigation systems, ensured the availability of water for agriculture and human consumption. The Luminese, with their advanced water purification technologies, made a significant contribution, ensuring that even in the face of scarcity, communities had access to clean and safe drinking water.

The role of technology extended beyond energy and infrastructure. Climate modeling and prediction became far more sophisticated, incorporating data from the Whispers' network and advanced AI algorithms. This enabled proactive adaptation strategies, allowing communities to prepare for extreme weather events and other climate-related hazards. Early warning systems, integrated with global communication networks, ensured that communities received timely alerts, minimizing loss of life and property. The deployment of drones equipped with sensors and cameras allowed for real-time monitoring of environmental conditions, assisting in the identification of potential risks and the rapid deployment of resources.

Beyond technological advancements, a profound societal transformation was necessary. Education played a vital role. Climate change education was integrated into curricula at all levels, fostering a deep understanding of the challenges and cultivating a sense of collective responsibility. Global collaborations, often facilitated by the Luminese and guided by the ethical frameworks developed with the Echoborn, addressed climate-related issues across borders, promoting cooperation and mutual support.

Economic policies were reformed, incentivizing sustainable practices and penalizing environmentally damaging behaviors. Carbon pricing mechanisms, integrated with global trading systems, created a powerful incentive for emission reduction. The

Luminese's advanced technologies were integrated into these systems, making them more efficient and transparent.

However, the process was not without its challenges. The transition to a sustainable economy necessitated a significant economic shift, requiring investments in new technologies and the retraining of workers. Addressing social inequalities was crucial; the impacts of climate change disproportionately affected vulnerable populations, necessitating measures to ensure equitable access to resources and opportunities.

The complex relationship between humanity and the Whispers remained a delicate balancing act. While their contributions were invaluable, understanding their cryptic communications and predicting their reactions to human actions required constant vigilance and collaboration. Dr. Rafe Mallory's continued threats loomed, a reminder of the potential for human greed and ambition to derail the collective effort.

Despite these challenges, the progress toward mitigating climate change and adapting to a changing world was remarkable. The collaboration between humans, the Luminese, and the Whispers, fostered by Sarah Chen's leadership and guided by the ethical considerations of Dr. Eliza Grant and the wisdom of Ambassador

Nyla, built a foundation for a more sustainable future. The Echoborn, with their unique understanding of the planet's interconnected systems, provided invaluable insights and played a pivotal role in shaping the strategy and implementing the necessary changes.

The journey was far from over, but the collective effort, fueled by a shared commitment to a thriving planet, offered a beacon of hope in a world once teetering on the brink of collapse. The new ecology was not simply about restoring damaged ecosystems; it was about forging a new relationship between humanity and the planet, a partnership built on mutual respect, understanding, and a shared commitment to a sustainable future for all.

The whispers of the old world were fading, replaced by a symphony of cooperation and hope for a future that was, at last, genuinely sustainable.

A Thriving Planet

The air, once thick with the acrid bite of pollution, now carried the scent of pine and damp earth. Vast swathes of land, once barren and scarred, were now vibrant ecosystems teeming with life. Forests, meticulously replanted and nurtured, stretched as far as the eye could see, their canopies a tapestry of green and gold under the sun. Rivers, once choked with plastic and industrial waste, flowed clear and strong, their banks alive with the songs of birds and the murmur of insects. Oceans, once depleted and poisoned, pulsed with life, their coral reefs vibrant and teeming with fish. The transformation was breathtaking, a testament to the power of collective action and the profound interconnectedness of life on Earth.

This wasn't mere restoration; it was a renaissance. The new ecology wasn't simply about returning to a pristine past; it was about creating something new, something better. The Whispers, once enigmatic and unpredictable, had become trusted partners in this grand endeavor. Their understanding of the planet's intricate web of life, their ability to manipulate and nurture ecosystems with an almost magical precision, had proved invaluable. The Echoborn, with their unique blend of human ingenuity and Whisper wisdom, played a crucial role in this transformation, acting as bridges between the two worlds. They understood the language of the ecosystems, the subtle rhythms and harmonies that governed their health, and they could communicate these insights to the rest of humanity.

The Luminese, with their advanced technology and unwavering commitment to sustainability, provided the tools and resources necessary to bring about this transformation. Their bioengineered materials, their sophisticated energy systems, and their understanding of water management had proven instrumental in revitalizing damaged ecosystems and building resilient communities. Their advanced sensors monitored the planet's vital signs, constantly providing updates on ecosystem health, alerting communities to potential threats, and guiding the efforts of ecologists and environmental engineers. Their contribution was not merely technological; it was also philosophical. They had shared their wisdom, their understanding of symbiotic existence, and their commitment to the long-term health of the planet. Their philosophy of sustainable coexistence—learning to live with the planet, not just on it—underpinned much of the new ecology.

Agriculture, too, had undergone a radical transformation. The old, unsustainable practices were relegated to history. Monoculture farming, with its reliance on chemical fertilizers and pesticides, had given way to a polyculture approach, emphasizing biodiversity and soil health. Genetically modified crops, developed in collaboration with the Echoborn, thrived in diverse conditions, requiring less water and fewer resources. Vertical farming, utilizing advanced hydroponics and aeroponics, allowed for food production in urban areas, reducing transportation costs and emissions. Sustainable food systems, integrated with local communities and driven by a commitment to both ecological and social justice, became the norm.

Cities themselves were redesigned to incorporate the principles of the new ecology. Green spaces were abundant, providing vital habitats for wildlife and enhancing the quality of life for urban dwellers. Sustainable transportation systems, relying on electric vehicles and mass transit, reduced emissions and congestion. Buildings were designed to minimize energy consumption, incorporating passive solar heating and cooling and efficient water recycling systems. Waste management systems were innovative, utilizing biological processes to break down organic waste and recover valuable resources. These cities were not just human settlements; they were integrated into the broader ecosystem, functioning as vibrant and self-sustaining components of the planet's overall health.

The success of the new ecology was not simply a matter of technological innovation or ecological restoration; it was fundamentally a cultural shift. A new ethos of respect for the environment permeated every aspect of human society. Education played a crucial role in this transformation. From early childhood, children learned about the interconnectedness of life and the importance of environmental stewardship. The curriculum wasn't just about facts and figures; it was about fostering a deep sense of connection to the natural world. It encouraged creative thinking, problem-solving, and collaboration—essential skills for building a sustainable future.

The economic model also underwent a radical transformation. The pursuit of endless economic growth, with its relentless consumption of resources, was replaced by a focus on sustainable development. The circular economy, emphasizing resource efficiency and waste minimization, became the dominant paradigm. Economies were redesigned to value ecological services, recognizing the importance of healthy ecosystems for human wellbeing. This shift required a fundamental change in how we define wealth and progress. The old metrics of GDP and economic growth were replaced by more holistic measures that took into account environmental sustainability, social equity, and human well-being.

Yet, challenges remained. The scars of the old world were deep. Rebuilding trust, repairing damaged social structures, and achieving true equality in resource distribution remained daunting tasks. The legacy of environmental injustice—the unequal distribution of resources and the disproportionate impact of climate change on vulnerable populations—needed to be addressed proactively and with sustained commitment. The ongoing threat posed by individuals and organizations still resistant to the new paradigm, those clinging to outdated models of progress and refusing to accept the urgency of the situation, kept vigilance a necessity. The memory of Dr. Rafe Mallory's actions served as a stark reminder of the fragility of this hard-won peace and the ever-present danger of regression.

But the overall picture was one of remarkable progress, a testament to human ingenuity and resilience. The Convergence Protocol, once a hidden hope, was now a living reality. The integration of human society with the intricate rhythms of the planet was ongoing, a dynamic process of adaptation and evolution. The whispers of the old world were fading, replaced by a new symphony—a chorus of life, a harmony born of cooperation, a vibrant, thriving testament to a world finally in balance. The future was uncertain, of course, but the possibility of a sustainable world— a world where humanity and nature coexisted in harmony—was now a palpable, breathtaking reality. The planet, once battered and scarred, was healing, thriving, and brimming with the promise of a future where both humans and nature could flourish.

CHAPTER FIFTEEN

LOOKING FORWARD:

A SUSTAINABLE FUTURE

The air hummed with a quiet energy, a symphony of rustling leaves, chirping crickets, and the gentle rush of wind through newly planted forests. Gone were the choking fumes of industrial pollution, replaced by the clean, crisp scent of a revitalized Earth. This wasn't simply a restoration of the past; it was a reimagining of the future, a testament to the extraordinary resilience of both humanity and the planet itself.

Cities, once concrete jungles suffocating under their own weight, now breathed. Green spaces snaked through their hearts, vibrant oases of biodiversity interwoven with human life. Buildings, crafted from bioengineered materials, blended seamlessly with their surroundings, harnessing solar energy and recycling water with remarkable efficiency. Vertical farms, rising like shimmering towers, provided fresh, locally grown food, eliminating the need for vast, resource-intensive agricultural lands. Transportation systems, powered by renewable energy, moved with a quiet grace, a stark contrast to the cacophony of the past.

The economic model had undergone a profound shift. The relentless pursuit of growth had given way to a more holistic approach, one

323

that valued ecological well-being alongside human prosperity. The circular economy, a paradigm shift that prioritized resource efficiency and waste minimization, was now the dominant force. Businesses, once driven solely by profit, now incorporated environmental and social responsibility into their core values. The emphasis was on sustainability, collaboration, and equitable distribution of resources.

New metrics replaced GDP as the primary indicators of progress, measuring not only economic output but also environmental health, social equity, and the overall well-being of the population. Innovation flourished, driven by a desire to create sustainable solutions to global challenges. This new economy was not only environmentally sound but also socially just, ensuring that the benefits of progress were shared by all.

Education, too, had undergone a radical transformation. The curriculum was no longer a mere catalog of facts and figures, but a vibrant exploration of interconnectedness, a journey into the wonders of the natural world. Children were taught not only about the science of ecology but also about the ethical responsibility of environmental stewardship. Creative problem-solving, collaboration, and critical thinking were at the heart of the educational system, nurturing the next generation of innovators, entrepreneurs, and environmental champions.

Schools were designed as living laboratories, integrating nature into the learning process, encouraging hands-on engagement with the environment, and fostering a deep sense of respect for the planet. The old hierarchies of knowledge were dismantled, replaced by a collaborative approach that valued diverse perspectives and encouraged interdisciplinary learning.

The arts flourished in this new world. Artists, inspired by the beauty and resilience of the natural world, created works that celebrated the interconnectedness of life. Music echoed the rhythms of the ecosystems, reflecting the delicate balance of nature. Literature explored the complexities of human relationships with the environment, reflecting the hopes and anxieties of a generation grappling with the legacy of environmental destruction. Theatre showcased stories of resilience and cooperation, inspiring audiences to embrace a sustainable future.

The arts, in all their forms, served as powerful tools for communication, education, and social change, forging a collective identity based on respect for the environment and a shared commitment to a sustainable future.

The Echoborn, the remarkable beings born from the merging of human consciousness and the Whisper's wisdom, played a pivotal role in this transformed world. They acted as bridges, translating the intricate language of ecosystems into human understanding. Their deep connection to nature guided humanity's efforts in ecological restoration and helped foster a more harmonious relationship between humans and the planet.

They became guardians of the natural world, ensuring that the planet's delicate balance remained undisturbed. Their unique perspective, blending human ingenuity with the wisdom of nature, shaped the way humanity interacted with its environment, ensuring that the hard-won peace was maintained. They served not as rulers but as wise advisors, guiding humanity's journey toward a future of coexistence and collaboration.

The Luminese, with their advanced technology and their unwavering commitment to sustainable development, played a crucial role in bringing about this future. Their sophisticated sensors continuously monitored the planet's health, providing real-time updates on ecosystem stability and helping to avert potential crises. Their advanced bioengineered materials and sustainable energy systems were critical in the rebuilding of cities and the restoration of ecosystems.

Their contribution, however, was not solely technological; they also shared their wisdom, their deep understanding of symbiotic relationships, and their philosophy of respectful coexistence. Their influence extended far beyond the realm of technology; they became the philosophers and guides, shaping a new worldview centered around environmental harmony and the ethical treatment of the planet. Their wisdom helped to shape a sustainable future where technology served humanity and nature, not dominated it.

However, this sustainable future was not without its challenges. The scars of the past remained, reminding everyone of the precarious balance they had achieved. Social inequalities persisted, requiring constant vigilance to ensure fair distribution of resources and opportunities. The legacy of environmental injustice—the unequal impact of climate change on vulnerable populations— needed ongoing attention and proactive solutions.

A constant threat remained, a latent distrust, the ever-present possibility of regression—a stark reminder that the transition to a sustainable future was an ongoing process, requiring continual adaptation, vigilance, and a shared commitment to maintaining the hard-won peace. The memory of Dr. Rafe Mallory and his ambitions served as a cautionary tale, a constant reminder of the need for unity and the dangers of unchecked ambition.

Yet, despite these challenges, the overall vision was one of profound hope. The Convergence Protocol, the very heart of the planetary regeneration project, had not only succeeded but had evolved into a dynamic system of interaction between human civilization and the natural world. It was not a static endpoint but a living process, constantly adapting to the ever-changing needs of the planet.

The planet, once scarred and wounded, was healing. Its ecosystems thrived, teeming with a vibrant tapestry of life. The harmony between humans and nature was not a passive coexistence but a dynamic dance of interdependence, a shared journey toward a future where both could flourish. The old anxieties about extinction were being replaced by a new understanding of partnership, a future of mutual respect and shared responsibility.

This future was not a utopian fantasy, but a tangible possibility, a testament to humanity's capacity for resilience, ingenuity, and collaboration. The journey had been long and arduous, fraught with peril and sacrifice. But the destination—a world where humanity lived in balance with nature—was now within reach.

The future remained uncertain, with its share of unforeseen challenges. Yet, the prevailing sentiment was one of cautious optimism, a shared belief in the possibility of a sustainable future, a world where the symphony of life could continue to play on, vibrant and strong, a testament to the enduring power of hope and the transformative potential of human resilience. It was a future born from the ashes of destruction, a testament to humanity's ability to learn from its mistakes and build a future worthy of its potential, a future where humanity and nature danced in harmony, a shared rhythm echoing through the ages.

Lessons Learned

The air, cleansed of its former toxicity, carried the scent of pine and damp earth, a stark contrast to the acrid smog that had once choked the cities. The scars of the past, however, remained etched into the landscape: the skeletal remains of abandoned factories, the ghostly outlines of once-thriving coastal communities swallowed by the rising tides. These weren't merely physical reminders; they were potent symbols, serving as constant reminders of the fragility of our existence and the devastating consequences of unchecked industrialization and environmental disregard. These scars, however, were not monuments to defeat, but rather, deeply ingrained lessons etched into the very fabric of the new world.

The most profound lesson, perhaps, was the interconnectedness of all things. The collapse hadn't been a series of isolated events, but a cascading failure, a domino effect triggered by seemingly minor imbalances in the delicate web of life. The depletion of the ozone layer, the acidification of the oceans, the collapse of fisheries—these weren't isolated problems, but symptoms of a deeper malaise, a systemic disregard for the planetary boundaries that sustain all life. The Whispers, in their wisdom, had starkly demonstrated this interconnectedness, revealing how every action, no matter how seemingly insignificant, could ripple outward, impacting entire ecosystems and, eventually, the entire planet.

The initial blindness to this interconnectedness had been humanity's fatal flaw. The new world understood this profound truth, incorporating it into every aspect of its existence—from its economic models to its educational systems.

Economically, the shift had been revolutionary. The relentless pursuit of GDP growth, the cornerstone of the old world's economic dogma, had been replaced by a holistic approach that measured prosperity not solely in monetary terms, but also in terms of environmental health, social equity, and overall well-being. The circular economy, once a niche concept, became the dominant model, prioritizing resource efficiency, waste minimization, and the regeneration of natural resources. Businesses, once solely focused on profit maximization, now integrated environmental and social responsibility into their core values, recognizing that their long-term survival was inextricably linked to the health of the planet.

Metrics like the Genuine Progress Indicator (GPI) and the Human Development Index (HDI) gained prominence, providing a more nuanced and comprehensive picture of societal progress than the narrow focus on GDP had allowed. This shift not only improved the environment but also fostered a more just and equitable society, ensuring that the benefits of progress were shared by all. The old model of infinite growth on a finite planet was finally abandoned, replaced by the more realistic and sustainable goal of living within planetary boundaries.

Education was radically transformed as well. The old system, characterized by rote learning and a fragmented curriculum, was replaced by an approach that emphasized critical thinking, problemsolving, and interdisciplinary learning. Children were taught the intricacies of ecological systems, the importance of biodiversity, and the ethical responsibilities of environmental stewardship.

Schools weren't merely places of formal education, but vibrant hubs of community engagement, where students learned through hands-on experiences, participated in restoration projects, engaged in citizen science initiatives, and directly contributed to the health of their local ecosystems. The curriculum fostered a deep understanding of environmental justice, ensuring that future generations would be equipped to address the inequalities that had exacerbated the environmental crisis. This wasn't simply an education about nature; it was an education in nature, fostering a profound respect for the natural world and a sense of responsibility toward its well-being.

The role of technology was also re-evaluated. While advanced technology played a crucial role in the planet's recovery—in the development of sustainable energy systems, the creation of bioengineered materials, and the monitoring of ecosystems—its use was guided by ethical considerations and a deep respect for the natural world. The old paradigm of technological dominance was abandoned, replaced by a more harmonious approach, where technology served as a tool to enhance human-nature interaction rather than to exploit or control it.

The Luminese's contribution, alongside human ingenuity, was instrumental in developing this harmonious relationship. They didn't impose their solutions, but rather, shared their knowledge and collaborated with humanity, ensuring that technology was used responsibly and sustainably.

The Echoborn, the bridge between humanity and the Whispers, represented the pinnacle of this new understanding. Their unique perspective, a blend of human intellect and ecological wisdom, provided invaluable insights into the functioning of ecosystems and guided humanity toward a more symbiotic relationship with nature. They were not rulers or controllers, but rather wise advisors, guiding humanity's journey toward a future of coexistence and mutual respect. They were living embodiments of the lessons learned, demonstrating the potential for human-nature symbiosis and the transformative power of collaboration.

Yet, the new world was not without its challenges. Social inequalities, deeply rooted in the past, persisted and required continuous effort to address. The legacy of environmental injustice—the disproportionate impact of climate change on vulnerable populations—demanded ongoing attention. The constant vigilance against potential backsliding, the ever-present possibility of regression toward unsustainable practices, remained a vital aspect of maintaining the hard-won balance.

The memory of Dr. Mallory's actions served as a potent warning, a stark reminder of the dangers of unchecked ambition and the importance of maintaining unity and collaborative decisionmaking. The path toward sustainability was not a destination, but a continuous journey, requiring constant adaptation, vigilance, and a shared commitment to preserving the hard-won equilibrium.

The Convergence Protocol, once the key to planetary regeneration, evolved into a dynamic system, constantly adapting to the planet's changing needs. It wasn't merely a technological solution, but a living testament to the interconnectedness of humanity and the natural world—a dynamic interaction that required constant learning, adaptation, and respect.

The future remained uncertain, with unforeseen challenges bound to arise. Yet the overall sentiment was one of cautious optimism, a belief in humanity's capacity for resilience, ingenuity, and collaboration, a collective acknowledgment that the path to a sustainable future was a shared journey requiring ongoing commitment and vigilance.

The lessons learned were deeply ingrained, not merely as abstract concepts, but as fundamental principles shaping every aspect of life. The most crucial lesson, perhaps, was the imperative to prevent future disasters. The path ahead was one of continuous learning, of adapting to ever-changing challenges, and of maintaining a profound respect for the delicate balance of the natural world.

This wasn't a utopia, but a fragile yet hopeful new beginning, a world reborn from the ashes of destruction, a testament to humanity's ability to learn from its mistakes and forge a future worthy of its potential—a future where the symphony of life continued to play on, vibrant and strong. It was a future where humanity and nature danced in harmony, a shared rhythm echoing through the ages, a constant reminder of the interconnectedness of all life and the profound responsibility that humanity bore toward the planet.

The scars of the past, while ever-present, were now also a powerful catalyst for change, guiding humanity on its path toward a more sustainable and harmonious future—a testament to the enduring power of hope and the remarkable resilience of both humanity and the Earth itself.

Global Cooperation

The revitalization of Earth wasn't solely a triumph of scientific ingenuity or technological prowess; it was a testament to the power of global cooperation. The shared understanding of the planetary crisis, born from the ashes of near-catastrophe, transcended national borders and ideological differences. The old paradigm of national self-interest gave way to a new era of collective responsibility, a recognition that the fate of each nation was inextricably linked to the fate of all.

This wasn't a sudden, miraculous transformation. The initial steps were hesitant, fraught with suspicion and mistrust. Years of conflict, fueled by resource scarcity and environmental degradation, had left deep scars on the global community. Reconciling competing interests, overcoming deeply ingrained prejudices, and establishing a framework for genuine collaboration proved to be a monumental task. Early attempts at international cooperation often faltered, hampered by conflicting priorities, bureaucratic inertia, and the lingering shadow of nationalistic agendas.

The turning point arrived not through grand pronouncements or sweeping declarations, but through a gradual shift in perspective. The shared experience of near-extinction forced nations to confront the brutal reality of their interdependence. The devastating consequences of unchecked environmental destruction, experienced universally, became a powerful catalyst for change, fostering a sense of shared vulnerability and the urgent need for collective action.

The Luminese played a pivotal role in this transformation. Their advanced technology, coupled with their profound understanding of planetary systems, provided crucial support, but more importantly, their wisdom and patience helped bridge the chasm of distrust between nations. They didn't impose solutions but facilitated dialogue, offering their expertise and knowledge without demanding political concessions. They acted as facilitators, promoting collaboration and fostering a sense of shared purpose among disparate nations. Their approach emphasized mutual respect and understanding, recognizing the diverse perspectives and unique challenges faced by different countries.

The establishment of the Global Environmental Restoration Authority (GERA) marked a significant milestone in this collaborative effort. GERA, a truly international body, transcended the limitations of traditional geopolitical structures. Its mandate encompassed a wide range of environmental challenges, from mitigating climate change and restoring damaged ecosystems to promoting sustainable development and ensuring environmental justice. It was designed to be a flexible, adaptive organization, capable of responding to evolving threats and integrating the latest scientific knowledge. GERA wasn't merely a bureaucratic entity; it became a powerful symbol of global unity, a tangible representation of the shared commitment to a sustainable future.

The success of GERA wasn't solely reliant on its organizational structure. Its effectiveness stemmed from a fundamental shift in global governance paradigms. Decisions were made not through the imposition of power, but through inclusive dialogue and consensusbuilding. Nations, large and small, were given a voice in shaping environmental policy, ensuring that the interests of all were taken into consideration. This inclusive approach addressed the historical injustices that had exacerbated the environmental crisis, recognizing that some nations had contributed disproportionately to the problem while bearing a greater brunt of its consequences.

One of GERA's most significant achievements was the equitable distribution of resources and technological support. Developed nations, recognizing their historical responsibility, provided financial and technical assistance to developing countries, enabling them to participate fully in the global restoration efforts. This wasn't merely charity; it was a recognition that the global environmental crisis demanded a collective response, requiring the coordinated efforts of all nations, regardless of their level of development.

The role of technology in this global endeavor was carefully managed. The advanced technologies developed by the Luminese and human scientists alike were shared openly and equitably, ensuring that the benefits of technological advancement were accessible to all nations. Strict regulations prevented the misuse of these technologies, promoting sustainable and responsible use.

Transparency and accountability were paramount, guaranteeing that technology served humanity, not the other way around.

The process of global cooperation wasn't without its challenges. Disputes arose over resource allocation, technological sharing, and the implementation of environmental policies. Differing national interests, cultural values, and political ideologies occasionally threatened to undermine the collaborative spirit. However, the lessons learned from the near-catastrophic events of the past served as a powerful reminder of the interconnectedness of the planet and the necessity of collective action.

These disputes, however, were resolved not through coercion but through dialogue and compromise. A new diplomatic approach emerged, one based on empathy, understanding, and a shared commitment to a sustainable future. Mediation efforts, guided by the Luminese elders and representatives from GERA, played a crucial role in resolving conflicts and fostering a sense of common purpose among nations. The focus shifted from asserting national dominance to building bridges of cooperation and mutual respect.

The revitalization of Earth's ecosystems provided a tangible demonstration of the effectiveness of global collaboration. Reforestation projects, spearheaded by GERA and supported by international partnerships, transformed barren landscapes into thriving forests. Ocean restoration initiatives, utilizing advanced technologies and traditional ecological knowledge, helped revive damaged marine environments. Sustainable agricultural practices, promoted globally, ensured food security while minimizing environmental impact. These were not isolated successes but interconnected elements of a larger, global effort.

This new era of global cooperation wasn't a utopian vision devoid of conflict. Challenges remained, new threats emerged, and the vigilance required for maintaining the hard-won balance was constant. However, the foundation for a sustainable future had been laid—a foundation built on shared responsibility, mutual respect, and unwavering commitment to the health of the planet. The collective spirit of global cooperation, once a distant dream, had become the driving force behind a new era of hope and resilience, a testament to humanity's capacity for collaboration and its determination to safeguard the future of life on Earth.

The scars of the past, while serving as a constant reminder of the fragility of the planet, also served as a testament to the resilience and collaborative spirit that rebuilt a world teetering on the brink of collapse.

Technological Responsibility

The revitalization of Earth wasn't just a matter of repairing the damage; it was a fundamental shift in the human relationship with technology. The near-extinction event served as a harsh lesson, highlighting the potential for technological advancement to both solve and create problems on a planetary scale. The unchecked pursuit of technological progress, divorced from ethical considerations and long-term consequences, had nearly brought about humanity's downfall. The rebuilding process, therefore, required a profound reevaluation of humanity's technological responsibility.

This reevaluation began with a critical examination of existing technological infrastructure. Many systems, built for short-term gains and unsustainable practices, needed radical overhauls or complete replacements. The transition wasn't easy. Resistance from vested interests, entrenched habits, and the inertia of existing systems created significant hurdles. The global community, however, was committed to a more sustainable path, recognizing that technological innovation needed to align with the planet's ecological carrying capacity.

One of the most significant changes was the adoption of circular economy principles. The linear "take-make-dispose" model of the past, responsible for massive waste generation and resource depletion, was replaced by a closed-loop system emphasizing resource efficiency, waste reduction, and material reuse. Advanced technologies, such as bio-based materials, 3D printing with recycled materials, and automated recycling systems, played a crucial role in this transformation. These innovations, coupled with robust waste management strategies and international cooperation, helped minimize the environmental footprint of human activities.

The development and deployment of new technologies were guided by rigorous ethical frameworks. Before any new technology was introduced, its potential environmental impact, social implications, and long-term consequences were carefully assessed. This involved not only scientific and technological expertise but also input from social scientists, ethicists, and representatives of affected communities. The focus shifted from simply maximizing technological capabilities to optimizing technological solutions within the constraints of planetary boundaries. Technological responsibility became a core principle guiding all research and development efforts, ensuring that technological advancements served humanity and the planet rather than perpetuating unsustainable practices.

Transparency and accountability were crucial aspects of this new technological paradigm. The development, deployment, and use of all technologies were subject to strict oversight and rigorous monitoring. Open-source initiatives were encouraged, promoting collaborative innovation and preventing the concentration of power in the hands of a few. Data sharing and open access to scientific research helped foster collaboration, facilitate rapid innovation, and ensure the responsible use of technological advancements. This transparency aimed to prevent technological advancements from being weaponized or used to exacerbate existing inequalities.

The Luminese played a pivotal role in this technological transformation. Their expertise in sustainable technologies, coupled with their commitment to ecological responsibility, provided invaluable guidance and support. Their advanced knowledge of planetary systems informed the development of sustainable energy sources, advanced water purification systems, and resilient agricultural practices. However, they shared this knowledge not as a means of technological dominance but as a contribution to a collective effort. They emphasized the importance of cultural sensitivity and local adaptation, recognizing that technology should not be imposed on communities but developed in collaboration with them.

Education and public awareness played a crucial role in shaping the responsible use of technology. Global educational initiatives, integrated into school curricula worldwide, emphasized the importance of ecological literacy, technological awareness, and responsible citizenship. These programs aimed to foster critical thinking skills, encouraging individuals to question the assumptions behind technological innovations and evaluate their long-term consequences. Public engagement campaigns helped raise awareness about the importance of sustainable practices and informed consumers about the ethical implications of their choices. The goal was to empower individuals to make informed decisions and to hold technology developers accountable.

The integration of traditional knowledge with advanced technologies proved to be a key driver of innovation. Indigenous communities, long stewards of their environments, shared their invaluable insights into sustainable practices, resource management, and ecological harmony. These traditional techniques, combined with modern technological innovations, resulted in robust and adaptable solutions. The collaboration of traditional and modern approaches fostered a sense of cultural respect and mutual understanding, creating a path forward that honored the wisdom of the past while embracing the possibilities of the future.

However, the shift toward technological responsibility wasn't without its challenges. Disputes arose regarding resource allocation, intellectual property rights, and the distribution of benefits derived from technological advancements. Developing countries, often bearing the brunt of environmental degradation, needed significant technological support and capacity-building to participate fully in the global transition. The equitable distribution of technological benefits became a central point of contention, necessitating a reimagining of global cooperation and the redistribution of resources. International organizations, building on the foundations laid by GERA, played a key role in resolving these disputes through collaborative dialogues and consensus building.

The threat of technological misuse continued to loom large. The legacy of past conflicts, fueled by technological advancements, served as a potent reminder of the potential dangers associated with unchecked innovation. The Global Environmental Restoration Authority (GERA) and other international bodies established stringent regulations, monitoring systems, and accountability mechanisms to prevent misuse and to ensure responsible development and deployment of technology. The focus was not on suppressing innovation but on channeling technological progress toward environmentally responsible and socially equitable outcomes.

In conclusion, the responsible use of technology became the cornerstone of Earth's revitalization. It wasn't merely about inventing new technologies, but about fundamentally altering the relationship between humanity and technology, ensuring that technological advancement served the common good, promoted ecological sustainability, and fostered social justice. This transformation required not only scientific and technological innovation but also profound changes in ethical frameworks, governance structures, and public awareness. The scars of the past remained, but they served as a constant reminder of the importance of technological responsibility in ensuring a sustainable and equitable future for all. The path forward was not without its challenges, but the collaborative spirit, borne from the brink of catastrophe, proved to be humanity's greatest strength—and technology, when wielded responsibly, was its most potent tool.

A New Beginning

The rhythmic pulse of the Convergence Protocol, a gentle thrumming that resonated deep within the Earth's core, marked a turning point. The planet, scarred yet resilient, began to breathe again. The oceans, once choked with pollution and ravaged by acidification, slowly started to clear, their vibrant ecosystems showing tentative signs of recovery. Coral reefs, once bleached skeletons, began to regain their color, teeming with life once more. Forests, once desolate wastelands, sprouted new growth, their leaves a vibrant testament to the planet's renewed vitality.

This wasn't a sudden miracle, but a gradual, painstaking process. The Protocol wasn't a magic wand, but a carefully calibrated system, a symphony of technological interventions and ecological restoration.

Jonah, still awestruck by the complexity of the Whispers' code, continued to refine the system, ensuring its smooth operation and adapting it to the ever-changing needs of the planet. His understanding of the Whispers, once a source of fear, had evolved into a deep respect and even a form of kinship. He had learned to listen to their silent language, the subtle shifts in the planet's energy, interpreting their needs and translating them into the Protocol's algorithms.

Eliza, her heart filled with a profound sense of relief and wonder, oversaw the reintroduction of keystone species, carefully monitoring their integration into the revitalizing ecosystems. She witnessed the return of creatures long thought extinct, their presence a symbol of the planet's remarkable resilience. Her scientific expertise, combined with her unwavering empathy for the natural world, guided the delicate balance of restoration, ensuring that the planet's biodiversity flourished once more.

The Luminese, masters of sustainable technology, continued to contribute their advanced knowledge and resources to the ongoing restoration efforts. Ambassador Nyla, her wisdom unwavering, played a crucial role in bridging the gap between human ambition and planetary needs, ensuring that technological advancements were implemented with respect for the Earth's delicate equilibrium. Their contribution transcended mere technological assistance; it was a profound act of interspecies cooperation, a testament to their belief in a shared future.

The Echoborn, once feared as anomalies, now played a vital role in the planetary restoration. Their unique connection to the Whispers enabled them to directly interact with the planet's energy systems, facilitating the Protocol's adaptation and ensuring its ongoing effectiveness. They became the living bridge between human ingenuity and the planet's innate wisdom. Their existence challenged the old definitions of humanity, blurring the lines between human and nature, demonstrating the potential for symbiotic evolution.

Sarah, her leadership unwavering, guided the global community toward a new era of planetary stewardship. She championed a radical shift in human values, prioritizing ecological sustainability, social justice, and interspecies cooperation. Her leadership was not based on authority but on her ability to inspire hope and foster collaboration. She understood that the planet's recovery was not just a technological challenge but a profound ethical imperative.

The defeat of Rafe Mallory and his misguided quest for technological control served as a stark reminder of the dangers of unchecked ambition. His actions, driven by a desire for power and control, had nearly brought about humanity's ultimate demise. His downfall wasn't a celebratory moment but a somber lesson, emphasizing the crucial need for ethical considerations in all aspects of technological development. The global community, having learned from its past mistakes, established robust safeguards against technological misuse, prioritizing safety, transparency, and accountability.

The reconstruction of human societies followed a similarly transformative path. The old systems, built on unsustainable practices and exploitative ideologies, were dismantled and replaced with more equitable and sustainable alternatives. Circular economy principles, supported by advanced recycling technologies and a new ethic of resource conservation, were adopted globally. Food systems were redesigned, focusing on local production, sustainable agriculture, and the reduction of food waste.

Education played a critical role in this transformation. Global curricula integrated ecological literacy, technological awareness, and ethical decision-making. Children were taught not only the science of planetary restoration but also the responsibility that came with wielding advanced technologies. They were encouraged to be critical thinkers, questioning the assumptions behind technological innovations and examining their long-term societal and ecological implications.

However, the path toward a sustainable future was not without its challenges. The scars of the past remained, both physical and emotional. Economic inequalities persisted, necessitating policies aimed at redistributing resources and wealth. Social and political divisions still existed, demanding continued dialogue and reconciliation. The ongoing threat of climate change, though mitigated by the Protocol, remained a constant reminder of the fragility of the planetary balance.

Yet, amidst these challenges, a renewed sense of hope emerged. Humanity, humbled by its near-extinction, had rediscovered its capacity for resilience, collaboration, and innovation. The collective effort, fueled by shared determination and a profound respect for the natural world, offered a testament to the enduring spirit of humanity. The transformation wasn't simply about restoring the planet; it was about transforming humanity itself.

The future was uncertain, yet it held the promise of a brighter tomorrow. The revitalized Earth offered an opportunity for humanity to build a truly sustainable and equitable civilization. It was a future built on cooperation, not competition; on collaboration, not domination; on respect for nature, not exploitation. The Convergence Protocol, a symbol of human ingenuity and interspecies cooperation, stood as a testament to humanity's potential for both self-destruction and self-redemption.

The story of the near-extinction and the subsequent planetary restoration became a cautionary tale, a lesson learned at a tremendous cost. It served as a constant reminder of the importance of planetary stewardship, urging future generations to exercise caution, responsibility, and a profound respect for the intricate web of life that supports all existence. The echoes of the past served as a guide, ensuring that the mistakes of the past were not repeated, reminding all that the future was a collaborative endeavor, a testament to the power of interspecies collaboration and technological responsibility.

The future, though uncertain, held the glimmer of hope, a testament to the resilience of both humanity and the planet itself. The path forward was long, requiring continued vigilance and dedication. But for the first time in a long time, the future felt possible—a future where humanity and the planet coexisted in a delicate but sustainable harmony, a future where the lessons learned in the crucible of near-extinction would guide the path toward a truly brighter tomorrow. The journey had been arduous, filled with loss and hardship, but the destination—a healed planet, a transformed humanity—offered a vision of hope that shone brighter than ever before. The seeds of a new beginning had been sown, and the future, though uncertain, held the potential to blossom into something truly magnificent.

ACKNOWLEDGMENTS

My deepest gratitude goes to my family and friends for their unwavering support and patience throughout the long process of writing this novel. Their encouragement and understanding were invaluable, particularly during those periods of doubt and frustration.

Special thanks to my editor, Maxwell Ambrose, for their insightful feedback and guidance, which helped to shape the narrative and refine the characters.

I am also indebted to the numerous scientists and environmental activists whose work inspired this story, and whose dedication to planetary health continues to inspire hope.

Finally, thank you to the readers for your curiosity and your willingness to engage with the complex issues explored in this book. Your engagement fuels the creative process and inspires me to continue exploring these important themes.

APPENDIX

This appendix contains supplementary materials related to the Convergence Protocol and the Whispers' language. Specifically, it includes a simplified diagram of the Protocol's core functions (Figure A.1), a glossary of key terms in the Whispers' language (Table A.1), and a collection of decoded fragments of the Whispers' ancient code (Appendix A.2).

This material is intended to provide a deeper understanding of the scientific and linguistic underpinnings of the narrative for those readers interested in delving further into the complexities of the fictional world presented in this book.

GLOSSARY

Convergence Protocol: A planetary regeneration plan designed to restore Earth's ecological balance.

Luminese: A technologically advanced extraterrestrial species with a deep understanding of sustainable technology.

Whispers: Sentient ecosystems capable of communication through subtle shifts in the planet's energy fields.

Echoborn: Humans who have developed a symbiotic relationship with the Whispers, resulting in enhanced abilities and a deeper understanding of the planet's systems.

Oceanic Resonance: The interconnected energy fields of

Earth's oceans, crucial to the planet's overall health.

Keystone Species: Species that play a crucial role in maintaining the balance of their ecosystems.

Circular Economy: An economic system designed to minimize waste and maximize the reuse of resources.

REFERENCES

While this novel is a work of fiction, it draws inspiration from a wide range of scientific and philosophical sources. A detailed bibliography of relevant works is available on my website at *dianekann.com*

This bibliography includes references to works on climate change, ecological restoration, symbiotic relationships, and the philosophy of technology, which provide a deeper understanding of the scientific and philosophical basis of the narrative.

AUTHOR BIOGRAPHY

Diane Kann is a eco–science fantasy author and environmental researcher with a passion for exploring the intersection of science, technology, and the environment.

Her work is characterized by richly detailed world building, complex characters, and a commitment to examining the ethical implications of scientific and technological advancements. Diane believes that science fiction has the power to raise awareness of critical environmental and social issues and to inspire hope for a more sustainable future.

She currently resides in central Florida and is working on her next novel.